GODOLPHIN

GODOLPHIN

SIR EDWARD BULWER-LYTTON

WILDSIDE PRESS

Published by Wildside Press LLC.
www.wildsidebooks.com

TO COUNT ALFRED D'ORSAY.

My dear Count d'Orsay, — When the parentage of Godolphin was still unconfessed and unknown, you were pleased to encourage his first struggles with the world; now, will you permit the father he has just discovered to re-introduce him to your notice? I am sorry to say, however, that my unfilial offspring, having been so long disowned, is not sufficiently grateful for being acknowledged at last; he says that he belongs to a very numerous family, and, wishing to be distinguished from his brothers, desires not only to reclaim your acquaintance, but to borrow your name. Nothing less will content his ambition than the most public opportunity in his power of parading his obligations to the most accomplished gentleman of our time. Will you, then, allow him to make his new appearance in the world under your wing, and thus suffer the son as well as the father to attest the kindness of your heart and to boast the honour of your friendship?

Believe me, my dear Count d'Orsay, with the sincerest regard,

Yours, very faithfully and truly,

E. B. L.

PREFACE TO GODOLPHIN.

In the Prefaces to this edition of my works, I have occasionally so far availed myself of that privilege of self-criticism which the French comic writer M. Picord maintains or exemplifies in the collection of his plays, — as, if not actually to sit in judgment on my own performances, still to insinuate some excuse for their faults by extenuatory depositions as to their character and intentions. Indeed, a writer looking back to the past is unconsciously inclined to think that he may separate himself from those children of his brain which have long gone forth to the world; and though he may not expatiate on the merits his paternal affection would ascribe to them, that he may speak at least of the mode in which they were trained and reared, — of the hopes he cherished, or the objects he entertained, when he finally dismissed them to the opinions of others and the ordeal of Fate or Time.

For my part, I own that even when I have thought but little of the value of a work, I have always felt an interest in the author's account of its origin and formation; and willing to suppose that what thus affords a gratification to my own curiosity may not be wholly unattractive to others, I shall thus continue from time to time to play the Showman to my own machinery, and explain the principle of the mainspring and the movement of the wheels.

This novel was begun somewhere in the third year of my authorship, and completed in the fourth. It was, therefore, composed almost simultaneously with "Eugene Aram," and afforded to me at least some relief from the gloom of that village tragedy. It is needless to observe how dissimilar in point of scene, character, and fable the one is from the other; yet they are alike in this, — that both attempt to deal with one of the most striking problems in the spiritual history of man; namely, the frustration or abuse of power in a superior intellect originally inclined to good. Perhaps there is no problem that more fascinates the attention of a man of some earnestness at that period of his life when his eye first disengages itself from the external phenomena around him, and his curiosity leads him to examine the cause and account for the effect; when, to cite reverently the words of the wisest, "He applies his heart to know and to search, and to seek out wisdom and the reason of things, and to know the wickedness of folly, even of foolishness and madness."

In "Eugene Aram," the natural career of genius is arrested by a single crime; in "Godolphin," a mind of inferior order, but more fanciful colouring, is wasted away by the indulgence of those morbid sentiments which are the nourishment of egotism, and the gradual influence of the frivolities which make the business of the idle. Here, the Demon tempts or destroys the hermit in his solitary cell; there, he glides amidst the pomps and vanities of the world, and whispers away the soul in the voice of his soft familiars, Indolence and Pleasure.

Of all my numerous novels, "Pelham" and "Godolphin" are the only ones which take their absolute groundwork in what is called "The Fashionable World." I have sought in each to make the general composition in some harmony with the principal figure in the foreground. Pelham is represented as almost wholly unsusceptible to the more poetical influences. He has the physical compound, which, versatile and joyous, amalgamates easily with the world; he views life with the lenient philosophy that Horace commends in Aristippus; he laughs at the follies he shares, and is ever ready to turn into uses ultimately (if indirectly) serious the frivolities that only serve to sharpen his wit, and augment that peculiar expression which we term "knowledge of the world." In a word, dispel all his fopperies, real or assumed, he is still the active man of crowds and cities, determined to succeed, and gifted with the ordinary qualities of success. Godolphin, on the contrary, is the man of poetical temperament, out of his place alike among the trifling idlers and the bustling actors of the world; wanting the stimulus of necessity, or the higher motive which springs from benevolence, to give energy to his powers or definite purpose to his fluctuating desires; not strong enough to break the bonds that confine his genius, not supple enough to accommodate its movements to their purpose. He is the moral antipodes to Pelham. In evading the struggles of the world, he grows indifferent to its duties; he strives with no obstacles; he can triumph in no career. Represented as possessing mental qualities of a higher and a richer nature than those to which Pelham can pretend, he is also represented as very inferior to him in constitution of character, and he is certainly a more ordinary type of the intellectual trifler.

The characters grouped around Godolphin are those with which such a man usually associates his life. They are designed to have a certain grace, a certain harmony with one form or the other of his two-fold temperament; namely, either its conventional elegance of taste or its constitutional poetry of idea. But all alike are brought under varying operations of similar influences; for whether in Saville, Constance, Fanny, or Lucilla, the picture presented is still the picture of gifts misapplied, of life misunderstood.

The Preacher who exclaimed "Vanity of vanities! all is vanity" perhaps solved his own mournful saying, when he added elsewhere, "This only have I found, that God made men upright, but they have sought out many inventions."

This work was first published anonymously, and for that reason perhaps it has been slow in attaining to its rightful station amongst its brethren, whose parentage at first was openly acknowledged. If compared with "Pelham" it might lose, at the first glance, but would perhaps gain on any attentive reperusal.

For although it must follow from the inherent difference in the design of the two works thus referred to that in "Godolphin" there can be little of the satire or vivacity which have given popularity to its predecessor, yet, on the other hand, in "Godolphin" there ought to be a more faithful illustration of the even polish that belongs to luxurious life, of the satiety that pleasure inflicts upon such of its votaries as are worthy of a higher service. The subject selected cannot admit the same facility for observation of things that lie on the surface; but it may well lend itself to subtler investigation of character, allow more attempt at pathos, and more appeal to reflection.

Regarded as a story, the defects of "Godolphin" most apparent to myself are in the manner in which Lucilla is re-introduced in the later chapters, and in the final catastrophe of the hero. There is an exaggerated romance in the one, and the admission of *accident* as a crowning agency in the other, which my maturer judgment would certainly condemn, and which at all events appear to me out of keeping with the natural events, and the more patient investigation of moral causes and their consequences, from which the previous interest of the tale is sought to be attained. On the other hand, if I may presume to conjecture the most probable claim to favour which the work, regarded as a whole, may possess, it may possibly be found in a tolerably accurate description of certain phases of modern civilization, and in the suggestion of some truths that may be worth considering in our examination of social influences or individual conduct.

CONTENTS.

GODOLPHIN.

CHAPTER I.

THE DEATH-BED OF JOHN VERNON. — HIS DYING WORDS. — DESCRIPTION OF HIS DAUGHTER, THE HEROINE. — THE OATH.

"Is the night calm, Constance?"

"Beautiful! the moon is up."

"Open the shutters wider, there. It *is* a beautiful night. How beautiful! Come hither, my child."

The rich moonlight that now shone through the windows streamed on little that it could invest with poetical attraction. The room was small, though not squalid in its character and appliances. The bed-curtains, of a dull chintz, were drawn back, and showed the form of a man, past middle age, propped by pillows, and bearing on his countenance the marks of approaching death. But what a countenance it still was! The broad, pale, lofty brow; the fine, straight, Grecian nose; the short, curved lip; the full, dimpled chin; the stamp of genius in every line and lineament,— these still defied disease, or rather borrowed from its very ghastliness a more impressive majesty. Beside the bed was a table spread with books of a motley character,— here an abstruse system of Calculations on Finance; there a volume of wild Bacchanalian Songs; here the lofty aspirations of Plato's "Phædon;" and there the last speech of some County Paris on a Malt Tax: old newspapers and dusty pamphlets completed the intellectual litter; and above them rose, mournfully enough, the tall spectral form of a half-emptied phial, and a chamber candle-stick, crested by its extinguisher.

A light step approached the bedside, and opposite the dying man now stood a girl, who might have seen her thirteenth year. But her features — of an exceeding, and what may be termed a regal beauty — were as fully developed as those of one who had told twice her years; and not a trace of the bloom or the softness of girlhood could be marked on her countenance. Her complexion was pale as the whitest marble, but clear and lustrous; and her raven hair, parted over her brow in a fashion then uncommon, increased the statue-like and classic effect of her noble features. The expression of her countenance seemed cold, sedate, and somewhat stern; but it might, in some measure, have belied her heart; for, when turned to the moonlight, you might see that her eyes were filled with tears, though she did not weep; and you might tell by the quivering of her lip, that a little hesitation in replying to any remark from the sufferer arose from her difficulty in commanding her emotions.

"Constance," said the invalid, after a pause, in which he seemed to have been gazing with a quiet heart on the soft skies, that, blue and eloquent with stars, he beheld through the unclosed windows, — "Constance, the hour is coming; I feel it by signs which I cannot mistake. I shall die this night."

"O God! my Father! my dear, dear Father!" broke from Constance's lips, "do not speak thus — do not; I will go to Doctor — "

"No, child, no! I loathe, I detest the thought of help. They denied it me while it was yet time. They left me to starve or to rot in jail, or to hang myself! They left me like a dog, and like a dog I will die! I would not have one iota taken from the justice, the deadly and dooming weight, of my dying curse." Here violent spasms broke on the speech of the sufferer; and when, by medicine and his daughter's attentions, he had recovered, he said, in a lower and calmer key: "Is all quiet below, Constance? Are all in bed,— the landlady, the servants, our fellow-lodgers?"

"All, my Father."

"Ay; then I shall die happy. Thank Heaven, you are my

only nurse and attendant. I remember the day when I was ill after one of their rude debauches. Ill!—a sick headache, a fit of the spleen, a spoiled lapdog's illness! Well: they wanted me that night to support one of their paltry measures,—their parliamentary measures; and I had a prince feeling my pulse, and a duke mixing my draught, and a dozen earls sending their doctors to me. I was of use to them then! Poor me! Read me that note, Constance,—Flamborough's note. Do you hesitate? Read it, I say!"

Constance trembled and complied.

My dear Vernon,—I am really *au désespoir* to hear of your melancholy state,—so sorry I cannot assist you; but you know my embarrassed circumstances. By the by, I saw his Royal Highness yesterday. "Poor Vernon!" said he; "would a hundred pounds do him any good?" So we don't forget you, *mon cher*. Ah, how we missed you at the Beefsteak! Never shall we know again so glorious a *bon vivant*. You would laugh to hear L—— attempting to echo your old jokes. But time presses: I must be off to the House. You know what a motion it is! Would to Heaven you were to bring it on instead of that ass T——. Adieu! I wish I could come and see you; but it would break my heart. Can I send you any books from Hookham's?

Yours ever,

Flamborough.

"This is the man whom I made Secretary of State," said Vernon. "Very well! oh, it's very well,—very well indeed. Let me kiss thee, my girl. Poor Constance! You will have good friends when I am dead! They will be proud enough to be kind to Vernon's daughter, when Death has shown them that Vernon is a loss. You are very handsome,—your poor mother's eyes and hair, my father's splendid brow and lip; and your figure even now so stately! They will court you: you will have lords and great men enough at your feet; but you will never forget this night, nor the agony of your father's death-bed face, and the brand they have burned in his heart. And now, Constance, give me the Bible in which you read to me this morning: that will do. Stand away from the light and fix your eyes on mine, and listen as if your soul were in your ears.

"When I was a young man, toiling my way to fortune through the labours of the Bar,—prudent, cautious, indefatigable, confident of success,—certain lords, who heard I possessed genius and thought I might become their tool, came to me, and besought me to enter parliament. I told them I was poor, was lately married, that my public ambition must not be encouraged at the expense of my private fortunes. They answered that they pledged themselves those fortunes should be their care. I yielded; I deserted my profession; I obeyed their wishes; I became famous—and a ruined man! They could not dine without me; they could not sup without me; they could not get drunk without me; no pleasure was sweet but in my company. What mattered it that, while I ministered to their amusement, I was necessarily heaping debt upon debt, accumulating miseries for future years, laying up bankruptcy, and care and shame and a broken heart and an early death? But listen, Constance! *Are* you listening,—attentively? Well! note now, I am a just man. I do not blame my noble friends, my gentle patrons, for this. No; if I were forgetful of my interests, if I preferred their pleasure to my happiness and honour, that was *my* crime, and I deserve the punishment! But look you: time went by, and my constitution was broken; debts came upon me; I could not pay; men mistrusted my word; my name in the country fell! With my health, my genius deserted me; I was no longer useful to my party; I lost my seat in parliament; and when I was on a sick-bed—you remember it, Constance—the bailiffs came, and tore me away for a paltry debt,—the value of one of those suppers the prince used to beg me to give him. From that time my familiars forsook me!—not a visit, not a kind act, not a service for him whose day of work was over! 'Poor Vernon's character was gone! Shockingly involved, could not perform his promises to his creditors, always so extravagant, quite unprincipled, must give him up!'

"In those sentences lies the secret of their conduct. They did not remember that *for* them, *by* them, the character was gone, the promises broken, the ruin incurred! They thought not how I had served them; how my best years had been devoted to advance them,—to ennoble their cause in the lying page of History! All this was not thought of: my life was reduced to two epochs,—that of use to them, that not. During the first, I was honoured; during the last, I was left to starve, to rot! Who freed me from prison; who protects me now? One of my 'party,' my 'noble friends,' my 'honourable, right honourable friends'? No! a tradesman whom I once served in my holiday, and who alone, of all the world, forgets me not in my penance. You see gratitude, friendship, spring up only in middle life; they grow not in high stations!

"And now, come nearer, for my voice falters, and I would have these words distinctly heard. Child, girl as you are, you I consider pledged to record, to fulfil my desire, my curse! Lay your hand on mine: swear that through life to death,—swear! You speak not! repeat my words after me" —Constance obeyed—"through life to death; through good, through ill, through weakness, through power, you will devote yourself to humble, to abase that party from whom your father received ingratitude, mortification, and death! Swear that you will not marry a poor and powerless man, who cannot minister to the ends of that solemn retribution I invoke! Swear that you will seek to marry from amongst the great; not through love. not through ambition, but through hate, and for revenge! You will seek to rise that you may humble those who have betrayed me! In the social walks of life you will delight to gall their vanities; in state intrigues you will embrace every measure that can bring them to their eternal downfall. For this great end you will pursue all means.—What! you hesitate? Repeat, repeat, repeat!—You will lie, cringe, fawn, and think viee not vice, if it bring you one jot nearer to Revenge! With this curse on my foes, I entwine my blessing, dear, dear Constance, on you,—you, who have nursed, watched, all but saved me! God, God bless you, my child!" And Vernon burst into tears.

It was two hours after this singular scene, and exactly in the third hour of morning, that Vernon woke from a short and troubled sleep. The gray dawn (for the time was the height of summer) already began to labour through the shades and against the stars of night. A raw and comfortless chill crept over the earth, and saddened the air in the death-chamber. Constance sat by her father's bed, her eyes fixed upon him, and her cheek more wan than ever by the pale light of that crude and cheerless dawn. When Vernon woke, his eyes, glazed with death, rolled faintly towards her, fixing and dimming in their sockets as they gazed; his throat rattled. But for one moment his voice found vent; a ray shot across his countenance as he uttered his last words,—words that sank at once and eternally to the core of his daughter's heart, —words that ruled her life, and sealed her destiny: "Constance, remember—the Oath—Revenge!"

CHAPTER II.

REMARK ON THE TENURE OF LIFE.—THE COFFINS OF GREAT MEN SELDOM NEGLECTED.—CONSTANCE TAKES REFUGE WITH LADY ERPINGHAM.—THE HEROINE'S ACCOMPLISHMENTS AND CHARACTER.—THE MANŒUVRING TEMPERAMENT.

What a strange life this is! What puppets we are! How terrible an enigma is Fate! I never set my foot without my door but what the fearful darkness that broods over the next moment rushes upon me. How awful an event may hang over our hearts! The sword is always above us, seen or invisible!

And with this life, this scene of darkness and dread, some men would have us so contented as to desire, to ask for no other!

Constance was now without a near relation in the world. But her father predicted rightly: vanity supplied the place of affection. Vernon, who for eighteen months preceding his death had struggled with the sharpest afflictions of want,—Vernon, deserted in life by all, was interred with the insulting ceremonials of pomp and state. Six nobles bore his pall; long trains of carriages attended his funeral; the journals were filled with outlines of his biography and lamentations at his decease. They buried him in Westminster Abbey, and they made subscriptions for a monument in the very best sort of marble. Lady Erpingham, a distant connection of the deceased, invited Constance to live with her; and Constance of course consented, for she had no alternative.

On the day that she arrived at Lady Erpingham's house, in Hill Street, there were several persons present in the drawing-room.

"I fear, poor girl," said Lady Erpingham,—for they were talking of Constance's expected arrival,—"I fear that she will be quite abashed by seeing so many of us, and under such unhappy circumstances."

"How old is she?" asked a beauty.

"About thirteen, I believe."

"Handsome?"

"I have not seen her since she was seven years old. She promised then to be very beautiful; but she was a remarkably shy, silent child."

"Miss Vernon," said the groom of the chambers, throwing open the door.

With the slow step and self-possessed air of womanhood, but with a far haughtier and far colder mien than women commonly assume, Constance Vernon walked through the long apartment, and greeted her future guardian. Though every eye was on her, she did not blush; though the Queens of the London World were round her, her gait and air were more royal than all. Every one present experienced a revulsion of feeling. They were prepared for pity; this was no case in which pity could be given. Even the words of protection died on Lady Erpingham's lip, and *she* it was who felt bashful and disconcerted.

I intend to pass rapidly over the years that elapsed till Constance became a woman. Let us glance at her education.

Vernon had not only had her instructed in the French and Italian, but, a deep and impassioned scholar himself, he had taught her the elements of the two great languages of the ancient world. The treasures of those languages she afterwards conquered of her own accord.

Lady Erpingham had one daughter, who married when Constance had reached the age of sixteen. The advantages Lady Eleanor Erpingham possessed in her masters and her governess Constance shared. Miss Vernon drew well, and sang divinely; but she made no very great proficiency in the science of music. To say truth, her mind was somewhat too stern, and somewhat too intent on other subjects, to surrender to that most jealous of accomplishments the exclusive devotion it requires.

But of all her attractions, and of all the evidences of her cultivated mind, none equalled the extraordinary grace of her conversation. Wholly disregarding the conventional leading-strings in which the minds of young ladies are accustomed to be held,—leading-strings, disguised by the name of "proper diffidence" and "becoming modesty,"—she never scrupled to share, nay, to lead, discussions even of a grave and solid nature. Still less did she scruple to adorn the common trifles that make the sum of conversation with the fascinations of a wit, which, playful, yet deep, rivalled even the paternal source from which it was inherited.

It seems sometimes odd enough to me, that while young ladies are so sedulously taught the accomplishments that a husband disregards, they are never taught the great one he would prize. They are taught to be *exhibitors;* he wants a *companion.* He wants neither a singing animal, nor a drawing animal, nor a dancing animal: he wants a talking animal. But to talk they are never taught; all they know of conversation is slander, and that "comes by nature."

But Constance *did* talk *beautifully,*—not like a pedant or *blue* or a Frenchwoman. A child would have been as much charmed with her as a scholar; but *both* would have been charmed. Her father's eloquence had descended to her; but in him eloquence commanded, in her it won. There was another trait she possessed in common with her father: Vernon (as most disappointed men are wont) had done the world injustice by his accusations. It was not his poverty and his distresses alone which had induced his party to look coolly on his declining day. They were not without some apparent excuse for desertion,—they doubted his *sincerity.* It is true that it was without actual cause. No modern politician had ever been more consistent. He had refused bribes, though poor; and place, though ambitious. But he was essentially—here is the secret—essentially an *intriguant.* Bred in the old school of policy, he thought that manœuvring was wisdom, and duplicity the art of governing. Like Lysander,[1] he loved plotting, yet neglected self-interest. There was not a man less open, or more honest. This character, so rare in all countries, is especially so in England. Your blunt squires, your politicians at Bellamy's, do not comprehend it. They saw in Vernon the arts which deceive enemies, and they dreaded lest, though his friends, they themselves should be deceived. This disposition, so fatal to Vernon, his daughter inherited. With a dark, bold, and passionate genius, which in a man would have led to the highest enterprises, she linked the feminine love of secrecy and scheming. To borrow again from Plutarch and Lysander, "When the skin of the lion fell short, she was quite of opinion that it should be eked out with the fox's."

[1] Plutarch: Life of Lysander.

CHAPTER III.

THE HERO INTRODUCED TO OUR READER'S NOTICE. — DIALOGUE BETWEEN HIMSELF AND HIS FATHER. — PERCY GODOLPHIN'S CHARACTER AS A BOY. — THE CATASTROPHE OF HIS SCHOOL LIFE.

"Percy, remember that it is to-morrow you will return to school," said Mr. Godolphin to his only son.

Percy pouted, and after a momentary silence replied, "No, Father, I think I shall go to Mr. Saville's. He has asked me to spend a month with him; and he says rightly that I shall learn more with him than at Dr. Shallowell's, where I am already head of the sixth form."

"Mr. Saville is a coxcomb, and you are another!" replied the father, who, dressed in an old flannel dressing-gown, with a worn velvet cap on his head, and cowering gloomily over a wretched fire, seemed no bad personification of that mixture of half-hypochondriac, half-miser, which he was in reality. "Don't talk to me of going to town, sir, or —"

"Father," interrupted Percy, in a cool and *nonchalant* tone, as he folded his arms, and looked straight and shrewdly on the paternal face,—"Father, let us understand each other. My schooling, I suppose, is rather an expensive affair?"

"You may well say that, sir! Expensive! it is frightful, horrible, ruinous! Expensive! £20 a year board and Latin; five guineas washing; five more for writing and arithmetic. Sir, if I were not resolved that you should not want education, though you may want fortune, I should—yes, I should— What do you mean, sir?—you are laughing! Is this your respect, your gratitude to your father?"

A slight shade fell over the bright and intelligent countenance of the boy.

"Don't let us talk of gratitude," said he, sadly; "Heaven knows what either you or I have to be grateful for! Fortune has left to your proud name but these bare walls and a handful of barren acres; to me she gave a father's affection,—not such as Nature had made it, but cramped and soured by misfortunes."

Here Percy paused, and his father seemed also struck and affected. "Let us," renewed in a lighter strain this singular boy, who might have passed, by some months, his sixteenth year,—"let us see if we cannot accommodate matters to our mutual satisfaction. You can ill afford my schooling, and I am resolved that at school I will not stay. Saville is a relation of ours; he has taken a fancy to me; he has even hinted that he may leave me his fortune; and he has promised, at least, to afford me a home and his tuition as long as I like. Give me free passport hereafter to come and go as I list, and I in turn will engage never to cost you another shilling. Come, sir, shall it be a compact?"

"You wound me, Percy," said the father, with a mournful pride in his tone; "I have not deserved this, at least from you. You know not, boy, you know not all that has hardened this heart; but to you it has *not* been hard, and a taunt from you,—yes, that *is* the serpent's tooth!"

Percy in an instant was at his father's feet; he seized both his hands, and burst into a passionate fit of tears. "Forgive me," he said, in broken words; "I—I meant not to taunt you. I am but a giddy boy! Send me to school! do with me as you will!"

"Ay," said the old man, shaking his head gently, "you know not what pain a son's bitter word can send to a parent's heart. But it is all natural, perfectly natural! You would reproach me with a love of money, it is the sin to which youth is the least lenient. But what! can I look round the world and not see its value, its necessity? Year after year, from my first manhood, I have toiled and toiled to preserve from the hammer these last remnants of my ancestors' remains. Year after year fortune has slipped from my grasp; and, after all my efforts, and towards the close of a long life, I stand on the very verge of penury. But you cannot tell—no man whose heart is not seared with many years can tell or can appreciate — the motives that have formed my character. You, however," — and his voice softened as he laid his hand on his son's head,— "you, however,— the gay, the bold, the young,— should not have your brow crossed and your eye dimmed by the cares that surround me. Go! I will accompany you to town; I will see Saville myself. If he be one with whom my son can at so tender an age be safely trusted, you shall pay him the visit you wish."

Percy would have replied, but his father checked him; and before the end of the evening, the father had resolved to forget as much as he pleased of the conversation.

The elder Godolphin was one of those characters on whom it is vain to attempt making a permanent impression. The habits of his mind were durably formed: like waters, they yielded to any sudden intrusion, but closed instantly again. Early in life he had been taught that he ought to marry an heiress for the benefit of his estate,— his ancestral estate; the restoration of which he had been bred to consider the grand object and ambition of life. His views had been strangely baffled; but the more they were thwarted the more pertinaciously he clung to them. Naturally kind, generous, and social, he had sunk at length into the anchorite and the miser. All other speculations that should retrieve his ancestral honours had failed; but there is one speculation that never fails,— the speculation of *saving!* It was to this that he now indissolubly attached himself. At moments he was open to all his old habits; but such moments were rare and few. A cold, hard, frosty penuriousness was his prevalent characteristic. He had sent his son, with eighteenpence in his pocket, to a school of £20 a year, where, naturally enough, he learned nothing but mischief and cricket; yet he conceived that his son owed him eternal obligations.

Luckily for Percy, he was an especial favourite with a certain not uncelebrated character of the name of Saville; and Saville claimed the privilege of a relation to supply him with money and receive him at his home. Wild, passionate, fond to excess of pleasure, the young Godolphin caught eagerly at these occasional visits; and at each his mind, keen and penetrating as it naturally was, took new flights, and revelled in new views. He was already the leader of his school, the torment of the master, and the lover of the master's daughter. He was sixteen years old, but a character. A secret pride, a secret bitterness, and an open wit and recklessness of bearing, rendered him to all seeming a boy more endowed with energies than affections; yet a kind word from a friend's lips was never without its effect on him, and he might have been led by the silk while he would have snapped the chain. But these were his boyish traits of mind: the world soon altered them.

The subject of the visit to Saville was not again touched upon. A little reflection showed Mr. Godolphin how nugatory were the promises of a schoolboy that he should not cost his father another shilling; and he knew that Saville's house was not exactly the spot in which economy was best learned. He thought it, therefore, more prudent that his son should return to school.

To school went Percy Godolphin; and about three weeks afterwards, Percy Godolphin was condemned to expulsion for returning, with considerable unction, a slap in the face that he had received from Dr. Shallowell. Instead of waiting for his father's arrival, Percy made up a small bundle of clothes, let himself drop, by the help of the bed-curtains, from the window of the room in which he was confined, and towards the close of a fine summer's evening found himself on the highroad between —— and London, with independence at his heart and — Saville's last gift — ten guineas in his pocket.

CHAPTER IV.

PERCY'S FIRST ADVENTURE AS A FREE AGENT.

It was a fine, picturesque outline of road on which the young outcast found himself journeying, whither he neither knew nor cared. His heart was full of enterprise and the unfledged valour of inexperience. He had proceeded several miles, and the dusk of the evening was setting in, when he observed a stage-coach crawling heavily up a hill, a little ahead of him, and a tall, well-shaped man walking alongside of it, and gesticulating somewhat violently. Godolphin remarked him with some curiosity; and the man, turning abruptly round, perceived, and in his turn noticed very inquisitively, the person and aspect of the young traveller.

"And how now?" said he, presently, and in an agreeable, though familiar and unceremonious tone of voice; "whither are you bound this time of day?"

"It is no business of yours, friend," said the boy, with the proud petulance of his age; "mind what belongs to yourself."

"You are sharp on me, young sir," returned the other; "but it is our business to be loquacious. Know, sir," — and the stranger frowned, — "that we have ordered many a taller fellow than yourself to execution for a much smaller insolence than you seem capable of."

A laugh from the coach caused Godolphin to lift up his eyes, and he saw the door of the vehicle half-open, as if for coolness, and an arch female face looking down on him.

"You are merry on me, I see," said Percy; "come out, and I 'll be even with you, pretty one."

The lady laughed yet more loudly at the premature gallantry of the traveller; but the man, without heeding her, and laying his hand on Percy's shoulder, said,—

"Pray, sir, do you live at B——?" naming the town they were now approaching.

"Not I," said Godolphin, freeing himself from the intrusion.

"You will, perhaps, sleep there?"

"Perhaps I shall."

"You are too young to travel alone."

"And you are too old to make such impertinent remarks," retorted Godolphin, reddening with anger.

"Faith, I like this spirit, my Hotspur," said the stranger, coolly. "If you are really going to put up for the night at B——, suppose we sup together?"

"And who and what are you?" asked Percy, bluntly.

"Anything and everything! in other words, an actor!"

"And the young lady?"

"Is our *prima donna*. In fact, except the driver, the coach holds none but the ladies and gentlemen of our company. We have made an excellent harvest at A——, and we are now on our way to the theatre at B——; pretty theatre it is too, and has been known to hold seventy-one pounds eight shillings." Here the actor fell into a revery; and Percy, moving nearer to the coach-door, glanced at the damsel, who returned the look with a laugh which, though coquettish, was too low and musical to be called bold.

"So that gentleman, so free and easy in his manners, is not your husband?"

"Heaven forbid! Do you think I should be so gay if he were? But, pooh! what can you know of married life? No!" she continued, with a pretty air of mock dignity; "I am the Belvidera, the Calista, of the company,—above all control, all husbanding, and reaping thirty-three shillings a week."

"But are you above lovers as well as husbands?" asked Percy, with a rakish air, borrowed from Saville.

"Bless the boy! No; but then my lovers must be at least as tall, and at least as rich, and, I am afraid, at least as old, as myself."

"Don't frighten yourself, my dear," returned Percy; "*I* was not about to make love to you."

"Were you not? Yes, you were, and you know it. But why will you not sup with us?"

"Why not, indeed?" thought Percy, as the idea, thus more enticingly put than it was at first, pressed upon him. "If *you* ask me," he said, "I will."

"I *do* ask you, then," said the actress; and here the hero of the company turned abruptly round with a theatrical start, and exclaimed, "To sup or not to sup? that is the question."

"To sup, sir," said Godolphin.

"Very well! I am glad to hear it. Had you not better mount and rest yourself in the coach? You can take my place — I am studying a new part. We have two miles farther to B—— yet."

Percy accepted the invitation, and was soon by the side of the pretty actress. The horses broke into a slow trot, and thus delighted with his adventure, the son of the ascetic Godolphin, the pupil of the courtly Saville, entered the town of B——, and commenced his first independent campaign in *the great world.*

CHAPTER V.

THE MUMMERS. — GODOLPHIN IN LOVE. — THE EFFECT OF FANNY MILLINGER'S ACTING UPON HIM. — THE TWO OFFERS. — GODOLPHIN QUITS THE PLAYERS.

Our travellers stopped at the first inn in the outskirts of the town. Here they were shown into a large room on the ground-floor, sanded, with a long table in the centre; and before the supper was served, Percy had leisure to examine all the companions with whom he had associated himself.

In the first place, there was an old gentleman, of the age of sixty-three, in a bob-wig, and inclined to be stout, who always played the *lover.* He was equally excellent in the pensive Romeo and the bustling Rapid. He had an ill way of talking off the stage, partly because he had lost all his front teeth,— a circumstance which made him avoid, in general, those parts in which he had to force a great deal of laughter. Next, there was a little girl of about fourteen, who played angels, fairies, and, at a pinch, was very effective as an old woman. Thirdly, there was our free-and-easy cavalier, who, having a loud voice and a manly presence, usually performed the tyrant. He was great in Macbeth, greater in Bombastes Furioso. Fourthly, came this gentleman's wife, a pretty, slatternish woman, much painted. She usually performed the second female,—the confidante, the chambermaid,—the Emilia to the Desdemona. And fifthly, was Percy's new inamorata,—a girl of about one-and-twenty, fair, with a *nez retroussé*: beautiful auburn hair, that was always a little dishevelled; the prettiest mouth, teeth, and dimple imaginable; a natural colour; and a person that promised to incline hereafter towards that roundness of proportion which is more dear to the sensual than the romantic. This girl, whose name was Fanny Millinger, was of so frank, good-humoured, and lively a turn, that she was the idol of the whole company, and her superiority in acting was never made a matter of jealousy. Actors may believe this, or not, as they please.

"But is this all your company?" said Percy.

"All? no!" replied Fanny, taking off her bonnet, and curling up her tresses by the help of a dim glass. "The rest are provided at the theatre along with the candle-snuffer and scene-shifters part of the fixed property. Why won't *you* take to the stage? I wish you would! you would make a very respectable—page."

"Upon my word!" said Percy, exceedingly offended.

"Come, come!" cried the actress, clapping her hands, and perfectly unheeding his displeasure, "why don't you help me off with my cloak; why don't you set me a chair; why don't you take this great box out of my way; why don't you—Heaven help me!" and she stamped her little foot quite seriously on the floor. "A pretty person for a lover you are!"

"Oho! then I *am* a lover, you acknowledge?"

"Nonsense! get a chair next me at supper."

The young Godolphin was perfectly fascinated by the lively actress; and it was with no small interest that he stationed himself the following night in the stage-box of the little theatre at ——, to see how his Fanny acted. The house was tolerably well filled, and the play was "She Stoops to Conquer." The male parts were, on the whole, respectably managed; though Percy was somewhat surprised to observe that a man, who had joined the corps that morning, blessed with the most solemn countenance in the world,—a fine Roman nose, and a forehead like a sage's,—was now dressed in nankeen tights, and a coat without skirts, splitting the sides of the gallery in the part of Tony Lumpkin. But into the heroine Fanny Millinger threw a grace, a sweetness, a simple yet dignified spirit of true love, that at once charmed and astonished all present. The applause was unbounded; and Percy Godolphin felt proud of himself for having admired one whom every one else seemed also resolved upon admiring.

When the comedy was finished, he went behind the scenes, and for the first time felt the rank which intellect bestows. This idle girl, with whom he had before been so familiar; who had seemed to him, boy as he was, only made for jesting and coquetry and trifling, he now felt to be raised to a sudden eminence that startled and abashed him. He became shy and awkward, and stood at a distance stealing a glance towards her, but without the courage to approach and compliment her.

The quick eye of the actress detected the effect she had produced. She was naturally pleased at it, and coming up to Godolphin, she touched his shoulder, and with a smile rendered still more brilliant by the rouge yet unwashed from the dimpled cheeks, said, "Well, most awkward swain, no flattery ready for me? Go to! you won't suit me: get yourself another empress."

"You have pleased me into respecting you," said Godolphin.

There was a delicacy in the expression that was very characteristic of the real mind of the speaker, though that mind was not yet developed; and the pretty actress was touched by it at the moment, though, despite the grace of her acting, she was by nature far too volatile to think it at all advantageous to be *respected* in the long run. She did not act in the after-piece, and Godolphin escorted her home to the inn.

So long as his ten guineas lasted — which the reader will conceive was not very long — Godolphin stayed with the gay troop, as the welcome lover of its chief ornament. To her he confided his name and history: she laughed heartily at the latter, — for she was one of Venus's true children, fond of striking mirth out of all subjects. "But what," said she, patting his cheek affectionately, "what should hinder you from joining us for a little while? I could teach you to be an actor in three lessons. Come now, attend! It is but a mere series of tricks,— this art that seems to you so admirable."

Godolphin grew embarrassed. There was in him a sort of hidden pride that could never endure to subject itself to the censure of others. He had no propensity to imitation, and he had a strong susceptibility to the ridiculous. These traits of mind thus early developed — which in later life prevented his ever finding fit scope for his natural powers, which made him too proud to bustle, and too philosophical to shine — were of service to him on this occasion, and preserved him from the danger into which he might otherwise have fallen. He could not be persuaded to act: the fair Fanny gave up the attempt in despair. "Yet stay with us," said she, tenderly, "and share my poor earnings."

Godolphin started; and in the wonderful contradictions of the proud human heart, this generous offer from the poor actress gave him a distaste, a displeasure, that almost reconciled him to parting from her. It seemed to open to him at once the equivocal mode of life he had entered upon. "No, Fanny," said he, after a pause, "I am here because I resolved to be independent; I cannot, therefore, choose dependence."

"Miss Millinger is wanted instantly for rehearsal," said the little girl who acted fairies and old women, putting her head suddenly into the room.

"Bless me!" cried Fanny, starting up; "is it so late? Well, I must go now. Good-by! look in upon us,— do!"

But Godolphin, moody and thoughtful, walked into the street; and lo! the first thing that greeted his eyes was a handbill on the wall, describing his own person, and offering twenty guineas reward for his detention. "Let him return to his afflicted parent," was the conclusion of the bill, "and all shall be forgiven."

Godolphin crept back to his apartment; wrote a long, affectionate letter to Fanny; enclosed her his watch, as the only keepsake in his power; gave her his address at Saville's; and then, towards dusk, once more sallied forth, and took a place in the mail for London. He had no money for his passage, but his appearance was such that the coachman readily trusted him; and the next morning at daybreak he was under Saville's roof.

CHAPTER VI.

PERCY GODOLPHIN THE GUEST OF SAVILLE. — HE ENTERS THE LIFE-GUARDS AND BECOMES THE FASHION.

"And so," said Saville, laughing, "you really gave them the slip: excellent! But I envy you your adventures with the player folk. 'Gad! if I were some years younger, I would join them myself; I should act Sir Pertinax Macsycophant famously; I have a touch of the mime in me. Well! but what do you propose to do,— live with me, eh?"

"Why, I think that might be the best, and certainly it would be the pleasantest, mode of passing my life. But—"

"But what?"

"Why, I can scarcely quarter myself on your courtesy; I should soon grow discontented. So I shall write to my father, whom I, kindly and considerately, by the way, informed of my safety the very first day of my arrival at B——. I told him to direct his letters to your house; but I regret to find that the handbill which so frightened me from my propriety is the only notice he has deigned to take of my whereabout. I shall write to him therefore again, begging him to let me enter the army. It is not a profession I much fancy; but what then? I shall be my own master."

"Very well said!" answered Saville; "and here I hope I can serve you. If your father will pay the lawful sum for a commission in the Guards, why, I think I have interest to get you in for that sum alone,— no trifling favour."

Godolphin was enchanted at this proposal, and instantly wrote to his father, urging it strongly upon him; Saville, in a separate epistle, seconded the motion. "You see," wrote the latter,— "you see, my dear sir, that your son is a wild, resolute scapegrace. You can do nothing with him by schools and coercion: put him to discipline in the king's service, and condemn him to live on his pay. It is a cheap mode, after all, of providing for a reprobate; and as he will have the good fortune to enter the army at so early an age, by the time he is thirty, he may be a colonel on full pay. Seriously, this is the best thing you can do with him,— unless you have a living in your family."

The old gentleman was much discomposed by these letters, and by his son's previous elopement. He could not, however, but foresee that if he resisted the boy's wishes, he was likely to have a troublesome time of it. Scrape after scrape, difficulty following difficulty, might ensue, all costing both anxiety and money. The present offer furnished him with a fair excuse for ridding himself, for a long time to come, of further provision for his offspring; and now growing daily more and more attached to the indolent routine of solitary economies in which he moved, he was glad of an opportunity to deliver himself from future interruption, and surrender his whole soul to his favourite occupation.

At length, after a fortnight's delay and meditation, he wrote shortly to Saville and his son, saying, after much reproach to the latter, that if the commission could really be purchased at the sum specified he was willing to make a sacrifice, for which he must pinch himself, and conclude the business. This touched the son, but Saville laughed him out of the twinge of good feeling; and very shortly afterwards, Percy Godolphin was gazetted as a cornet in the —— Life-Guards.

The life of a soldier, in peace, is indolent enough, Heaven knows! Percy liked the new uniforms and the new horses — all of which were bought on credit. He liked his new companions; he liked balls; he liked flirting; he did not dislike Hyde Park from four o'clock till six; and he was not very much bored by drills and parade. It was much to his credit in the world that he was the *protégé* of a man who had so great a character for profligacy and gambling as Augustus Saville; and under such auspices he found himself launched at once into the full tide of "good society."

Young, romantic, high-spirited, with the classic features of an Antinous, and a very pretty knack of complimenting and writing verses, Percy Godolphin soon became, while yet more fit in years for the nursery than the world, "the curled darling" of that wide class of high-born women who have nothing to do but to hear love made to them, and who, all artifice themselves, think the love sweetest which springs from the most natural source. They like boyhood when it is not bashful; and from sixteen to twenty, a Juan need scarcely go to Seville to find a Julia.

But love was not the worst danger that menaced the intoxicated boy. Saville, the most seductive of tutors,—Saville who, in his wit, his *bon ton*, his control over the great world, seemed as a god to all less elevated and less aspiring,—Saville was Godolphin's constant companion; and Saville was worse than a profligate,—he was a gambler! One would think that gaming was the last vice that could fascinate the young: its avarice, its grasping, its hideous selfishness, its cold, calculating meanness, would, one might imagine, scare away all who have yet other and softer deities to worship. But, in fact, the fault of youth is that it can rarely resist whatever is the Mode. Gaming, in all countries, is the vice of an aristocracy. The young find it already established in the best circles; they are enticed by the habit of others, and ruined when the habit becomes their own.

"You look feverish, Percy," said Saville, as he met his pupil in the Park. "I don't wonder at it; you lost infernally last night."

"More than I can pay," replied Percy, with a quivering lip.

"No! you shall pay it to-morrow, for you shall go shares with me to-night. Observe," continued Saville, lowering his voice, "I *never lose.*"

"How *never?*"

"Never, unless by design. I play at no game where chance

only presides. Whist is my favourite game: it is not popular; I am sorry for it. I take up with other games,—I am forced to do it; but even at *rouge-et-noir* I carry about with me the rules of whist. I calculate, I remember."

"But hazard?"

"I never play at that," said Saville, solemnly. "It is the devil's game; it defies skill. Forsake hazard, and let me teach you *écarté;* it is coming into fashion."

Saville took great pains with Godolphin; and Godolphin, who was by nature of a contemplative, not hasty mood, was no superficial disciple. As his biographer, I grieve to confess that he became, though a punctiliously honest, a wise and fortunate gamester; and thus he eked out betimes the slender profits of a subaltern's pay.

This was the first great deterioration in Percy's mind,—a mind which ought to have made him a very different being from what he became, but which no vice, no evil example, could ever entirely pervert.

CHAPTER VII.

SAVILLE EXCUSED FOR HAVING HUMAN AFFECTIONS.—GODOLPHIN SEES ONE WHOM HE NEVER SEES AGAIN.—THE NEW ACTRESS.

SAVILLE was deemed the consummate man of the world,—wise and heartless. How came he to take such gratuitous pains with the boy Godolphin? In the first place, Saville had no legitimate children; Godolphin was his relation: in the second place, it may be observed, that hackneyed and sated men of the world are fond of the young, in whom they recognize something—a better something—belonging to themselves. In Godolphin's gentleness and courage, Saville thought he saw the mirror of his own crusted urbanity and scheming perseverance; in Godolphin's fine imagination and subtle intellect he beheld his own cunning and hypocrisy. The boy's popularity flattered him; the boy's conversation amused. No man is so heartless but that he is capable of strong likings, when they do not put him much out of his way; it was this sort of liking that Saville had for Godolphin. Besides, there was yet another reason for attachment, which might at first seem too delicate to actuate the refined voluptuary; but examined closely, the delicacy vanished. Saville had loved, at least had offered his hand to, Godolphin's mother (she was supposed an heiress!). He thought he had just missed being Godolphin's father; his vanity made him like to show the boy what a much better father he would have been than the one that Providence had given him. His resentment, too, against the accepted suitor, made him love to exercise a little spiteful revenge against Godolphin's father; he was glad to show that the son preferred where the mother rejected. All these motives combined made Saville take, as it were, to the young Percy; and being rich, and habitually profuse, though prudent, and a shrewd speculator withal, the pecuniary part of his kindness cost him no pain. But Godolphin, who was not ostentatious, did not trust himself largely to the capricious fount of the worldling's generosity. Fortune smiled on her boyish votary; and during the short time he was obliged to cultivate her favours, showered on him at least a sufficiency for support, or even for display.

Crowded with fine people, and blazing with light, were the rooms of the Countess of B——, as, flushed from a late dinner at Saville's, young Godolphin made his appearance in the scene. He was not of those numerous gentlemen, the stock-flowers of the *parterre*, who stick themselves up against walls in the panoply of neckclothed silence. He came not to balls from the vulgar motive of being seen there in the most conspicuous situation,—a motive so apparent among the stiff exquisites of England. He came to amuse himself; and if he found no one capable of amusing him, he saw no necessity in staying. He was always seen, therefore, conversing or dancing, or listening to music—or he was not seen at all.

In exchanging a few words with a Colonel D——, a noted *roué* and gamester, he observed, gazing on him very intently —and as Percy thought, very rudely—an old gentleman in a dress of the last century. Turn where he would, Godolphin could not rid himself of the gaze; so at length he met it with a look of equal scrutiny and courage. The old gentleman slowly approached. "Percy Godolphin, I think?" said he.

"That is *my* name, sir," replied Percy. "Yours—"

"No matter! Yet stay! you shall know it. I am Henry Johnstone,—old Harry Johnstone. You have heard of him? —your father's first cousin. Well, I grieve, young sir, to find that you associate with that rascal Saville.—Nay, never interrupt me, sir!—I grieve to find that you, thus young, thus unguarded, are left to be ruined in heart and corrupted in nature by any one who will take the trouble! Yet I like your countenance! I like your countenance!—it is open, yet thoughtful; frank, and yet it has something of melancholy. You have not Charles's coloured hair; but you are much younger,—much. I am glad I have seen you; I came here on purpose; good-night!" and without waiting for an answer, the old man disappeared.

Godolphin, recovering from his surprise, recollected that he had often heard his father speak of a rich and eccentric relation named Johnstone. This singular interview made a strong but momentary impression on him. He intended to seek out the old man's residence; but one thing or another drove away the fulfilment of the intention, and in this world the relations never met again.

Percy, now musingly gliding through the crowd, sank into a seat beside a lady of forty-five, who sometimes amused herself in making love to him—because there could be no harm in such a mere boy! And presently afterwards, a Lord George Somebody sauntering up asked the lady if he had not seen her at the play on the previous night.

"Oh, yes! we went to see the new actress. How pretty she is! so unaffected too! how well she sings!"

"Pretty well—er!" replied Lord George, passing his

hand through his hair. "Very nice girl — er! — good ankles. Devilish hot — er, is it not — er — er? What a bore this is, eh! Ah, Godolphin! don't forget Wattier's — er!" and his lordship *er'd* himself off.

"What actress is this?"

"Oh, a very good one indeed! — came out in 'The Belle's Stratagem.' We are going to see her to-morrow; will you dine with us early, and be our cavalier?"

"Nothing will please me more! Your ladyship has dropped your handkerchief."

"Thank you!" said the lady, bending till her hair touched Godolphin's cheek, and gently pressing the hand that was extended to her. It was a wonder that Godolphin never became a coxcomb.

He dined at Wattier's the next day according to appointment; he went to the play; and at the moment his eye first turned to the stage, a universal burst of applause indicated the entrance of the new actress, — Fanny Millinger!

CHAPTER VIII.

GODOLPHIN'S PASSION FOR THE STAGE. — THE DIFFERENCE IT ENGENDERED IN HIS HABITS OF LIFE.

Now this event produced a great influence over Godolphin's habits, — and I suppose, therefore, I may add, over his character. He renewed his acquaintance with the lively actress.

"What a change!" cried both.

"The strolling player risen into celebrity!"

"And the runaway boy polished into fashion!"

"You are handsomer than ever, Fanny."

"I return the compliment," replied Fanny, with a courtesy.

And now Godolphin became a constant attendant at the theatre. This led him into a mode of life quite different from that which he had lately cultivated.

There are in London two sets of idle men: one set, the butterflies of balls, the loungers of the regular walks of society, diners out, the "old familiar faces," seen everywhere, known to every one; the other set, a more wild, irregular, careless race, who go little into parties, and vote balls a nuisance, who live in clubs, frequent theatres, drive about late o' nights in mysterious-looking vehicles, and enjoy a vast acquaintance among the Aspasias of pleasure. These are the men who are the critics of theatricals; black-neckclothed and well-booted, they sit in their boxes and decide on the ankles of a dancer or the voice of a singer. They have a smattering of literature, and use a great deal of French in their conversation; they have something of romance in their composition, and have been known to marry for love. In short, there is in their whole nature a more roving, liberal, Continental character of dissipation than belongs to the cold, tame, dull, prim, hedge-clipped indolence of more national exquisitism. Into this set, out of the other set, fell young Godolphin; and oh! the merry mornings at actresses' houses; the jovial suppers after the play; the buoyancy, the brilliancy, the *esprit,* with which the hours, from midnight to cockcrow, were often pelted with rose-leaves and drowned in Rhenish.

By degrees, however, as Godolphin warmed into his attendance at the playhouses, the fine intellectual something that lay yet undestroyed at his heart stirred up emotions which he felt his more vulgar associates were unfitted to share.

There is that in theatrical representation which perpetually awakens whatever romance belongs to our character. The magic lights, the pomp of scene, the palace, the camp, the forest, the midnight wold, the moonlight reflected on the water, the melody of the tragic rhythm, the grace of the comic wit, the strange art that gives such meaning to the poet's lightest word; the fair, false, exciting life that is detailed before us, crowding into some three little hours all that our most busy ambition could desire — love, enterprise, war, glory; the kindling exaggeration of the sentiments which belong to the stage like our own in our boldest moments,— all these appeals to our finer senses are not made in vain. Our taste for castle-building and visions deepens upon us; and we chew a mental opium which stagnates all the other faculties, but wakens that of the ideal.

Godolphin was peculiarly fascinated by the stage; he loved to steal away from his companions, and, alone and unheeded, to feast his mind on the unreal stream of existence that mirrored images so beautiful. And oh! while yet we are young; while yet the dew lingers on the green leaf of spring; while all the brighter, the more enterprising part of the future is to come; while we know not whether the true life may not be visionary and excited as the false,— how deep and rich a transport is it to see, to feel, to hear Shakspeare's conceptions made *actual*, though all imperfectly, and only for an hour! Sweet Arden! are we in thy forest,— thy "shadowy groves and unfrequented glens"? Rosalind, Jaques, Orlando, have you indeed a being upon earth? Ah, this is true enchantment! And when we turn back to life, we turn from the colours which the Claude glass breathes over a winter's landscape to the nakedness of the landscape itself!

CHAPTER IX.

THE LEGACY. — A NEW DEFORMITY IN SAVILLE. — THE NATURE OF WORLDLY LIAISONS. — GODOLPHIN LEAVES ENGLAND.

But then it is not always a sustainer of the stage delusion to be enamoured of an actress: it takes us too much behind the scenes. Godolphin felt this so strongly that he liked those plays least in which Fanny performed. Off the stage her character had so little romance that he could not deceive himself into the romance of her character before the lamps. Luckily, however, Fanny did not attempt Shakspeare. She was inimitable in vaudeville, in farce, and in the lighter comedy; but she had prudently abandoned tragedy in deserting the barn. She was a girl of much talent and quickness, and discovered exactly the paths in which her vanity could walk without being wounded. And there was a simplicity, a frankness, about her manner, that made her a most agreeable companion.

The attachment between her and Godolphin was not very violent; it was a silken tie, which opportunity could knit and snap a hundred times over without doing much wrong to the hearts it so lightly united. Over Godolphin the attachment itself had no influence, while the *effects* of the attachment had an influence so great.

One night, after an absence from town of two or three days, Godolphin returned home from the theatre, and found among the letters waiting his arrival one from his father. It was edged with black; the seal, too, was black. Godolphin's heart misgave him: tremblingly he opened it, and read as follows: —

Dear Percy, — I have news for you, which I do not know whether I should call good or bad. On the one hand, your cousin, that old oddity, Harry Johnstone, is dead, and has left you, out of his immense fortune, the poor sum of £20,000. But mark! on condition that you leave the Guards, and either reside with me, or at least leave London, till your majority is attained. If you refuse these conditions you lose the legacy. It is rather strange that this curious character should take such pains with your morals, and yet not leave *me* a single shilling. But justice is out of fashion nowadays; your showy virtues only are the rage. I beg, if you choose to come down here, that you will get me twelve yards of house-flannel; I inclose a pattern of the quality. Snug, in Oxford Street, near Tottenham Court Road, is my man. It is certainly a handsome thing in old Johnstone; but so odd to omit me. How did you get acquainted with him? The £20,000 will, however, do much for the poor property. Pray take care of it, Percy, — pray do.

I have had a touch of the gout, for the first time. I have been too luxurious; by proper abstinence, I trust to bring it down. Compliments to that smooth rogue, Saville.

Your affectionate, A. G

P. S.— Discharged Old Sally for flirting with the butcher's boy,— flirtations of that sort make meat weigh much heavier. Bess is my only she-helpmate now, besides the old creature who shows the ruins: so much the better. What an eccentric creature that Johnstone was! I hate eccentric people.

The letter fell from Percy's hands. And this, then, was the issue of his single interview with the poor old man! It was events like these, wayward and strange (events which checkered his whole life), that, secretly to himself, tinged Godolphin's character with superstition. He afterwards dealt *con amore* with fatalities and influences.

You may be sure that he did not sleep much that night. Early the next morning he sought Saville, and imparted to him the intelligence he had received.

"Droll enough!" said Saville, languidly, and more than a little displeased at this generosity to Godolphin from another; for, like all small-hearted persons, he was jealous; "droll enough! Hem! and you never knew him but once, and then he abused me! I wonder at that; I was very obliging to his vulgar son."

"What! he had a son, then?"

"Some two-legged creature of that sort, raw and bony, dropped into London, like a ptarmigan, wild, and scared out of his wits. Old Johnstone was in the country, taking care of his wife, who had lost the use of her limbs ever since she had been married,— caught a violent — husband — the first day of wedlock! The boy, sole son and heir, came up to town at the age of discretion; got introduced to me; I patronized him; brought him into a decent degree of fashion; played a few games at cards with him; won some money; would not win any more; advised him to leave off,— too young to play; neglected my advice; went on, and, d—n the fellow! if he did not cut his throat one morning; and the father, to my astonishment, laid the blame upon me!"

Godolphin stood appalled in speechless disgust. He never *loved* Saville from that hour.

"In fact," resumed Saville, carelessly, "he had lost very considerably. His father was a stern, hard man, and the poor boy was frightened at the thought of his displeasure. I suppose Monsieur Papa imagined me a sort of moral ogre, eating up all the little youths that fall in my way, since he leaves you £ 20,000 on condition that you take care of yourself and shun the castle I live in! Well, well! 't is all very flattering! And where will you go? To Spain?"

This story affected Percy sensibly. He regretted deeply that he had not sought out the bereaved father, and been of some comfort to his later hours. He appreciated all that warmth of sympathy, that delicacy of heart, which had made the old man compassionate his young relation's unfriended lot, and couple his gift with a condition, likely perhaps to limit Percy's desires to the independence thus bestowed, and certain to remove his more tender years from a scene of constant contagion. Thus melancholy and thoughtful, Godolphin repaired to the house of the now famous, the now admired Miss Millinger.

Fanny received the good news of his fortune with a smile, and the bad news of his departure from England with a tear. There are some attachments, of which we so easily sound the depth that the one never thinks of exacting from the other the sacrifices that seem inevitable to more earnest affections. Fanny never dreamed of leaving her theatrical career, and accompanying Godolphin; Godolphin never dreamed of demanding it. These are the connections of the great world: my good reader, learn the great world as you look at them!

All was soon settled. Godolphin was easily disembarrassed of his commission. Six hundred a year from his fortune was allowed him during his minority. He insisted on sharing this allowance with his father; the moiety left to himself was quite sufficient for all that a man so young could require. At the age of little more than seventeen, but with a character which premature independence had half formed, and also half enervated, the young Godolphin saw the shores of England recede before him, and felt himself alone in the universe,—the lord of his own fate.

CHAPTER X.

THE EDUCATION OF CONSTANCE'S MIND.

MEANWHILE, Constance Vernon grew up in womanhood and beauty. All around her contributed to feed that stern remembrance which her father's dying words had bequeathed. Naturally proud, quick, susceptible, she felt slights, often merely incidental, with a deep and brooding resentment. The forlorn and dependent girl could not, indeed, fail to meet with many bitter proofs that her situation was not forgotten by a world in which prosperity and station are the cardinal virtues. Many a loud whisper, many an intentional "aside," reached her haughty ear and coloured her pale cheek. Such accidents increased her early-formed asperity of thought, chilled the gushing flood of her young affections, and sharpened with a relentless edge her bitter and caustic hatred to a society she deemed at once insolent and worthless. To a taste intuitively fine and noble, the essential vulgarities — the fierceness to-day, the cringing to-morrow; the veneration for power; the indifference to virtue, — which characterized the framers and rulers of "society" could not but bring contempt as well as anger; and amidst the brilliant circles to which so many aspirers looked up with hopeless ambition, Constance moved only to ridicule, to loathe, to despise.

So strong, so constantly nourished, was this sentiment of contempt, that it lasted with equal bitterness when Constance afterwards became the queen and presider over that great world in which she now shone, — to dazzle, but not to rule. What at first might have seemed an exaggerated and insane prayer on the part of her father grew, as her experience ripened, a natural and laudable command. She was thrown entirely with that party amongst whom were his early friends and his late deserters. She resolved to humble the crested arrogance around her, as much from her own desire as from the wish to obey and avenge her father. From contempt for rank rose naturally the ambition of rank. The young beauty resolved to banish love from her heart; to devote herself to one aim and object; to win title and station, that she might be able to give power and permanence to her disdain of those qualities in others; and in the secrecy of night she repeated the vow which had consoled her father's death-bed, and solemnly resolved to crush love within her heart and marry solely for station and for power.

As the daughter of so celebrated a politician, it was natural that Constance should take interest in politics. She lent to every discussion of state events an eager and thirsty ear. She embraced with masculine ardour such sentiments as were then considered the extreme of liberality; and she looked on that career which society limits to *man*, as the noblest, the loftiest in the world. She regretted that she was a woman, and prevented from personally carrying into effect the sentiments she passionately espoused. Meanwhile, she did not neglect, nor suffer to rust, the bright weapon of a wit which embodied at times all the biting energies of her contempt. To insolence she retorted sarcasm; and, early able to see that society, like virtue, must be trampled upon in order to yield forth its incense, she rose into respect by the *hauteur* of her manner, the bluntness of her satire, the independence of her mind, far more than by her various accomplishments and her unrivalled beauty.

Of Lady Erpingham she had nothing to complain: kind, easy, and characterless, her protectress sometimes wounded her by carelessness, but never through design; on the contrary, the countess at once loved and admired her, and was as anxious that her *protégée* should form a brilliant alliance as if she had been her own daughter. Constance, therefore, loved Lady Erpingham with sincere and earnest warmth, and endeavoured to forget all the commonplaces and littlenesses which made up the mind of her protectress, and which, otherwise, would have been precisely of that nature to which one like Constance would have been the least indulgent.

CHAPTER XI.

CONVERSATION BETWEEN LADY ERPINGHAM AND CONSTANCE. — FURTHER PARTICULARS OF GODOLPHIN'S FAMILY, ETC.

Lady Erpingham was a widow; her jointure, for she had been an heiress and a duke's daughter, was large; and the noblest mansion of all the various seats possessed by the wealthy and powerful house of Erpingham had been allotted by her late lord for her widowed residence. Thither she went punctually on the first of every August, and quitted it punctually on the eighth of every January.

It was some years after the date of Godolphin's departure from England, and the summer following the spring in which Constance had been "brought out;" and after a *début* of such splendour that at this day (many years subsequent to that period) the sensation she created is not only a matter of remembrance but of conversation, Constance, despite the triumph of her vanity, was not displeased to seek some refuge, even from admiration, among the shades of Wendover Castle.

"When," said she one morning, as she was walking with Lady Erpingham upon a terrace beneath the windows of the castle, which overlooked the country for miles,— "when will you go with me, dear Lady Erpingham, to see those ruins of which I have heard so much and so often, and which I have never been able to persuade you to visit? Look! the day is so clear that we can see their outline now — there, to the right of that church! — they cannot be so very far from Wendover."

"Godolphin Priory is about twelve miles off," said Lady Erpingham; "but it may seem nearer, for it is situated on the highest spot of the county. Poor Arthur Godolphin! he is lately dead!" Lady Erpingham sighed.

"I never heard you speak of him before."

"There might be a reason for my silence, Constance. He was the person, of all whom I ever saw, who appeared to me when I was at your age the most fascinating. Not, Constance, that I was in love with him, or that he gave me any reason to become so through gratitude for any affection on his part. It was a girl's fancy, idle and short-lived,—nothing more!"

"And the young Godolphin,—the boy who, at so early an age, has made himself known for his eccentric life abroad?"

"Is his son; the present owner of those ruins, and, I fear, of little more, unless it be the remains of a legacy received from a relation."

"Was the father extravagant, then?"

"Not he! But *his* father had exceeded a patrimony greatly involved, and greatly reduced from its ancient importance. All the lands we see yonder — those villages, those woods — once belonged to the Godolphins. They were the most ancient and the most powerful family in this part of England; but the estates dwindled away with each successive generation, and when Arthur Godolphin, *my* Godolphin, succeeded to the property, nothing was left for him but the choice of three evils,—a profession, obscurity, or a wealthy marriage. My father, who had long destined me for Lord Erpingham, insinuated that it was in me that Mr. Godolphin wished to find the resource I have last mentioned, and that in such resource was my only attraction in his eyes. I have some reason to believe he proposed to the duke; but he was silent to me, from whom, girl as I was, he might have been less certain of refusal."

"What did he at last?"

"Married a lady who was supposed to be an heiress; but he had scarcely enjoyed her fortune a year before it became the subject of a lawsuit. He lost the cause and the dowry; and, what was worse, the expenses of litigation, and the sums he was obliged to refund, reduced him to what, for a man of his rank, might be considered absolute poverty. He was thoroughly chagrined and soured by this event; retired to those ruins, or rather to the small cottage that adjoins them, and there lived to the day of his death, shunning society, and certainly not exceeding his income."

"I understand you: he became parsimonious."

"To the excess which his neighbours called miserly."

"And his wife?"

"Poor woman! she was a mere fine lady, and died, I believe, of the same vexation which nipped, not the life, but the heart of her husband."

"Had they only one son?"

"Only the present owner: Percy, I think, — yes, Percy; it was his mother's surname, — Percy Godolphin."

"And how came this poor boy to be thrown so early on the world? Did he quarrel with Mr. Godolphin?"

"I believe not; but when Percy was about sixteen, he left the obscure school at which he was educated, and resided for some little time with a relation, Augustus Saville. He stayed with him in London for about a year, and went everywhere with him, though so mere a boy. His manners were, I well remember, assured and formed. A relation left him some moderate legacy, and afterwards he went abroad alone."

"But the ruins? The late Mr. Godolphin, notwithstanding his reserve, did not object to indulging the curiosity of his neighbours?"

"No; he was proud of the interest the ruins of his hereditary mansion so generally excited, — proud of their celebrity in print-shops and in tours; but he himself was never seen. The cottage in which he lived, though it adjoins the ruins, was, of course, sacred from intrusion, and is so walled in, that that great delight of English visitors at show-places, — peeping in at windows, — was utterly forbidden. However that be, during Mr. Godolphin's life I never had courage to visit what, to me, would have been a melancholy scene; now, the pain would be somewhat less; and since you wish it, suppose we drive over and visit the ruins to-morrow? It is the regular day for seeing them, by the by."

"Not, dear Lady Erpingham, if it give you the least — "

"My sweet girl," interrupted Lady Erpingham, when a servant approached to announce visitors at the castle.

"Will you go into the saloon, Constance?" said the elder lady, as, thinking still of love and Arthur Godolphin, she took her way to her dressing-room to renovate her rouge.

It would have been a pretty amusement to one of the lesser devils, if, during the early romance of Lady Erpingham's feelings towards Arthur Godolphin, he had foretold her the hour when she would tell how Arthur Godolphin died a miser,— just five minutes before she repaired to the toilette to decorate the cheek of age for the heedless eyes of a common acquaintance. 'T is the world's way! For my part, I would undertake to find a better world in that rookery opposite my windows.

CHAPTER XII.

DESCRIPTION OF GODOLPHIN'S HOUSE. — THE FIRST INTERVIEW. — ITS EFFECT ON CONSTANCE.

"BUT," asked Constance, as, the next day, Lady Erpingham and herself were performing the appointed pilgrimage to the ruins of Godolphin Priory, "if the late Mr. Godolphin, as he grew in years, acquired a turn of mind so penurious, was he not enabled to leave his son some addition to the *pied de terre* we are about to visit?"

"He must certainly have left some ready money," answered Lady Erpingham. "But is it, after all, likely that so young a man as Percy Godolphin could have lived in the manner he has done without incurring debts? It is most probable that he had some recourse to those persons so willing to encourage the young and extravagant, and that repayment to them will more than swallow up any savings his father might have amassed."

"True enough!" said Constance; and the conversation glided into remarks on avaricious fathers and prodigal sons.

Constance was witty on the subject, and Lady Erpingham laughed herself into excellent humour.

It was considerably past noon when they arrived at the ruins.

The carriage stopped before a small inn, at the entrance of a dismantled park; and taking advantage of the beauty of the day, Lady Erpingham and Constance walked slowly towards the remains of the Priory.

The scene, as they approached, was wild and picturesque in the extreme. A wide and glassy lake lay stretched beneath them; on the opposite side stood the ruins. The large oriel window, the Gothic arch, the broken yet still majestic column, all embrowned and mossed with age, were still spared, and now mirrored themselves in the waveless and silent tide. Fragments of stone lay around, for some considerable distance, and the whole was backed by hills, covered with gloomy and thick woods of pine and fir. To the left, they saw the stream which fed the lake stealing away through grassy banks, overgrown with the willow and pollard oak; and there, from one or two cottages, only caught in glimpses, thin wreaths of smoke rose in spires against the clear sky. To the right, the ground was broken into a thousand glens and hollows; the deer-loved fern, the golden broom, were scattered about profusely; and here and there were dense groves of pollards; or, at very rare intervals, some single tree decaying (for all round bore the seal of vassalage to Time), but mighty, and greenly venerable in its decay.

As they passed over a bridge that, on either side of the stream, emerged, as it were, from a thick copse, they caught a view of the small abode that adjoined the ruins. It seemed covered entirely with ivy; and so far from diminishing, tended rather to increase the romantic and imposing effect of the crumbling pile from which it grew.

They opened a little gate at the other extremity of the bridge, and in a few minutes more, they stood at the entrance to the Priory.

It was an oak door, studded with nails. The jessamine

grew upon either side; and, to descend to a commonplace matter, they had some difficulty in finding the bell among the leaves in which it was imbedded. When they had found and touched it, its clear and lively sound rang out in that still and lovely though desolate spot with an effect startling and impressive from its contrast. There is something very fairy-like in the cheerful voice of a bell sounding among the wilder scenes of nature, particularly where Time advances his claim to the sovereignty of the landscape; for the cheerfulness is a little ghostly, and might serve well enough for a tocsin to the elfish hordes whom our footsteps may be supposed to disturb.

An old woman, in the neat peasant dress of our country, when, taking a little from the fashion of the last century (the cap and the kerchief), it assumes no ungraceful costume, replied to their summons. She was the solitary cicerone of the place. She had lived there, a lone and childless widow, for thirty years; and of all the persons I have ever seen would furnish forth the best heroine to one of those pictures of homely life which Wordsworth has dignified with the patriarchal tenderness of his genius.

They wound a narrow passage, and came to the ruins of the great hall. Its gothic arches still sprang lightly upward on either side; and opening a large stone box that stood in a recess, the old woman showed them the gloves and the helmet and the tattered banners, which had belonged to that Godolphin who had fought side by side with Sidney, when he, whose life — as the noblest of British lyrists hath somewhere said — was "poetry put into action,"[1] received his death-wound in the field of Zutphen.

Thence they ascended by the dilapidated and crumbling staircase to a small room, in which the visitors were always expected to rest themselves, and enjoy the scene in the garden below. A large chasm yawned where the casement once was; and round this aperture the ivy wreathed itself in fantastic luxuriance. A sort of ladder, suspended from this chasm to the ground, afforded a convenience for those who were tempted to a short excursion by the view without.

[1] Campbell.

And the view *was* tempting! A smooth green lawn, surrounded by shrubs and flowers, was ornamented in the centre by a fountain. The waters were, it is true, dried up; but the basin, and the "Triton with his wreathed shell," still remained. A little to the right was an old monkish sun-dial; and through the green vista you caught the glimpse of one of those gray, grotesque statues with which the taste of Elizabeth's day shamed the classic chisel.

There was something quiet and venerable about the whole place; and when the old woman said to Constance, "Would you not like, my lady, to walk down and look at the sun-dial and the fountain?" Constance felt she required nothing more to yield to her inclination. Lady Erpingham, less adventurous, remained in the ruined chamber; and the old woman, naturally enough, honoured the elder lady with her company.

Constance, therefore, descended the rude steps alone. As she paused by the fountain, an indescribable and delicious feeling of repose stole over a mind that seldom experienced any sentiment so natural or so soft. The hour, the stillness, the scene,—all conspired to lull the heart into that dreaming and half-unconscious revery in which poets would suppose the hermits of elder times to have wasted a life, indolent, and yet scarcely, after all, unwise. "Methinks," she inly soliloquized, "while I look around, I feel as if I could give up my objects of life; renounce my hopes; forget to be artificial and ambitious; live in these ruins, and" (whispered the spirit within), "loved and loving, fulfil the ordinary doom of woman."

Indulging a mood which the proud and restless Constance, who despised love as the poorest of human weaknesses, though easily susceptible to all other species of romance, had scarcely ever known before, she wandered away from the lawn into one of the alleys cut amidst the grove around. Caught by the murmur of an unseen brook, she tracked it through the trees, as its sound grew louder and louder on her ear, till at length it stole upon her sight. The sun, only winning through the trees at intervals, played capriciously upon the cold and dark waters as they glided on, and gave to her, as the same effect has done to a thousand poets, ample matter for a simile or a moral.

She approached the brook, and came unawares upon the figure of a young man, leaning against a stunted tree that overhung the waters, and occupied with the idle amusement of dropping pebbles in the stream. She saw only his profile; but that view is, in a fine countenance, almost always the most striking and impressive, and it was eminently so in the face before her. The stranger, who was scarcely removed from boyhood, was dressed in deep mourning. He seemed slight, and small of stature. A travelling cap of sables contrasted, not hid, light brown hair of singular richness and beauty. His features were of that pure and severe Greek of which the only fault is that in the very perfection of the chiselling of the features there seems something hard and stern. The complexion was pale, even to wanness; and the whole cast and contour of the head were full of intellect, and betokening that absorption of mind which cannot be marked in any one without exciting a certain vague curiosity and interest.

So dark and wondrous are the workings of our nature, that there are scarcely any of us, however light and unthinking, who would not be arrested by the countenance of one in deep reflection; who would not pause, and long to pierce into the mysteries that were agitating that world, most illimitable by nature, but often most narrowed by custom,—the world within.

And this interest, powerful as it is, spelled and arrested Constance at once. She remained for a minute gazing on the countenance of the young stranger, and then she — the most self-possessed and stately of human creatures — blushing deeply, and confused though unseen, turned lightly away and stopped not on her road till she regained the old chamber and Lady Erpingham.

The old woman was descanting upon the merits of the late lord of Godolphin Priory.

"For though they called him close, and so forth, my lady, yet he was generous to others; it was only himself he pinched.

But, to be sure, the present squire won't take after him there."

"Has Mr. Percy Godolphin been here lately?" asked Lady Erpingham.

"He is at the cottage now, my lady," replied the old woman. "He came two days ago."

"Is he like his father?"

"Oh, not near so fine-looking a gentleman! much smaller, and quite pale-like. He seems sickly: them foreign parts do nobody no good. He was as fine a lad at sixteen years old as ever I seed; but now he is not like the same thing."

So then it was evidently Percy Godolphin whom Constance had seen by the brook,—the owner of a home without coffers, and estates without a rent-roll; the Percy Godolphin, of whom, before he had attained the age when others have left the college, or even the school, every one had learned to speak,—some favourably, all with eagerness. Constance felt a vague interest respecting him spring up in her mind. She checked it, for it was a sin in her eye to think with interest on a man neither rich nor powerful; and as she quitted the ruins with Lady Erpingham, she communicated to the latter her adventure. She was, however, disingenuous, for though Godolphin's countenance was exactly of that cast which Constance most admired, she described him just as the old woman had done; and Lady Erpingham figured to herself, from the description, a little yellow man, with white hair and a turned-up nose. O Truth! what a hard path is thine! Does any keep it for three inches together in the commonest trifle?—and yet two sides of my library are filled with histories!

CHAPTER XIII.

A BALL ANNOUNCED. — GODOLPHIN'S VISIT TO WENDOVER CASTLE.—HIS MANNERS AND CONVERSATION.

Lady Erpingham (besides her daughter, Lady Eleanor, married to Mr. Clare, a county member, of large fortune) was blessed with one son.

The present earl had been for the last two years abroad. He had never, since his accession to his title, visited Wendover Castle; and Lady Erpingham one morning experienced the delight of receiving a letter from him, dated Dover, and signifying his intention of paying her a visit. In honour of this event, Lady Erpingham resolved to give a grand ball. Cards were issued to all the families in the county; and, among others, to Mr. Godolphin.

On the third day after this invitation had been sent to the person I have last named, as Lady Erpingham and Constance were alone in the saloon, Mr. Percy Godolphin was announced. Constance blushed as she looked up, and Lady Erpingham was struck by the nobleness of his address, and the perfect self-possession of his manner. And yet nothing could be so different as was his deportment from that which she had been accustomed to admire, from that manifested by the exquisites of the day. The calm, the *nonchalance*, the artificial smile of languor, the evenness, so insipid, yet so irreproachable, of English manners when considered most polished,—all this was the reverse of Godolphin's address and air. In short, in all he said or did there was something foreign, something unfamiliar. He was abrupt and enthusiastic in conversation, and used gestures in speaking. His countenance lighted up at every word that broke from him on the graver subjects of discussion. You felt, indeed, with him that you were with a man of genius,— a wayward and a spoiled man, who had acquired his habits in solitude, but his graces in the world.

They conversed about the ruins of the Priory, and Constance expressed her admiration of their romantic and picturesque beauty. "Ah," said he, smiling, but with a slight blush, in which Constance detected something of pain, "I heard of your visit to my poor heaps of stone. My father took great pleasure in the notice they attracted. When a proud man has not riches to be proud of, he grows proud of the signs of his poverty itself. This was the case with my poor father. Had he been rich, the ruins would not have existed,—he would have rebuilt the old mansion. As he was poor, he valued himself on their existence, and fancied magnificence in every handful of moss. But all life is delusion; all pride, all vanity, all pomp, are equally deceit. Like the Spanish hidalgo, we put on spectacles when we eat our cherries, in order that they may seem ten times as big as they are!"

Constance smiled; and Lady Erpingham, who had more kindness than delicacy, continued her praises of the Priory and the scenery round it.

"The old park," said she, "with its wood and water, is so beautiful! It wants nothing but a few deer, just tame enough to come near the ruins, and wild enough to start away as you approach."

"Now you would borrow an attraction from wealth," said Godolphin, who, unlike English persons in general, seemed to love alluding to his poverty. "It is not for the owner of a ruined Priory to consult the aristocratic enchantments of that costly luxury, the Picturesque. Alas! I have not even wherewithal to feed a few solitary partridges; and I hear that if I go beyond the green turf, once a park, I shall be warned off forthwith, and my very qualification disputed."

"Are you fond of shooting?" said Lady Erpingham.

"I fancy I should be; but I have never enjoyed the sport in England."

"Do pray come, then," said Lady Erpingham, kindly, "and spend your first week in September here. Let me see: the first of the month will be next Thursday; dine with us on Wednesday. We have keepers and dogs here enough, thanks to Robert; so you need only bring your gun."

"You are very kind, dear Lady Erpingham," said Godolphin, warmly; "I accept your invitation at once."

"Your father was a very old friend of mine," said the lady with a sigh.

"He was an old admirer," said the gentleman, with a bow.

CHAPTER XIV.

CONVERSATION BETWEEN GODOLPHIN AND CONSTANCE. — THE COUNTRY LIFE AND THE TOWN LIFE.

And Godolphin came on the appointed Wednesday. He was animated that day even to brilliancy. Lady Erpingham thought him the most charming of men; and even Constance forgot that he was no match for herself. Gifted and cultivated as she was, it was not without delight that she listened to his glowing descriptions of scenery, and to his playful, yet somewhat melancholy strain of irony upon men and their pursuits. The peculiar features of her mind made her, indeed, like the latter more than she could appreciate the former; for in her nature there was more bitterness than sentiment. Still, his rich language and fluent periods, even in description, touched her ear and fancy, though they sank not to her heart; and she yielded insensibly to the spells she would almost have despised in another.

The next day, Constance, who was no very early riser, tempted by the beauty of the noon, strolled into the gardens. She was surprised to hear Godolphin's voice behind her: she turned round and he joined her.

"I thought you were on your shooting expedition?"

"I *have* been shooting, and I am returned. I was out by

daybreak, and I came back at noon in the hope of being allowed to join you in your ride or walk."

Constance smilingly acknowledged the compliment; and as they passed up the straight walks of the old-fashioned and stately gardens, Godolphin turned the conversation upon the varieties of garden scenery; upon the poets who have described those varieties best; upon that difference between the town life and the country, on which the brothers of the minstrel craft have, in all ages, so glowingly insisted. In this conversation, certain points of contrast between the characters of these two young persons might be observed.

"I confess to you," said Godolphin, "that I have little faith in the permanence of any attachment professed for the country by the inhabitants of cities. If we can occupy our minds solely with the objects around us, if the brook and the old tree, and the golden sunset and the summer night, and the animal and homely life that we survey,—if these can fill our contemplation, and take away from us the feverish schemes of the future,—then indeed I can fully understand the reality of that tranquil and happy state which our elder poets have described as incident to a country life. But if we carry with us to the shade all the restless and perturbed desires of the city; if we only employ present leisure in schemes for an agitated future,—then it is in vain that we affect the hermit and fly to the retreat. The moment the novelty of green fields is over, and our projects are formed, we wish to hurry to the city to execute them. We have, in a word, made our retirement only a nursery for schemes now springing up, and requiring to be transplanted."

"You are right," said Constance, quickly; "and who would pass life as if it were a dream? It seems to me that we put retirement to the right use when we make it only subservient to our aims in the world."

"A strange doctrine for a young beauty," thought Godolphin, "whose head ought to be full of groves and love.—Then," said he aloud, "I must rank among those who abuse the purposes of retirement; for I have hitherto been flattered to think that I enjoy it for itself. Despite the artificial life

I have led, everything that speaks of Nature has a voice that I can rarely resist. What feelings created in a city can compare with those that rise so gently and so unbidden within us when the trees and the waters are our only companions, our only sources of excitement and intoxication? Is not contemplation better than ambition?"

"Can you believe it?" said Constance, incredulously.

"I do."

Constance smiled; and there would have been contempt in that beautiful smile, had not Godolphin interested her in spite of herself.

CHAPTER XV.

THE FEELINGS OF CONSTANCE AND GODOLPHIN TOWARDS EACH OTHER. — THE DISTINCTION IN THEIR CHARACTERS. — REMARKS ON THE EFFECTS PRODUCED BY THE WORLD UPON GODOLPHIN. — THE RIDE. — RURAL DESCRIPTIONS. — OMENS. — THE FIRST INDISTINCT CONFESSION.

Every day, at the hour in which Constance was visible, Godolphin had loaded the keeper, and had returned to attend upon her movements. They walked and rode together; and in the evening, Godolphin hung over her chair, and listened to her songs; for though, as I have before said, she had but little science in instrumental music, her voice was rich and soft beyond the pathos of ordinary singers.

Lady Erpingham saw, with secret delight, what she believed to be a growing attachment. She loved Constance for herself, and Godolphin for his father's memory. She thought again and again what a charming couple they would make,— so handsome, so gifted: and if Prudence whispered also — so poor, the kind countess remembered that she herself had saved from her ample jointure a sum which she had always designed as a dowry for Constance, and which, should Godolphin be the bridegroom, she felt she should have a tenfold pleasure in bestowing. With this fortune, which would place them, at least, in independence, she united in her kindly imagination the importance which she imagined Godolphin's talents must ultimately acquire; and for which, in her aristocratic estimation, she conceived the senate the only legitimate sphere. She said, she hinted, nothing to Constance; but she suffered nature, youth, and companionship to exercise their sway.

And the complexion of Godolphin's feelings for Constance Vernon did indeed resemble love,— was love itself, though rather love in its romance than its reality. What were those of Constance for him? She knew not herself at that time. Had she been of a character one shade less ambitious or less powerful, they would have been love, and love of no common character. But within her musing and self-possessed and singularly constituted mind there was, as yet, a limit to every sentiment, a chain to the wings of every thought, save those of one order; and that order was not of love. There was a marked difference, in all respects, between the characters of the two; and it was singular enough that that of the woman was the less romantic, and composed of the simpler materials.

A volume of Wordsworth's most exquisite poetry had then just appeared. "Is not this wonderful?" said Godolphin, reciting some of those lofty but refining thoughts which characterize the Pastor of modern poets.

Constance shook her head.

"What! you do not admire it?"

"I do not understand it."

"What poetry do you admire?"

"This."

It was Pope's translation of the "Iliad."

"Yes, yes, to be sure," said Godolphin, a little vexed; "we all admire this in its way: but what else?"

Constance pointed to a passage in the "Palamon and Arcite" of Dryden.

Godolphin threw down his Wordsworth. "You take an ungenerous advantage of me," said he. "Tell me something you admire, which, at least, I may have the privilege of disputing,—something that you think generally neglected."

"I admire few things that are generally neglected," answered Constance, with her bright and proud smile. "Fame gives its stamp to all metal that is of intrinsic value."

This answer was quite characteristic of Constance; she worshipped fame far more than the genius which won it.

"Well, then," said Godolphin, "let us see *now* if we can come to a compromise of sentiment;" and he took up the "Comus" of Milton.

No one read poetry so beautifully: his voice was so deep and flexible; and his countenance answered so well to every modulation of his voice. Constance was touched by the reader, but not by the verse. Godolphin had great penetration; he perceived it, and turned to the speeches of Satan in "Paradise Lost." The noble countenance before him grew luminous at once; the lip quivered, the eye sparkled; the enthusiasm of Godolphin was not comparable to that of Constance. The fact was, that the broad and common emotions of the intellectual character struck upon the right key. Courage, defiance, ambition,—these she comprehended to their fullest extent; but the rich subtleties of thought which mark the cold and bright page of the "Comus," the noble Platonism, the high and rare love for what is abstractedly good,—these were not "sonorous and trumpet-speaking" enough for the heart of one meant by Nature for a heroine or a queen, not a poetess or a philosopher.

But all that in literature was delicate and half-seen and abstruse had its peculiar charm for Godolphin. Of a reflective and refining mind, he had early learned to despise the common emotions of men: glory touched him not, and to ambition he had shut his heart. Love, with him—even though he had been deemed, nor unjustly, a man of gallantry and pleasure—love was not compounded of the ordinary elements of the passions. Full of dreams and refinements and intense abstractions, it was a love that seemed not homely enough for endurance, and of too rare a nature to hope for sympathy in return.

And so it was in his intercourse with Constance both were continually disappointed. "You do not feel this," said Constance. "She cannot understand me," sighed Godolphin.

But we must not suppose — despite his refinements and his reveries and his love for the intellectual and the pure — that Godolphin was of a stainless character or mind. He was one who, naturally full of decided and marked qualities, was, by the peculiar elements of our society, rendered a doubtful, motley, and indistinct character, tinctured by the frailties that leave us in a wavering state between vice and virtue. The energies that had marked his boyhood were dulled and crippled in the indolent life of the world. His wandering habits for the last few years, the soft and poetical existence of the South, had fed his natural romance, and nourished that passion for contemplation which the intellectual man of pleasure so commonly forms; for pleasure has a philosophy of its own,— a sad, a fanciful, yet deep persuasion of the vanity of all things, a craving after the bright ideal —

"The desire of the moth for the star."

Solomon's thirst for pleasure was the companion of his wisdom: satiety was the offspring of the one, discontent of the other. But this philosophy, though seductive, is of no wholesome nor useful character; it is the philosophy of feelings, not principles; of the heart, not head. So with Godolphin: he was too refined in his moralizing to cling to what was moral. The simply good and the simply bad he left for us plain folks to discover. He was unattracted by the doctrines of right and wrong which serve for all men; but he had some obscure and shadowy standard in his own mind by which he compared the actions of others. He had imagination, genius, even heart; was brilliant always, sometimes profound; graceful in society, yet seldom social; a lonely man, yet a man of the world; generous to individuals, selfish to the mass. How many fine qualities worse than thrown away!

Who will not allow that he has met many such men?— and who will not follow this man to his end?

One day (it was the last of Godolphin's protracted visit),

as the sun was waning to its close, and the time was unusually soft and tranquil, Constance and Godolphin were returning slowly home from their customary ride. They passed by a small inn, bearing the common sign of the Chequers, round which a crowd of peasants were assembled, listening to the rude music which a wandering Italian boy drew from his guitar. The scene was rustic and picturesque; and as Godolphin reined in his horse and gazed on the group, he little dreamed of the fierce and dark emotions with which, at a far distant period, he was destined to revisit that spot.

"Our peasants," said he, as they rode on, "require some humanizing relaxation like that we have witnessed. The music and the morris-dance have gone from England; and instead of providing, as formerly, for the amusement of the grinded labourer, our legislators now regard with the most watchful jealousy his most distant approach to festivity. They cannot bear the rustic to be merry: disorder and amusement are words for the same offence."

"I doubt," said the earnest Constance, "whether the legislators are not right; for men given to amusement are easily enslaved. All noble thoughts are grave."

Thus talking, they passed a shallow ford in the stream. "We are not far from the Priory," said Godolphin, pointing to its ruins, that rose grayly in the evening skies from the green woods around it.

Constance sighed involuntarily. She felt pain in being reminded of the slender fortunes of her companion. Ascending the gentle hill that swelled from the stream, she now, to turn the current of her thoughts, pointed admiringly to the blue course of the waters, as they wound through their shagged banks. And deep, dark, rushing, even at that still hour, went the stream through the boughs that swept over its surface. Here and there the banks suddenly shelved down, mingling with the waves; then abruptly they rose, overspread with thick and tangled umbrage, several feet above the level of the river.

"How strange it is," said Godolphin, "that at times a feeling comes over us, as we gaze upon certain places, which associates the scene either with some dim-remembered and dream-like images of the Past, or with a prophetic and fearful omen of the Future! As I gaze now upon this spot — those banks, that whirling river — it seems as if my destiny claimed a mysterious sympathy with the scene: when, how, wherefore, I know not, guess not; only this shadowy and chilling sentiment unaccountably creeps over me. Every one has known a similar strange, indistinct feeling at certain times and places, and with a similar inability to trace the cause. And yet, is it not singular that in poetry, which wears most feelings to an echo, I have never met with any attempt to describe it?"

"Because poetry," said Constance, "is, after all, but a hackneyed imitation of the most common thoughts, giving them merely a gloss by the brilliancy of verse. And yet how little poets *know!* They *imagine*, and they *imitate*,— behold all their secrets!"

"Perhaps you are right," said Godolphin, musingly; "and I, who have often vainly fancied I had the poetical temperament, have been so chilled and sickened by the characteristics of the tribe that I have checked its impulses with a sort of disdain; and thus the Ideal, having no vent in me, preys within, creating a thousand undefined dreams and unwilling superstitions, making me enamoured of the Shadowy and Unknown, and dissatisfying me with the petty ambitions of the world."

"You will awake hereafter," said Constance, earnestly.

Godolphin shook his head, and replied not.

Their way now lay along a green lane that gradually wound round a hill commanding a view of great richness and beauty. Cottages and spires and groves gave life — but it was scattered and remote life — to the scene; and the broad stream, whose waves, softened in the distance, did not seem to break the even surface of the tide, flowed onward, glowing in the sunlight, till it was lost among dark and luxuriant woods.

Both once more arrested their horses by a common impulse, and both became suddenly silent as they gazed. Godolphin was the first to speak; it brought to his memory a scene in that delicious land, whose Southern loveliness Claude has transfused to the canvas, and De Staël to the page. With his own impassioned and earnest language, he spoke to Constance of that scene and that country. Every tree before him furnished matter for his illustration or his contrast; and as she heard that magic voice, and speaking, too, of a country dedicated to love, Constance listened with glistening eyes, and a cheek which he — consummate master of the secrets of womanhood — perceived was eloquent with thoughts which *she* knew not, but which *he* interpreted to the letter.

"And in such a spot," said he, continuing, and fixing his deep and animated gaze on her,— "in such a spot I could have stayed forever but for one recollection, one feeling,— I *should have been too much alone!* In a wild or a grand or even a barren country, we may live in solitude, and find fit food for thought; but not in one so soft, so subduing, as that which I saw and see. Love comes over us then in spite of ourselves; and I feel — I feel now — " his voice trembled as he spoke — "that any secret we may before have nursed, though hitherto unacknowledged, makes itself at length a voice. We are oppressed with the desire to be loved; we long for the courage to say we love."

Never before had Godolphin, though constantly verging into sentiment, spoken to Constance in so plain a language. Eye, voice, cheek,— *all* spoke. She felt that he had confessed he loved her! And was she not happy at that thought? She was; it was her happiest moment. But, in that sort of vague and indistinct shrinking from the subject with which a woman who loves hears a disclosure of love from him on whose lips it is most sweet, she muttered some confused attempt to change the subject, and quickened her horse's pace. Godolphin did not renew the topic so interesting and so dangerous, only, as with the winding of the road the landscape gradually faded from their view, he said in a low voice, as if to himself,— "How long, how fondly, shall I remember this day!"

CHAPTER XVI.

GODOLPHIN'S RETURN HOME. — HIS SOLILOQUY. — LORD ERPINGHAM'S ARRIVAL AT WENDOVER CASTLE. — THE EARL DESCRIBED. — HIS ACCOUNT OF GODOLPHIN'S LIFE AT ROME.

WITH a listless step, Godolphin re-entered the threshold of his cottage-home. He passed into a small chamber, which was yet the largest in his house. The poor and scanty furniture scattered around; the old, tuneless, broken harpsichord; the worn and tattered carpet; the tenantless birdcage in the recess by the window; the book-shelves, containing some dozens of worthless volumes; the sofa of the last century (when, if people knew comfort, they placed it not in lounging), small, narrow, highbacked, hard, and knotted,— these, just as his father had left, just as his boyhood had seen, them, greeted him with a comfortless and chill though familiar welcome. It was evening. He ordered a fire and lights; and leaning his face on his hand as he contemplated the fitful and dusky outbreakings of the flame through the bars of the niggard and contracted grate, he sat himself down to hold commune with his heart.

"So, I love this woman," said he, "do I? Have I not deceived myself? She is poor,— no connection; she has nothing whereby to reinstate my house's fortunes, to rebuild this mansion, or repurchase yonder demesnes. I love her! *I* who have known the value of her sex so well, that I have said, again and again, I would not shackle life with a princess! Love may withstand possession,— true; but not time. In three years there would be no glory in the face of Constance, and I should be — what? My fortunes, broken as they are, can support *me* alone, and with my few wants. But if married! the haughty Constance my wife! Nay, nay, nay! this must not be thought of! I, the hero of Paris! the pupil of

Saville! I, to be so beguiled as even to *dream* of such a madness!

"Yet I have that within me that might make a stir in the world; I might rise. Professions are open; the Diplomacy, the House of Commons. What! Percy Godolphin be ass enough to grow ambitious! to toil, to fret, to slave, to answer fools on a first principle, and die at length of a broken heart or a lost place! Pooh, pooh! I, who despise your prime ministers, can scarcely stoop to their apprenticeship. Life is too short for toil. And what do men strive for? — to enjoy; but why not enjoy without the toil? And relinquish Constance? Ay, it is but one woman lost!"

So ended the soliloquy of a man scarcely of age. The world teaches us its last lessons betimes; but then, lest we should have nothing left to acquire from its wisdom, it employs the rest of our life in unlearning all that it first taught.

Meanwhile, the time approached when Lord Erpingham was to arrive at Wendover Castle; and at length came the day itself. Naturally anxious to enjoy as exclusively as possible the company of her son the first day of his return from so long an absence, Lady Erpingham had asked no one to meet him. The earl's heavy travelling-carriage at length rolled clattering up the courtyard; and in a few minutes a tall man, in the prime of life, and borrowing some favourable effect as to person from the large cloak of velvet and furs which hung round him, entered the room, and Lady Erpingham embraced her son. The kind and familiar manner with which he answered her inquiries and congratulations was somewhat changed when he suddenly perceived Constance. Lord Erpingham was a cold man, and, like most cold men, ashamed of the evidence of affection. He greeted Constance very quietly, and as she thought, slightly; but his eyes turned to her far more often than any friend of Lord Erpingham's might ever have remarked those large round hazel eyes turn to any one before.

When the earl withdrew to adjust his toilet for dinner, Lady Erpingham, as she wiped her eyes, could not help exclaiming to Constance, "Is he not handsome? What a figure!"

Constance was a little addicted to flattery where she liked the one who was to be flattered, and she assented readily enough to the maternal remark. Hitherto, however, she had not observed anything more in Lord Erpingham than his height and his cloak; as he re-entered and led her to the dining-room she took a better, though still but a casual, survey.

Lord Erpingham was that sort of person of whom *men* always say, "What a prodigiously fine fellow!" He was above six feet high, stout in proportion: not, indeed, accurately formed, nor graceful in bearing, but quite as much so as a man of six feet high need be. He had a manly complexion of brown, yellow, and red. His whiskers were exceedingly large, black, and well arranged. His eyes, as I have before said, were round, large, and hazel; they were also unmeaning. His teeth were good; and his nose, neither aquiline nor Grecian, was yet a very showy nose upon the whole. All the maidservants admired him; and you felt, in looking at him, that it was a pity our army should lose so good a grenadier.

Lord Erpingham was a Whig of the old school: he thought the Tory boroughs ought to be thrown open. He was generally considered a sensible man. He had read Blackstone, Montesquieu, Cowper's Poems, and "The Rambler;" and he was always heard with great attention in the House of Lords. In his moral character he was a *bon vivant*, as far as wine is concerned; for choice *eating* he cared nothing. He was good-natured, but close; brave enough to fight a duel, if necessary; and religious enough to go to church once a week — in the country.

So far Lord Erpingham might seem modelled from one of Sir Walter's heroes: we must reverse the medal, and show the points in which he differed from those patterns of propriety.

Like the generality of his class, he was peculiarly loose in his notions of women, though not ardent in pursuit of them. His amours had been among opera-dancers, "because," as he was wont to say, "there was no d—d bore with *them*." Lord Erpingham was always considered a high-minded man. People chose him as an umpire in quarrels; and told a story (which was not true) of his having held some state office for a whole year, and insisted on returning the emoluments.

Such was Robert Earl of Erpingham. During dinner, at which he displayed, to his mother's great delight, a most excellent appetite, he listened, as well as he might, considering the more legitimate occupation of the time and season, to Lady Erpingham's recitals of county history, her long answers to his brief inquiries whether old friends were dead and young ones married; and his countenance brightened up to an expression of interest — almost of intelligence — when he was told that birds were said to be plentiful.

As the servants left the room, and Lord Erpingham took his first glass of claret, the conversation fell upon Percy Godolphin.

"He has been staying with us a whole fortnight," said Lady Erpingham; "and, by the by, he said he had met you in Italy, and mentioned your name as it deserved."

"Indeed! And did he really condescend to praise me?" said Lord Erpingham, with eagerness; for there was that about Godolphin, and his reputation for fastidiousness, which gave a rarity and a value to his praise, at least to lordly ears. "Ah, he 's a queer fellow; he led a very singular life in Italy."

"So I have always heard," said Lady Erpingham. "But of what description,— was he very wild?"

"No, not exactly; there was a good deal of mystery about him; he saw very few English, and those were chiefly men who played high. He was said to have a great deal of learning and so forth."

"Oh, then he was surrounded, I suppose, by those medallists and picture-sellers and other impostors, who live upon such of our countrymen as think themselves blessed with a taste or afflicted with a genius," said Lady Erpingham, — who, having lived with the wits and orators of the time, had caught mechanically their way of rounding a period.

"Far from it!" returned the earl. "Godolphin is much too deep a fellow for that; he 's not easily taken in, I assure you.

I confess I don't like him the worse for that," added the close noble. "But he lived with the Italian doctors and men of science; and encouraged, in particular, one strange fellow who affected sorcery, I fancy, or something very like it. Godolphin resided in a very lonely spot at Rome: and I believe laboratories and caldrons, and all sorts of devilish things, were always at work there — at least so people said."

"And yet," said Constance, "you thought him too sensible to be easily taken in?"

"Indeed I do, Miss Vernon; and the proof of it is, that no man has less fortune or is made more of. He plays, it is true, but only occasionally; though as a player at games of skill — piquet, billiards, whist — he has no equal, unless it be Saville. But then Saville, *entre nous*, is suspected of playing unfairly."

"And you are quite sure," said the placid Lady Erpingham, "that Mr. Godolphin is only indebted to skill for his success?"

Constance darted a glance of fire at the speaker.

"Why, faith, I believe so! No one ever accused him of a single shabby or even suspicious trick; and indeed, as I said before, no one was ever more sought after in society, though he shuns it; and he 's devilish right, for it 's a cursed bore!"

"My dear Robert! at your age!" exclaimed the mother.

"But," continued the earl, turning to Constance,— "but, Miss Vernon, a man may have his weak point; and the cunning Italian may have hit on Godolphin's, clever as he is in general; though, for my part, I will tell you frankly, I think he only encouraged him to mystify and perplex people, just to get talked of — vanity, in short. He 's a good-looking fellow, that Godolphin, eh?" continued the earl, in the tone of a man who meant you to deny what he asserted.

"Oh, beautiful!" said Lady Erpingham. "Such a countenance!"

"Deuced pale, though! — eh? — and not the best of figures thin, narrow-shouldered, eh, eh?"

Godolphin's proportions were faultless; but your strapping heroes think of a moderate-sized man as mathematicians define a point,—declare that he has no length nor breadth whatsoever.

"What say *you*, Constance?" asked Lady Erpingham, meaningly.

Constance felt the meaning, and replied calmly that Mr. Godolphin appeared to her handsomer than any one she had seen lately.

Lord Erpingham played with his neckcloth, and Lady Erpingham rose to leave the room. "D—d fine girl!" said the earl, as he shut the door upon Constance; "but d—d sharp!" added he, as he resettled himself on his chair.

CHAPTER XVII.

CONSTANCE AT HER TOILET. — HER FEELINGS. — HER CHARACTER OF BEAUTY DESCRIBED. — THE BALL. — THE DUCHESS OF WINSTOUN AND HER DAUGHTER. — AN INDUCTION FROM THE NATURE OF FEMALE RIVALRIES. — JEALOUSY IN A LOVER. — IMPERTINENCE RETORTED. — LISTENERS NEVER HEAR GOOD OF THEMSELVES. — REMARKS ON THE AMUSEMENTS OF A PUBLIC ASSEMBLY. — THE SUPPER. — THE FALSENESS OF SEEMING GAYETY. — VARIOUS REFLECTIONS, NEW AND TRUE. — WHAT PASSES BETWEEN GODOLPHIN AND CONSTANCE.

It was the evening of the ball to be given in honour of Lord Erpingham's arrival. Constance, dressed for conquest, sat alone in her dressing-room. Her woman had just left her. The lights still burned in profusion about the antique chamber (antique, for it was situated in the oldest part of the castle); those lights streamed full upon the broad brow and exquisite features of Miss Vernon. As she leaned back in her chair — the fairy foot upon the low Gothic stool, and the hands drooping beside her despondingly — her countenance betrayed much but not serene thought; and mixed with that thought was something of irresolution and of great and real sadness.

It is not, as I have before hinted, to be supposed that Constance's lot had been hitherto a proud one, even though she was the most admired beauty of her day; even though she lived with, and received adulation from, the high and noble and haughty of her land. Often in the glittering crowd that she attracted around her, her ear, sharpened by the jealousy and pride of her nature, caught words that dashed the cup of pleasure and of vanity with shame and anger. "What! that *the* Vernon's daughter? Poor girl! dependent entirely on Lady Erpingham! Ah, she 'll take in some rich *roturier*, I hope."

Such words from ill-tempered dowagers and faded beauties were no unfrequent interruption to her brief-lived and wearisome triumphs. She heard manœuvring mothers caution their booby sons, whom Constance would have looked into the dust had they dared but to touch her hand, against her untitled and undowried charms. She saw cautious earls, who were all courtesy one night, all coldness another, as some report had reached them accusing their hearts of feeling too deeply her attractions, or as they themselves suspected for the first time that a heart was not a word for a poetical nothing, and that to look on so beautiful and glorious a creature was sufficient to convince them, even yet, of the possibility of emotion. She had felt to the quick the condescending patronage of duchesses and chaperons; the oblique hint; the nice and fine distinction which, in polished circles, divides each grade from the other, and allows you to be galled without the pleasure of feeling justified in offence.

All this, which, in the flush and heyday of youth and gayety and loveliness, would have been unnoticed by other women, rankled deep in the mind of Constance Vernon. The image of her dying father, his complaints, his accusations (the justice of which she never for an instant questioned), rose up before her in the brightest hours of the dance and the revel. She was not one of those women whose meek and gentle nature would fly what wounds them: Constance had resolved to conquer. Despising glitter and gayety and show, she burned, she thirsted for power,—a power which could retaliate the insults she fancied she had received, and should turn condescension into homage. This object, which every casual word, every heedless glance from another, fixed deeper and deeper in her heart, took a sort of sanctity from the associations with which she linked it,—her father's memory and his dying breath.

At this moment in which we have portrayed her, all these restless and sore and haughty feelings were busy within; but they were combated, even while the more fiercely aroused, by one soft and tender thought,—the image of Godolphin,—of Godolphin, the spendthrift heir of a broken fortune and a fallen house. She felt too deeply that she loved him; and ignorant of his worldlier qualities, imagined that he loved her with all the devotion of that romance, and the ardour of that genius, which appeared to her to compose his character. But this persuasion gave her now no delightful emotion. Convinced that she ought to reject him, his image only coloured with sadness those objects and that ambition which she had hitherto regarded with an exulting pride. She was not the less bent on the lofty ends of her destiny; but the glory and the illusion had fallen from them. She had taken an insight into futurity, and felt that to enjoy power was to lose happiness. Yet, with this full conviction, she forsook the happiness and clung to the power. Alas! for our best and wisest theories, our problems, our systems, our philosophy! Human beings will never cease to mistake the means for the end; and despite the dogmas of sages, our conduct does *not* depend on our convictions.

Carriage after carriage had rolled beneath the windows of the room where Constance sat, and still she moved not; until at length a certain composure, as if the result of some determination, stole over her features. The brilliant and transparent hues returned to her cheek; and as she rose and stood erect, with a certain calmness and energy on her lip and forehead, perhaps her beauty had never seemed of so lofty and august a cast. In passing through the chamber, she stopped for a moment opposite the mirror that reflected her stately shape in its full height. Beauty is so truly the weapon of woman that it is as impossible for her, even in grief, wholly to forget its effect, as it is for the dying warrior to look with indifference on the sword with which he has won his trophies or his fame. Nor was Constance that evening *disposed* to be indifferent to the effect she should produce. She looked on the reflection of herself with a feeling of triumph, not arising from vanity alone.

And when did mirror ever give back a form more worthy of a Pericles to worship, or an Apelles to paint? Though but little removed from the common height, the impression Constance always gave was that of a person much taller than she really was. A certain majesty in the turn of the head, the fall of the shoulders, the breadth of the brow, and the exceeding calmness of the features invested her with an air which I have never seen equalled by any one, but which, had Pasta been a beauty, she might have possessed. But there was nothing hard or harsh in this majesty. Whatsoever of a masculine nature Constance might have inherited, nothing masculine, nothing not exquisitely feminine, was visible in her person. Her shape was rounded, and sufficiently full to show that in middle age its beauty would be preserved by that richness and freshness which a moderate increase of the proportions always gives to the sex. Her arms and hands were, and are, even to this day, of a beauty the more striking, because it is so rare. Nothing in any European country is more uncommon than an arm really beautiful both in hue and shape. In any assembly we go to, what miserable bones, what angular elbows, what red skins, do we see under the cover of those capacious sleeves, which are only one whit less ugly. At the time I speak of, those coverings were not worn; and the white, round, dazzling arm of Constance, bare almost to the shoulder, was girded by dazzling gems, which at once set off, and were foiled by, the beauty of nature. Her hair was of the most luxuriant and of the deepest black; and it was worn in a fashion — then uncommon, without being bizarre — now hackneyed by the plainest faces, though suit

CONSTANCE.

ing only the highest order of beauty,—I mean that simple and classic fashion to which the French have given a name borrowed from Calypso, but which appears to me suited rather to an intellectual than a voluptuous goddess. Her long lashes, and a brow delicately but darkly pencilled, gave additional eloquence to an eye of the deepest blue, and a classic contour to a profile so slightly aquiline that it was commonly considered Grecian. That necessary completion to all real beauty of either sex, the short and curved upper lip, terminated in the most dazzling teeth, and the ripe and dewy under lip added to what was noble in her beauty that charm also which is exclusively feminine. Her complexion was capricious; now pale, now tinged with the pink of the sea-shell, or the softest shade of the rose leaf: but in either it was so transparent that you doubted which became her the most. To these attractions add a throat, a bust of the most dazzling whiteness, and the justest proportions; a foot, whose least beauty was its smallness, and a waist narrow,—not the narrowness of tenuity or constraint, but round, gradual, insensibly less in its compression,—and the person of Constance Vernon, in the bloom of her youth, is before you.

She passed with her quiet and stately step from her room, through one adjoining it, and which we stop to notice, because it was her customary sitting-room when not with Lady Erpingham. There had Godolphin, with the foreign but courtly freedom, the respectful and chivalric ease of his manners, often sought her; there had he lingered in order to detain her yet a moment and a moment longer from other company, seeking a sweet excuse in some remark on the books that strewed the tables, or the music in that recess, or the forest scene from those windows through which the moon of autumn now stole with its own peculiar power to soften and subdue. As these recollections came across her, her step faltered and her colour faded from its glow: she paused a moment, cast a mournful glance round the room, and then tore herself away, descended the lofty staircase, passed the stone hall, melancholy with old banners and rusted crests, and bore her beauty and her busy heart into the thickening and gay crowd.

Her eye looked once more round for the graceful form of Godolphin: but he was not visible; and she had scarcely satisfied herself of this before Lord Erpingham, the hero of the evening, approached and claimed her hand.

"I have just performed my duty," said he, with a gallantry of speech not common to him, "now for my reward. I have danced the first dance with Lady Margaret Midgecombe: I come, according to your promise, to dance the second with you."

There was something in these words that stung one of the morbid remembrances in Miss Vernon's mind. Lady Margaret Midgecombe, in ordinary life, would have been thought a good-looking, vulgar girl; she was a duke's daughter, and she was termed a Hebe. Her little nose and her fresh colour and her silly but not unmalicious laugh were called enchanting; and all irregularities of feature and faults of shape were absolutely turned into merits by that odd commendation, so common with us,—"A deuced fine girl; none of your regular beauties."

Not only in the county of —— shire, but in London, had Lady Margaret Midgecombe been set up as the rival beauty of Constance Vernon. And Constance, far too lovely, too cold, too proud, not to acknowledge beauty in others where it really existed, was nevertheless unaffectedly indignant at a comparison so unworthy; she even, at times, despised her own claims to admiration, since claims so immeasurably inferior could be put into competition with them. Added to this sore feeling for Lady Margaret, was one created by Lady Margaret's mother. The Duchess of Winstoun was a woman of ordinary birth,—the daughter of a peer of great wealth but new family. She had married, however, one of the most powerful dukes in the peerage,—a stupid, heavy, pompous man, with four castles, eight parks, a coal-mine, a tin-mine, six boroughs, and about thirty livings. Inactive and reserved, the duke was seldom seen in public; the care of supporting his rank devolved on the duchess, and she supported it with as much solemnity of purpose as if she had been a cheesemonger's daughter. Stately, insolent, and coarse; asked everywhere; insulting all; hated and courted,— such was the Duchess of Winstoun, and such, perhaps, have been other duchesses before her.

Be it understood that, at that day, Fashion had not risen to the despotism it now enjoys: it took its colouring from Power, not controlled it. I shall show, indeed, how much of its present condition that *Fashion* owes to the Heroine of these Memoirs. The Duchess of Winstoun could not now be that great person she was then; there is a certain good taste in Fashion which repels the mere insolence of Rank, which requires persons to be either agreeable or brilliant or at least original, which weighs stupid dukes in a righteous balance and finds vulgar duchesses wanting. But in lack of this new authority, this moral sebastocrator between the Sovereign and the dignity hitherto considered next to the Sovereign's, her Grace of Winstoun exercised with impunity the rights of insolence. She had taken an especial dislike to Constance: partly because the few good judges of beauty, who care neither for rank nor report, had very unreservedly placed Miss Vernon beyond the reach of all competition with her daughter; and principally because the high spirit and keen irony of Constance had given more than once to the duchess's effrontery so cutting and so public a check, that she had felt with astonishment and rage there was one woman in that world — that woman too unmarried — who could retort the rudeness of the Duchess of Winstoun. Spiteful, however, and numerous were the things she said of Miss Vernon, when Miss Vernon was absent; and haughty beyond measure were the inclination of her head and the tone of her voice when Miss Vernon was present. If, therefore, Constance was disliked by the duchess, we may readily believe that she returned the dislike. The very name roused her spleen and her pride; and it was with a feeling all a woman's, though scarcely feminine in the amiable sense of the word, that she learned to whom the honour of Lord Erpingham's precedence had been (though necessarily) given.

As Lord Erpingham led her to her place, a buzz of admiration and enthusiasm followed her steps. This pleased Erpingham more than, at that moment, it did Constance. Already intoxicated by her beauty, he was proud of the effect it produced on others, for that effect was a compliment to his taste. He exerted himself to be agreeable; nay, more, to be fascinating: he affected a low voice; and he attempted — poor man! — to flatter.

The Duchess of Winstoun and her daughter sat behind on an elevated bench. They saw with especial advantage the attentions with which one of the greatest of England's earls honoured the daughter of one of the greatest of England's orators. They were shocked at his want of dignity. Constance perceived their chagrin, and she lent a more pleased and attentive notice to Lord Erpingham's compliments; her eyes sparkled and her cheek blushed; and the good folks around, admiring Lord Erpingham's immense whiskers, thought Constance in love.

It was just at this time that Percy Godolphin entered the room.

Although Godolphin's person was not of a showy order, there was something about him that always arrested attention. His air, his carriage, his long fair locks, his rich and foreign habits of dress, which his high bearing and intellectual countenance redeemed from coxcombry,—all, united, gave something remarkable and distinguished to his appearance; and the interest attached to his fortunes, and to his social reputation for genius and eccentricity, could not fail of increasing the effect he produced when his name was known.

From the throng of idlers that gathered around him, from the bows of the great and the smiles of the fair, Godolphin, however, directed his whole notice — his whole soul — to the spot which was hallowed by Constance Vernon. He saw her engaged with a man rich, powerful, and handsome; he saw that she listened to her partner with evident interest, that he addressed her with evident admiration. His heart sank within him; he felt faint and sick; then came anger, mortification; then agony and despair. All his former resolutions, all his prudence, his worldliness, his caution, vanished at once; he felt only that he loved, that he was supplanted, that he was undone. The dark and fierce passions of his youth, of a nature in reality wild and vehement, swept away at once the projects and the fabrics of that shallow and chill philosophy he had borrowed from the world, and deemed the wisdom of the closet. A cottage and a desert with Constance — Constance all his, heart and hand — would have been Paradise; he would have nursed no other ambition, nor dreamed of a reward beyond. Such effect has jealousy upon us. We confide, and we hesitate to accept a boon; we are jealous, and we would lay down life to attain it.

"What a handsome fellow Erpingham is!" said a young man in a cavalry regiment.

Godolphin heard and groaned audibly.

"And what a devilish handsome girl he is dancing with!" said another young man, from Oxford.

"Oh, Miss Vernon! By Jove, Erpingham seems smitten. What a capital thing it would be for her!"

"And for him, too!" cried the more chivalrous Oxonian.

"Humph!" said the officer.

"I heard," renewed the Oxonian, "that she was to be married to young Godolphin. He was staying here a short time ago. They rode and walked together. What a lucky fellow he has been! I don't know any one I should so much like to see."

"Hush!" said a third person, looking at Godolphin.

Percy moved on. Accomplished and self-collected as he usually was, he could not wholly conceal the hell within. His brow grew knit and gloomy; he scarcely returned the salutations he received; and moving out of the crowd, he stole to a seat behind a large pillar, and, scarcely seen by any one, fixed his eyes on the form and movements of Miss Vernon.

It so happened that he had placed himself in the vicinity of the Duchess of Winstoun, and within hearing of the conversation that I am about to record.

The dance being over, Lord Erpingham led Constance to a seat close by Lady Margaret Midgecombe. The duchess had formed her plan of attack; and, rising as she saw Constance *within reach*, approached her with an air that affected civility.

"How do you do, Miss Vernon? I am happy to see you

looking so well. What truth in the report, eh?" And the duchess showed her teeth,— *videlicet*, smiled.

"What report does your grace allude to?"

"Nay, nay; I am sure Lord Erpingham has heard it as well as myself; and I wish for *your* sake (a slight emphasis), indeed, for both your sakes, that it may be true."

"To wait till the Duchess of Winstoun speaks intelligibly would be a waste of her time and my own," said the haughty Constance, with the rudeness in which she then delighted, and for which she has since become known. But the duchess was not to be offended until she had completed her manœuvre.

"Well, now," said she, turning to Lord Erpingham, "I appeal to you; is not Miss Vernon to be married very soon to Mr. Godolphin? I am sure [with an affected good-nature and compassion that stung Constance to the quick], I am sure I *hope* so."

"Upon my word you amaze me," said Lord Erpingham, opening to their fullest extent the large, round, hazel eyes for which he was so justly celebrated. "I never heard this before."

"Oh, a secret as yet?" said the duchess; "very well! I can keep a secret."

Lady Margaret looked down, and laughed prettily.

"I thought till now," said Constance, with grave composure, "that no person could be more contemptible than one who *collects* idle reports: I now find I was wrong: a person infinitely more contemptible is one who *invents* them."

The rude duchess, beat at her own weapons, blushed with anger even through her rouge; but Constance turned away, and, still leaning on Lord Erpingham's arm, sought another seat; that seat, on the opposite side of the pillar behind which Godolphin sat, was still within his hearing.

"Upon my word, Miss Vernon," said Erpingham, "I admire your spirit. Nothing like setting down those absurd people who try to tease one, and think one dares not retort. But pray — I hope I 'm not impertinent — pray, may I ask if this rumour have *any* truth in it?"

"Certainly not," said Constance, with great effort, but in a clear tone.

"No; I should have thought not, I should have thought not. Godolphin 's much too poor,—much too poor for you. Miss Vernon is not born to marry for love in a cottage, is she?"

Constance sighed.

That soft, low tone thrilled to Godolphin's very heart. He bent forward: he held his breath; he thirsted for her voice, for some tone, some word in answer; it came not at that moment.

"You remember," renewed the earl,—"you remember Miss L——? No? she was before your time. Well, she married S——, much such another fellow as Godolphin. He had not a shilling; but he lived well, had a house in Mayfair, gave dinners, hunted at Melton, and so forth,—in short, he played high. She had about £10,000. They married, and lived for two years so comfortably, you have no idea. Every one envied them. They did not keep a close carriage, but he used to drive her out to dinners in his French cabriolet.[1] There was no show, no pomp: everything deuced neat, though; quite love in a cottage,—only the cottage was in Curzon Street. At length, however, the cards turned; S—— lost everything: owed more than he could ever pay. We were forced to cut him; and his relation, Lord ——, coming into the ministry a year afterwards, got him a place in the Customs. They live at Brompton; he wears a pepper-and-salt coat, and she a mob-cap, with pink ribbons; they have five hundred a year, and ten children. Such was the fate of S——'s wife; such may be the fate of Godolphin's. Oh, Miss Vernon could not marry *him!*"

"You are right, Lord Erpingham," said Constance with emphasis; "but you take too much license in expressing your opinion."

Before Lord Erpingham could stammer forth his apology, they heard a slight noise behind. They turned; Godolphin had risen. His countenance, always inclined to a calm se-

[1] Then uncommon.

verity — for thought is usually severe in its outward aspect — bent now on both the speakers with so dark and menacing an aspect that the stout earl felt his heart stand still for a moment; and Constance was appalled as if it had been the apparition, and not the living form, of her lover that she beheld. But scarcely had they seen this expression of countenance ere it changed. With a cold and polished smile, a relaxed brow, and profound inclination of his form, Godolphin greeted the two; and passing from his seat with a slow step glided among the crowd and vanished.

What a strange thing, after all, is a great assembly! An immense mob of persons, who feel for each other the profoundest indifference, met together to join in amusements which the large majority of them consider wearisome beyond conception. How unintellectual, how uncivilized, such a scene and such actors! What a remnant of barbarous times, when people danced because they had nothing to say! Were there nothing ridiculous in dancing, there would be nothing ridiculous in seeing wise men dance. But that sight would be ludicrous because of the disparity between the mind and the occupation. However, we have some excuse; we go to these assemblies to sell our daughters, or flirt with our neighbours' wives. A ballroom is nothing more or less than a great market-place of beauty. For my part, were I a buyer, I should like making my purchases in a less public mart.

"Come, Godolphin, a glass of champagne," cried the young Lord Belvoir, as they sat near each other at the splendid supper.

"With all my heart; but not from that bottle! We must have a new one; for this glass is pledged to Lady Delmour, and I would not drink to her health but from the first sparkle! Nothing tame, nothing insipid, nothing that has lost its first freshness, can be dedicated to one so beauiful and young."

The fresh bottle was opened, and Godolphin bowed over his glass to Lord Belvoir's sister,— a Beauty and a Blue. Lady Delmour admired Godolphin, and she was flattered by a compliment that no one wholly educated in England would have had the gallant courage to utter across a crowded table.

"You have been dancing?" said she.

"No!"

"What then?"

"What then?" said Godolphin. "Ah, Lady Delmour, do not ask." The look that accompanied the words supplied them with a meaning. "Need I add," said he, in a lower voice, "that I have been thinking of the most beautiful person present?"

"Pooh," said Lady Delmour, turning away her head.

Now, that *pooh* is a very significant word. On the lips of a man of business, it denotes contempt for romance; on the lips of a politician it rebukes a theory; with that monosyllable a philosopher massacres a fallacy; by those four letters a rich man gets rid of a beggar. But in the rosy mouth of a woman the harshness vanishes, the disdain becomes encouragement. "Pooh!" says the lady, when you tell her she is handsome; but she smiles when she says it. With the same reply she receives your protestation of love, and blushes as she receives. With men it is the sternest, with women the softest, exclamation in the language.

"Pooh!" said Lady Delmour, turning away her head,—and Godolphin was in singular spirits. What a strange thing that we should call such hilarity from our gloom! The stroke induces the flash; excite the nerves by jealousy, by despair, and with the proud you only trace the excitement by the mad mirth and hysterical laughter it creates.

Godolphin was charming *comme un amour*, and the young countess was delighted with his gallantry.

"Did you ever love?" asked she, tenderly, as they sat alone after supper.

"Alas, yes!" said he.

"How often?"

"Read Marmontel's story of the 'Four Phials;' I have no other answer."

"Oh, what a beautiful tale that is! The whole history of a man's heart is contained in it."

While Godolphin was thus talking with Lady Delmour, his whole soul was with Constance; of her only he thought, and on her he thirsted for revenge. There is a curious phenomenon in love, showing how much vanity has to do with even the best species of it, when, for your mistress to prefer another, changes all your affection into hatred: — is it the *loss* of the mistress, or her *preference* to the other? The last, to be sure: for if the former, you would only grieve; but jealousy does not make you grieve, it makes you enraged; it does not sadden, it stings. After all, as we grow old, and look back on the "master passion," how we smile at the fools it made of us, at the importance we attach to it, of the millions that have been governed by it! When we examine the passion of love, it is like examining the character of some great man; we are astonished to perceive the littlenesses that belong to it. We ask in wonder, "How come such effects from such a cause?"

Godolphin continued talking sentiment with Lady Delmour, until her lord, who was very fond of his carriage-horses, came up and took her away; and then, perhaps, glad to be relieved, Percy sauntered into the ballroom, where, though the crowd was somewhat thinned, the dance was continued with that spirit which always seems to increase as the night advances.

For my own part, I now and then look late in at a ball as a warning and grave memento of the flight of time. No amusement belongs of right so essentially to the young in their first youth, to the unthinking, the intoxicated, to those whose blood is an elixir.

"If Constance be woman," said Godolphin to himself, as he returned to the ballroom, "I will yet humble her to my will. I have not learned the science so long to be now foiled in the first moment I have seriously wished to triumph."

As this thought inspired and excited him, he moved along at some distance from but carefully within the sight of Constance. He paused by Lady Margaret Midgecombe. He addressed her. Notwithstanding the insolence and the ignorance of the Duchess of Winstoun, he was well received by both mother and daughter. Some persons there are, in all times and in all spheres, who command a certain respect, bought neither by riches, rank, nor even scrupulous morality of conduct. They win it by the reputation that talent alone can win them, and which yet is not always the reputation of talent. No man, even in the frivolous societies of the great, obtains homage without certain qualities, which, had they been happily directed, would have conducted him to fame. Had the attention of a Grammont, or of a ——, been early turned towards what *ought* to be the objects desired, who can doubt that, instead of the heroes of a circle, they might have been worthy of becoming names of posterity?

Thus the genius of Godolphin had drawn around him an *éclat* which made even the haughtiest willing to receive and to repay his notice; and Lady Margaret actually blushed with pleasure when he asked her to dance. A foreign dance, then only very partially known in England, had been called for: few were acquainted with it,—those only who had been abroad; and as the movements seemed to require peculiar grace of person, some even among those few declined, through modesty, the exhibition.

To this dance Godolphin led Lady Margaret. All crowded round to see the performers; and as each went through the giddy and intoxicating maze, they made remarks on the awkwardness or the singularity or the impropriety of the dance. But when Godolphin began, the murmurs changed. The slow and stately measure then adapted to the steps was one in which the graceful symmetry of his person might eminently display itself. Lady Margaret was at least as well acquainted with the dance: and the couple altogether so immeasurably excelled all competitors, that the rest, as if sensible of it, stopped one after the other; and when Godolphin, perceiving that they were alone, stopped also, the spectators made their approbation more audible than approbation usually is in polished society.

As Godolphin paused, his eyes met those of Constance. There was not there the expression he had anticipated: there was neither the anger of jealousy, nor the restlessness of offended vanity, nor the desire of conciliation, visible in those large and speaking orbs. A deep, a penetrating, a sad inquiry seemed to dwell in her gaze,—seemed anxious to pierce into his heart, and to discover whether there she possessed the power to wound, or whether each had been deceived: so at least seemed that fixed and melancholy intenseness of look to Godolphin. He left Lady Margaret abruptly; in an instant he was by the side of Constance.

"You must be delighted with this evening," said he, bitterly. "Wherever I go I hear your praises: every one admires you; and he who does not admire so much as worship you, *he* alone is beneath your notice. He, born to such shattered fortunes,—he indeed might never *aspire* to that which titled and wealthy idiots deem they may *command*,—the hand of Constance Vernon."

It was with a low and calm tone that Godolphin spoke. Constance turned deadly pale: her frame trembled; but she did not answer immediately. She moved to a seat retired a little from the busy crowd; Godolphin followed and sat himself beside her; and then, with a slight effort, Constance spoke.

"You heard what was said, Mr. Godolphin, and I grieve to think you did. If I offended you, however, forgive me, I pray you; I pray it sincerely, warmly. God knows I have suffered myself enough from idle words, and from the slighting opinion with which this hard world visits the poor, not to feel deep regret and shame if I wound, by like means, another, more especially"—Constance's voice trembled,—"more especially *you!*"

As she spoke, she turned her eyes on Godolphin, and they were full of tears. The tenderness of her voice, her look, melted him at once. Was it to him, indeed, that the haughty Constance addressed the words of kindness and apology,—to him whose intrinsic circumstances she had heard described as so unworthy of her, and, his reason told him, with such justice?

"Oh, Miss Vernon!" said he, passionately; "Miss Vernon—Constance—dear, dear Constance! dare I call you so? hear me one word. I love you with a love which leaves me no words to tell it. I know my faults, my poverty, my unworthiness; but—but—may I—may I hope?"

And all the woman was in Constance's cheek, as she listened. That cheek, how richly was it dyed! Her eyes drooped; her bosom heaved. How every word in those broken sentences sank into her heart! never was a tone forgotten. The child may forget its mother, and the mother desert the child; but never, never from a woman's heart departs the memory of the first confession of love from him whom she first loves! She lifted her eyes, and again withdrew them, and again gazed.

"This must not be," at last she said; "no, no! it is folly, madness in both!"

"Not so; nay, not so!" whispered Godolphin, in the softest notes of a voice that could never be harsh. "It may seem folly, madness if you will, that the brilliant and all-idolized Miss Vernon should listen to the vows of so lowly an adorer; but try me, prove me, and own — yes, you *will* own some years hence — that that folly has been happy beyond the happiness of prudence or ambition."

"This," answered Constance, struggling with her emotions,— "this is no spot or hour for such a conference. Let us meet to-morrow — the western chamber."

"And the hour?"

"Twelve!"

"And I may hope — till then?"

Constance again grew pale; and in a voice that, though it scarcely left her lips, struck coldness and dismay into his sudden and delighted confidence, answered,—

"No, Percy, there is no hope! — none!"

CHAPTER XVIII.

THE INTERVIEW. — THE CRISIS OF A LIFE.

The western chamber was that I have mentioned as the one in which Constance usually fixed her retreat, when neither sociability nor state summoned her to the more public apartments. I should have said that Godolphin slept in the house; for, coming from a distance and through country roads, Lady Erpingham had proffered him that hospitality, and he had willingly accepted it. Before the appointed hour, he was at the appointed spot.

He had passed the hours till then without even seeking his pillow. In restless strides across his chamber, he had revolved those words with which Constance had seemed to deny the hopes she herself had created. All private and more selfish schemes or reflections had vanished, as by magic, from the mind of a man prematurely formed, but not yet wholly hardened in the mould of worldly speculation. He thought no more of what he should relinquish in obtaining her hand; with the ardour of boyish and real love, he thought only of her. It was as if there existed no world but the little spot in which she breathed and moved.

Poverty, privation, toil, the change of the manners and habits of his whole previous life, to those of professional enterprise and self-denial,—to all this he looked forward, not so much with calmness as with triumph.

"Be but Constance mine!" said he again and again; and again and again those fatal words knocked at his heart, "No hope,—none!" and he gnashed his teeth in very anguish, and muttered, "But mine she will not—she will never be!"

Still, however, before the hour of noon, something of his habitual confidence returned to him. He had succeeded, though but partially, in reasoning away the obvious meaning of the words; and he ascended to the chamber from the gardens, in which he had sought, by the air, to cool his mental fever, with a sentiment, ominous and doubtful indeed, but still removed from despondency and despair.

The day was sad and heavy. A low, drizzling rain, and labouring yet settled clouds, which denied all glimpse of the sky, and seemed cursed into stagnancy by the absence of all wind or even breeze, increased, by those associations we endeavour in vain to resist, the dark and oppressive sadness of his thoughts.

He paused as he laid his hand on the door of the chamber:

he listened; and in the acute and painful life which seemed breathed into all his senses, he felt as if he could have heard — though without the room — the very breath of Constance, or known, as by an inspiration, the presence of her beauty. He opened the door gently: all was silence and desolation for him,— Constance was not there!

He felt, however, as if that absence was a relief. He breathed more freely, and seemed to himself more prepared for the meeting. He took his station by the recess of the window: in vain,— he could rest in no spot; he walked to and fro, pausing only for a moment as some object before him reminded him of past and more tranquil hours. The books he had admired, and which, at his departure, had been left in their usual receptacle at another part of the house, he now discovered on the tables; they opened of themselves at the passages he had read aloud to Constance: those passages, in his presence, she had not seemed to admire; he was inexpressibly touched to perceive that, in his absence, they had become dear to her. As he turned with a beating heart from this silent proof of affection, he was startled by the sudden and almost living resemblance to Constance, which struck upon him in a full-length picture opposite,— the picture of her father. That picture, by one of the best of our great modern masters of the art, had been taken of Vernon in the proudest epoch of his prosperity and fame. He was portrayed in the attitude in which he had uttered one of the most striking sentences of one of his most brilliant orations: the hand was raised, the foot advanced, the chest expanded. Life, energy, command, flashed from the dark eye, breathed from the dilated nostril, broke from the inspired lip. That noble brow, those modelled features, that air, so full of the royalty of genius — how startlingly did they resemble the softer lineaments of Constance!

Arrested, in spite of himself, by the skill of the limner, and the characteristic of the portrait, Godolphin stood motionless and gazing till the door opened, and Constance herself stood before him. She smiled faintly, but with sweetness as she approached; and seating herself, motioned him to a chair at a little distance. He obeyed the gesture in silence.

"Godolphin!" said she, softly. At the sound of her voice he raised his eyes from the ground, and fixed them on her countenance with a look so full of an imploring and earnest meaning, so expressive of the passion, the suspense of his heart, that Constance felt her voice cease at once. But he saw as he gazed how powerful had been his influence. Not a vestige of bloom was on her cheek: her very lips were colourless; her eyes were swollen with weeping; and though she seemed very calm and self-possessed, all her wonted majesty of mien was gone. The form seemed to shrink within itself. Humbleness and sorrow — deep, passionate, but quiet sorrow — had supplanted the haughtiness and the elastic freshness of her beauty. "Mr. Godolphin," she repeated, after a pause, "answer me truly and with candour; not with the world's gallantry, but with a sincere, a plain avowal. Were you not — in your unguarded expressions last night — were you not excited by the surprise, the passion, of the moment? Were you not uttering what, had you been actuated only by a calm and premeditated prudence, you would at least have suppressed?"

"Miss Vernon," replied Godolphin, "all that I said last night, I now, in calmness, and with deliberate premeditation, repeat: all that I can dream of happiness is in your hands."

"I would, indeed, that I could disbelieve you," said Constance, sorrowfully; "I have considered deeply on your words. I am touched, made grateful, proud — yes, truly proud, by your confessed affection — but — "

"Oh, Constance!" cried Godolphin, in a sudden and agonized voice, and rising, he flung himself impetuously at her feet, — "Constance! do not reject me!"

He seized her hand; it struggled not with his. He gazed on her countenance: it was dyed in blushes; and before those blushes vanished, her agitation found relief in tears, which flowed fast and full.

"Beloved!" said Godolphin, with a solemn tenderness, "why struggle with your heart? That heart I read at this moment: *that* is not averse to me." Constance wept on. "I know what you would say, and what you feel," continued Godolphin; "you think that I — that we both are poor; that you could ill bear the humiliations of that haughty poverty which those born to higher fortunes so irksomely endure. You tremble to link your fate with one who has been imprudent, lavish,— selfish, if you will. You recoil before you intrust your happiness to a man who, if he wreck *that*, can offer you nothing in return,— no rank, no station, nothing to heal a bruised heart, or cover its wound, at least, in the rich disguises of power and wealth. Am I not right, Constance? Do I not read your mind?"

"No!" said Constance, with energy. "Had I been born any man's daughter but his from whom I take my name; were I the same in all things, mind and heart, save in one feeling, one remembrance, one object, that I am now,— Heaven is my witness that I would not cast a thought upon poverty, upon privation; that I would — nay, I do — I *do* confide in your vows, your affection. If you have erred, I know it not. If any but you tell me you have erred, I believe them not. You I trust wholly and implicitly. Heaven, I say, is my witness that, did I obey the voice of my selfish heart, I would gladly, proudly, share and follow your fortunes. You mistake me if you think sordid and vulgar ambition can only influence me. No! I could be worthy of you! The daughter of John Vernon could be a worthy wife to the man of indigence and genius. In your poverty I could soothe you; in your labour I could support you; in your reverses console, in your prosperity triumph. But — but, it must not be. Go, Godolphin — dear Godolphin! There are thousands better and fairer than I am, who will do for you as I would have done; but who possess the power I have not, who, instead of sharing, can raise your fortunes. Go! — and if it comfort, if it soothe you, believe that I have not been insensible to your generosity, your love. My best wishes, my fondest prayers, my dearest hopes, are yours."

Blinded by her tears, subdued by her emotions, Constance was still herself. She rose; she extricated her hand from

Godolphin's; she turned to leave the room. But Godolphin, still kneeling, caught hold of her robe, and gently but effectually detained her.

"The picture you have painted," said he, "do not destroy at once. You have portrayed yourself my soother, guide, restorer. You *can*, indeed you can, be this. You do not know me, Constance. Let me say one word for myself. Hitherto, I have shunned fame and avoided ambition. Life has seemed to me so short, and all that even glory wins so poor, that I have thought no labour worth the price of a single hour of pleasure and enjoyment. For you, how joyfully will I renounce my code! For myself I could ask no honour; for you, I will labour for all. No toil shall be dry to me, no pleasure shall decoy. I will renounce my idle and desultory pursuits. I will enter the great public arena, where all who come armed with patience and with energy are sure to win. Constance, I am not without talents, though they have slept within me; say but the word, and you know not what they can produce."

An irresolution in Constance was felt as a sympathy by Godolphin; he continued,—

"We are both desolate in the world, Constance; we are orphans,— friendless, fortuneless. Yet both have made our way without friends, and commanded our associates, though without fortune. Does not this declare we have that within us which, when we are united, can still exalt or conquer our destiny? And we — we — alone in the noisy and contentious world with which we strive — we shall turn, after each effort, to our own hearts, and find there a comfort and a shelter. All things will bind us closer and closer to each other. The thought of our past solitude, the hope of our future objects, will only feed the fountain of our present love. And how much sweeter, Constance, will be honours to you, if we thus win them,— sanctified as they will be by the sacrifices we have made; by the thought of the many hours in which we desponded, yet took consolation from each other; by the thought how we sweetened mortifications by sympathy, and made even the lowest successes noble by the endearing associations with which we allied them! How much sweeter to you will be such honours than those which you might command at once, but accompanied by a cold heart; rendered wearisome because won with ease and low because undignified by fame! Oh, Constance! am I not heard? Have not love, nature, sense, triumphed?"

As he spoke, he had risen gently, and wound his arms around her not reluctant form: her head reclined upon his bosom; her hand was surrendered to his; and his kiss stole softly and unchidden to her cheek. At that instant, the fate of both hung on a very hair. How different might the lot, the character, of each have been, had Constance's lips pronounced the words that her heart already recorded! And she might have done so; but as she raised her eyes, the same object that had before affected Godolphin came vividly upon her, and changed, as by an electric shock, the whole current of her thoughts. Full and immediately before her was the picture of her father. The attitude there delineated, so striking at all times, seemed to Constance at that moment more than ever impressive, and even awful in the *livingness* of its command. It was the face of Vernon in the act of speech, of warning, of reproof; such as she had seen it often in private life; such as she had seen it in his bitter maledictions on his hollow friends at the close of his existence; nay, such as she had seen it — only more fearful, and ghastly with the hues of death — in his last hours; in those hours in which he had pledged her to the performance of his revenge, and bade her live not for love but the memory of her sire.

With the sight of that face rushed upon her the dark and solemn recollections of that time and of that vow. The weakness of love vanished before the returning force of a sentiment nursed through her earliest years, fed by her dreams, strengthened by her studies, and hardened by the daring energies of a nature lofty yet fanatical, into the rule, the end, nay, the very religion of life! She tore herself away from the surprised and dismayed Godolphin; she threw herself on her knees before the picture; her lips moved rapidly; the rapid and brief prayer for forgiveness was over, and Constance rose a new being. She turned to Godolphin, and, lifting her arm towards the picture, as she regarded, with her bright and kindling eyes, the face of her lover, she said,—

"As you think now, thought he whose voice speaks to you from the canvas; he, who pursued the path that you would tread; who, through the same toil, the same pursuit, that you would endure, used the same powers and the same genius you would command; he, who won — what you might win also at last — the smile of princes, the trust of nobles, the shifting and sandy elevation which the best, the wisest, and greatest statesmen in this country, if unbacked by a sordid and caballing faction, can alone obtain,— he warns you from that hollow distinction, from its wretched consummation. Oh, Godolphin!" she continued, subdued, and sinking from a high-wrought but momentary paroxysm, uncommon to her collected character, "oh, Godolphin! I saw that man dying, deserted, lonely, cursed by his genius, ruined by his prosperity. I saw him dying — *die* — of a broken and trampled heart. Could I doom another victim to the same course and the same perfidy and the same fate? Could I, with a silent heart, watch by that victim; could I, viewing his certain doom, elate him with false hopes? No, no! fly from me,— from the thought of such a destiny. Marry one who can bring you wealth, and support you with rank; *then* be ambitious if you will. Leave me to fulfil my doom,— MY VOW; and to think, however wretched I may be, that I have not inflicted a permanent wretchedness on you."

Godolphin sprang forward; but the door closed upon his eyes; and he saw Constance — as Constance *Vernon* — no more.

CHAPTER XIX.

A RAKE AND EXQUISITE OF THE BEST (WORST) SCHOOL. — A CONVERSATION ON A THOUSAND MATTERS. — THE DECLENSION OF THE "SUI PROFUSUS" INTO THE "ALIENI APPETENS."

There was, in the day I now refer to, a certain house in Chesterfield Street, Mayfair, which few young men anxious for the *éclat* of society passed without a wish for the acquaintance of the inmate. To that small and dingy mansion, with its verandas of dusky green and its blinds perpetually drawn, there attached an interest, a consideration, and a mystery. Thither, at the dusk of night, were the hired carriages of intrigue wont to repair, and dames to alight, careful seemingly of concealment, yet wanting, perhaps, even a reputation to conceal. Few, at the early hours of morn, passed that street on their way home from some glittering revel without noticing some three or four chariots in waiting, or without hearing from within the walls the sounds of protracted festivity. That house was the residence of a man who had never done anything in public, and yet was the most noted personage in "Society:" in early life, the all-accomplished *Lovelace!* in later years mingling the graces with the decayed heart and the want of principle of a *Grammont.* Feared, contemned, loved, hated, ridiculed, honoured, the very genius, the very personification, of a civilized and profligate life seemed embodied in Augustus Saville. Hitherto we have spoken of, let us now describe him.

Born to the poor fortunes and equivocal station of cadet in a noble but impoverished house, he had passed his existence in a round of lavish, but never inelegant, dissipation. Unlike other men, whom youth and money and the flush of health and aristocratic indulgence allure to follies which shock the taste as well as the morality of the wise, Augustus

Saville had never committed an error which was not varnished by grace, and limited by a profound and worldly discretion. A systematic votary of pleasure, no woman had ever through him lost her reputation or her sphere,— whether it was that he corrupted into fortunate dissimulation the minds that he betrayed into guilt, or whether he chose his victims with so just a knowledge of their characters and of the circumstances round them, that he might be sure the secrecy maintained by himself would scarcely be divulged elsewhere. All the world attributed to Augustus Saville the most various and consummate success in that quarter in which success is most envied by the lighter part of the world; yet no one could say exactly who, amongst the many he addressed, had been the object of his triumph. The same quiet and yet victorious discretion waited upon all he did. Never had he stooped to win celebrity from horses or from carriages; nothing in his equipages showed the ambition to be distinguished from another; least of all did he affect that most displeasing of minor ostentations, that offensive exaggeration of neatness, that *outré* simplicity, which our young nobles and aspiring bankers so ridiculously think it *bon ton* to assume. No harness industriously avoiding brass; no liveries pretending to the tranquillity of a gentleman's dress; no panels disdaining the armorial attributes of which real dignity should neither be ashamed nor proud, converted plain taste into a display of plainness. He seldom appeared at races, and never hunted; though he was profound master of the calculations in the first, and was, as regarded the second, allowed to be one of the most perfect masters of horsemanship in his time. So, in his dress, while he chose even sedulously what became him most, he avoided the appearance of coxcombry, by a disregard to minutiæ. He did not value himself on the perfection of his boot, and suffered a wrinkle in his coat without a sigh; yet even the exquisites of the time allowed that no one was more gentleman-like in the *tout-ensemble;* and while he sought by other means than dress to attract, he never even in dress offended. Carefully shunning the character of the professed wit or the general talker, he was yet piquant, shrewd, and animated to the few persons whom he addressed, or with whom he associated; and though he had refused all offers to enter public life, he was sufficiently master of the graver subjects that agitated the times to impress even those practically engaged in them with a belief in his information and his talents.

But he was born poor; and yet he had lived for nearly thirty years as a rich man! What was his secret? — he had lived upon others. At all games of science he played with a masterly skill; and in those wherein luck preponderates, there are always chances for a cool and systematic calculation. He had been, indeed, suspected of unfair play; but the charge had never cooled the eagerness with which he had been courted. With far better taste, and in far higher estimation than Brummell, he obtained an equal though a more secret sway. Every one was desirous to know him: without his acquaintance, the young *débutant* felt that he wanted the qualification to social success; by his intimacy, even vulgarity became the rage. It was true that, as no woman's disgrace was confessedly traced to him, so neither was any man's ruin — save only in the doubtful instance of the unfortunate Johnstone. He never won of any person, however ardent, more than a certain portion of his fortune, — the rest of his undoing Saville left to his satellites; nay, even those who had in reality most reason to complain of him never perceived his due share in their impoverishment. It was common enough to hear men say, "Ah, Saville, I wish I had taken your advice, and left off while I had yet half my fortune!" They did not accurately heed that the first half was Saville's, because the first half had excited, not ruined them.

Besides this method of making money, so strictly social, Saville had also applied his keen intellect and shrewd sense to other speculations. Cheap houses, cheap horses, fluctuations in the funds, all descriptions of property (except perhaps stolen goods), had passed under his earnest attention; and in most cases such speculations had eminently succeeded. He was therefore now, in his middle age, and still unmarried, a man decidedly wealthy; having, without ever playing the miser, without ever stinting a luxury or denying a wish, turned nothing into something, poverty into opulence.

It was noon; and Saville was slowly finishing his morning repast, and conversing with a young man stretched on a sofa opposite in a listless attitude. The room was in perfect keeping with the owner: there was neither velvet nor gilding nor *buhl* nor *marquetrie* — all of which would have been inconsistent with the moderate size of the apartment. But the furniture was new, massive, costly, and luxurious without the ostentation of luxury. A few good pictures, and several exquisite busts and figures in bronze, upon marble pedestals, gave something classic and graceful to the aspect of the room. Annexed to the back drawing-room, looking over Lord Chesterfield's gardens, a small conservatory, filled with rich exotics, made the only feature in the apartment that might have seemed, to a fastidious person, effeminate or unduly voluptuous.

Saville himself was about forty-seven years of age: of a person slight and thin, without being emaciated; a not ungraceful, though habitual stoop, diminished his height, which might be a little above the ordinary standard. In his youth he had been handsome; but in his person there was now little trace of any attraction beyond that of a manner remarkably soft and insinuating: yet in his narrow though high forehead, his sharp aquiline nose, gray eye, and slightly sarcastic curve of lip, something of his character betrayed itself. You saw, or fancied you saw, in them the shrewdness, the delicacy of tact; the consciousness of duping others; the subtle and intuitive, yet bland and noiseless penetration into the characters around him, which made the prominent features of his mind. And, indeed, of all qualities, dissimulation is that which betrays itself the most often in the physiognomy. A fortunate thing, that the long habit of betraying should find at times the index in which to betray itself.

"But you don't tell me, my dear Godolphin," said Saville, as he broke the toast into his chocolate,— "you don't tell me how the world employed itself at Rome. Were there any of the true calibre there,— steady fellows, yet ardent, like myself; men who make us feel our strength and put it forth, with whom we cannot dally nor idle, who require our coolness of head, clearness of memory, ingenuity of stratagem,— in a word, men of my ART, the art of play: were there any such?"

"Not many, but enough for honour," said Godolphin; "for myself, I have long forsworn gambling for profit."

"Ah, I always thought you wanted that perseverance which belongs to strength of character. And how stand your resources now,— sufficient to recommence the world here with credit and *éclat?*"

"Ay, were I so disposed, Saville. But I shall return to Italy. Within a month hence, I shall depart."

"What! and only just arrived in town! An heir in possession!"

"Of what?"

"The reputation of having succeeded to a property, the extent of which, if wise, you will tell to no one! Are you so young, Godolphin, as to imagine that it signifies one crumb of this bread what be the rent-roll of your estate, so long as you can obtain credit for any sum to which you are pleased to extend it? Credit! beautiful invention!— the moral new world to which we fly when banished from the old. Credit! — the true charity of Providence, by which they who otherwise would starve live in plenty, and despise the indigent rich. Credit! — admirable system, alike for those who live on it and the wiser few who live by it. Will you borrow some money of me, Godolphin?"

"At what percentage?"

"Why, let me see: funds are low; I 'll be moderate. But stay; be it with you as I did with George Sinclair. You shall have all you want, and pay me with a premium, when you marry an heiress. Why, man, you wince at the word 'marry'!"

"'T is a sore subject, Saville: one that makes a man think of halters."

"You are right,— I recognize my young pupil. Your old play-writers talked nonsense when they said men lost liberty of person by marriage. Men lose liberty, but it is the liberty of the mind. We cease to be independent of the world's word, when we grow respectable with a wife, a fat butler, two children, and a family coach. It makes a gentleman little better than a grocer or a king! But you have seen Constance Vernon. Why, out on this folly, Godolphin! You turn away. Do you fancy that I did not penetrate your weakness the moment you mentioned her name; still less, do you fancy, my dear young friend, that I, who have lived through nearly half a century, and know our nature, and the whole thermometer of our blood, think one jot the worse of you for forming a caprice — or a passion, if you will — for a woman who would set an anchoret, or, what is still colder, a worn-out debauchee, on fire? Bah! Godolphin, I am wiser than you take me for. And I will tell you more. For your sake, I am *happy* that you have incurred already this, our common folly (which we all have once in a life), and that the fit is over. I do not pry into your secrets,— I know their delicacy. I do not ask which of you drew back; for, to have gone forward, to have married, would have been madness in both. Nay, it was an *impossibility:* it could not have happened to my pupil,— the ablest, the subtlest, the wisest of my pupils. But, however it was broken off, I repeat that I am glad it happened. One is never sure of a man's wisdom till he has been really and vainly in love. You know what that moralizing lump of absurdity, Lord Edouard, has said in the 'Julie,' — 'The path of the passions conducts us to philosophy!' It is true, very true: and now that the path has been fairly trod, the goal is at hand. *Now,* I can confide in your steadiness; now, I can feel that you will run no chance in future of over-appreciating that bauble, Woman. You will beg, borrow, steal, and exchange or lose the jewel, with the same delicious excitement, coupled with the same steady indifference, with which we play at a more scientific game, and for a more comprehensive reward. I say more comprehensive reward: for how many women may we be able to buy by a judicious bet on the odd trick!"

"Your turn is sudden," said Godolphin, smiling; "and

there is some justice in your reasoning. The fit *is* over; and if ever I can be wise, I have entered on wisdom now. But talk of this no more."

"I will not," said Saville, whose unerring tact had reached just the point where to stop, and who had led Godolphin through just that vein of conversation, half sentimentalizing, half sensible, all profligate, which seldom fails to win the ear of a man both of imagination and of the world. "I will not; and, to vary the topic, I will turn egotist, and tell you *my* adventures."

With this, Saville began a light and amusing recital of his various and singular life for the last three years. Anecdote, jest, maxim, remark, interspersed, gave a zest and piquancy to the narration. An accomplished *roué* always affects to moralize; it is a part of his character. There is a vague and shrewd sentiment that pervades his *morale* and his system. Frequent excitement, and its attendant relaxation; the conviction of the folly of all pursuits; the insipidity of all life; the hollowness of all love; the faithlessness in all ties; the disbelief in all worth,—these consequences of a dissipated existence on a thoughtful mind produce some remarkable, while they make so many wretched, characters. They coloured some of the most attractive prose among the French, and the most fascinating verse in the pages of Byron. It might be asked, by a profane inquirer (and I have touched on this before), what effect a life nearly similar—a life of luxury, indolence, lassitude, profuse, but heartless love—imparted to the deep and touching wisdom in *his* page, whom we consider the wisest of men, and who has left us the most melancholy of doctrines?

It was this turn of mind that made Saville's conversation peculiarly agreeable to Godolphin in his present humour; and the latter invested it, from his own mood, with a charm which in reality it wanted. For, as I shall show in Godolphin what deterioration the habits of frivolous and worldly life produce on the mind of a man of genius, I show only in Saville the effect they produce on a man of sense.

"Well, Godolphin," said Saville, as he saw the former rise

to depart; "you will at least dine with me to-day,—a punctual eight. I think I can promise you an agreeable evening. The Linettini and that dear little Fanny Millinger (your old *flame*) are coming; and I have asked old Stracey, the poet, to say *bons mots* for them. Poor old Stracey! He goes about to all his former friends and fellow-liberals, boasting of his favour with the Great, and does not see that we only use him as we would a puppet-show or a dancing-dog."

"What folly," said Godolphin, "it is in any man of genius (not also of birth) to think the Great of this country can possibly esteem him! Nothing can equal the secret enmity with which dull men regard an intellect above their comprehension. Party politics, and the tact, the shifting, the commonplace that Party politics alone require,—these they *can* appreciate; and they feel respect for an orator, even though he be not a county member, for he can assist them in their paltry ambition for place and pension: but an author or a man of science—the rogues positively jeer at him!"

"And yet," said Saville, "how few men of letters perceive a truth so evident to us, so hackneyed even in the conversations of society! For a little reputation at a dinner-table, for a coaxing note from some titled demirep affecting the De Staël, they forget not only to be glorious but even to be respectable. And this, too, not only for so petty a gratification, but for one that rarely lasts above a London season. We allow the low-born author to be the *lion* this year, but we dub him a *bore* the next. We shut our doors upon his twice-told jests, and send for the Prague minstrels to sing to us after dinner instead."

"However," said Godolphin, "it is only poets you find so foolish as to be deceived by you. There is not a single prose writer of real genius so absurd."

"And why is that?"

"Because," replied Godolphin, philosophizing, "poets address themselves more to women than men; and insensibly they acquire the weaknesses which they are accustomed to address. A poet whose verses delight the women will be found, if we closely analyze his character, to be very like a woman himself."

"You don't love poets?" said Saville.

"The glory of old has departed from them,—I mean less from their pages than their minds. We have plenty of beautiful poets, but how little poetry breathing of a great soul!"

Here the door opened, and a Mr. Glosson was announced. There entered a little, smirking, neat-dressed man, prim as a lawyer or a house-agent.

"Ah, Glosson, is that you?" said Saville, with something like animation; "sit down, my good sir,—sit down. Well! well! [rubbing his hands] what news? what news?"

"Why, Mr. Saville, I think we may get the land from old ——. He has the right of the *job*. I have been with him all this morning. He asks £6,000 for it."

"The unconscionable dog! He got it from the crown for two."

"Ah, very true,—very true: but you don't see, sir,—you don't see, that it is well worth nine. Sad times, sad times: jobs from the crown are growing scarcer every day, Mr. Saville."

"Humph! that 's all a chance, a speculation. Times are bad indeed, as you say: no money in the market; go, Glosson, offer him five; your percentage shall be one per cent higher than if I pay six thousand, and shall be counted up to the latter sum."

"He, he, he! sir!" grinned Glosson; "you are fond of your joke, Mr. Saville."

"Well, now; what else in the market? Never mind my friend: Mr. Godolphin—Mr. Glosson; now all *gêne* is over; proceed,—proceed."

Glosson hummed and bowed and hummed again, and then glided on to speak of houses and crown lands and properties in Wales, and places at court (for some of the subordinate posts at the palace were then—perhaps are now—regular matter of barter); and Saville, bending over the table, with his thin delicate hands clasped intently, and his brow denoting his interest, and his sharp shrewd eye fixed on the agent, furnished to the contemplative Godolphin a picture which he did not fail to note, to moralize on, to despise!

What a spectacle is that of the prodigal rake, hardening and sharpening into the grasping speculator!

CHAPTER XX.

FANNY MILLINGER ONCE MORE. — LOVE. — WOMAN. — BOOKS. — A HUNDRED TOPICS TOUCHED ON THE SURFACE. — GODOLPHIN'S STATE OF MIND MORE MINUTELY EXAMINED. — THE DINNER AT SAVILLE'S.

Godolphin went to see and converse with Fanny Millinger. She was still unmarried, and still the fashion. There was a sort of allegory of real life, in the manner in which, at certain epochs, our Idealist was brought into contact with the fair actress of ideal creations. There was, in short, something of a moral in the way these two streams of existence — the one belonging to the Actual, the other to the Imaginary — flowed on, crossing each other at stated times. Which was the more really imaginative,— the life of the stage, or that of the world's stage?

The gay Fanny was rejoiced to welcome back again her early lover. She ran on, talking of a thousand topics, without remarking the absent mind and musing eye of Godolphin, till he himself stopped her somewhat abruptly,—

"Well, Fanny, well, and what do you know of Saville? You have grown intimate with him, eh? We shall meet at his house this evening."

"Oh, yes, he is a charming person in his little way; and the only man who allows me to be a friend without dreaming of becoming a lover. Now that 's what I like. We poor actresses have so much would-be love in the course of our lives, that a little friendship now and then is a novelty which other and soberer people can never appreciate. On reading 'Gil

Blas' the other day — I am no great reader, as you may remember — I was struck by that part in which the dear Santillane assures us that there was never any love between him and Laura the actress. I thought it so true to nature, so probable, that they should have formed so strong an intimacy for each other, lived in the same house, had every opportunity for love, yet never loved. And it was exactly because she was an actress and a light good-for-nothing creature that it so happened; the very multiplicity of lovers prevented her falling in love; the very carelessness of her life, poor girl, rendered a friend so charming to her. It would have spoiled the friend to have made him an adorer; it would have turned the rarity into the every-day character. Now, so it is with me and Saville; I like his wit, he likes my good temper. We see each other as often as if we were in love; and yet I do not believe it even possible that he should ever kiss my hand. After all," continued Fanny, laughing, "love is not so necessary to us women as people think. Fine writers say, 'Oh, men have a thousand objects, women but one!' That's nonsense, dear Percy; women have their thousand objects too. They have not the Bar, but they have the milliner's shop; they can't fight, but they can sit by the window and embroider a work-bag; they don't rush into politics, but they plunge their souls into love for a parrot or a lap-dog. Don't let men flatter themselves; Providence has been just as kind in that respect to one sex as to the other: our objects are small, yours great; but a small object may occupy the mind just as much as the loftiest."

"Ours great! pshaw!" said Godolphin, who was rather struck with Fanny's remarks; "there is nothing great in those professions which man is pleased to extol. Is selfishness great? Are the low trickery, the organized lies of the Bar, a great calling? Is the mechanical slavery of the soldier — fighting because he is in the way of fighting, without knowing the cause, without an object, save a dim, foolish vanity which he calls glory, and cannot analyze — is that a great aim and vocation? Well: the senate! look at the outcry which wise men make against the loathesome corruption of that arena; then look at the dull hours, the tedious talk, the empty boasts, the poor and flat rewards, and tell me where is the greatness? No, Fanny! the embroidered work-bag and the petted parrot afford just as great — morally great — occupations as those of the Bar, the army, the senate. It is only the frivolous who talk of frivolities; there is nothing frivolous; all earthly occupations are on a par,— alike important if they alike occupy; for to the wise all are poor and valueless."

"I fancy you are very wrong," said the actress, pressing her pretty fingers to her forehead, as if to understand him; "but I cannot tell you why, and I never argue. I ramble on in my odd way, casting out my shrewd things without defending them if any one chooses to quarrel with them. What I do I let others do. My maxim in talk is my maxim in life. I claim liberty for myself, and give indulgence to others."

"I see," said Godolphin, "that you have plenty of books about you, though you plead *not guilty* to reading. Do you learn your philosophy from them,— for I think you have contracted a vein of reflection since we parted which I scarcely recognize as an old characteristic."

"Why," answered Fanny, "though I don't read, I skim. Sometimes I canter through a dozen novels in a morning. I am disappointed, I confess, in all these works; I want to see more real knowledge of the world than they ever display. They tell us how Lord Arthur looked, and Lady Lucy dressed, and what was the colour of those curtains, and these eyes, and so forth; and then the better sort, perhaps, *do* also tell us what the heroine felt as well as wore, and try with might and main to pull some string of the internal machine; but still I am not enlightened, not touched. I don't recognize men and women; they are puppets with holiday phrases: and I tell you what, Percy, these novelists make the last mistake you would suppose them guilty of,— they have not *romance* enough in them to paint the truths of society. Old gentlemen say novels are bad teachers of life, because they make it too ideal; quite the reverse: novels are too trite! too superficial! Their very talk about love, and the fuss they make about it, show

how shallow real romance is with them; for they say nothing new on it, and real romance is forever striking out new thoughts. Am I not right, Percy? No! life, be it worldly as it may, has a vast deal of romance in it. Every one of us (even poor I) have a mine of thoughts and fancies and wishes, that books are too dull and commonplace to reach: the heart is a romance in itself."

"A philosophical romance, my Fanny; full of mysteries and conceits and refinements, mixed up with its deeper passages. But how came you so wise?"

"Thank you!" answered Fanny, with a profound courtesy. "The fact is — though you, as in duty bound, don't perceive it — that I am older than I was when we last met. I reflect where I then felt. Besides, the stage fills our heads with a half sort of wisdom, and gives us that strange *mélange* of shrewd experience and romantic notions which is, in fact, the real representation of nine human hearts out of ten. Talking of books, I want some one to write a novel which shall be a metaphysical 'Gil Blas;' which shall deal more with the mind than Le Sage's book, and less with the actions; which shall make its hero the creature of the world, but a different creation, though equally true; which shall give a faithful picture in the character of one man of the aspect and the effects of our social system,— making that man of a better sort of clay than the amusing lacquey was, and the produce of a more artificial grade of society. The book I mean would be a sadder one than Le Sage's, but equally faithful to life."

"And it would have more of romance, if I rightly understand what you mean?"

"Precisely: romance of idea as well as incident,— natural romance. By the way, how few know what natural romance is: so that you feel the ideas in a book or play are true and faithful to the characters they are ascribed to, why mind whether the incidents are probable? Yet common readers only go by the incidents; as if the incidents in three-fourths of Shakspeare's plays were even ordinarily possible! But people have so little nature in them that they don't know what *is* natural!"

Thus Fanny ran on, in no very connected manner; stringing together those remarks which, unless I am mistaken, show how much better an uneducated, clever girl, whose very nature is a quick perception of art, can play the critic than the pedants who assume the office.

But it was only for the moment that the heavy heart of Godolphin could forget its load. It was in vain that he sought to be amused while yet smarting under the freshness of regret. A great shock had been given to his nature; he had loved against his will; and as we have seen, on his return to the Priory, he had even resolved on curing himself of a passion so unprofitable and unwise. But the jealousy of a night had shivered into dust a prudence which never of right belonged to a very ardent and generous nature: that jealousy was soothed, allayed; but how fierce, how stunning was the blow that succeeded it! Constance had confessed love, and yet had refused him — forever! Clear and noble as to herself her motives might seem in that refusal, it was impossible that they should appear in the same light to Godolphin. Unable to penetrate into the effect which her father's deathbed and her own oath had produced on the mind of Constance; how indissolubly that remembrance had united itself with all her schemes and prospects for the future; how marvellously, yet how naturally, it had converted worldly ambition into a sacred duty,— unable, I say, to comprehend all these various and powerful and governing motives, Godolphin beheld in her refusal only the aversion to share his slender income, and the desire for loftier station. He considered, therefore, that sorrow was a tribute to her unworthy of himself; he deemed it a part of his dignity to strive to forget. That hallowed sentiment which, in some losses of the heart, makes it a duty to remember, and preaches a soothing and soft lesson from the very text of regret, was not for the wrung and stricken soul of Godolphin. He only strove to dissipate his grief, and shut out from his mental sight the charmed vision of the first, the only woman he had deeply loved.

Godolphin felt, too, that the sole impulse which could have united the fast-expiring energy and enterprise of his youth to the ambition of life was forever gone. With Constance—with the proud thoughts that belonged to her — the aspirings after earthly honours were linked, and with her were broken. He felt his old philosophy — the love of ease, the profound contempt for fame — close like the deep waters over those glittering hosts for whose passage they had been severed for a moment, whelming the crested and gorgeous visions forever beneath the wave! Conscious of his talents — nay, swayed to and fro by the unquiet stirrings of no common genius — Godolphin yet foresaw that he was not henceforth destined to play a shining part in the crowded drama of life. His career was already closed; he might be contented, prosperous, happy, but never great. He had seen enough of authors, and of the thorns that beset the paths of literature, to experience none of those delusions which cheat the blinded aspirer into the wilderness of publication,—that mode of obtaining fame and hatred to which those who feel unfitted for more bustling concerns are impelled. Write he might: and he was fond (as disappointment increased his propensities to dreaming) of brightening his solitude with the golden palaces and winged shapes that lie glassed within the fancy,—the soul's fairy-land. But the vision with him was only evoked one hour to be destroyed the next. Happy had it been for Godolphin, and not unfortunate perhaps for the world, had he learned at that exact moment the true motive for human action which he afterwards, and too late, discovered. Happy had it been for him to have learned that there is an ambition to *do good*, — an ambition to raise the wretched as well as to rise.

Alas! either in letters or in politics, how utterly poor, barren, and untempting is every path that points upward to the mockery of public eminence, when looked upon by a soul that has any real elements of wise or noble, unless we have an impulse within, which mortification chills not,— a reward without, which selfish defeat does not destroy.

But, unblest by one friend really wise or good, spoilt by the world, soured by disappointment, Godolphin's very faculties made him inert, and his very wisdom taught him to be useless. Again and again — as the spider in some cell where no winged insect ever wanders builds and rebuilds his mesh —the scheming heart of the Idealist was doomed to weave net after net for those visions of the Lovely and the Perfect which can never descend to the gloomy regions wherein mortality is cast. The most common disease to genius is nympholepsy,—the saddening for a spirit that the world knows not. Ah, how those outward disappointments which should cure only feed the disease!

The dinner at Saville's was gay and lively, as such entertainments with such participators usually are. If nothing in the world is more heavy than your formal banquet, nothing, on the other hand, is more agreeable than those well-chosen *laissez-aller* feasts at which the guests are as happily selected as the wines; where there is no form, no reserve, no effort; and people having met to sit still for a few hours are willing to be as pleasant to each other as if they were never to meet again. Yet the conversation in all companies not literary turns upon persons rather than things; and your wits learn their art only in the School for Scandal.

"Only think, Fanny," said Saville, "of Clavers turning beau in his old age! He commenced with being a jockey; then he became an electioneerer; then a Methodist parson; then a builder of houses; and now he has dashed suddenly up to London, rushed into the clubs, mounted a wig, studied an ogle, and walks about the Opera House swinging a cane, and, at the age of fifty-six, punching young minors in the side, and saying tremulously, '*We* young fellows!' "

"He hires pages to come to him in the Park with three-cornered notes," said Fanny; "he opens each with affected *nonchalance;* looks full at the bearer, and cries aloud, 'Tell your mistress I cannot refuse her;' then canters off, with the air of a man persecuted to death!"

"But did you see what an immense pair of whiskers Chester has mounted?"

"Yes," answered a Mr. de Lacy; "A—— says he has cultivated them in order to 'plant out' his ugliness."

"But vy *you* no talk, Monsieur de Dauphin?" said the Linettini gently, turning to Percy; "you ver silent."

"Unhappily, I have been so long out of town, that these anecdotes of the day are *caviare* to me."

"But so," cried Saville, "would a volume of French Memoirs be to any one that took it up for the first time; yet the French Memoirs amuse one exactly as much as if one had lived with the persons written of. Now that ought to be the case with conversations upon persons. I flatter myself, Fanny, that you and I hit off characters so well by a word or two, that no one who hears us wants to know anything more about them."

"I believe you," said Godolphin; "and that is the reason you never talk of yourselves."

"Bah! *À propos* of egoism, did you meet Jack Barabel in Rome?"

"Yes, writing his travels. 'Pray,' said he to me (seizing me by the button) in the Colisseum, 'what do you think is the highest order of literary composition?' 'Why, an epic, I fancy,' said I; 'or perhaps a tragedy, or a great history, or a novel like "Don Quixote."' 'Pooh!' quoth Barabel, looking important, 'there's nothing so high in literature as a good book of travels;' then sinking his voice into a whisper and laying his finger wisely on his nose, he hissed out, '*I* have a quarto, sir, in the press!'"

"Ha, ha!" laughed Stracey, the old wit, picking his teeth, and speaking for the first time; "if you tell Barabel you have seen a handsome woman, he says, mysteriously frowning, 'Handsome, sir! has she *travelled?* — answer me that!'"

"But have you seen Paulton's new equipage? Brown carriage, brown liveries, brown harness, brown horses, while Paulton and his wife sit within dressed in brown *cap-à-pie.* The best of it is that Paulton went to his coachmaker, to order his carriage, saying, 'Mr. Houlditch, I am growing old,— too old to be eccentric any longer; I must have something remarkably plain;' and to this hour Paulton goes *brown*-ing about the town, crying out to every one, 'Nothing like simplicity, believe me.'"

"He discharged his coachman for wearing white gloves instead of brown," said Stracey. "'What do you mean, sir,' cried he, 'with your d—d showy vulgarities? Don't you see me toiling my soul out to be plain and quiet, and you must spoil all, by not being *brown* enough!'"

"Ah, Godolphin, you seem pensive," whispered Fanny; "yet we are tolerably amusing, too."

"My dear Fanny," answered Godolphin, rousing himself, "the dialogue is gay, the actors know their parts, the lights are brilliant; but — the scene — the scene cannot shift for me! Call it what you will, I am not deceived. I see the paint and the canvas, but — and yet, away these thoughts! Shall I fill your glass, Fanny?"

CHAPTER XXI.

AN EVENT OF GREAT IMPORTANCE TO THE PRINCIPAL ACTORS IN THIS HISTORY. — GODOLPHIN A SECOND TIME LEAVES ENGLAND.

Godolphin was welcomed with enthusiasm by the London world. His graces, his manners, his genius, his *bon ton*, and his *bonnes fortunes* were the theme of every society. Verses imputed to him — some erroneously, some truly — were mysteriously circulated from hand to hand; and every one envied the fair inspirers to whom they were supposed to be addressed.

It is not my intention to reiterate the wearisome echo of novelists who descant on fashion and term it life. No description of rose-coloured curtains and buhl cabinets; no miniature paintings of boudoirs and sàlons; no recital of conventional insipidities, interlarded with affected criticisms, and honoured by the name of dramatic dialogue, shall lend their fascination to these pages. Far other and far deeper aims are mine in stooping to delineate the customs and springs of polite life. The reader must give himself wholly up to me; he must prepare to go with me through the grave as through the gay, and unresistingly to thread the dark and subtle interest which alone I can impart to these memoirs, or — let him close the book at once. I promise him novelty; but it is not, when duly scanned, a novelty of a light and frivolous cast.

But throughout that routine of dissipation in which he chased the phantom Forgetfulness, Godolphin sighed for the time he had fixed on for leaving the scenes in which it was pursued. Of Constance's present existence he heard nothing; of her former triumphs and conquests he heard everywhere. And when did he ever meet one face, however fair, which could awaken a single thought of admiration while hers was yet all faithfully glassed in his remembrance? I know nothing that so utterly converts society into "the gallery of pictures" as the recollection of one loved and lost. That recollection has but two cures,—Time and the hermitage. Foreigners impute to us the turn for sentiment; alas! there are no people who have it less. We seek forever after amusement; and there is not one popular prosebook in our language in which the more tender and yearning secrets of the heart form the subject-matter. The "Corinne" and the "Julie" weary us, or we turn them into sorry jests!

One evening, a little before his departure from England — that a lingering and vague hope, of which Constance was the object, had considerably protracted beyond the allotted time — Godolphin was at a house in which the hostess was a relation to Lord Erpingham.

"Have you heard," asked Lady G——, "that my cousin Erpingham is to be married?"

"No, indeed; to whom?" said Godolphin, eagerly.

"To Miss Vernon."

Sudden as was the shock, Godolphin heard, and changed neither hue nor muscle.

"Are you certain of this?" asked a lady present.

"Quite: Lady Erpingham is my authority; I received the news from herself this very day."

"And does she seem pleased with the match?"

"Why, I can scarcely say, for the letter contradicts itself in every passage. Now, she congratulates herself on having so charming a daughter-in-law; now, she suddenly stops short to observe what a pity it is that young men should be so precipitate! Now, she says what a great match it will be for her dear ward! and now, what a happy one it will be for Erpingham! In short, she does not know whether to be pleased or vexed; and that, *pour dire vrai*, is my case also."

"Why, indeed," observed the former speaker, "Miss Vernon has played her cards well. Lord Erpingham would have been a great match in himself, with his person and reputation. Ah, she was always an ambitious girl."

"And a proud one," said Lady G——. "Well, I suppose Erpingham House will be the rendezvous to all the blues and wits and *savans*. Miss Vernon is another Aspasia, I hear."

"I hate girls who are so designing," said the lady who spoke before, and had only one daughter, very ugly, who, at the age of thirty-five, was about to accept her first offer, and marry a younger son in the Guards. "I think she 's rather vulgar; for my part, I doubt if — I shall patronize her."

"Well, what do *you* think of it, Mr. Godolphin? — you have seen Miss Vernon."

Godolphin was gone.

It was about ten days after this conversation that Godolphin, waiting at a hotel in Dover the hour at which the packet set sail for Calais, took up the "Morning Post;" and the first passage that met his eye was the one which I transcribe: —

"*Marriage in High Life.* — On Thursday last, at Wendover Castle, the Earl of Erpingham, to Constance, only daughter of the celebrated Mr. Vernon. The bride was dressed, etc."

And then followed the trite, yet pompous pageantry of words, the sounding nothings, with which ladies who become countesses are knelled into marriage.

"The dream is over!" said Godolphin mournfully, as the paper fell to the ground; and burying his face within his hands, he remained motionless till they came to announce the moment of departure.

And thus Percy Godolphin left, for the second time, his

native shores. When we return to him, what changes will the feelings now awakened within him have worked in his character! The drops that trickle within the cavern harden, yet brighten into spars as they indurate. Nothing is more polished, nothing more cold, than that wisdom which is the work of former tears, of former passions, and is formed within a musing and solitary mind!

CHAPTER XXII.

THE BRIDE ALONE. — A DIALOGUE POLITICAL AND MATRIMONIAL. — CONSTANCE'S GENIUS FOR DIPLOMACY. — THE CHARACTER OF HER ASSEMBLIES. — HER CONQUEST OVER LADY DELVILLE.

"Bring me that book, place that table nearer, and leave me."

The abigail obeyed the orders, and the young Countess of Erpingham was alone. Alone! what a word for a young and beautiful bride in the first months of her marriage! Alone! and in the heart of that mighty city in which rank and wealth — and they were hers — are the idols adored by millions.

It was a room fancifully and splendidly decorated. Flowers and perfumes were, however, its chief luxury; and from the open window you might see the trees in the old Mall deepening into the rich verdure of June. That haunt, too — a classical haunt for London — was at the hour I speak of full of gay and idle life; and there was something fresh and joyous in the air, the sun, and the crowd of foot and horse that swept below.

Was the glory gone from your brow, Constance, or the proud gladness from your eye? Alas! are not the blessings of the world like the enchanted bullets, — that which pierces our heart is united with the gift which our heart desired!

Lord Erpingham entered the room. "Well, Constance," said he, "shall you ride on horseback to-day?"

"I think not."

"Then I wish you would call on Lady Delville. You see Delville is of my party: we sit together. You should be very civil to her, and I did not think you were so the other night."

"You wish Lady Delville to support your political interest; and, if I mistake not, you think her at present lukewarm?"

"Precisely."

"Then, my dear lord, will you place confidence in my discretion? I promise you if you will leave me undisturbed in my own plans, that Lady Delville shall be the most devoted of your party before the season is half over; but then, the means will not be those you advise."

"Why, I advise none."

"Yes, civility,— a very poor policy."

"D—n it, Constance! why, you would not *frown* a great person like Lady Delville into affection for us?"

"Leave it to me."

"Nonsense!"

"My dear lord, only try. Three months is all I ask. You will leave the management of politics to me ever afterwards! I was born a schemer. Am I not John Vernon's daughter?"

"Well, well, do as you will," said Lord Erpingham; "but I see how it will end. However, you will call on Lady Delville to-day?"

"If you wish it, certainly."

"I do."

Lady Delville was a proud, great lady; not very much liked and not so often invited by her equals as if she had been agreeable and a flirt.

Constance knew with whom she had to treat. She called on Lady Delville that day. Lady Delville was at home; a pretty and popular Mrs. Trevor was with her.

Lady Delville received her coolly,— Constance was haughtiness itself.

"You go to the Duchess of Daubigny's to-night?" said Lady Delville, in the course of their broken conversation.

"Indeed I do not. I like agreeable society. It shall be my object to form a circle that not one displeasing person shall obtain access to. Will you assist me, my dear Mrs. Trevor?" — and Constance turned, with her softest smile, to the lady she addressed.

Mrs. Trevor was flattered; Lady Delville drew herself up.

"It is a small party at the duchess's," said the latter; "merely to meet the Duke and Duchess of C——."

"Ah, few people are capable of giving a suitable entertainment to the royal family."

"But surely none more so than the Duchess of Daubigny,— her house so large, her rank so great!"

"These are but poor ingredients towards the forming of an agreeable party," said Constance, coldly. "The mistake made by common minds is to suppose titles the only rank. Royal dukes love, above all other persons, to be amused; and amusement is the last thing generally provided for them."

The conversation fell into other channels. Constance rose to depart. She warmly pressed the hand of Mrs. Trevor, whom she had only seen once before.

"A few persons come to me to-morrow evening," said she; "*do* waive ceremony, and join us. I can promise you that not one disagreeable person shall be present, and that the Duchess of Daubigny shall write for an invitation and be refused."

Mrs. Trevor accepted the invitation.

Lady Delville was enraged beyond measure. Never was female tongue more bitter than hers at the expense of that insolent Lady Erpingham! Yet Lady Delville was secretly in grief; for the first time in her life, she was hurt at not having been asked to a party: and being hurt because she was not going, she longed most eagerly to go.

The next evening came. Erpingham House was not large, but it was well adapted to the description of assembly its beautiful owner had invited. Statues, busts, pictures, books, scattered or arranged about the apartments, furnished matter for intellectual conversation, or gave at least an intellectual air to the meeting.

About a hundred persons were present. They were selected from the most distinguished ornaments of the time,—musicians, painters, authors, orators, fine gentlemen, dukes, princes, and beauties. One thing, however, was imperatively necessary in order to admit them,—the profession of liberal opinions. No Tory, however wise, eloquent, or beautiful, could, that evening, have obtained the *sesame* to those apartments.

Constance never seemed more lovely, and never before was she so winning. The coldness and the arrogance of her manner had wholly vanished. To every one she spoke; and to every one her voice, her manner, were kind, cordial, familiar, but familiar with a soft dignity that heightened the charm. Ambitious not only to please but to dazzle, she breathed into her conversation all the grace and culture of her mind. They who admired her the most were the most accomplished themselves.

Now exchanging with foreign nobles that brilliant trifling of the world in which there is often so much penetration, wisdom, and research into character; now with a kindling eye and animated cheek commenting, with poets and critics, on literature and the arts; now, in a more remote and quiet corner, seriously discussing, with hoary politicians, those affairs in which even they allowed her shrewdness and her grasp of intellect; and combining with every grace and every accomplishment a rare and dazzling order of beauty,—we may readily imagine the sensation she created, and the sudden and novel zest which so splendid an Armida must have given to the tameness of society.

The whole of the next week, the party at Erpingham House was the theme of every conversation. Each person who had been there had met the *lion* he had been most anxious to see. The beauty had conversed with the poet, who had charmed her; the young *débutant* in science had paid homage to the great professor of its loftiest mysteries; the statesman had thanked the author who had defended his measures; the author had been delighted with the compliment of the statesman. Every one then agreed that, while the highest rank in the kingdom had been there, rank had been the least attraction; and those who before had found Constance repellent were the very persons who now expatiated with the greatest rapture on the sweetness of her manners. Then, too, every one who had been admitted to the *coterie* dwelt on the *rarity* of the admission; and thus, all the world were dying for an introduction to Erpingham House,—partly, because it was agreeable; principally, because it was difficult.

It soon became a compliment to the understanding to say of a person, "He goes to Lady Erpingham's!" They who valued themselves on their understandings moved heaven and earth to become popular with the beautiful countess. Lady Delville was not asked; Lady Delville was furious: she affected disdain, but no one gave her credit for it. Lord Erpingham teazed Constance on this point.

"You see I was right, for you have affronted Lady Delville. She has made Delville look coolly on me; in a few weeks he will be a Tory; think of that, Lady Erpingham!"

"One month more," answered Constance, with a smile, "and you shall see."

One night, Lady Delville and Lady Erpingham met at a large party. The latter seated herself by her haughty enemy; not seeming to heed Lady Delville's coolness, Constance entered into conversation with her. She dwelt upon books, pictures, music: her manner was animated, and her wit playful. Pleased, in spite of herself, Lady Delville warmed from her reserve.

"My dear Lady Delville," said Constance, suddenly turning her bright countenance on the countess with an expression of delighted surprise, "will you forgive me?—I never dreamed before that you were so charming a person! I never conceal my sentiments; and I own with regret and shame that, till this moment, I had never seen in your mind—whatever I might in your person—those claims to admiration which were constantly dinned into my ear."

Lady Delville actually coloured.

"Pray," continued Constance, "condescend to permit me to a nearer acquaintance. Will you dine with us on Thursday? — we shall have only nine persons beside yourself; but they are the nine persons whom I most esteem and admire."

Lady Delville accepted the invitation. From that hour, Lady Delville — who had at first resented, from the deepest recess of her heart, Constance Vernon's accession to rank and wealth; who, had Constance deferred to her early acquaintance, would have always found something in her she could have affected to despise,— from that hour, Lady Delville was the warmest advocate, and a little time after, the sincerest follower, of the youthful countess.

CHAPTER XXIII.

AN INSIGHT INTO THE REAL GRANDE MONDE, — BEING A SEARCH BEHIND THE ROSE-COLOURED CURTAINS.

The time we now speak of was the most brilliant the English world, during the last half century, has known. Lord Byron was in his brief and dazzling zenith; De Staël was in London; the Peace had turned the attention of rich idlers to social enjoyment and to letters. There was an excitement and a brilliancy and a *spirituality* about our circles, which we do not recognize now. Never had a young and ambitious woman — a beauty and a genius — a finer moment for the commencement of her power. It was Constance's early and bold resolution to push to the utmost — even to exaggeration — a power existing in all polished states, but now mostly in this,— the power of fashion! This mysterious and subtle engine she was eminently skilled to move according to her will. Her intuitive penetration into character, her tact, and her grace were exactly the talents Fashion most demands; and they were at present devoted only to that sphere. The rudeness that she mingled, at times, with the bewitching softness and ease of manner she could command at others increased the effect of her power. It is much to intimidate as well as to win. And her rudeness in a very little while grew popular; for it was never exercised but on those whom the world loves to see humbled. Modest merit in any rank, and even insolence, if accompanied with merit, were always safe from her satire. It was the *hauteur* of foolish duchesses or purse-proud *roturiers* that she loved, and scrupled not, to abase.

And the independence of her character was mixed with extraordinary sweetness of temper. Constance could not be in a passion: it was out of her nature. If she was stung, she could utter a sarcasm; but she could not frown or raise her voice. There was that magic in her, that she was always feminine. She did not stare young men out of countenance; she never addressed them by their Christian names; she never flirted, never coquetted: the bloom and flush of modesty was yet all virgin upon her youth. She, the founder of a new dynasty, avoided what her successors and contemporaries have deemed it necessary to incur. She was the leader of fashion; but — it is a miraculous union — she was respectable!

. At this period, some new dances were brought into England. These dances found much favour in the eyes of several great ladies young enough to dance them. They met at each other's houses in the morning to practise the steps. Among these was Lady Erpingham; her house became the favourite rendezvous.

The young Marquess of Dartington was one of the little knot. Celebrated for his great fortune, his personal beauty, and his general success, he resolved to fall in love with Lady Erpingham. He devoted himself exclusively to her; he joined her in the morning in her rides, in the evening in her gayeties. He had fallen in love with her? — yes! Did he love her? — not the least. But he was excessively idle! — what else could he do?

Constance early saw the attentions and designs of Lord Dartington. There is one difficulty in repressing advances in great society, — one so easily becomes ridiculous by being a prude. But Constance dismissed Lord Dartington with great dexterity. This was the occasion.

One of the apartments in Erpingham House communicated with a conservatory. In this conservatory Constance was alone one morning, when Lord Dartington, who had entered the house with Lord Erpingham, joined her. He was not a man who could ever become sentimental; he was rather the gay lover, — rather the Don Gaolor than the Amadis; but he was a little abashed before Constance. He trusted, however, to his fine eyes and his good complexion; plucked up courage; and, picking a flower from the same plant Constance was tending, said,—

"I believe there is a custom in some part of the world to express love by flowers. May I, dear Lady Erpingham, trust to this flower to express what I dare not utter?"

Constance did not blush nor look confused, as Lord Dartington had hoped and expected. One who had been loved by Godolphin was not likely to feel much agitation at the gallantry of Lord Dartington; but she looked gravely in his face, paused a little before she answered, and then said, with a smile that abashed the suitor more than severity could possibly have done,—

"My dear Lord Dartington, do not let us mistake each other. I live in the world like other women, but I am not altogether like them. Not another word of gallantry to me alone, as you value my friendship. In a crowded room, pay me as many compliments as you like. It will flatter my vanity to have you in my train. And now, just do me the favour to take these scissors and cut the dead leaves off that plant."

Lord Dartington, to use a common phrase, "hummed and hawed." He looked, too, a little angry. An artful and shrewd politician, it was not Constance's wish to cool the devotion, though she might the attachment, of a single member of her husband's party. With a kind look — but a look so superior, so queenlike, so free from the petty and coquettish condescension of the sex, that the gay lord wondered from that hour how he could ever have dreamed of Constance as of certain other ladies — she stretched her hand to him.

"We are friends, Lord Dartington?—and now we know each other, we shall be so always."

Lord Dartington bowed confusedly over the beautiful hand he touched; and Constance, walking into the drawing-room, sent for Lord Erpingham on business. Dartington took his leave.

CHAPTER XXIV.

THE MARRIED STATE OF CONSTANCE.

Constance, Countess of Erpingham, was young, rich, lovely as a dream, worshipped as a goddess. Was she happy; and was her whole heart occupied with the trifles that surrounded her?

Deep within her memory was buried one fatal image that she could not exorcise. The reproaching and mournful countenance of Godolphin rose before her at all times and seasons. The charm of his presence no other human being could renew. His eloquent and noble features, living and glorious with genius and with passion; his sweet deep voice; his conversation, so rich with mind and knowledge, and the subtle delicacy with which he applied its graces to some sentiment dedicated to her (delicious flattery, of all flatteries the most attractive to a sensitive and intellectual woman!),—these occurred to her again and again, and rendered all she saw around her flat, wearisome, insipid. Nor was this deep-seated and tender weakness the only serpent—if I may use so confused a metaphor—in the roses of her lot.

And here I invoke the reader's graver attention. The fate of women in all the more polished circles of society is eminently unnatural and unhappy. The peasant and his dame are on terms of equality,—equality even of ambition; no career is open to one and shut to the other: equality even of hardship, and hardship is employment; no labour occupies the whole energies of the man but leaves those of the woman unemployed. Is this the case with the wives in a higher station,— the wives of the lawyer, the merchant, the senator, the noble? There, the men have their occupations; and the women (unless, like poor Fanny, work-bags and parrots can employ them) none. They are idle. They employ the imagination and the heart. They fall in love and are wretched; or they remain virtuous, and are either wearied by an eternal monotony or they fritter away intellect, mind, character, in the minutest frivolities,— frivolities being their only refuge from stagnation. Yes, there is one very curious curse for the sex which men don't consider! Once married, the more aspiring of them have no real scope for ambition; the ambition gnaws away their content, and never finds elsewhere wherewithal to feed on.

This was Constance's especial misfortune. Her lofty and restless and soaring spirit pined for a sphere of action, and ballrooms and boudoirs met it on every side. One hope she did indeed cherish; that hope was the source of her intriguings and schemes, of her care for seeming trifles, the waste of her energies on seeming frivolities. This hope, this object, was to diminish, to crush, not only the party which had forsaken her father, but the power of that order to which she belonged herself; which she had entered only to humble. But this hope was a distant and chill vision. She was too rational to anticipate an early and effectual change in our social state, and too rich in the treasures of mind to be the creature of one idea. Satiety — the common curse of the great — crept over her day by day. The powers within her lay stagnant, the keen intellect rusted in its sheath.

"How is it," said she to the beautiful Countess of ——, "that you seem always so gay and so animated; that with all your vivacity and tenderness, you are never at a loss for occupation? You never seem weary — *ennuyée* — why is this?"

"I will tell you," said the pretty countess, archly; "I change my lovers every month." Constance blushed and asked no more.

Many women in her state, influenced by contagious example, wearied by a life in which the heart had no share; without children, without a guide; assailed and wooed on all sides, in all shapes,—many women might have ventured, if not into love, at least into coquetry. But Constance remained as bright and cold as ever,—"the unsunned snow!" It might be, indeed, that the memory of Godolphin preserved her safe from all lesser dangers. The asbestos once conquered by fire can never be consumed by it; but there was also another cause in Constance's very nature,—it was pride!

Oh, if men could but dream of what a proud woman endures in those caresses which humble her, they would not wonder why proud women are so difficult to subdue. This is a matter on which we all ponder much, but we dare not write honestly upon it. But imagine a young, haughty, guileless beauty, married to a man whom she neither loves nor honours; and so far from that want of love rendering her likely to fall hereafter, it is more probable that it will make her recoil from the very name of love.

About this time the Dowager Lady Erpingham died,—an event sincerely mourned by Constance, and which broke the strongest tie that united the young countess to her lord. Lord Erpingham and Constance, indeed, now saw but little of each other. Like most men six feet high, with large black whiskers, the earl was vain of his person; and like most rich noblemen, he found plenty of ladies who assured him he was irresistible. He had soon grown angry at the unadmiring and calm urbanity of Constance; and, living a great deal with single men, he formed *liaisons* of the same order as they do. He was, however, sensible that he had been fortunate in the choice of a wife. His political importance the wisdom of Constance had quadrupled, at the least; his house she had rendered the most brilliant in London, and his name the most courted in the lists of the peerage. Though munificent, she was not extravagant; though a beauty, she did not intrigue; neither, though his inconstancy was open, did she appear jealous; nor, whatever the errors of his conduct, did she ever disregard his interest, disobey his wishes, or waver from the smooth and continuous sweetness of her temper. Of such a wife Lord Erpingham could not complain: he esteemed her, praised her, asked her advice, and stood a little in awe of her.

Ah, Constance! had you been the daughter of a noble or a peasant, had you been the daughter of any man but John Vernon, what a treasure beyond price, without parallel, would that heart, that beauty, that genius, have been!

CHAPTER XXV.

THE PLEASURE OF RETALIATING HUMILIATION. — CONSTANCE'S DEFENCE OF FASHION. — REMARKS ON FASHION. — GODOLPHIN'S WHEREABOUT. — FANNY MILLINGER'S CHARACTER OF HERSELF. — WANT OF COURAGE IN MORALISTS.

IT was a proud moment for Constance when the Duchess of Winstoun and Lady Margaret Midgecombe wrote to her, worried her, beset her, for a smile, a courtesy, an invitation, or a ticket to Almack's.

They had at first thought to cry her down; to declare that she was plebeian, mad, bizarre, and a blue. It was all in vain. Constance rose every hour. They struggled against the conviction, but it would not do. The first person who confounded them with a sense of their error was the late King, then Regent; he devoted himself to Lady Erpingham for a whole evening, at a ball given by himself. From that hour they were assured they had been wrong: they accordingly called on her the next day. Constance received them with the same coldness she had always evinced; but they went away declaring they never saw any one whose manners were so improved. They then sent her an invitation! she refused it; a second! she refused; a third, begging her to fix the day! she fixed the day, and disappointed them. Lord bless us! how sorry they were, how alarmed, how terrified! — their dear Lady Erpingham must be ill! they sent every day for the next week to know how she was!

"Why," said Mrs. Trevor to Lady Erpingham,—"why do you continue so cruel to these poor people? I know they were very impertinent, and so forth, once; but it is surely wiser and more dignified now to forgive; to appear unconscious of the past: people of the world ought not to quarrel with each other."

"You are right, and yet you are mistaken," said Constance; "I do forgive, and I don't quarrel; but my opinion, my contempt, remain the same, or are rather more disdainful than ever. These people are not worth losing the luxury we all experience in expressing contempt. I continue, therefore, but quietly and without affectation, to indulge that luxury. Besides, I own to you, my dear Mrs. Trevor, I do think that the mere insolence of titles must fairly and thoroughly be put down, if we sincerely wish to render society agreeable; and where can we find a better example for punishment than the Duchess of Winstoun?"

"But, my dear Lady Erpingham, *you* are thought insolent; your friend, Lady ——, is called insolent, too,—are you sure the charge is not merited?"

"I allow the justice of the charge; but you will observe, ours is not the insolence of rank: we have made it a point to protect, to the utmost, the poor and unfriended of all circles. Are *we* ever rude to governesses or companions or poor writers or musicians? When a man marries below him, do we turn our backs on the poor wife? Do we not, on the contrary, lavish our attention on her, and throw round her equivocal and joyless state the protection of Fashion? No, no! *our* insolence is JUSTICE! it is the chalice returned to the lips which prepared it; it is insolence to the insolent; reflect, and you will allow it."

The fashion that Constance set and fostered was of a generous order; but it was not suited to the majority; it was corrupted by her followers into a thousand basenesses. In vain do we make a law, if the general spirit is averse to the law. Constance could humble the great, could loosen the links of extrinsic rank, could undermine the power of titles; but that was all! She could abase the proud, but not elevate the general tone: for one slavery she only substituted another,—people hugged the chains of Fashion as before they hugged those of Titular Arrogance.

Amidst the gossip of the day Constance heard much of Godolphin, and all spoke of him with interest,—even those who could not comprehend his very intricate and peculiar character. Separated from her by lands and seas, there seemed no danger in allowing herself the sweet pleasure of hearing his actions and his mind discussed. She fancied she did not permit herself to *love* him; she was too pure not to start at such an idea; but her mind was not so regulated, so trained and educated in sacred principle, that she forbade herself the luxury to *remember*. Of his present mode of life she heard little. He was traced from city to city, from shore to shore; from the haughty *noblesse* of Vienna to the gloomy shrines of Memphis, by occasional report, and seemed to tarry long in no place. This roving and unsettled life, which secretly assured her of her power, suffused his image in all tender and remorseful dyes. Ah, where is that one person to be envied, could we read the heart?

The actress had heard incidentally from Saville of Godolphin's attachment to the beautiful countess. She longed to see her; and when, one night at the theatre, she was informed that Lady Erpingham was in the Lord Chamberlain's box close before her, she could scarcely command her self-possession sufficiently to perform with her wonted brilliancy of effect.

She was greatly struck by the singular nobleness of Lady Erpingham's face and person; and Godolphin rose in her estimation from the justice of the homage he had rendered to so fair a shrine. What a curious trait, by the by, that is in women,—their exaggerated anxiety to see one who has been loved by the man in whom they themselves take interest: and the manner in which the said man rises or falls in their estimation, according as they admire, or are disappointed in, the object of his love.

"And so," said Saville, supping one night with the actress, "you think the world does not overlaud Lady Erpingham?"

"No; she is what Medea would have been, if innocent,—full of majesty, and yet of sweetness. It is the face of a queen of some three thousand years back. I could have worshipped her."

"My little Fanny, you are a strange creature. Methinks you have a dash of poetry in you."

"Nobody who has not written poetry could ever read my character," answered Fanny, with *naïveté*, yet with truth.

"Yet you have not much of the ideal about you, pretty one."

"No; because I was so early thrown on myself, that I was forced to make independence my chief good. I soon saw that if I followed my heart to and fro, wherever it led me, I should be the creature of every breath, the victim of every accident; I should have been the very soul of romance; lived on a smile, and died, perhaps, in a ditch at last. Accordingly, I set to work with my feelings, and pared and cut them down to a convenient compass. Happy for me that I did so! What would have become of me if, years ago, when I loved Godolphin, I had thrown the whole world of my heart upon him?"

"Why, he has generosity; he would not have deserted you."

"But I should have wearied him," answered Fanny; "and that would have been quite enough for me. But I did love him well, and purely — ah! you may smile! — and disinterestedly. I was only fortified in my resolution not to love any one too much, by perceiving that he had *affection* but no *sympathy* for me. His nature was different from mine. I am *woman* in everything, and Godolphin is always sighing for a *goddess!*"

"I should like to sketch your character, Fanny. It is original, though not strongly marked. I never met with it in any book; yet it is true to your sex, and to the world."

"Few people could paint me exactly," answered Fanny. "The danger is, that they would make too much or too little of me. But such as I am, the world ought to know what is so common, and, as you think, so undescribed."

And now, beautiful Constance, farewell for the present! I leave you surrounded by power and pomp and adulation. Enjoy as you may that for which you sacrificed affection!

CHAPTER XXVI.

THE VISIONARY AND HIS DAUGHTER. — AN ENGLISHMAN, SUCH AS FOREIGNERS IMAGINE THE ENGLISH.

We must now present the reader to characters very different from those which have hitherto passed before his eye.

Without the immortal city, along the Appia Via, there dwelt a singular and romantic visionary, of the name of Volktman. He was by birth a Dane; and Nature had bestowed on him that frame of mind which might have won him a distinguished career, had she placed the period of his birth in the eleventh century. Volktman was essentially a man belonging to the past time: the character of his enthusiasm was weird and Gothic; with beings of the present day he had no sympathy; their loves, their hatreds, their politics, their literature, awoke no echo in his breast. He did not affect to herd with them; his life was solitude, and its occupation study,— and study of that nature which every day unfitted him more and more for the purposes of existence. In a word, he was a reader of the stars, a believer in the occult and dreamy science of astrology. Bred up to the art of sculpture, he had early in life sought Rome, as the nurse of inspiration; but even then he had brought with him the dark and brooding temper of his northern tribe. The images of the classic world; the bright and cold and beautiful divinities, whose natures as well as shapes the marble simulation of life is so especially adapted to represent, spoke but little to Volktman's pre-occupied and gloomy imagination. Faithful to the superstitions and the warriors of the North, the loveliness and majesty of the southern creations but called forth in him the desire to apply the principles by which they were formed to the embodying those stern visions which his haggard and dim fancies only could invoke. This train of inspiration preserved him, at least, from the deadliest vice in a worshipper of the arts,—commonplace. He was no servile and trite imitator; his very faults were solemn and commanding. But before he had gained that long experience which can alone perfect genius, his natural energies were directed to new channels. In an illness which prevented his applying to his art, he had accidentally sought entertainment in a certain work upon astrology. The wild and imposing theories of the science — if science it may be called — especially charmed and invited him. The clear bright nights of his fatherland were brought back to his remembrance; he recalled the mystic and unanalyzed impressions with which he had gazed upon the lights of heaven, and he imagined that the very vagueness of his feelings was a proof of the certainty of the science.

The sons of the North are pre-eminently liable to be affected by that romance of emotion which the hushed and starry aspect of night is calculated to excite. The long-broken luxurious silence that, in their frozen climate, reigns from the going down of the sun to its rise; the wandering and sudden meteors that disport, as with an impish life, along the noiseless and solemn heaven; the peculiar radiance of the stars; and even the sterile and severe features of the earth, which those stars light up with their chill and ghostly serenity, serve to deepen the effect of the wizard tales which are instilled into the ear of childhood, and to connect the less known and more visionary impulses of life with the influences, or at least with the associations, of Night and Heaven.

To Volktman, more alive than even his countrymen are wont to be to superstitious impressions, the science on which he had chanced came with an all-absorbing interest and fascination. He surrendered himself wholly to his new pursuit. By degrees the block and the chisel were neglected, and, though he still worked from time to time, he ceased to consider the sculptor's art as the vocation of his life and the end of his ambition. Fortunately, though not rich, Volktman was not without the means of existence, nor even without the decent and proper comforts; so that he was enabled, as few men are, to indulge his ardour for unprofitable speculations, albeit to the exclusion of lucrative pursuits. It may be noted that when a man is addicted to an occupation that withdraws him from the world, any great affliction tends to confirm, without hope of cure, his inclinations to solitude. The world, distasteful in that it gave no pleasure, becomes irremediably hateful when it is coupled with the remembrance of pain. Volktman had married an Italian, a woman who loved him entirely, and whom he loved with that strong though uncaressing affection common to men of his peculiar temper. Of the gay and social habits and constitution of her country, the Italian was not disposed to suffer the astrologer to dwell only among the stars. She sought, playfully and kindly, to attract him towards human society; and Volktman could not always resist — as what man earth-born can do? — the influence of the fair presider over his house and hearth. It happened, that on one day in which she peculiarly wished his attendance at some one of those parties in which Englishmen think the notion of festivity strange — for it includes conversation — Volktman had foretold the menace of some great misfortune. Uncertain, from the character of the prediction, whether to wish his wife to remain at home or to go abroad, he yielded to her wish, and accompanied her to her friend's house. A young Englishman lately arrived at Rome, and already celebrated in the circles of that city for his eccentricity of life and his passion for beauty, was of the party. He appeared struck with the sculptor's wife; and in his attentions, Volktman, for the first and the last time, experienced the pangs of jealousy; he hurried his wife away.

On their return home, whether or not a jewel worn by the signora had attracted the cupidity of some of the lawless race who live through gaining, and profiting by, such information, they were attacked by two robbers in the obscure and ill-lighted suburb. Though Volktman offered no resistance, the manner of their assailants was rude and violent. The signora was fearfully alarmed; her shrieks brought a stranger to their assistance; it was the English youth who had so alarmed the jealousy of Volktman. Accustomed to danger in his profession of a gallant, the Englishman seldom, in those foreign lands, went from home at night without the protection of pistols. At the sight of firearms, the ruffians felt their courage evaporate; they fled from their prey; and the Englishman assisted Volktman in conveying the Italian to her home. But the terror of the encounter operated fatally on a delicate frame; and within three weeks from that night Volktman was a widower.

His marriage had been blessed with but one daughter, who at the time of this catastrophe was about eight years of age. His love for his child in some measure reconciled Volktman to life; and as the shock of the event subsided, he returned with a pertinacity which was now subjected to no interruption to his beloved occupations and mysterious researches. One visitor alone found it possible to win frequent ingress to his seclusion; it was the young Englishman. A sentiment of remorse at the jealous feelings he had experienced, and for which his wife, though an Italian, had never given him even the shadow of a cause, had softened into a feeling rendered kind by the associations of the deceased, and a vague desire to atone to her for an acknowledged error, the dislike he had at first conceived against the young man. This was rapidly confirmed by the gentle and winning manners of the stranger, by his attentions to the deceased, to whom he had sent an English physician of great skill, and, as their acquaintance expanded, by the animated interest which he testified in the darling theories of the astrologer.

It happened also that Volktman's mother had been the daughter of Scotch parents. She had taught him the English tongue; and it was the only language, save his own, which he spoke as a native. This circumstance tended greatly to facilitate his intercourse with the traveller; and he found in the society of a man ardent, sensitive, melancholy, and addicted to all abstract contemplation, a pleasure which, among the keen but uncultivated intellects of Italy, he had never enjoyed.

Frequently, then, came the young Englishman to the lone house on the Appia Via; and the mysterious and unearthly conversation of the starry visionary afforded to him, who had early learned to scrutinize the varieties of his kind, a strange delight, heightened by the contrast it presented to the worldly natures with which he usually associated, and the commonplace occupations of a life in pursuit of pleasure.

And there was one who, child as she was, watched the coming of that young and beautiful stranger with emotion beyond her years. Brought up alone; mixing, since her mother's death, with no companions of her age; catching dim and solemn glimpses of her father's wild but lofty speculations; his books, filled with strange characters and imposing "words of mighty sound," open forever to her young and curious gaze,— it can scarce be matter of wonder that something strange and unworldly mingled with the elements of character which Lucilla Volktman early developed,— a character that was nature itself, yet of a nature erratic and bizarre. Her impulses she obeyed spontaneously, but none fathomed their origin. She was not of a quiet and meek order of mind; but passionate, changeful, and restless. She would laugh and weep without apparent cause, and the colour on her cheek never seemed for two minutes the same; and the most fitful changes of an April heaven were immutability itself compared with the play and lustre of expression that undulated in her features and her wild, deep, eloquent eyes.

Her person resembled her mind; it was beautiful, but the beauty struck you less than the singularity of its character. Her eyes were of a darkness that at night seemed black, but her hair was of the brightest and purest auburn; her complexion, sometimes pale, sometimes radiant even to the flush of a fever, was delicate and clear; her teeth and mouth were lovely beyond all words; her hands and feet were small to a fault; and as she grew up (for we have forestalled her age in this description) her shape, though wanting in height, was in such harmony and proportion, that the mind of the sculptor would sometimes escape from the absorption of the astrologer, and Volktman would gaze upon her with the same admiration that he would have bestowed, in spite of the subject, on the goddess-forms of Phidias or Canova. But then, this beauty was accompanied with such endless variety of gesture, often so wild, though always necessarily graceful, that the eye ached for that repose requisite for prolonged admiration.

When she was spoken to, she did not often answer to the purpose, but rather appeared to reply as to some interrogatory of her own; in the midst of one occupation, she would start up to another; leave that, in turn, undone, and sit down in silence lasting for hours. Her voice, in singing, was exquisitely melodious; she had, too, an intuitive talent for painting; and she read all the books that came in her way with an avidity that bespoke at once the restlessness and the genius of her mind.

This description of Lucilla must, I need scarcely repeat, be considered as applicable to her at some years distant from the time in which the young Englishman first attracted her childish but ardent imagination. To her, that face, with its regular and harmonious features, its golden hair, and soft, shy, melancholy aspect, seemed as belonging to a higher and brighter order of beings than those who, with exaggerated lineaments and swarthy hues, surrounded and displeased her. She took a strange and thrilling pleasure in creeping to his side, and looking up when unobserved at the countenance which in his absence she loved to imitate with her pencil by day, and to recall in her dreams at night. But she seldom spoke to him, and she shrank, covered with painful blushes, from his arms, whenever he attempted to bestow on her those caresses which children are wont to claim as an attention. Once, however, she summoned courage to ask him to teach her English, and he complied. She learned that language with surprising facility; and as Volktman loved its sound she grew familiar with its difficulties by always addressing her father in a tongue which became inexpressibly dear to her. And the young stranger delighted to hear that soft and melodious voice, with its trembling, Italian accent, make music from the nervous and masculine language of his native land. Scarce accountably to himself, a certain tender and peculiar interest in the fortunes of this singular and bewitching child grew up within him,—peculiar and not easily accounted for, in that it was not wholly the interest we feel in an engaging child, and yet was of no more interested nor sinister order. Were there truth in the science of the stars, I should say that they had told him her fate was to have affinity with his; and with that persuasion, something mysterious and more than ordinarily tender entered into the affection he felt for the daughter of his friend.

The Englishman was himself of a romantic character. He had been self-taught; and his studies, irregular though often deep, had given directions to his intellect frequently enthusiastic and unsound. His imagination preponderated over his judgment; and any pursuit that attracted his imagination won his entire devotion, until his natural sagacity proved it deceitful. If at times, living as he did in that daily world which so sharpens our common-sense, he smiled at the persevering fervour of the astrologer, he more often shared it; and he became his pupil in "the poetry of heaven," with a secret but deep belief in the mysteries cultivated by his master. Carrying the delusion to its height, I fear that the enthusiast entered upon ground still more shadowy and benighted,—the old secrets of the alchemist, and perhaps even of those arcana yet more gloomy and less rational, were subjected to their serious contemplation; and night after night, they delivered themselves wholly up to that fearful and charmed fascination which the desire and effort to overleap our mortal boundaries produce even in the hardest and best regulated minds. The train of thought so long nursed by the abstruse and solitary Dane was, perhaps, a better apology for the weakness of credulity than the youth and wandering fancy of the Englishman. But the scene around — not alluring to the one — fed to overflowing the romantic aspirations of the other.

On his way home, as the stars (which night had been spent in reading) began to wink and fade, the Englishman crossed the haunted Almo, renowned of yore for its healing virtues, and in whose stream the far-famed *simulacrum* (the image of Cybele), which fell from heaven, was wont to be laved with every coming spring: and around his steps, till he gained his home, were the relics and monuments of that superstition which sheds so much beauty over all that, in harsh reasoning, it may be said to degrade; so that his mind, always peculiarly alive to external impressions, was girt, as it were, with an atmosphere favourable both to the lofty speculation and the graceful credulities of romance.

The Englishman remained at Rome, with slight intervals of absence, for nearly three years. On the night before the day in which he received intelligence of an event that recalled him to his native country, he repaired at an hour accidentally later than usual to the astrologer's abode.

CHAPTER XXVII.

A CONVERSATION LITTLE APPERTAINING TO THE NINETEENTH CENTURY. — RESEARCHES INTO HUMAN FATE. — THE PREDICTION.

On entering the apartment, he found Lucilla seated on a low stool beside the astrologer. She looked up when she heard his footsteps; but her countenance seemed so dejected, that he turned involuntarily to that of Volktman for explanation. Volktman met his gaze with a steadfast and mournful aspect.

"What has happened?" asked the Englishman. "You seem sad, — you do not greet me as usual."

"I have been with the stars," replied the visionary.

"They seem but poor company," rejoined the Englishman; "and do not appear to have much heightened your spirits."

"Jest not, my friend," said Volktman; "it was for the loss of thee I looked sorrowful. I perceive that thou wilt take a journey soon, and that it will be of no pleasant nature."

"Indeed!" answered the Englishman, smilingly. "I ask leave to question the fact: you know better than any man, how often, through an error in our calculations, through haste, even through an over-attention, astrological predictions are exposed to falsification; and at present I foresee so little chance of my quitting Rome that I prefer the earthly probabilities to the celestial."

"My schemes are just, and the Heavens wrote their decrees in their clearest language," answered the astrologer. "Thou art on the eve of quitting Rome."

"On what occasion?"

The astrologer hesitated; the young visitor pressed the question.

"The lord of the fourth house," said Volktman, reluctantly, "is located in the eleventh house. Thou knowest to whom the position portends disaster."

"My father!" said the Englishman, anxiously, and turning pale; "I think that position would relate to him."

"It doth," said the astrologer, slowly.

"Impossible! I heard from him to-day; he is well. Let me see the figures."

The young man looked over the mystic hieroglyphics of the art, inscribed on a paper that was placed before the visionary, with deep and scrutinizing attention. Without bewildering the reader with those words and figures of weird sound and import which perplex the uninitiated, and entangle the disciple of astrology, I shall merely observe that there was one point in which the judgment appeared to admit doubt as to the signification. The Englishman insisted on the doubt; and a very learned and edifying debate was carried on between pupil and master, in the heat of which all recollection of the point in dispute (as is usual in such cases) evaporated.

"I know not how it is," said the Englishman, "that I should give any credence to a faith which (craving your forgiveness) most men out of Bedlam concur, at this day, in condemning as wholly idle and absurd. For it may be presumed that men only incline to some unpopular theory in proportion as it flatters or favours them; and as for this theory of yours — of ours, if you will — it has foretold me nothing but misfortune."

"Thy horoscope," replied the astrologer, "is indeed singular and ominous: but, like my daughter, the exact minute (within almost a whole hour) of thy birth seems unknown; and however ingeniously we, following the ancients, have contrived means for correcting nativities, our predictions (so long as the exact period of birth is not ascertained) remain in my mind always liable to some uncertainty. Indeed, the surest method of reducing the supposed time to the true — that of 'Accidents' — is but partially given, as in thy case; for, with a negligence that cannot be too severely blamed or too deeply lamented, thou hast omitted to mark down, or remember, the days on which accidents — fevers, broken limbs, etc. — occurred to thee; and this omission leaves a cloud over the bright chapters of fate — "

"Which," interrupted the young man, "is so much the happier for me, in that it allows me some loophole for hope."

"Yet," renewed the astrologer, as if resolved to deny his friend any consolation, "thy character, and the bias of thy habits, as well as the peculiarities of thy person,— nay, even the moles upon thy skin,— accord with thy proposed horoscope."

"Be it so!" said the Englishman, gayly. "You grant me, at least, the fairest of earthly gifts,— the happiness of pleasing that sex which alone sweetens our human misfortunes. That gift I would sooner have, even accompanied as it is, than all the benign influences without it."

"Yet," said the astrologer, "shalt thou even there be met with affliction; for Saturn had the power to thwart the star Venus, that was disposed to favour thee, and evil may be the result of the love thou inspirest. There is one thing remarkable in our science, which is especially worthy of notice in thy lot. The ancients, unacquainted with the star of Herschel, seem also scarcely acquainted with the character which the influence of that wayward and melancholy orb creates.

Thus, the aspect of Herschel neutralizes, in great measure, the boldness and ambition and pride of heart thou wouldst otherwise have drawn from the felicitous configuration of the stars around the Moon and Mercury at thy birth. That yearning for something beyond the narrow bounds of the world, that love for revery, that passionate romance, yea, thy very leaning, despite thy worldly sense, to these occult and starry mysteries,— all are bestowed on thee by this new and potential planet."

"And hence, I suppose," said the Englishman, interested (as the astrologer had declared) in spite of himself, "hence that opposition in my nature of the worldly and romantic; hence, with you, I am the dreaming enthusiast, but the instant I regain the living and motley crowd, I shake off the influence with ease, and become the gay pursuer of social pleasures."

"Never *at heart gay*," muttered the astrologer; "Saturn and Herschel make not sincere mirth-makers." The Englishman did not hear or seem to hear him.

"No," resumed the young man, musingly, "no! it is true that there is some counteraction of what, at times, I should have called my natural bent. Thus, I am bold enough, and covetous of knowledge, and not deaf to vanity; and yet I have no ambition. The desire to rise seems to me wholly unalluring: I scorn and contemn it as a weakness. But what matters it? So much the happier for me if, as you predict, my life be short. But how, if so unambitious and so quiet of habit, how can I imagine that my death will be violent as well as premature?"

It was as he spoke that the young Lucilla, who, with fixed eyes and lips apart, had been drinking in their conversation, suddenly rose and left the room. They were used to her comings in and her goings out without cause or speech, and continued their conversation.

"Alas!" said the visionary, "can tranquillity of life or care or prudence preserve us from our destiny? No sign is more deadly, whether by accident or murder, than that which couples Hyleg with Orion and Saturn. Yet thou mayest pass the year in which that danger is foretold thee; and beyond that time peace, honour, good fortune, await thee. Better to have the menace of ill in early life than in its decline. Youth bears up against misfortune; but it withers the heart, and crushes the soul of age!"

"After all," said the young guest, haughtily, "we must do our best to contradict the starry evils by our own internal philosophy. We can make ourselves independent of fate; that independence is better than prosperity!" Then, changing his tone, he added, "But you imagine that, by the power of other arts, we may control and counteract the prophecies of the stars —"

"How meanest thou?" said the astrologer, hastily. "Thou dost not suppose that alchemy, which is the servant of the heavenly host, is their opponent?"

"Nay," answered the disciple; "but you allow that we may be enabled to ward off evils, and to cure diseases, otherwise fatal to us, by the gift of Uriel and the charm of the Cabala?"

"Surely," replied the visionary; "but then I opine that the discovery of these precious secrets was foretold to us by the Omniscient Book at our nativity; and, therefore, though the menace of evils be held out to us, so also is the probability of their correction or our escape. And I must own," pursued the enthusiast, "that, to me, the very culture of those divine arts hath given a consolation amidst the evils to which I have been fated; so true seems it that it is not in the outer nature, in the great elements, and in the bowels of the earth, but also within ourselves, that we must look for the preparations whereby we are to achieve the wisdom of Zoroaster and Hermes. We must abstract ourselves from passion and earthly desires. Lapped in a celestial revery, we must work out, by contemplation, the essence from the matter of things: nor can we dart into the soul of the Mystic World until we ourselves have forgotten the body; and by fast, by purity, and by thought have become, in the flesh itself, a living soul."

Much more, and with an equal wildness of metaphysical

eloquence, did the astrologer declare in praise of those arts condemned by the old Church; and it doth indeed appear from reference to the numerous works of the alchemists and magians yet extant, somewhat hastily and unjustly. For those books all unite in dwelling on the necessity of virtue, subdued passions, and a clear mind, in order to become a fortunate and accomplished cabalist,—a precept, by the way, not without its policy; for, if the disciple failed, the failure might be attributed to his own fleshy imperfections, not to any deficiency in the truth of the science.

The young man listened to the visionary with an earnest and fascinated attention. Independent of the dark interest always attached to discourses of supernatural things more especially, we must allow, in the mouth of a fervent and rapt believer, there was that in the language and very person of the astrologer which inexpressibly enhanced the effect of the theme. Like most men acquainted with the literature of a country, but not accustomed to daily conversation with its natives, the English words and fashion of periods that occurred to Volktman were rather those used in books than in colloquy; and a certain solemnity and slowness of tone accompanied with the frequent, almost constant use of the pronoun singular,—the *thou* and the *thee*,—gave a strangeness and unfamiliar majesty to his dialect that suited well with the subjects on which he so loved to dwell. He himself was lean, gaunt, and wan; his cheeks were drawn and hollow; and thin locks, prematurely bleached to gray, fell in disorder round high, bare temples, in which the thought that is not of this world had paled the hue and furrowed the surface. But, as may be noted in many imaginative men, the life that seemed faint and chill in the rest of the frame collected itself, as in a citadel, within the eye. Bright, wild, and deep, the expression of those blue large orbs told the intense enthusiasm of the mind within, and even somewhat thrillingly communicated a part of that emotion to those on whom they dwelt. No painter could have devised, nor even Volktman himself, in the fulness of his northern fantasy, have sculptured forth a better image of those pale and unearthly students who, in the darker ages, applied life and learning to one unhallowed vigil, the Hermes or the Gebir of the alchemist's empty science,—dreamers, and the martyrs of their dreams.

In the discussion of mysteries which to detail would only weary while it perplexed the reader, the enthusiasts passed the greater portion of the night; and when at length the Englishman rose to depart, it cannot be denied that a solemn and boding emotion agitated his breast..

"We have talked," said he, attempting a smile, "of things above this nether life; and here we are lost, uncertain. On one thing, however, we can decide,—life itself is encompassed with gloom; sorrow and anxiety await even those upon whom the stars shed their most golden influence. We know not one day what the next shall bring!—no; I repeat it; no,—in spite of your scheme and your ephemeris and your election of happy moments. But, come what will, Volktman, come all that you foretell to me,—crosses in my love, disappointment in my life, melancholy in my blood, and a violent death in the very flush of my manhood,—ME at least, ME! my soul, my heart, my better part, you shall never cast down nor darken nor deject. I move in a certain and serene circle; ambition cannot tempt me above it, nor misfortune cast me below!"

Volktman looked at the speaker with surprise and admiration; the enthusiasm of a brave mind is the only fire broader and brighter than that of a fanatical one.

"Alas! my young friend," he said, as he clasped the hand of his guest, "I would to Heaven that my predictions may be wrong: often and often they have been erroneous," added he, bowing his head humbly; "they may be so in their reference to thee. So young, so brilliant, so beautiful too; so brave, yet so romantic of heart, I feel for all that may happen to thee,—ay, far, far more deeply than aught which may be fated to myself; for I am an old man now, and long inured to disappointment; all the greenness of my life is gone: even could I attain to the Grand Secret, the knowledge methinks would be too late. And, at my birth, my lot was portioned out unto me in characters so clear, that, while I have had time to acquiesce in it, I have had no hope to correct and change it. For Jupiter in Cancer, removed from the Ascendant, and not impedited of any other star, betokened me indeed some expertness in science, but a life of seclusion, and one that should bring not forth the fruits that its labour deserved. But there is so much in thy fate that ought to be bright and glorious, that it will be no common destiny marred, should the evil influences and the ominous seasons prevail against thee. But thou speakest boldly,—boldly, and as one of a high soul, though it be sometimes clouded and led astray. And I, therefore, again and again impress upon thee, it is from *thine own self*, thine own character, thine own habits, that all evil, save that of death, will come. Wear, then, I implore thee, wear in thy memory, as a jewel, the first great maxim of alchemist and magian,—'SEARCH THYSELF; CORRECT THYSELF; SUBDUE THYSELF:' it is only through the lamp of crystal that the light will shine duly out."

"It is more likely that the stars should err," returned the Englishman, "than that the human heart should correct itself of error: adieu!"

He left the room, and proceeded along a passage that led to the outer door. Ere he reached it, another door opened suddenly, and the face of Lucilla broke forth upon him. She held a light in her hand; and as she gazed on the Englishman, he saw that her face was very pale, and that she had been weeping. She looked at him long and earnestly, and the look affected him strangely; he broke silence, which at first it appeared to him difficult to do.

"Good-night, my pretty friend," said he: "shall I bring you some flowers to-morrow?"

Lucilla burst into a wild eldrich laugh; and abruptly closing the door, left him in darkness.

The cool air of the breaking dawn came freshly to the cheek of our countryman; yet, still, an unpleasant and heavy sensation sat at his heart. His nerves, previously weakened by his long commune with the visionary, and the effect it had produced, yet tingled and thrilled with the abrupt laugh and meaning countenance of that strange girl, who differed so widely from all others of her years. The stars were growing pale and ghostly, and there was a mournful and dim haze around the moon.

"Ye look ominously upon me," said he, half aloud, as his eyes fixed their gaze above; and the excitement of his spirit spread to his language,—"ye on whom, if our lore be faithful, the Most High hath written the letters of our mortal doom. And if ye rule the tides of the great deep, and the changes of the rolling year, what is there out of reason or nature in our belief that ye hold the same sympathetic and unseen influence over the blood and heart, which are the character (and the character makes the conduct) of man?" Pursuing his soliloquy of thought, and finding reasons for a credulity that afforded to him but little cause for pleasure or hope, the Englishman took his way to St. Sebastian's gate.

There was, in truth, much in the traveller's character that corresponded with that which was attributed and destined to one to whom the heavens had given a horoscope answering to his own; and it was this conviction, rather than any accidental coincidence in events, which had first led him to pore with a deep attention over the vain but imposing prophecies of judicial astrology. Possessed of all the powers that enable men to rise; ardent, yet ordinarily shrewd; eloquent, witty, brave, and, though not what may be termed versatile, possessing that rare art of concentrating the faculties which enables the possessor rapidly and thoroughly to master whatsoever once arrests the attention, he yet despised all that would have brought these endowments into full and legitimate display. He lived only for enjoyment. A passionate lover of women, music, letters, and the arts, it was society, not the world, which made the sphere and end of his existence. Yet was he no vulgar and commonplace epicurean: he lived for enjoyment; but that enjoyment was mainly formed from elements wearisome to more ordinary natures. Revery, contemplation, loneliness, were at times dearer to him than the softer and more Aristippean delights. His energies were called forth in society, but he was scarcely social. Trained from his early boyhood to solitude, he was seldom weary of being alone. He sought the crowd, not to amuse himself, but to observe others. The world to him was less as a theatre on which he was to play a part than as a book in which he loved to decipher the enigmas of wisdom. He observed all that passed around him. No sprightly cavalier at any time, the charm that he exercised at will over his companions was that of softness, not vivacity. But amidst that silken blandness of demeanour, the lynx eye of Remark never slept. He penetrated character at a glance, but he seldom made use of his knowledge. He found a pleasure in reading men, but a fatigue in governing them. And thus, consummately skilled as he was in the *science du monde,* he often allowed himself to appear ignorant of its practice. Forming in his mind a beau-ideal of friendship and of love, he never found enough in the realities long to engage his affection. Thus with women he was considered fickle, and with men he had no intimate companionship. This trait of character is common with persons of genius; and, owing to too large an overflow of heart, they are frequently considered heartless. There is always, however, danger that a character of this kind should become with years what it seems,— what it soon learns to despise. Nothing steels the affections like contempt.

The next morning an express from England reached the young traveller. His father was dangerously ill; nor was it expected that the utmost diligence would enable the young man to receive his last blessing. The Englishman, appalled and terror-stricken, recalled his interview with the astrologer. Nothing so effectually dismays us as to feel a confirmation of some idea of supernatural dread that has already found entrance within our reason; and of all supernatural belief, that of being compelled by a predecree, and thus being the mere tools and puppets of a dark and relentless fate, seems the most fraught at once with abasement and with horror.

The Englishman left Rome that morning, and sent only a verbal and hasty message to the astrologer, announcing the cause of his departure. Volktman was a man of excellent heart; but one would scarcely like to inquire whether exultation at the triumph of his prediction was not with him a far more powerful sentiment than grief at the misfortune to his friend!

CHAPTER XXVIII.

THE YOUTH OF LUCILLA VOLKTMAN. — A MYSTERIOUS CONVERSATION. — THE RETURN OF ONE UNLOOKED FOR.

Time went slowly on, and Lucilla grew up in beauty. The stranger traits of her character increased in strength, but perhaps in the natural bashfulness of maidenhood they became more latent. At the age of fifteen, her elastic shape had grown round and full, and the wild girl had already ripened to the woman. An expression of thought, when the play of her features was in repose, that dwelt upon her lip and forehead, gave her the appearance of being two or three years older than she was; but again, when her natural vivacity returned, when the clear and buoyant music of her gay laugh rang out, or when the cool air and bright sky of morning sent the blood to her cheek and the zephyr to her step, her face became as the face of childhood, and contrasted with a singular and dangerous loveliness the rich development of her form.

And still was Lucilla Volktman a stranger to all that savoured of the world; the company of others of her sex and age never drew forth her emotions from their resting-place: —

"And Nature said, a lovelier flower
On earth was never sown:
. . . .
"Myself will to my darling be
Both law and impulse; and with me
The girl, in rock and plain,
In earth and heaven, in glade and bower,
Shall feel an overseeing power
To kindle or restrain.

"The stars of midnight shall be dear
To her; and she shall lean her ear
In many a secret place;
Where rivulets dance their wayward round,
And beauty, born of murmuring sound,
Shall pass into her face."[1]

These lines have occurred to me again and again, as I looked on the face of her to whom I have applied them. And remembering as I do its radiance and glory in her happier moments, I can scarcely persuade myself to notice the faults and heats of temper which at times dashed away all its lustre and gladness. Unrestrained and fervid, she gave way to the irritation or grief of the moment with a violence that would have terrified any one who beheld her at such times. But it rarely happened that the scene had its witness even in her father, for she fled to the loneliest spot she could find to indulge these emotions; and perhaps even the agony they occasioned — an agony convulsing the heart and whole of her impassioned frame — took a sort of luxury from the solitary and unchecked nature of its indulgence.

Volktman continued his pursuits with an ardour that increased — as do all species of monomania — with increasing years; and in the accidental truth of some of his predictions, he forgot the erroneous result of the rest. He corresponded at times with the Englishman, who, after a short sojourn in England, had returned to the Continent, and was now making a prolonged tour through its northern capitals.

Very different, indeed, from the astrologer's occupations were those of the wanderer; and time, dissipation, and a maturer intellect had cured the latter of his boyish tendency to studies so idle and so vain. Yet he always looked back with an undefined and unconquered interest to the period of his acquaintance with the astrologer; to their long and thrilling watches in the night season; to the contagious fervour of faith breathing from the visionary; his dark and restless excursions into that remote science associated with the legends of eldest time, and of —

[1] Wordsworth.

"The crew, who, under names of old renown,
Osiris, Isis, Orus, and their train,
With monstrous shapes and sorceries, abused
Fanatic Egypt and her priests."

One night, four years after the last scene we have described in the astrologer's house, Volktman was sitting alone in his favourite room. Before him was a calculation on which the ink was scarcely dry. His face leaned on his breast, and he seemed buried in thought. His health had been of late gradually declining; and it might be seen upon his worn brow and attenuated frame that death was already preparing to withdraw the visionary from a world whose substantial enjoyments he had so sparingly tasted.

Lucilla had been banished from his chamber during the day. She now knew that his occupation was over, and entered the room with his evening repast; that frugal meal, common with the Italians,—the *polenta* (made of Indian corn), the bread and the fruits, which after the fashion of students, he devoured unconsciously, and would not have remembered one hour after whether or not it had been tasted!

"Sit thee down, child," said he to Lucilla, kindly,—"sit thee down."

Lucilla obeyed, and took her seat upon the very stool on which she had been seated the last night on which the Englishman had seen her.

"I have been thinking," said Volktman, as he placed his hand on his daughter's head, "that I shall soon leave thee; and I should like to see thee protected by another before my own departure."

"Ah, Father," said Lucilla, as the tears rushed to her eyes, "do not talk thus! indeed, indeed, you must not indulge in this perpetual gloom and seclusion of life. You promised to take me with you some day this week to the Vatican. Do let it be to-morrow; the weather has been so fine lately; and who knows how long it may last?"

"True," said Volktman; "and to-morrow will not, I think, be unfavourable to our stirring abroad, for the moon will be of the same age as at my birth,—an accident that thou wilt note, my child, to be especially auspicious towards any enterprise."

The poor astrologer so rarely stirred from his home, that he did well to consider a walk of a mile or two in the light of an enterprise. "I have wished," continued he, after a pause, "that I might see our English friend once more,—that is, ere long; for, to tell thee the truth, Lucilla, certain events happening unto him do, strangely enough, occur about the same time as that in which events equally boding will befall thee. This coincidence it was which contributed to make me assume so warm an interest in the lot of a stranger. I would I might see him soon."

Lucilla's beautiful breast heaved, and her face was covered with blushes: these were symptoms of a disorder that never occurred to the recluse.

"Thou rememberest the foreigner?" asked Volktman, after a pause.

"Yes," said Lucilla, half inaudibly.

"I have not heard from him of late: I will make question concerning him ere the cock crow."

"Nay, my father!" said Lucilla, quickly: "not to-night; you want rest, your eyes are heavy."

"Girl," said the mystic, "the soul sleepeth not, nor wanteth sleep; even as the stars, to which (as the Arabian saith) there is also a soul, wherewith an intent passion of our own doth make a union, so that we by an unslumbering diligence do constitute ourselves a part of the heaven itself,—even, I say, as the stars may vanish from the human eye nor be seen in the common day, though all the while their course is stopped not nor their voices dumb, even so doth the soul of man retire, as it were, into a seeming sleep and torpor; yet it worketh all the same, and perhaps with a less impeded power, in that it is more free from common obstruction and trivial hindrance. And if I purpose to confer this night with the '*Intelligence*' that ruleth earth and earth's beings concerning this stranger, it will not be by the vigil and the scheme, but by the very sleep which thou imaginest, in thy mental darkness, would deprive me of the resources of my art."

"Can you really, then, my father," said Lucilla, in a tone half anxious, half timid,—"can you really, at will, conjure up in your dreams the persons you wish to see; or draw, from sleep, any oracle concerning their present state?"

"Of a surety," answered the astrologer; "it is one of the great—though not perchance the most gifted—of our endowments."

"Can you teach me the method?" asked Lucilla, gravely.

"All that relates to the art I can," rejoined the mystic: "but the chief and main power rests with thyself. For know, my daughter, that one who seeks the wisdom that is above the earth must cultivate and excite, with long labour and deep thought, his least earthly faculty."

Here the visionary, observing that the countenance of Lucilla was stamped with a fixed attention, which she did not often bestow upon his metaphysical exordiums, paused for a moment; and then pursued the theme with the tone of one desirous of making himself at once as clear and impressive as the nature of an abstruse science would allow.

"There are two things in the outer creation, which, according to the great Hermes, suffice for the operation of all that is wonderful and glorious,—Fire and Earth. Even so, my child, there are in the human mind two powers that affect all of which our nature is capable,—REASON and IMAGINATION. Now mankind—less wise in themselves than in the outer world—have cultivated, for the most part, but one of these faculties, and that the inferior and more passive,—REASON. They have tilled the *earth* of the human heart, but suffered its *fire* to remain dormant, or waste itself in chance and frivolous directions. Hence the insufficiency of human knowledge. Inventions founded only on reason move within a circle from which their escape is momentary and trivial. When some few, endowed with a just instinct, have had recourse to the diviner element, IMAGINATION, thou wilt observe that they have used it only in the service of the lighter arts, and those chiefly disconnected from REASON. Such is poetry and music, and other delicious fabrications of genius, that amuse men, soften men, but *advance* them not. They have—with but rare exceptions — left this glorious and winged faculty utterly passive in the service of Philosophy. There, REASON alone has been admitted, and IMAGINATION hath been carefully banished, as an erratic and deceitful meteor. Now mark me, child: I, noting this our error in early youth, did resolve to see what might be effected by the culture of this renounced and maltreated element; and finding, as I proceeded in the studies that grew from this desire, by the occult yet guiding writings of the great philosophers of old, that they had forestalled me in this discovery, I resolved to learn from their experience by what means the imagination is best fostered, and, as it were, sublimed.

"Anxiously following their precepts — the truth of which soon appeared — I found that solitude, fast, intense revery upon the one theme on which we desired knowledge, were the true elements and purifiers of this glorious faculty. It was by these means and by this power that men so far behind us in lesser lore achieved, on the mooned plains of Chaldea and by the dark waters of Egypt, their penetration into the womb of Event; by these means and this power the solitaries of the Gothic time not only attained to the most intricate arcana of the stars, but to the empire of the spirits about, above, and beneath the earth, — a power, indeed, disputed by the presumptuous sophists of the present time, but of which their writings yet contain ample proof. Nay, by the constant feeding and impressing and moulding and refining and heightening the imaginative power, I do conceive that even the false prophets and the evil practitioners of the blacker cabala clomb into the power seemingly inconceivable, — the power of accomplishing miracles and prodigies, that to appearance belie, but in truth verify, the course of nature. By this spirit within the flesh, we grow *from* the flesh, and may see, and at length invoke the souls, of the dead, and receive warnings, and hear omens, and girdle our sleep with dreams.

"Not unto me," continued the cabalist, in a lowlier tone, "have been vouchsafed all these gifts; for I began the art when the first fire of youth was dim within me; and it was therefore with duller and already earth-clogged pinions that

I sought to rise. Something, however, I have won as a recompense for austere abstinence and much labour; and this power over the land of dreams is at least within my command."

"Then," said Lucilla, in a disappointed tone, "it is only by a long course of indulgence to the fervour of the imagination, and not by spell or charm, that one can gain a similar power?"

"Not wholly so, my daughter," replied the mystic; "they who do so excite, and have so raised the diviner faculty, can alone possess the *certain and invariable* power over dreams, even without charms and talismans; but the most dull or idle may hope to do so with just confidence (though not certainty) by help of skill, and by directing the full force of their half-roused fancy towards the person or object they wish to see reflected in the glass of Sleep."

"And what means should the uninitiated employ?" asked Lucilla, in a tone betokening her interest.

"I will tell thee," answered the astrologer. "Thou must inscribe on a white parchment an image of the sun."

"As how?" interrupted Lucilla.

"Thus!" said the astrologer, drawing from among his papers one inscribed with the figure of a man asleep on the bosom of an angel. "This was made at the potential and appointed time, when the sun was in the Ninth of the Celestial Houses, and the Lion shook his bright mane as he ascended the blue mount. Observe, that on the figure must be written thy desire,—the name of the person thou wishest to see, or the thing thou wouldst have foreshown; then, having prepared and brought the mind to a faith in the effect,—for without faith the imagination lies inert and lifeless,—this image will be placed under the head of the invoker, and when the moon goeth through the sign which was in the Ninth House of his nativity, the Dream will glide into him, and his soul walk with the spirit of the vision."

"Give me the image," said Lucilla, eagerly.

The mystic hesitated. "No, Lucilla," said he, at length; "no, it is a dark and comfortless path, that of prescience and unearthly knowledge, save to the few that walk it with a gifted light and a fearless soul. It is not for women or children,—nay, for few amongst men; it withers up the sap of life, and makes the hair gray before its time. No, no; take the broad sunshine, and the brief but sweet flowers of earth; they are better for thee, my child, and for thy years, than the fever and hope of the night-dream and the planetary influence."

So saying, the astrologer replaced the image within the leaves of one of his books; and with a prudence not common to him, thrust the volume into a drawer, which he locked. The fair face of Lucilla became clouded, but the ill health of her father imposed a restraint on her wild temper.

Just at that moment the door slowly opened, and the Englishman stood before the daughter and sire. They did not note him at first. The solitary servant of the sage had admitted him; he had proceeded, without ceremony, to the well-remembered apartment.

As he now stood gazing on the pair, he observed with an inward smile how exactly their present attitudes (as well as the old aspect of the scene) resembled those in which he had broken upon them on the last evening he had visited that chamber,—the father bending over the old, worn, quaint table; and the daughter seated beside him on the same low stool. The character of their countenances struck him, too, as wearing the same ominous expression as when those countenances had chilled him on that evening. For Volktman's features were impressed with the sadness that breathed from, and caused, his prohibition to his daughter; and that prohibition had given to her features an abstraction and shadow similar to the dejection they had worn on the night we recur to.

This remembered coincidence did not cheer the spirits of the young traveller; he muttered to himself; and then, as if anxious to break the silence, moved forward with a heavy step.

Volktman started at the sound; and looking up, seemed literally electrified by this sudden apparition of one whom he had so lately expressed his desire to see. His lips muttered the intruder's name, one well known to the reader (it was the name of Godolphin), and then closed; but Lucilla sprang from her seat, and clasping her hands joyously together, darted forward till she came within a foot of the unexpected visitor. There she abruptly arrested herself, blushed deeply, and stood before him humbled, agitated, but all vivid with delight.

"What, is this Lucilla?" said Godolphin, admiringly; "how beautiful she is grown!" and advancing, he saluted, with a light and fraternal kiss, her girlish and damask cheek; then, without heeding her confusion, he turned to the astrologer, who by this time had a little recovered from his amaze.

CHAPTER XXIX.

THE EFFECT OF YEARS AND EXPERIENCE. — THE ITALIAN CHARACTER.

Godolphin now came almost daily to the astrologer's abode. He was shocked to perceive the physical alteration four years had wrought in his singular friend; and with the warmth of a heart naturally kind, he sought to contribute to the comfort and enjoyment of a life that was evidently drawing to a close.

Godolphin's company seemed to give Volktman a pleasure which nothing else could afford him. He loved to converse on the various incidents that had occurred to each since they met; and in whatsoever Godolphin communicated to him, the mystic sought to impress upon his friend's attention the fulfilment of an astrological prediction.

Godolphin, though no longer impressed with a belief in the visionary's science, did not affect to combat his assertions. He had not, in his progress through life, found much to shake his habitual indolence in ordinary affairs; and it was no easy matter to provoke one of his quiet temper and self-indulging wisdom into conversational dispute. Besides, who argues with fanaticism?

Since the young idealist had left England, the elements of his character had been slowly performing the ordination of time, and working their due change in its general aspect. The warm fountains of youth flowed not so freely as before: the selfishness that always comes, sooner or later, to solitary men of the world, had gradually mingled itself with all the channels of his heart. The brooding and thoughtful disposition of his faculties having turned from romance to what he deemed philosophy, that which once was enthusiasm had hardened into wisdom. He neither hated men nor loved them with a sanguine philanthropy; he viewed them with cool and discerning eyes. He did not think it within the power of governments to make the mass, in any country, much happier or more elevated than they are. Republics, he was wont to say, favoured *aristocratic* virtues, and despotisms extinguished them; but, whether in a monarchy or republic, the hewers of wood and the drawers of water, *the multitude,* still remained intrinsically the same.

This theory heightened his indifference to ambition. The watchwords of party appeared to him ridiculous; and politics in general — what a great moralist termed one question in particular — a shuttlecock kept up by the contention of noisy children. His mind thus rested as to all public matters in a state of quietude, and covered over with the mantle of a most false, a most perilous philosophy. His appetites to pleasure had grown somewhat dulled by experience, but he was as yet neither sated nor discontented. One feeling at his breast still remained scarcely diminished of its effect, when the string was touched,— his tender remembrance of Constance; and this had prevented any subsequent but momentary attachment deepening into love. Thus, at the age of seven and twenty, Percy Godolphin reappears on our stage.

There was a great deal in the Italian character that our traveller liked: its love of ease, reduced into a system; its courtesy; its content with the world as it is; its moral apathy as regards all that agitates life, save one passion, and the universal tenderness, ardour, and delicacy which, in *that* passion, it ennobles itself in displaying. The commonest peasant of Rome or Naples, though not perhaps in the freer land of Tuscany, can comprehend all the romance and mystery of the most subtle species of love; all that it requires in England the idle habits of aristocracy, or the sensitive fibre of genius, even to conceive. And what is yet stranger, the worn-out debauchee, sage with an experience and variety of licentiousness, which come not within the compass of a northern profligacy, remains alive to the earliest and most innocent sentiments of the passion. And if Platonism in its coldest purity exist on earth, it is among the Aretins of southern Italy.

This unworldly refinement, amidst so much worldly callousness, was a peculiarity that afforded perpetual amusement to the nice eye and subtle judgment of Godolphin. He loved not to note the common elements of character; whatever was most abstract and difficult to analyze, pleased him most. He mixed then much with the Romans, and was a favourite amongst them; but during his present visit to the Immortal City, he did not, how distantly soever, associate with the English. His carelessness of show, and the independence of a single man from burdensome connections, rendered his income fully competent to his wants; but, like many proud men, he was not willing to make it seem even to himself as a comparative poverty, beside the lavish expenses of his ostentatious countrymen. Travel, moreover, had augmented those stores of reflection which rob solitude of *ennui*.

CHAPTER XXX.

MAGNETISM. — SYMPATHY. — THE RETURN OF ELEMENTS TO ELEMENTS.

DAILY did the health of Volktman decline; Lucilla was the only one ignorant of his danger. She had never seen the gradual approaches of death: her mother's abrupt and rapid illness made the whole of her experience of disease. Physicians and dark rooms were necessarily coupled in her mind with all graver maladies; and as the astrologer, rapt in his calculations, altered not any of his habits, and was insensible to pain, she fondly attributed his occasional complaints to the melancholy induced by seclusion. With sedentary men, diseases, being often those connected with the organization of the heart, do not usually terminate suddenly: it was so with Volktman.

One day he was alone with Godolphin, and their conversation turned upon one of the doctrines of the old Magnetism, a doctrine which, depending as it does so much upon a seeming reference to experience, survived the rest of its associates, and is still not wholly out of repute among the wild imaginations of Germany.

"One of the most remarkable and abstruse points in what students call metaphysics," said Volktman, "is *sympathy!* the first principle, according to some, of all human virtue. It is this, say they, which makes men just, humane, charitable. When one who has never heard of the duty of assisting his neighbour sees another drowning, he plunges into the water and saves him. Why? because involuntarily, and at once, his imagination places himself in the situation of the stranger: the pain *he* would experience in the watery death glances across him; from this pain he hastens, without analyzing its cause, to deliver himself.

"Humanity is thus taught him by sympathy: where is this sympathy placed? In the nerves. The nerves are the communicants with outward nature; the more delicate the nerves, the finer the sympathies; hence, women and children are more alive to sympathy than men. Well, mark me: do not these nerves have attraction and sympathy, not only with human suffering, but with the powers of what is falsely termed inanimate nature? Do not the winds, the influences of the weather and the seasons, act confessedly upon them? And if one part of nature, why not another, inseparably connected too with that part? If the weather and seasons have sympathy with the nerves, why not the moon and the stars, by which the weather and the seasons are influenced and changed? Ye of the schools may allow that sympathy originates some of our actions; I say it governs the whole world,— the whole creation! Before the child is born, it is this secret affinity which can mark and stamp him with the witness of his mother's terror or his mother's desire."

"Yet," said Godolphin, "you would scarcely, in your zeal for sympathy, advocate the same cause as Edricius Mohynnus, who cured wounds by a powder, not applied to the wound, but to the towel that had been dipped in its blood?"

"No," answered Volktman; "it is these quacks and pretenders that have wronged all sciences, by clamouring for false deductions. But I do believe of sympathy that it has a power to transport ourselves out of the body and reunite us with the absent. Hence, trances, and raptures, in which the patient, being sincere, will tell thee, in grave earnestness, and with minute detail, of all that he saw and heard and encountered, afar off, in other parts of the earth, or even above the earth. As thou knowest the accredited story of the youth, who, being transported with a vehement and long-nursed desire to see his mother, did through that same desire become as it were rapt, and beheld her, being at the distance of many miles, and giving and exchanging signs of their real and bodily conference."

Godolphin turned aside to conceal an involuntary smile at this grave affirmation; but the mystic, perhaps perceiving it, continued yet more eagerly:—

"Nay, I myself, at times, have experienced such trance, if trance it be; and have conversed with them who have passed from the outward earth,—with my father and my wife. And," continued he, after a moment's pause, "I do believe that we may, by means of this power of attraction—this elementary and all-penetrative sympathy—pass away, in our last moments, at once into the bosom of those we love. For, by the intent and rapt longing to behold the Blest and to be amongst them, we may be drawn insensibly into their presence, and the hour being come when the affinity between the spirit and the body shall be dissolved, the mind and desire, being so drawn upward, can return to earth no more. And this sympathy, refined and extended, will make, I imagine, our powers, our very being, in a future state. Our sympathy being only, then, with what is immortal, we shall partake necessarily of that nature which attracts us; and the body no longer clogging the intenseness of our desires, we shall be able by a wish to transport ourselves wheresoever we please,—from star to star, from glory to glory, charioted and winged by our wishes."

Godolphin did not reply, for he was struck with the growing paleness of the mystic, and with a dreaming and intent fixedness that seemed creeping over his eyes, which were usually bright and restless. The day was now fast declining. Lucilla entered the room, and came caressingly to her father's side.

"Is the evening warm, my child?" said the astrologer.

"Very mild and warm," answered Lucilla.

"Give me your arm, then," said he; "I will sit a little while without the threshold."

The Romans live in flats, as at Edinburgh, and with a common stair. Volktman's abode was in the *secondo piano*. He descended the stairs with a step lighter than it had been of late; and sinking into a seat without the house, seemed silently and gratefully to inhale the soft and purple air of an Italian sunset.

By and by the sun had entirely vanished: and that most brief but most delicious twilight, common to the clime, had succeeded. Veil-like and soft, the mist that floats at that hour between earth and heaven lent its transparent shadow to the scene around them; it seemed to tremble as for a moment, and then was gone. The moon arose, and cast its light over Volktman's earnest countenance, over the rich bloom and watchful eye of Lucilla, over the contemplative brow and motionless figure of Godolphin. It was a group of indefinable interest: the Earth was so still, that the visionary might well have fancied it had hushed itself, to drink within its quiet heart the voices of that Heaven in whose oracles he believed. Not one of the group spoke: the astrologer's mind and gaze were riveted above; and neither of his companions wished to break the meditations of the old and dreaming man.

Godolphin, with folded arms and downcast eyes, was pursuing his own thoughts; and Lucilla, to whom Godolphin's presence was a subtle and subduing intoxication, looked indeed upward to the soft and tender heavens, but with the soul of the loving daughter of earth.

Slowly, nor marked by his companions, the gaze of the mystic deepened and deepened in its fixedness.

The minutes went on; and the evening waned, till a chill breeze, floating down from the Latian Hills, recalled Lucilla's attention to her father. She covered him tenderly with her own mantle, and whispered gently in his ear her admonition to shun the coldness of the coming night. He did not answer; and on raising her voice a little higher, with the same result, she looked appealingly to Godolphin. He laid his hand on Volktman's shoulder; and, bending forward to address him, was struck dumb by the glazed and fixed expression of the mystic's eyes. The certainty flashed across him; he hastily felt Volktman's pulse,—it was still. There was no doubt left on his mind; and yet the daughter, looking at him all the while, did not even dream of this sudden and awful stroke. In silence, and unconsciously, the strange and solitary spirit of the mystic had passed from its home, in what exact instant of time, or by what last contest of nature, was not known.

CHAPTER XXXI.

A SCENE.—LUCILLA'S STRANGE CONDUCT.—GODOLPHIN PASSES THROUGH A SEVERE ORDEAL.—EGERIA'S GROTTO, AND WHAT THERE HAPPENS.

Let us pass over Godolphin's most painful task. What Lucilla's feelings were, the reader may imagine; and yet, her wayward and unanalyzed temper mocked at once imagination and expression to depict its sufferings or its joys.

The brother of Volktman's wife was sent for: he and his wife took possession of the abode of death. This, if possible, heightened Lucilla's anguish. The apathetic and vain character of the middle classes in Rome, which her relations shared, stung her heart by contrasting its own desolate abandonment to grief. Above all, she was revolted by the unnatural ceremonies of a Roman funeral. The corpse exposed, the cheeks painted, the parading procession,—all shocked the delicacy of her real and reckless affliction. But when this was over; when the rite of death was done, and when, in the house wherein her sire had presided, and she herself had been left to a liberty wholly unrestricted, she saw strangers (for such comparatively her relatives were to her) settling themselves down, with vacant countenances and light words, to the common occupations of life; when she saw them move, alter (nay, talk calmly, and sometimes with jests, of selling), those little household articles of furniture which, homely and worn as they were, were hallowed to her by a thousand dear and infantine and filial recollections; when, too, she found herself treated as a child, and, in some measure, as a dependant; when she, the wild, the free, saw herself subjected to restraint,—nay, heard the commonest actions of her life chidden and reproved; when she saw the trite and mean natures which thus presumed to lord it over her, and assume empire in the house of one, of whose wild and lofty, though erring speculations, of whose generous though abstract elements of character, she could comprehend enough to respect, while what she did *not* comprehend heightened the respect into awe,— then the more vehement and indignant passions of her mind broke forth! her flashing eye, her scornful gesture, her mysterious threat, and her open defiance astonished always, sometimes amused, but more often terrified, the apathetic and superstitious Italians.

Godolphin, moved by interest and pity for the daughter of his friend, called once or twice after the funeral at the house; and commended, with promises and gifts, the desolate girl to the tenderness and commiseration of her relations. There is nothing an Italian will not promise, nothing he will not sell; and Godolphin thus purchased, in reality, a forbearance to Lucilla's strange temper (as it was considered) which otherwise, assuredly, would not have been displayed.

More than a month had elapsed since the astrologer's decease; and, the season of the malaria verging to its commencement, Godolphin meditated a removal to Naples. He strolled, two days prior to his departure, to the house on the Appia Via, in order to take leave of Lucilla, and bequeath to her relations his parting injunctions.

It was a strange and harsh face that peered forth on him through the iron grating of the door before he obtained admittance; and when he entered, he heard the sound of voices in loud altercation. Among the rest, the naturally dulcet and silver tones of Lucilla were strained beyond their wonted key, and breathed the accents of passion and disdain.

He entered the room whence the sounds of dispute proceeded, and the first face that presented itself to him was that of Lucilla. It was flushed with anger; the veins in the smooth forehead were swelled; the short lip breathed beautiful contempt. She stood at some little distance from the rest of the inmates of the room, who were seated; and her posture was erect and even stately, though in wrath: her arms were folded upon her bosom, and the composed excitement of her figure contrasted with the play and fire and energy of her features.

At Godolphin's appearance, a sudden silence fell upon the conclave; the uncle and the aunt (the latter of whom had seemed the noisiest) subsided into apologetic respect to the rich (he was rich to them) young Englishman; and Lucilla sank into a seat, covered her face with her small and beautiful hands, and — humbled from her anger and her vehemence — burst into tears.

"And what is this?" said Godolphin, pityingly.

The Italians hastened to inform him. Lucilla had chosen to absent herself from home every evening; she had been seen, the last night, on the Corso, crowded as that street was with the young, the profligate, and the idle. They could not but reprove "the dear girl" for this indiscretion (Italians, indifferent as to the conduct of the married, are generally attentive to that of their single, women); and she announced her resolution to persevere in it.

"Is this true, my pupil?" said Godolphin, turning to Lucilla; the poor girl sobbed on, but returned no answer. "Leave me to reprimand and admonish her," said he to the aunt and uncle; and they, without appearing to notice the incongruity of reprimand in the mouth of a man of seven-and-twenty to a girl of fifteen, chattered forth a Babel of conciliation and left the apartment.

Godolphin, young as he might be, was not unfitted for his task. There was a great deal of quiet dignity mingled with the kindness of his manner; and his affection for Lucilla had hitherto been so pure that he felt no embarrassment in addressing her as a brother. He approached the corner of the room in which she sat; he drew a chair near to her, and took her reluctant and trembling hand with a gentleness that made her weep with a yet wilder vehemence.

"My dear Lucilla," said he, "you know your father honoured me with his regard: let me presume on that regard, and on my long acquaintance with yourself, to address you as your friend, as your brother." Lucilla drew away her hand; but again, as if ashamed of the impulse, extended it towards him.

"You cannot know the world as I do, dear Lucilla," continued Godolphin; "for experience in its affairs is bought at some little expense, which I pray that it may never cost you. In all countries, Lucilla, an unmarried female is exposed to dangers which, without any actual fault of her own, may embitter her future life. One of the greatest of these dangers lies in deviating from custom. With the woman who does this, every man thinks himself entitled to give his thoughts, his words, nay, even his actions, a license which you cannot but dread to incur. Your uncle and aunt, therefore, do right to advise your not going alone, to the public streets of Rome more especially, except in the broad daylight; and though their advice be irksomely intruded, and ungracefully couched, it is good in its principle, and — yes, dearest Lucilla — even *necessary* for you to follow."

"But," said Lucilla, through her tears, "you cannot guess what insults, what unkindness, I have been forced to submit to from them. I, who never knew, till now, what insult and unkindness were! I, who — " here sobs checked her utterance.

"But how, my young and fair friend, how can you mend their manners by destroying their esteem for you? Respect yourself, Lucilla, if you wish others to respect you. But, perhaps," — and such a thought for the first time flashed across Godolphin, — "perhaps you did not seek the Corso for the *crowd*, but for *one;* perhaps you went there to meet — dare I guess the fact? — an admirer, a lover."

"Now *you* insult me!" cried Lucilla, angrily.

"I thank you for your anger; I accept it as a contradiction," said Godolphin. "But listen yet a while, and forgive frankness. If there be any one, among the throng of Italian youths, whom you have seen, and could be happy with; one who loves you and whom you do not hate, remember that I am your father's friend; that I am rich; that I can — "

"Cruel, cruel!" interrupted Lucilla; and withdrawing herself from Godolphin, she walked to and fro with great and struggling agitation.

"Is it not so, then?" said Godolphin, doubtingly.

"No, sir; no!"

"Lucilla Volktman," said Godolphin, with a colder gravity than he had yet called forth, "I claim some attention from you, some confidence, nay, some esteem,— for the sake of your father, for the sake of your early years, when I assisted to teach you my native tongue, and loved you as a brother. Promise me that you will not commit this indiscretion any more,— at least till we meet again; nay, that you will not stir abroad, save with one of your relations."

"Impossible! impossible!" cried Lucilla, vehemently; "it were to take away the only solace I have: it were to make life a privation, a curse."

"Not so, Lucilla; it is to make life respectable and safe. I, on the other hand, will engage that all within these walls shall behave to you with indulgence and kindness."

"I care not for their kindness! — for the kindness of any one, save — "

"Whom?" asked Godolphin, perceiving she would not proceed: but as she was still silent, he did not press the question. "Come!" said he, persuasively: "come, promise, and be friends with me; do not let us part angrily: I am about to take my leave of you for many months."

"Part! you! months! — O God, do not say so!"

With these words, she was by his side, and gazing on him with her large and pleading eyes, wherein was stamped a wildness, a terror, the cause of which he did not as yet decipher.

"No, no," said she, with a faint smile; "no! you mean to frighten me, to extort my promise. *You* are not going to desert me!"

"But, Lucilla, I will not leave you to unkindness; they shall not, they dare not wound you again."

"Say to me that you are not going from Rome; speak, quick!"

"I go in two days."

"Then let me die!" said Lucilla, in a tone of such deep despair that it chilled and appalled Godolphin, who did not, however, attribute her grief (the grief of this mere child,— a child so wayward and eccentric) to any other cause than that feeling of abandonment which the young so bitterly experience at being left utterly alone with persons unfamiliar to their habits and opposed to their liking.

He sought to soothe her, but she repelled him. Her features worked convulsively; she walked twice across the room; then stopped opposite to him, and a certain strained composure on her brow seemed to denote that she had arrived at some sudden resolution.

"Wouldst thou ask me," she said, "what cause took me into the streets as the shadows darkened, and enabled me lightly to bear threats at home and risk abroad?"

"Ay, Lucilla; will you tell me?"

"Thou wast the cause!" she said, in a low voice, trembling with emotion, and the next moment sank on her knees before him.

With a confusion that ill became so practised and favoured a gallant, Godolphin sought to raise her. "No! no!" she said; "you will despise me now; let me lie here, and die thinking of thee. Yes!" she continued, with an inward but rapid voice, as he lifted her reluctant frame from the earth, and hung over her with a cold and uncaressing attention, "yes! you I loved — I adored — from my very childhood. When you were by, life seemed changed to me; when absent, I longed for night, that I might dream of you. The spot you had touched I marked out in silence, that I might kiss it and address it when you were gone. You left us; four years passed away: and the recollection of you made and shaped my very nature. I loved solitude, for in solitude I saw you; in imagination I spoke to you, and methought you answered and did not chide. You returned — and — and — but no matter: to see you, at the hour you usually leave home, *to see you*, I wandered forth with the evening. I tracked you, myself unseen; I followed you at a distance; I marked you disappear within some of the proud palaces that never know what love is. I returned home weeping, but happy. And do you think — do you dare to think — that I should have told you this, had you not driven me mad; had you not left me reckless of what henceforth was thought of me, became of me? What will life be to me when you are gone? And now I have said all! Go! You do not love me: I know it; but do not say so. Go, leave me; why do you not leave me?"

Does there live one man who can hear a woman, young and beautiful, confess attachment to him, and not catch the contagion? Affected, flattered, and almost melted into love himself, Godolphin felt all the danger of the moment; but this young, inexperienced girl — the daughter of his friend — no! her he could not, loving, willing as she was, betray.

Yet it was some moments before he could command himself sufficiently to answer her. "Listen to me calmly," at length he said; "we are at least to each other dear friends; nay, listen, I beseech you. I, Lucilla, am a man whose heart is forestalled,— exhausted before its time. I have loved deeply and passionately; that love is over, but it has unfitted me for any species of love resembling itself, — any which I could offer to you. Dearest Lucilla, I will not disguise the truth from you. Were I to love you, it would be — not in the eyes of *your* countrymen (with whom such connections are common), but in the eyes of mine — it would be dishonour. Shall I confer even this partial dishonour on you? No! Lucilla, this feeling of yours towards me is (pardon me) but a young and childish fantasy; you will smile at it some years hence. I am not worthy of so pure and fresh a heart; but at least" — here he spoke in a lower voice, and as to himself — "at least I am not so unworthy as to wrong it."

"Go!" said Lucilla; "go, I implore you." She spoke, and stood hueless and motionless, as if the life (life's life was indeed gone!) had departed from her. Her features were set and rigid; the tears that stole in large drops down her cheeks were unfelt; a slight quivering of her lips only bespoke what passed within her.

"Ah!" cried Godolphin, stung from his usual calm, stung from the quiet kindness he had sought, from principle, to assume, "can I withstand this trial? — I, whose dream of life has been the love that I might now find! I, who have never before known an obstacle to a wish which I have not contended against, if not conquered; and, weakened as I am with the habitual indulgence to temptation, which has never been so strong as now — but no! I will — I will deserve this attachment by self-restraint, self-sacrifice."

He moved away; and then returning, dropped on his knee before Lucilla.

"Spare me!" said he, in an agitated voice, which brought back all the blood to that young and transparent cheek, which was now half averted from him — "spare me! spare yourself! Look around, when I am gone, for some one to replace my image: thousands younger, fairer, warmer of heart, will aspire to your love; that love for them will be exposed to no peril, no shame: forget me; select another; be happy and respected. Permit me alone to fill the place of your friend, your brother. I will provide for your comforts, your liberty; you shall be restrained, offended no more. God bless you, dear, dear Lucilla; and believe" (he said, almost in a whisper), "that, in thus flying you, I have acted generously, and with an effort worthy of your loveliness and your love."

He said, and hurried from the apartment. Lucilla turned slowly round as the door closed and then fell motionless on the ground.

Meanwhile Godolphin, mastering his emotion, sought the host and hostess; and begging them to visit his lodging that evening to receive certain directions and rewards, hastily left the house.

But instead of returning home, the desire for a brief solitude and self-commune, which usually follows strong excitement (and which, in all less ordinary events, suggested his sole counsellers or monitors to the musing Godolphin), led his steps in an opposite direction. Scarcely conscious whither he was wandering, he did not pause till he found himself in that green and still valley in which the pilgrim beholds the grotto of Egeria.

It was noon, and the day warm, but not overpowering. The leaf slept on the old trees that are scattered about that little valley; and amidst the soft and rich turf the wanderer's step disturbed the lizard, basking its brilliant hues in the noontide, and glancing rapidly through the herbage as it retreated. And from the trees and through the air, the occasional song of the birds (for in Italy their voices are rare) floated with a peculiar clearness, and even noisiness of music, along the deserted haunts of the Nymph.

The scene, rife with its beautiful associations, recalled Godolphin from his revery. "And here," thought he, "Fable has thrown its most lovely enduring enchantment; here, every one who has tasted the loves of earth, and sickened for the love that is ideal, finds a spell more attractive to his steps, more fraught with contemplation to his spirit, than aught raised by the palace of the Cæsars or the tomb of the Scipios."

Thus meditating, and softened by the late scene with Lucilla (to which his thoughts again recurred), he sauntered onward to the steep side of the bank, in which faith and tradition have hollowed out the grotto of the goddess. He entered the silent cavern, and bathed his temples in the delicious waters of the fountain.

It was perhaps well that it was not at that moment Lucilla made to him her strange and unlooked-for confession; again and again he said to himself (as if seeking for a justification of his self-sacrifice), "Her father was not Italian, and possessed feeling and honour: let me not forget that he loved me!" In truth, the avowal of this wild girl — an avowal made indeed with the ardour, but also breathing of the innocence, the inexperience of her character — had opened to his fancy new and not undelicious prospects. He had never loved her, save with a lukewarm kindness, before that last hour; but now, in recalling her beauty, her tears, her passionate abandonment, can we wonder that he felt a strange beating at his heart, and that he indulged that dissolved and luxurious vein of tender meditation which is the prelude to all love? We must recall, too, the recollection of his own temper, so constantly yearning for the unhackneyed, the untasted; and his deep and soft order of imagination, by which he involuntarily conjured up the delight of living with one, watching one, so different from the rest of the world, and

Lucilla.

whose thoughts and passions (wild as they might be) were all devoted to him!

And in what spot were these imaginings fed and coloured? In a spot which in the nature of its divine fascination could be found only beneath one sky, that sky the most balmy and loving upon earth! Who could think of love within the haunt and temple of —

"That Nympholepsy of some fond despair,"

and not feel that love enhanced, deepened, modulated, into at once a dream and a desire?

It was long that Godolphin indulged himself in recalling the image of Lucilla; but nerved at length and gradually, by harder, and we may hope better, sentiments than those of a love which he could scarcely indulge without criminality on the one hand, or what must have appeared to the man of the world derogatory folly on the other, he turned his thoughts into a less voluptuous channel, and prepared, though with a reluctant step, to depart homewards. But what was his amaze, his confusion, when, on reaching the mouth of the cave, he saw within a few steps of him Lucilla herself!

She was walking alone and slowly, her eyes bent upon the ground, and did not perceive him. According to a common custom with the middle classes of Rome, her rich hair, save by a single band, was uncovered; and as her slight and exquisite form moved along the velvet sod, so beautiful a shape, and a face so rare in its character and delicate in its expression, were in harmony with the sweet superstition of the spot, and seemed almost to restore to the deserted cave and the mourning stream their living Egeria.

Godolphin stood transfixed to the earth; and Lucilla, who was walking in the direction of the grotto, did not perceive, till she was almost immediately before him. She gave a faint scream as she lifted her eyes; and the first and most natural sentiment of the woman breaking forth involuntarily, she attempted to falter out her disavowal of all expectation of meeting him there.

"Indeed, indeed, I did not know — that is — I — I — " she could achieve no more.

"Is this a favourite spot with you?" said he, with the vague embarrassment of one at a loss for words.

"Yes," said Lucilla, faintly.

And so, in truth, it was: for its vicinity to her home, the beauty of the little valley, and the interest attached to it — an interest not the less to her in that she was but imperfectly acquainted with the true legend of the Nymph and her royal lover — had made it, even from her childhood, a chosen and beloved retreat, especially in that dangerous summer time, which drives the visitor from the spot, and leaves the scene, in great measure, to the solitude which befits it. Associated as the place was with the recollections of her earlier griefs, it was thither that her first instinct made her fly from the rude contact and displeasing companionship of her relations, to give vent to the various and conflicting passions which the late scene with Godolphin had called forth.

They now stood for a few moments silent and embarrassed, till Godolphin, resolved to end a scene which he began to feel was dangerous, said in a hurried tone,—

"Farewell, my sweet pupil! — farewell! May God bless you!" He extended his hand; Lucilla seized it, as if by impulse, and conveying it suddenly to her lips, bathed it with tears.

"I feel," said this wild and unregulated girl, "I feel, from your manner, that I ought to be grateful to you; yet I scarcely know why: you confess you cannot love me, that my affection distresses you — you fly — you desert me. Ah, if you felt one particle even of friendship for me, could you do so?"

"Lucilla, what can I say? — I cannot marry you."

"Do I wish it? I ask thee but to let me go with thee wherever thou goest."

"Poor child!" said Godolphin, gazing on her; "art thou not aware that thou askest thine own dishonour?"

Lucilla seemed surprised. "Is it dishonour to love? They do not think so in Italy. It is wrong for a maiden to confess it; but that thou hast forgiven me. And if to follow thee, to sit with thee, to be near thee, bring aught of evil to myself, not thee, let me incur the evil; it can be nothing compared to the agony of thy absence!"

She looked up timidly as she spoke, and saw, with a sort of terror, that his face worked with emotions which seemed to choke his answer. "If," she cried passionately, "if I have said what pains thee, if I have asked what would give dishonour, as thou callest it, or harm, to thyself, forgive me — I knew it not — and leave me. But if it were not of thyself that thou didst speak, believe that thou hast done me but a cruel mercy. Let me go with thee, I implore! I have no friend here: no one loves me. I hate the faces I gaze upon; I loathe the voices I hear. And, were it for nothing else, thou remindest me of him who is gone. Thou art familiar to me; every look of thee breathes of my home, of my household recollections. Take me with thee, beloved stranger! — or leave me to die — I will not survive thy loss!"

"You speak of your father: know you that, were I to grant what you, in your childish innocence, so unthinkingly request, he might curse me from his grave?"

"O God, not so! — mine is the prayer — be mine the guilt, if guilt there be. But is it not unkinder in thee to desert his daughter than to protect her?"

There was a great, a terrible struggle in Godolphin's breast. "What," said he, scarcely knowing what he said,— "what will the world think of you if you fly with a stranger?"

"There is no world to me but thee!"

"What will your uncle, your relations say?"

"I care not; for I shall not hear them."

"No, no; this must not be!" said Godolphin, proudly, and once more conquering himself. "Lucilla, I would give up every other dream or hope in life to feel that I might requite this devotion by passing my life with thee; to feel that I might grant what thou askest without wronging thy innocence; but — but —"

"You love me then! You love me!" cried Lucilla, joyously, and alive to no other interpretation of his words.

Godolphin was transported beyond himself; and clasping

Lucilla in his arms he covered her cheeks, her lips, with impassioned and burning kisses; then suddenly, as if stung by some irresistible impulse, he tore himself away, and fled from the spot.

CHAPTER XXXII.

THE WEAKNESS OF ALL VIRTUE SPRINGING ONLY FROM THE FEELINGS.

It was the evening before Godolphin left Rome. As he was entering his palazzo he descried, in the darkness, and at a little distance, a figure wrapped in a mantle, that reminded him of Lucilla; ere he could certify himself, it was gone.

On entering his rooms, he looked eagerly over the papers and notes on his table; he seemed disappointed with the result, and sat himself down in moody and discontented thought. He had written to Lucilla the day before, a long, a kind, nay, a noble outpouring of his thoughts and feelings. As far as he was able to one so simple in her experience, yet so wild in her fancy, he explained to her the nature of his struggles and his self-sacrifice. He did not disguise from her that, till the moment of her confession, he had never examined the state of his heart towards her; nor that, with that confession, a new and ardent train of sentiment had been kindled within him. He knew enough of women to be aware that the last avowal would be the sweetest consolation both to her vanity and her heart. He assured her of the promises he had received from her relations to grant her the liberty and the indulgence that her early and unrestrained habits required; and, in the most delicate and respectful terms, he inclosed an order for a sum of money sufficient at any time to command the regard of those with whom she lived, or to enable her to hoose, should she so desire (though he advised her not to adopt such a measure, save for the most urgent reasons), another residence.

"Send me in return," he said, as he concluded, "a lock of your hair. I want nothing to remind me of your beauty; but I want some token of the heart of whose affection I am so mournfully proud. I will wear it as a charm against the contamination of that world of which you are so happily ignorant; as a memento of one nature beyond the thought of self; as a surety that, in finding within this base and selfish quarter of earth one soul so warm, so pure as yours, I did not deceive myself, and dream. If we ever meet again, may you have then found some one happier than I am, and in his tenderness have forgotten all of me save one kind remembrance. Beautiful and dear Lucilla, adieu! If I have not given way to the luxury of being beloved by you, it is because your generous self-abandonment has awakened within a heart too selfish to others a real love for yourself."

To this letter Godolphin had, hour after hour, expected a reply. He received none,—not even the lock of hair for which he had pressed. He was disappointed, angry, with Lucilla, dissatisfied with himself. "How bitterly," thought he, "the wise Saville would smile at my folly! I have renounced the bliss of possessing this singular and beautiful being; for what?—a scruple which she cannot even comprehend, and at which, in her friendless and forlorn state, the most starched of her dissolute countrywomen would smile as a ridiculous punctilio. And, in truth, had I fled hence with her, should I not have made her throughout life happier—far happier—than she will be now? Nor would she, in that happiness, have felt, like an English girl, any pang of shame. *Here*, the tie would have never been regarded as a degradation; nor does she, recurring to the simple laws of nature, imagine that any one *could* so regard it. Besides, inexperienced as she is—the creature of impulse—will she not fall a victim to some more artful and less generous lover; to some one who in her innocence will see only forwardness; and who, far from protecting her as I should have done, will regard her but as the plaything of an hour, and cast her forth the moment his passion is sated!—sated! O bitter thought, that the head of another should rest upon that bosom now so wholly mine! After all, I have, in vainly adopting a seeming and sounding virtue, merely renounced my own happiness to leave her to the chances of being permanently rendered unhappy, and abandoned to want, shame, destitution, by another!"

These disagreeable and regretful thoughts were, in turn, but weakly combated by the occasional self-congratulation that belongs to a just or generous act, and were varied by a thousand conjectures — now of anxiety, now of anger — as to the silence of Lucilla. Sometimes he thought — but the thought only glanced partially across him, and was not distinctly acknowledged — that she might seek an interview with him ere he departed; and in this hope he did not retire to rest till the dawn broke over the ruins of the mighty and breathless city. He then flung himself on a sofa without undressing, but could not sleep, save in short and broken intervals.

The next day, he put off his departure till noon, still in the hope of hearing from Lucilla, but in vain. He could not flatter himself with the hope that Lucilla did not know the exact time for his journey,— he had expressly stated it. Sometimes he conceived the notion of seeking her again; but he knew too well the weakness of his generous resolution; and, though infirm of thought, was yet virtuous enough in act not to hazard it to certain defeat. At length in a momentary desperation, and muttering reproaches on Lucilla for her fickleness and inability to appreciate the magnanimity of his conduct, he threw himself into his carriage, and bade adieu to Rome.

As every grove that the traveller passes on that road was guarded once by a nymph, so now it is hallowed by a memory. In vain the air, heavy with death, creeps over the wood, the rivulet, and the shattered tower: the mind will not recur to the risk of its ignoble tenement; it flies back; it is with the Past! A subtle and speechless rapture fills and exalts the spirit. There — far to the West — spreads that purple sea, haunted by a million reminiscences of glory; there the mountains, with their sharp and snowy crests, rise into the bosom of the heavens; on that plain, the pilgrim yet hails the traditional tomb of the Curiatii and those immortal Twins who left to their brother the glory of conquest, and the shame by which it was succeeded; around the Lake of Nemi yet bloom the sacred groves by which Diana raised Hippolytus again into life. Poetry, Fable, History, watch over the land: it is a sepulchre; Death is within and around it; Decay writes defeature upon every stone; but the Past sits by the tomb as a mourning angel; a soul breathes through the desolation; a voice calls amidst the silence. Every age that hath passed away hath left a ghost behind it; and the beautiful land seems like that imagined clime beneath the earth in which man, glorious though it be, may not breathe and live, but which is populous with holy phantoms and illustrious shades.

On, on sped Godolphin. Night broke over him as he traversed the Pontine Marshes. There, the malaria broods over its rankest venom; solitude hath lost the soul that belonged to it; all life, save the deadly fertility of corruption, seems to have rotted away; the spirit falls stricken into gloom; a nightmare weighs upon the breast of Nature; and over the wrecks of Time, Silence sits motionless in the arms of Death.

He arrived at Terracina, and retired to rest. His sleep was filled with fearful dreams; he woke, late at noon, languid and dejected. As his servant, who had lived with him some years, attended him in rising, Godolphin observed on his countenance that expression common to persons of his class when they have something which they wish to communicate, and are watching their opportunity.

"Well, Malden!" said he, "you look important this morning: what has happened?"

"E—hem! Did not you observe, sir, a carriage behind us as we crossed the marshes? Sometimes you might just see it at a distance, in the moonlight."

"How the deuce should I, being within the carriage, see behind me? No; I know nothing of the carriage: what of it?"

"A person arrived in it, sir, a little after you, would not retire to bed, and waits you in your sitting-room."

"A *person!* what person?"

"A lady, sir,—a *young* lady;" said the servant, suppressing a smile.

"Good heavens!" ejaculated Godolphin; "leave me." The valet obeyed.

Godolphin, not for a moment doubting that it was Lucilla who had thus followed him, was struck to the heart by this proof of her resolute and reckless attachment. In any other woman, so bold a measure would, it is true, have revolted his fastidious and somewhat English taste. But in Lucilla, all that might have seemed immodest arose, in reality, from that pure and spotless ignorance which, of all species of modesty, is the most enchanting, the most dangerous to its possessor. The daughter of loneliness and seclusion, estranged wholly from all familiar or female intercourse, rather bewildered than in any way enlightened by the few books of poetry, or the lighter letters, she had by accident read,—the sense of impropriety was in her so vague a sentiment that every impulse of her wild and impassioned character effaced and swept it away. Ignorant of what is due to the reserve of the sex, and even of the opinions of the world—lax as the Italian world is on matters of love—she only saw occasion to glory in her tenderness, her devotion, to one so elevated in her fancy as the English stranger. Nor did there—however unconsciously to herself—mingle a single more derogatory or less pure emotion with her fanatical worship.

For my own part, I think that few men understand the real nature of a girl's love. Arising so vividly as it does from the imagination, nothing that the mind of the libertine would impute to it ever (or at least in most rare instances) sullies its weakness or debases its folly. I do not say the love is better for being thus solely the creature of imagination: I say only so it is in ninety-nine out of a hundred instances of girlish infatuation. In later life, it is different; in the experienced woman, forwardness is always depravity.

With trembling steps and palpitating heart, Godolphin sought the apartment in which he expected to find Lucilla. There, in one corner of the room, her face covered with her mantle, he beheld her. He hastened to that spot; he threw himself on his knees before her; with a timid hand he removed the covering from her face; and through tears and paleness and agitation, his heart was touched to the quick by its soft and loving expression.

"Wilt thou forgive me?" she faltered; "it was thine own letter that brought me hither. Now leave me, if thou canst!"

"Never, never!" cried Godolphin, clasping her to his heart. "It is fated, and I resist no more. Love, tend, cherish thee, I will to my last hour. I will be all to thee that human ties can afford,— father, brother, lover — all but —" He paused; "all but husband," whispered his conscience, but he silenced its voice.

"I may go with thee!" said Lucilla, in wild ecstasy; that was *her* only thought.

As, when the notion of escape occurs to the insane, their insanity appears to cease; courage, prudence, caution, invention (faculties which they knew not in sounder health), flash upon and support them as by an inspiration, so a new genius had seemed breathed into Lucilla by the idea of rejoining Godolphin. She imagined — not without justice — that, could she throw in the way of her return home an obstacle of that worldly nature which he seemed to dread she should encounter, his chief reason for resisting her attachment would be removed. Encouraged by this thought, and more than ever transported by her love since he had expressed a congenial sentiment; excited into emulation by the generous tone of his letter, and softened into yet deeper weakness by its tenderness, she had resolved upon the bold step she adopted. A *vetturino* lived near the gate of St. Sebastian. She had sought him; and at sight of the money which Godolphin had sent her, the *vetturino* willingly agreed to transport her to whatever point on the road to Naples she might desire,— nay, even to keep pace with the more rapid method of travelling which Godolphin pursued. Early on the morning of his departure, she had sought her station within sight of Godolphin's palazzo; and ten minutes after his departure the *vetturino* bore her, delighted but trembling, on the same road.

The Italians are ordinarily good-natured, especially when they are paid for it; and courteous to females, especially if they have any suspicion of the influence of the *belle passion.* The *vetturino's* foresight had supplied the deficiencies of her inexperience: he had reminded her of the necessity of procuring her passport; and he undertook that all other difficulties should solely devolve on him. And thus Lucilla was now under the same roof with one for whom, indeed, she was unaware of the sacrifice she made, but whom, despite of all that clouded and separated their after-lot, she loved to the last, with a love as reckless and strong as then,—a love passing the love of woman, and defying the common ordinances of time.

. . . .

On the blue waters that break with a deep and far voice along the rocks of that delicious shore, above which the mountain that rises behind Terracina scatters to the air the odours of the citron and the orange, on that sounding and immemorial sea the stars, like the hopes of a brighter world upon the darkness and unrest of life, shone down with a solemn but tender light. On that shore stood Lucilla and he—the wandering stranger—in whom she had hoarded the peace and the hopes of earth. Hers was the first and purple flush of the love which has attained its object; that sweet and quiet fulness of content, that heavenly, all-subduing and subdued delight, with which the heart slumbers in the excess of its own rapture. Care, the forethought of change, even the shadowy and vague mournfulness of passion, are felt not in those voluptuous but tranquil moments. Like the waters that rolled, deep and eloquent, before her, every feeling within was but the mirror of an all-gentle and cloudless heaven. Her head half-declined upon the breast of her young lover, she caught the beating of his heart, and in it heard all the sounds of what was now become to her the world.

And still and solitary deepened around them the mystic and lovely night. How divine was that sense and consciousness of solitude! how, as it thrilled within them, they clung closer to each other! Theirs as yet was that blissful and unsated time when the touch of their hands, clasped together, was in itself a happiness of emotion too deep for words. And ever, as his eyes sought hers, the tears which the sensitiveness of her frame, in the very luxury of her overflowing heart, called forth glittered in the tranquil stars a moment and were kissed away. "Do not look up to heaven, my love," whispered Godolphin, "lest thou shouldst think of any world but this!"

Poor Lucilla! will any one who idly glances over this page sympathize one moment with the springs of thy brief joys and thy bitter sorrow? The page on which, in stamping a record of thee, I would fain retain thy memory from oblivion, that page is an emblem of thyself,—a short existence, confounded with the herd to which it has no resemblance, and then, amidst the rush and tumult of the world, forgotten and cast away forever!

CHAPTER XXXIII.

RETURN TO LADY ERPINGHAM. — LADY ERPINGHAM FALLS ILL. — LORD ERPINGHAM RESOLVES TO GO ABROAD. — PLUTARCH UPON MUSICAL INSTRUMENTS. — PARTY AT ERPINGHAM HOUSE. — SAVILLE ON SOCIETY AND THE TASTE FOR THE LITTLE. — DAVID MANDEVILLE. — WOMEN, THEIR INFLUENCE AND EDUCATION. — THE NECESSITY OF AN OBJECT. — RELIGION.

As after a long dream, we rise to the occupations of life, even so, with an awakening and more active feeling, I return from characters removed from the ordinary world — like Volktman [1] and his daughter — to the brilliant heroine of my narrative.

[1] After all, an astrologer — nay, a cabalist — is not so monstrous a prodigy in the nineteenth century! In the year 1801, Lackington published a quarto, entitled "Magus: a Complete System of Occult Philosophy; treating of Alchemy, the Cabalistic Art, Natural and Celestial Magic," etc. — and a very

There is a certain tone about London society which enfeebles the mind without exciting it; and this state of temperament, more than all others, engenders satiety. In classes that border upon the highest this effect is less evident; for in them there is some object to contend for. Fashion gives them an inducement. They struggle to emulate the *ton* of their superiors. It is an ambition of trifles, it is true; but it is still ambition. It frets, it irritates, but it keeps them alive. The great are the true victims of *ennui*. The more firmly seated their rank, the more established their position, the more their life stagnates into insipidity. Constance was at the height of her wishes. No one was so courted, so adored. One after one, she had humbled and subdued all those who, before her marriage, had trampled on her pride, or who after it had resisted her pretensions: a look from her had become a triumph, and a smile conferred a rank on its receiver. But this empire palled upon her: of too large a mind to be satisfied with petty pleasures and unreal distinctions, she still felt the SOMETHING of life was wanting. She was not blessed or cursed (as it may be) with children, and she had no companion in her husband. There might be times in which she regretted her choice, dazzling as it had proved; but she complained not of sorrow, but monotony.

Political intrigue could not fill up the vacuum of which Constance daily complained; and of private intrigue the then purity of her nature was incapable. When people have really nothing to do, they generally fall ill upon it; and at length the rich colour grew faint upon Lady Erpingham's cheek, her form wasted; the physicians hinted at consumption, and recommended a warmer clime. Lord Erpingham seized at the proposition: he was fond of Italy; he was bored with England.

Very stupid people often become very musical: it is a sort of pretension to intellect that suits their capacities. Plutarch says somewhere that the best musical instruments are made

impudent publication it is too. That Raphael should put forth astrological manuels is not a proof of his belief in the science he professes; but that it should *answer* to Raphael to put them forth, shows a tendency to belief in his purchasers.

from the jaw-bones of asses. Plutarch never made a more sensible observation. Lord Erpingham had of late taken greatly to operas: he talked of writing one himself; and not being a performer, he consoled himself by becoming a patron. Italy, therefore, presented to him manifold captivations,— he thought of fiddling, but he talked only of his wife's health. Amidst the regrets of the London world, they made their arrangements, and prepared to set out at the end of the season for the land of Paganini and Julius Cæsar.

Two nights before their departure, Lady Erpingham gave a farewell party to her more intimate acquaintance. Saville, who always contrived to be well with every one who was worth the trouble it cost him, was of course among the guests. Years had somewhat scathed him since he last appeared on our stage. Women had ceased to possess much attraction for his jaded eyes: gaming and speculation had gradually spread over the tastes once directed to other pursuits. His vivacity had deserted him in great measure, as years and infirmity began to stagnate and knot up the current of his veins; but conversation still possessed for and derived from him its wonted attraction. The sparkling *jeu d'esprit* had only sobered down into the quiet sarcasm; and if his wit rippled less freshly to the breeze of the present moment, it was coloured more richly by the glittering sands which rolled down from the experience that overshadowed the current. For the wisdom of the worldly is like the mountains that, sterile without, conceal within them unprofitable ore: only the filings and particles escape to the daylight and sparkle in the wave; the rest wastes idly within. The Pactolus takes but the sand-drifts from the hoards lost to use in the Tmolus.

"And how," said Saville, seating himself by Lady Erpingham, "how shall we bear London when you are gone? When society, the everlasting draught, had begun to pall upon us, you threw your pearl into the cup; and now we are grown so luxurious, that we shall never bear the wine without the pearl."

"But the pearl gave no taste to the wine: it only dissolved itself,— idly, and in vain."

"Ah, my dear Lady Erpingham, the dullest of us, having once seen the pearl, could at least imagine that we were able to appreciate the subtleties of its influence. Where, in this little world of tedious realities, can we find anything even to imagine about, when you abandon us?"

"Nay! do you conceive that I am so ignorant of the framework of society as to suppose that I shall not be easily replaced? King succeeds king, without reference to the merits of either; so, in London, idol follows idol, though one be of jewels and the other of brass. Perhaps, when I return, I shall find you kneeling to the dull Lady A——, or worshipping the hideous Lady Z——."

> "'Le temps assez souvent a rendu légitime
> Ce qui sembloit d'abord ne se pouvoir sans crime;'"

answered Saville, with a mock heroic air. "The fact is, that we are an indolent people; the person who succeeds the most with us has but to push the most. You know how Mrs. ——, in spite of her red arms, her red gown, her city pronunciation, and her city connections, managed — by dint of perseverance alone — to become a dispenser of consequence to the very countesses whom she at first could scarcely coax into a courtesy. The person who can stand ridicule and rudeness has only to *desire* to become the fashion — she or he must be so sooner or later."

"Of the immutability of one thing among all the changes I may witness on my return, at least I am certain no one still will dare to think for himself. The great want of each individual is, the want of an opinion! For instance, who judges of a picture from his own knowledge of painting? Who does not wait to hear what Mr. ——, or Lord —— (one of the six or seven privileged connoisseurs), says of it? Nay, not only the fate of a single picture, but of a whole school of painting, depends upon the caprice of some one of the self-elected dictators. The King, or the Duke of ——, has but to love the Dutch school and ridicule the Italian, and behold a Raphael will not sell, and a Teniers rises into infinite value! Dutch representations of candlesticks and boors are sought after with the most rapturous delight; the most disagreeable objects of nature become the most worshipped treasures of art; and we emulate each other in testifying our exaltation of taste by contending for the pictured vulgarities by which taste itself is the most essentially degraded. In fact, too, the meaner the object, the more certain it is with us of becoming the rage. In the theatre, we run after the farce; in painting, we worship the Dutch school; in — "

"Literature?" said Saville.

"No! — our literature still breathes of something noble; but why? Because books do not always depend upon a clique. A book, in order to succeed, does not require the opinion of Mr. Saville or Lady Erpingham so much as a picture or a ballet."

"I am not sure of that," answered Saville, as he withdrew presently afterwards to a card-table, to share in the premeditated plunder of a young banker, who was proud of the honour of being ruined by persons of rank.

In another part of the rooms Constance found a certain old philosopher, whom I will call David Mandeville. There was something about this man that always charmed those who had sense enough to be discontented with the ordinary inhabitants of the Microcosm,— Society. The expression of his countenance was different from that of others; there was a breathing goodness in his face, an expansion of mind on his forehead. You perceived at once that he did not live among triflers, nor agitate himself with trifles. Serenity beamed from his look — but it was the serenity of thought. Constance sat down by him.

"Are you not sorry," said Mandeville, "to leave England, — you, who have made yourself the centre of a circle which, for the varieties of its fascination, has never perhaps been equalled in this country? Wealth, rank, even wit, others might assemble round them; but none ever before convened into one splendid galaxy all who were eminent in art, famous in letters, wise in politics, and even (for who but you were ever above rivalship?) attractive in beauty. I should have thought it easier for us to fly from the Armida, than for the

Armida to renounce the scene of her enchantment,—the scene in which De Staël bowed to the charms of her conversation, and Byron celebrated those of her person."

We may conceive the spell Constance had cast around her, when even philosophy (and Mandeville of all philosophers) had learned to flatter; but his flattery was sincerity.

"Alas!" said Constance, sighing, "even if your compliment were altogether true, you have mentioned nothing that should cause me regret. Vanity is one source of happiness, but it does not suffice to recompense us for the absence of all others. In leaving England, I leave the scene of everlasting weariness. I am the victim of a feeling of sameness, and I look with hope to the prospect of change."

"Poor thing!" said the old philosopher, gazing mournfully on a creature who, so resplendent with advantages, yet felt the crumpled rose-leaf more than the luxury of the couch. "Wherever you go the same polished society will present to you the same monotony. All courts are alike: men have change in action; but to women of your rank all scenes are alike. You must not look without for an object,—you must create one within. To be happy we must render ourselves independent of others."

"Like all philosophers, you advise the impossible," said Constance.

"How so? Have not the generality of your sex their peculiar object? One has the welfare of her children; another the interest of her husband; a third makes a passion of economy; a fourth of extravagance; a fifth of fashion; a sixth of solitude. Your friend yonder is always employed in nursing her own health: hypochondria supplies her with an object; she is really happy because she fancies herself ill. Every one you name has an object in life that drives away *ennui*, save yourself."

"I have one too," said Constance, smiling, "but it does not fill up all the spaces of time. The intervals between the acts are longer than the acts themselves."

"Is your object religion?" asked Mandeville, simply.

Constance was startled: the question was novel. "I fear

not," said she, after a moment's hesitation, and with a downcast face.

"As I thought," returned Mandeville. "Now listen. The reason why you feel weariness more than those around you, is solely because your mind is more expansive. Small minds easily find objects: trifles amuse them; but a high soul covets things beyond its daily reach: trifles occupy its aim mechanically; the thought still wanders restless. This is the case with you. Your intellect preys upon itself. You would have been happier if your rank had been less;" Constance winced —she thought of Godolphin; "for then you would have been ambitious, and aspired to the very rank that now palls upon you." Mandeville continued,—

"You women are at once debarred from public life, and yet influence it. You are the prisoners, and yet the despots of society. Have you talents? it is criminal to indulge them in public; and thus, as talent cannot be stifled, it is misdirected in private; you seek ascendency over your own limited circle; and what should have been genius degenerates into cunning. Brought up from your cradles to dissembling your most beautiful emotions, your finest principles are always tinctured with artifice. As your talents, being stripped of their wings, are driven to creep along the earth, and imbibe its mire and clay, so are your affections perpetually checked and tortured into conventional paths, and a spontaneous feeling is punished as a deliberate crime. You are untaught the broad and sound principles of life: all that you know of morals are its decencies and forms. Thus you are incapable of estimating the public virtues and the public deficiencies of a brother or a son; and one reason why *we* have no Brutus, is because *you* have no Portia. Turkey has its seraglio for the person; but Custom in Europe has also a seraglio for the mind."

Constance smiled at the philosopher's passion; but she was a woman, and she was moved by it.

"Perhaps," said she, "in the progress of events, the state of the women may be improved as well as that of the men."

"Doubtless, at some future stage of the world. And believe me, Lady Erpingham, politician and schemer as you are, that no legislative reform *alone* will improve mankind: it is the social state which requires reformation."

"But you asked me some minutes since," said Constance, after a pause, "if the object of my pursuit was religion. I disappointed but not surprised you by my answer."

"Yes: you grieved me, because, in your case, religion could alone fill the dreary vacuum of your time. For, with your enlarged and cultivated mind, you would not view the grandest of earthly questions in a narrow and sectarian light. You would not think religion consisted in a sanctified demeanour, in an ostentatious almsgiving, in a harsh judgment of all without the pale of your opinions. You would behold in it a benign and harmonious system of morality, which takes from ceremony enough not to render it tedious but impressive. The school of the Bayles and Voltaires is annihilated. Men begin now to feel that to philosophize is not to sneer. In Doubt we are stopped short at every outlet beyond the Sensual. In Belief lies the secret of all our valuable exertion. Two sentiments are enough to preserve even the idlest temper from stagnation,— a desire and a *hope*. What then can we say of the desire to be useful, and the hope to be immortal?"

This was language Constance had not often heard before, nor was it frequent on the lips of him who now uttered it. But an interest in the fate and happiness of one in whom he saw so much to admire, had made Mandeville anxious that she should entertain some principle which he could also esteem. And there was a fervour, a sincerity, in his voice and manner, that thrilled to the very heart of Lady Erpingham. She pressed his hand in silence. She thought afterwards over his words; but worldly life is not easily accessible to any lasting impressions save those of vanity and love. Religion has two sources,— the habit of early years, or the process of after thought. But to Constance had not been fated the advantage of the first; and how can deep thought of another world be a favourite employment with the scheming woman of this?

This is the only time that Mandeville appears in this

work,— a type of the rarity of the intervention of religious wisdom on the scenes of real life.

"By the way," said Saville, as, in departing, he encountered Constance by the door, and made his final adieus,— "by the way, you will perhaps meet, somewhere in Italy, my old young friend, Percy Godolphin. He has not been pleased to prate of his whereabout to me; but I hear that he has been seen lately at Naples."

Constance coloured, and her heart beat violently; but she answered indifferently, and turned away.

The next morning they set off for Italy. But within one week from that day, what a change awaited Constance!

CHAPTER XXXIV.

AMBITION VINDICATED. — THE HOME OF GODOLPHIN AND LUCILLA. — LUCILLA'S MIND. — THE EFFECT OF HAPPY LOVE ON FEMALE TALENT. — THE EVE OF FAREWELL. — LUCILLA ALONE. — TEST OF A WOMAN'S AFFECTION.

O MUCH-ABUSED and highly-slandered passion! — passion rather of the soul than the heart; hateful to the pseudo-moralist, but viewed with favouring though not undiscriminating eyes by the true philosopher,— bright-winged and august AMBITION! It is well for fools to revile thee, because thou art liable, like other utilities, to abuse! The wind uproots the oak,— but for every oak it uproots it scatters a thousand acorns. Ixion embraced the cloud, but from the embrace sprang a hero. Thou, too, hast thy fits of violence and storm; but without thee, life would stagnate. Thou, too, embracest thy clouds; but even thy clouds have the demigods for their offspring!

It was the great and prevailing misfortune of Godolphin's life that he had early taught himself to be superior to exertion. His talents, therefore, only preyed on himself; and instead of the vigorous and daring actor of the world, he was alternately the indolent sensualist or the solitary dreamer. He did not view the stir of the great Babel as a man with a wholesome mind should do; and thus from his infirmities we draw a moral. The moral is not the worse in that it opposes the trite moralities of those who would take from action its motive: the men of genius, who are not also men of ambition, are either humourists, or visionaries, or hypochondriacs.

By the side of one of the Italian lakes, Godolphin and Lucilla fixed their abode; and here the young idealist for some time imagined himself happy. Never until now so fond of Nature as of cities, he gave himself up to the enchantment of the Eden around him. He spent the long sunny hours of noon on the smooth lake, or among the sheltering trees by which it was encircled. The scenes he had witnessed in the world became to him the food of quiet meditation, and for the first time in his life, thought did not weary him with its sameness.

When his steps turned homeward, the anxious form of Lucilla waited for him; her eye brightened at his approach, her spirit escaped restraint and bounded into joy; and Godolphin, touched by her delight, became eager to witness it,— he felt the magnet of a Home. Yet as the first enthusiasm of passion died away, he could not but be sensible that Lucilla was scarcely a companion. Her fancy was indeed lively, and her capacity acute; but experience had set a confined limit to her ideas. She had nothing save love, and a fitful temperament, upon which she could draw for conversation. Those whose education debars them from deriving instruction from things have in general the power to extract amusement from persons,— they can talk of the ridiculous Mrs. So-and-so, or the absurd Mr. Blank. But our lovers saw no society, and thus their commune was thrown entirely on their internal resources.

There was always that in the peculiar mind of Godolphin which was inclined towards ideas too refined and subtle even for persons of cultivated intellect. If Constance could scarcely comprehend the tone of his character, we may believe that to

Lucilla he was wholly a mystery. This, perhaps, enhanced *her* love, but the consciousness of it disappointed *his*. He felt that what he considered the noblest faculties he possessed were unappreciated. He was sometimes angry with Lucilla that she loved only those qualities in his character which he shared with the rest of mankind. His speculative and *Hamlet*-like temper — let us here take Goethe's view of Hamlet, and combine a certain weakness with the finer traits of the royal dreamer — perpetually deserted the solid world, and flew to aërial creations. He could not appreciate the present. Had Godolphin loved Lucilla as he once thought that he should love her, the beauties of her character would have blinded him to its defects; but its passion had been too sudden to be thoroughly grounded. It had arisen from the knowledge of *her* affection, not grown step by step from the natural bias of his own. Between the interval of liking and possession, love (to be durable) should pass through many stages. The doubt, the fear, the first pressure of the hand, the first kiss, each should be an epoch for remembrance to cling to. In moments of after coolness or anger, the mind should fly from the sated present to the million tender and freshening associations of the past. With these associations the affection renews its youth. How vast a store of melting reflections, how countless an accumulation of the spells that preserve constancy, does that love forfeit, in which the memory only commences with possession!

And the more delicate and thoughtful our nature, the more powerful are these associations. Do they not constitute the immense difference between the love and the intrigue? All things that savour of youth make our most exquisite sensations, whether to experience, or recall: thus, in the seasons of the year, we prize the spring; and in the effusions of the heart, the courtship.

Beautiful, too, and tender — wild and fresh in her tenderness — as Lucilla was, there was that in her character, in addition to her want of education, which did not wholly accord with Godolphin's preconception of the being his fancy had conjured up. His calm and profound nature desired one in whom he could not only confide, but, as it were, repose. Thus one great charm that had attracted him to Constance was the evenness and smoothness of her temper. But the self-formed mind of Lucilla was ever in a bright, and to him a wearying, agitation; tears and smiles perpetually chased each other. Not comprehending his *character*, but thinking only and wholly of *him*, she distracted herself with conjectures and suspicions, which she was too ingenuous and too impassioned to conceal. After watching him for hours, she would weep that he did not turn from his books or his revery to search also for her, with eyes equally yearning and tender as her own. The fear in absence, the absorbed devotion when present, that absolutely made her existence, she was wretched because he did not reciprocate with the same intensity of soul. She could conceive nothing of love but that which she felt herself; and she saw, daily and hourly, that in that love he did not sympathize, and therefore she embittered her life by thinking that he did not return her affection.

"You wrong us both," said he, in answer to her tearful accusations; "but our sex love differently from yours."

"Ah," she replied, "I feel that love has no varieties: there is but one love, but there may be many counterfeits."

Godolphin smiled to think how the untutored daughter of nature had unconsciously uttered the sparkling aphorism of the most artificial of maxim-makers.[1] Lucilla saw the smile, and her tears flowed instantly.

"Thou mockest me."

"Thou art a little fool," said Godolphin, kindly, and he kissed away the storm.

And this was ever an easy matter. There was nothing unfeminine or sullen in Lucilla's irregulated moods; a kind word, a kind caress, allayed them in an instant, and turned the transient sorrow into sparkling delight. But they who know how irksome is the perpetual trouble of conciliation to a man meditative and indolent like Godolphin, will appreciate the pain that even her tenderness occasioned him.

[1] Rochefoucauld.

There is one thing very noticeable in women when they have once obtained the object of their life,—the sudden check that is given to the impulses of their genius. Content to have found the realization of their chief hope, they do not look beyond to other but lesser objects, as they had been wont to do before. Hence we see so many who, before marriage, strike us with admiration from the vividness of their talents, and after marriage settle down into the mere machine. We wonder that we ever feared, while we praised, the brilliancy of an intellect that seems now never to wander from the limits of house and hearth. So with poor Lucilla; her restless mind and ardent genius had once seized on every object within their reach: she had taught herself music; she had learned the colourings and lines of art; not a book came in her way, but she would have sought to extract from it a new idea. But she was now with Godolphin, and all other occupations for thought were gone; she had nothing beyond his love to wish for, nothing beyond his character to learn. He was the circle of hope, and her heart its centre; all lines were equal to that heart, so that they touched him. It is clear that this devotion prevented her, however, from fitting herself to be his companion; she did not seek to accomplish herself, but to study him: thus in her extreme love was another reason why that love was not adequately returned.

But Godolphin felt all the responsibility that he had taken on himself. He felt how utterly the happiness of this poor and solitary child — for a child she was in character, and almost in years — depended upon him. He roused himself, therefore, from his ordinary selfishness, and rarely, if ever, gave way to the irritation which she unknowingly but constantly kept alive. The balmy and delicious climate, the liquid serenity of the air, the majestic repose with which Nature invested the loveliness that surrounded their home, contributed to soften and calm his mind; and he had persuaded Lucilla to look without despair upon his occasional although short absences. Sometimes he passed two or three weeks at Rome, sometimes at Naples or Florence. He knew so well how necessary such intervals of absence are to the preservation of love, to the defeat of that satiety which creeps over us with custom, that he had resolutely enforced it as a necessity, although always under the excuse of business,— a plea that Lucilla could understand and not resist; for the word "business" seemed to her like destiny,— a call that, however odious, we cannot disobey. At first, indeed, she was disconsolate at the absence only of two days; but when she saw how eagerly her lover returned to her, with what a fresh charm he listened to her voice or her song, she began to confess that even in the evil might be good.

By degrees he accustomed her to longer intervals; and Lucilla relieved the dreariness of the time by the thousand little plans and surprises with which women delight in receiving the beloved wanderer after absence. His departure was a signal for a change in the house, the gardens, the arbour; and when she was tired with these occupations, she was not forbidden at least to write to him and receive his letters. Daily intoxication! and men's words are so much kinder when written than they are when uttered! Fortunately for Lucilla, her early habits, and her strange qualities of mind, rendered her independent of companionship, and fond of solitude.

Often Godolphin, who could not conceive how persons without education could entertain themselves, taking pity on her loneliness and seclusion, would say,—

"But how, Lucilla, have you passed this long day that I have spent away from you,— among the woods or on the lake?"

And Lucilla, delighted to recount to him the history of her hours, would go over each incident, and body forth every thought that had occurred to her, with a grave and serious minuteness that evinced her capabilities of dispensing with the world.

In this manner they passed somewhat more than two years; and, in spite of the human alloy, it was perhaps the happiest period of Godolphin's life, and the one that the least disappointed his too-exacting imagination. Lucilla had had one daughter, but she died a few weeks after birth. She wept over the perished flower, but was not inconsolable; for, before its loss, she had taught herself to think no affliction could be irremediable that did not happen to Godolphin. Perhaps Godolphin was the more grieved of the two; men of his character are fond of the occupation of watching the growth of minds; they put in practice their chimeras of education. Happy child, to have escaped an experiment!

It was the eve before one of Godolphin's periodical excursions, and it was Rome that he proposed to visit; Godolphin had lingered about the lake until the sun had set, and Lucilla, grown impatient, went forth to seek him. The day had been sultry, and now a sombre and breathless calm hung over the deepening eve. The pines, those gloomy children of the forest, which shed something of melancholy and somewhat of sternness over the brighter features of an Italian landscape, drooped heavily in the breezeless air. As she came on the border of the lake, its waves lay dark and voiceless; only, at intervals, the surf, fretting along the pebbles, made a low and dreary sound, or from the trees some lingering songster sent forth a shrill and momentary note, and then again all became —

> "An atmosphere without a breath,
> A silence sleeping there."

There was a spot where the trees, receding in a ring, left some bare and huge fragments of stone uncovered by verdure. It was the only spot around that rich and luxuriant scene that was not in harmony with the soft spirit of the place: might I indulge a fanciful comparison, I should say that it was like one desolate and gray remembrance in the midst of a career of pleasure. On this spot Godolphin now stood alone, looking along the still and purple waters that lay before him. Lucilla, with a light step, climbed the rugged stones, and touching his shoulder, reproached him with a tender playfulness for his truancy.

"Lucilla," said he, when peace was restored, "what impressions does this dreary and prophetic pause of nature before the upgathering of the storm create in you? Does it inspire you with melancholy, or thought, or fear?"

"I see my star," answered Lucilla, pointing to a far and solitary orb, which hung islanded in a sea of cloud, that swept slowly and blackly onward,—"I see my star, and I think more of that little light than of the darkness around it."

"But it will presently be buried among the clouds," said Godolphin, smiling at that superstition which Lucilla had borrowed from her father.

"But the clouds pass away, and the star endures."

"You are of a sanguine nature, my Lucilla." Lucilla sighed.

"Why that sigh, dearest?"

"Because I am thinking how little even those who love us most know of us! I never tell my disquiet and sorrow. There are times when thou wouldst not think me too warmly addicted to hope!"

"And what, poor idler, have you to fear?"

"Hast thou never felt it possible that thou couldst love me less?"

"Never!"

Lucilla raised her large searching eyes, and gazed eagerly on his face; but in its calm features and placid brow she saw no ground for augury, whether propitious or evil. She turned away.

"I cannot think, Lucilla," said Godolphin, "that you ever direct those thoughts of yours, wandering though they be, to the future. Do they ever extend to the space of some ten or twenty years?"

"No. But one year may contain the whole history of my future."

As she spoke, the clouds gathered round the solitary star to which Lucilla had pointed. The storm was at hand; they felt its approach, and turned homeward.

There is something more than ordinarily fearful in the tempests that visit those soft and garden climes. The unfrequency of such violent changes in the mood of Nature serves to appall us as with an omen; it is like a sudden affliction in the midst of happiness, or a wound from the hand of one we love. For the stroke for which we are not prepared we have rather despondency than resistance.

As they reached their home, the heavy raindrops began to fall. They stood for some minutes at the casement, watching the coruscations of the lightning as it played over the black and heavy waters of the lake. Lucilla, whom the influences of Nature always strangely and mysteriously affected, clung pale and almost trembling to Godolphin; but even in her fear there was delight in being so near to him in whose love alone she thought there was protection. Oh, what luxury so dear to a woman as is the sense of dependence! Poor Lucilla! it was the last evening she ever spent with one whom she worshipped so entirely.

Godolphin remained up longer than Lucilla. When he joined her in her room, the storm had ceased; and he found her standing by the open window, and gazing on the skies that were now bright and serene. Far in the deep stillness of midnight crept the waters of the lake, hushed once more into silence, and reflecting the solemn and unfathomable stars. That chain of hills, which but to name awakens countless memories of romance, stretched behind, their blue and dim summits melting into the skies; and over one, higher than the rest, paused the new-risen moon, silvering the first beneath, and farther down, breaking with one long and yet mellower track of light over the waters of the lake.

As Godolphin approached he did so, unconsciously, with a hushed and noiseless step. There is something in the quiet of nature like worship; it is as if, from the breathless heart of Things, went up a prayer or a homage to the Arch-Creator. One feels subdued by a stillness so utter and so august; it extends itself to our own sensations, and deepens into an awe.

Both, then, looked on in silence, indulging it may be different thoughts. At length, Lucilla said softly, "Tell me, hast thou really no faith in my father's creed? Are the stars quite dumb? Is there no truth in their movements, no prophecy in their lustre?"

"My Lucilla, reason and experience tell us that the astrologers nurse a dream that has no reality."

"Reason! well! — Experience! — why, did not *thy* father's mortal illness hurry thee from home at the very time in which *mine* foretold thy departure and its cause? I was then but a child; yet I shall never forget the paleness of thy cheek when my father uttered his prediction."

"I, too, was almost a child then, Lucilla."

"But that prediction was verified?"

"It was so; but how many did Volktman utter that were never verified? In true science there are no chances, no uncertainties."

"And my father," said Lucilla, unheeding the answer, "always foretold that thy lot and mine were to be entwined."

"And the prophecy, perhaps, disposed you to the fact. You might never have loved me, Lucilla, if your thoughts had not been driven to dwell upon me by the prediction."

"Nay; I thought of thee before I heard the prophecy."

"But your father foretold *me*, dearest, cross and disappointment in my love,—was he not wrong; am I not blest with you?"

Lucilla threw herself into her lover's arms, and, as she kissed him, murmured, "Ah, if I *could* make thee happy!"

The next day Godolphin departed for Rome. Lucilla was more dejected at his departure than she had been even in his earliest absence. The winter was now slowly approaching, and the weather was cold and dreary. That year it was unusually rainy and tempestuous, and as the wild gusts howled around her solitary home — how solitary now!— or she heard the big drops hurrying down on the agitated lake, she shuddered at her own despondent thoughts, and dreaded the gloom and loneliness of the lengthened night. For the first time since she had lived with Godolphin she turned, but disconsolately, to the company of books.

Works of all sorts filled their home, but the spell that once spoke to her from the page was broken. If the book was not of love, it possessed no interest; if of love, she thought the description both tame and false. No one ever painted love so as fully to satisfy another: to some it is too florid, to some too commonplace; the god, like other gods, has no likeness on earth, and every wave on which the star of passion beams breaks the lustre into different refractions of light.

As one day she was turning listlessly over some books that had been put aside by Godolphin in a closet, and hoping to find one that contained, as sometimes happened, his comments or at least his marks, she was somewhat startled to find among them several volumes which she remembered to have belonged to her father. Godolphin had bought them after Volktman's death, and put them by as relics of his singular friend, and as samples of the laborious and self-willed aberration of the human intellect.

Few among these works could Lucilla comprehend, for they were chiefly in other tongues than the only two with which she was acquainted. But some, among which were manuscripts by her father, beautifully written, and curiously ornamented (some of the chief works on the vainer sciences are only to be found in manuscript), she could contrive to decipher by a little assistance from her memory, in recalling the signs and hieroglyphics which her father had often explained to her, and, indeed, caused her to copy out for him in his calculations. Always possessing an untaxed and unquestioned belief in the astral powers, she now took some interest in reading of their mysteries. Her father, secretly, perhaps, hoping to bequeath his name to the gratitude of some future Hermes, had in his manuscripts reduced into a system many scattered theories of others, and many dogmas of his own. Over these, for they were simpler and easier than the crabbed and mystical speculations in the printed books, she more especially pored; and she was not sorry at finding fresh reasons for her untutored adoration of the stars and apparitions of the heavens.

Still, however, these bewildering researches made but a small part, comparatively speaking, of the occupation of her thoughts. To write to and hear from Godolphin had become to her more necessary than ever, and her letters were fuller and more minute in their details of love than even in the period of their first passion. Wouldst thou know if the woman thou lovest still loves thee, trust not her spoken words, her present smiles; examine her letters in absence, see if she dwells, as she once did, upon *trifles* — but trifles relating to *thee.* The things which the indifferent forget are among the most treasured meditations of love.

But Lucilla was not satisfied with the letters — frequent as they were — that she received in answer; they were kind, affectionate, but the something was wanting. "The best part of beauty is that which no picture can express." That which the heart most asks is that which no words can convey. Honesty, patriotism, religion,— these have had their hypocrites for life; but passion permits only momentary dissemblers.

CHAPTER XXXV.

GODOLPHIN AT ROME. — THE CURE FOR A MORBID IDEALISM. — HIS EMBARRASSMENT IN REGARD TO LUCILLA. — THE RENCONTRE WITH AN OLD FRIEND. — THE COLOSSEUM. — A SURPRISE.

Godolphin arrived at Rome: it was thronged with English. Among them were some whom he remembered with esteem in England. He had grown a little weary of his long solitude, and he entered with eagerness into the society of those who courted him. He was still an object of great interest to the idle; and as men grow older, they become less able to dispense with attention.

He was pleased to find his own importance, and he tasted the sweets of companionship with more gust than he had yet done. His talents, buried in obscurity, and uncalled for by the society of Lucilla, were now perpetually tempted into action, and stimulated by reward. It had never before appeared to him so charming a thing to shine; for before he had been sated with even that pleasure. Now, from long relaxation, it had become new; vanity had recovered its nice perception. He was no longer so absorbed as he had been by visionary images. He had given his fancy food in his long solitude, and with its wild co-mate; and being somewhat disappointed in the result, the living world became to him a fairer prospect than it had seemed while the world of imagination was untried. Nothing more confirms the health of the mind than indulging its favourite infirmity to its own cure. So Goethe, in his memoirs, speaking of "Werther," remarks, that "the composition of that extravagant work cured his character of extravagance."

Godolphin thought often of Lucilla; but perhaps, if the truth of his heart were known even to himself, a certain sentiment of pain and humiliation was associated with the tenderness of his remembrance. With her he had led a life, romantic, it is true, but somewhat effeminate; and he thought now, surrounded by the gay and freshening tide of the world, somewhat mawkish in its romance. He did not experience a desire to return to the still lake and the gloomy pines; he felt that Lucilla did not suffice to make his world. He would have wished to bring her to Rome; to live with her more in public than he had hitherto done; to conjoin, in short, her society with the more recreative dissipation of the world: but there were many obstacles to this plan in his fastidious imagination. So new to the world, its ways, its fashions, so strange and infantine in all things as Lucilla was, he trembled to expose her inexperience to the dangers that would beset it. He knew that his "friends" would pay very little respect to her reserve; and that for one so lovely and unhackneyed, the snares of the wildest and most subtle adepts of intrigue would be set. Godolphin did not undervalue Lucilla's pure and devoted heart; but he knew that the only sure antidote against the dangers of the world is the knowledge of the world. There was nothing in Lucilla that *ever* promised to attain that knowledge; her very nature seemed to depend on her ignorance of the nature of others. Joined to this fear and a confused sentiment of delicacy towards her, a certain remorseful feeling in himself made him dislike bringing their connection immediately before the curious and malignant world: so much had circumstance, and Lucilla's own self-willed temper and uncalculating love, contributed to drive the poor girl into his arms, and so truly had he chosen the generous not the selfish part, until passion and nature were exposed to a temptation that could have been withstood by none but the adherent to sterner principles than he (the creature of indolence and feeling) had ever clung to, that Godolphin, viewing his habits, his education, his whole bias and frame of mind, the estimates and customs of the world, may not, perhaps, be very rigidly judged for the nature of his tie to Lucilla. But I do not seek to excuse it, nor did he wholly excuse it to himself. The image of Volktman often occurred to him, and always in reproach. Living with Lucilla in a spot only trod by Italians, so indulgent to love, and where the whisper of shame could never reach *her* ear or awaken *his* remorse, her state did not, however, seem to her or himself degraded, and the purity of her girlish mind almost forbade the intrusion of the idea. But to bring her into public, among his own countrymen, and to feel that the generous and devoted girl, now so unconscious of sin, would be rated by English eyes with the basest and most abandoned of the sex, with the glorifiers in vice or the hypocrites for money,—this was a thought which he could not contemplate, and which he felt he would rather pass his life in solitude than endure. But this very feeling gave an embarrassment to his situation with Lucilla, and yet more fixedly combined her image with that of a wearisome seclusion and an eternal *ennui*.

From the thought of Lucilla, coupled with its many embarrassments, Godolphin turned with avidity to the easy enjoyments of life,—enjoyments that ask no care and dispense with the trouble of reflection.

But among the visitors to Rome, the one whose sight gave to Godolphin the greatest pleasure was his old friend, Augustus Saville. A decaying constitution, and a pulmonary attack in especial, had driven the accomplished voluptuary to a warmer climate. The meeting of the two friends was quite characteristic; it was at a *soirée* at an English house. Saville had managed to get up a whist-table.

"Look, Saville, there is Godolphin, your old friend!" cried the host, who was looking on the game, and waiting to cut in.

"Hist!" said Saville; "don't direct his attention to me until after the odd trick!"

Notwithstanding this coolness when a point was in question, Saville was extremely glad to meet his former pupil. They retired into a corner of the room, and talked over the world. Godolphin hastened to turn the conversation on Lady Erpingham.

"Ah," said Saville, "I see from your questions, and yet more your tone of voice, that although it is now several years since you met, you still preserve the sentiment, the weakness — Ah! bah!"

"Pshaw!" said Godolphin; "I owe her revenge, not love. But Erpingham? Does she love him? He is handsome."

"Erpingham? What — you have not heard —"

"Heard what?"

"Oh, nothing; but, pardon me, they wait for me at the card-table. I should like to stay with you, but you know one must not be selfish; the table would be broken up without me. No virtue without self-sacrifice, eh?"

"But one moment. What is the matter with the Erpinghams; have they quarrelled?"

"Quarrelled? Bah! Quarrelled? no; I dare say she likes him better now than ever she did before." And Saville limped away to the table.

Godolphin remained for some time abstracted and thoughtful. At length, just as he was going away, Saville, who, having an unplayable hand and a bad partner, had somewhat lost his interest in the game, looked up and beckoned to him.

"Godolphin, my dear fellow, I am to escort a lady to see *the lions* to-morrow; a widow,— a rich widow; handsome, too. Do, for charity's sake, accompany us, or meet us at the Colosseum. How well that sounds, eh? About two."

Godolphin refused at first, but being pressed, assented.

Not surrounded by the lesser glories of modern Rome, but girt with the mighty desolation of the old city of Romulus, stands the most wonderful monument, perhaps, in the world, of imperial magnificence, — the Flavian Amphitheatre, to which, it has been believed, the colossal statue of the worst of emperors gave that name (the Colosseum!), allied with the least ennobling remembrances yet giving food to the loftiest thoughts. The least ennobling remembrances; for what can be more degrading than the amusements of a degraded people, who reserved meekness for their tyrants, and lavished ferocity on their shows? From that of the wild beast to that of the Christian martyr, blood has been the only sanctification of this temple to the Arts. The history of the Past broods like an air over those mighty arches; but Memory can find no reminiscence worthy of the spot. The amphitheatre was not built until history had become a record of the vice and debasement of the human race. The Faun and the Dryad had deserted the earth; no sweet superstition, the faith of the grotto and the green hill, could stamp with a delicate and undying spell the labours of man. Nor could the ruder but august virtues of the heroic age give to the tradition of the arch and column some stirring remembrance or exalting thought. Not only the warmth of fancy, but the greatness of soul was gone; the only triumph left to genius was to fix on its page the gloomy vices which made the annals of the world. Tacitus is the historian of the Colosseum. But the very darkness of the past gives to the thoughts excited within that immense pile a lofty but mournful character. A sense of vastness — for which, as we gaze, we cannot find words, but which bequeaths thoughts that our higher faculties would not willingly forego — creeps within us as we gaze on this Titan relic of gigantic crimes forever passed away from the world.

And not only within the scene, but around the scene, what voices of old float upon the air! Yonder the triumphal arch of Constantine, its Corinthian arcades, and the history of Trajan sculptured upon its marble; the dark and gloomy verdure of the Palatine; the ruins of the palace of the Cæsars; the mount of Fable, of Fame, of Luxury (the Three Epochs of Nations); the habitation of Saturn; the home of Tully; the sight of the Golden House of Nero! Look at your feet, look around; the waving weed, the broken column,—Time's witness, and the Earthquake's. In that contrast between grandeur and decay, in the unutterable and awful solemnity that, while rife with the records of past ages, is sad also with their ravage, you have felt the nature of eternity!

Through this vast amphitheatre, and giving way to such meditations, Godolphin passed on alone, the day after his meeting with Saville; and at the hour he had promised the latter to seek him, he mounted the wooden staircase which conducts the stranger to the wonders above the arena, and by one of the arches that looked over the still pines that slept afar off in the sun of noon, he saw a female in deep mourning, whom Saville appeared to be addressing. He joined them; the female turned round, and he beheld, pale and saddened, but how glorious still, the face of Constance!

To him the interview was unexpected, by her foreseen. The colour flushed over her cheek, the voice sank inaudible within. But Godolphin's emotion was more powerful and uncontrolled: violent tremblings literally shook him as he stood; he gasped for breath; the sight of the dead returned to earth would have affected him less.

In this immense ruin, in the spot where, most of earth, man feels the insignificance of an individual life, or of the rapid years over which it extends, he had encountered, suddenly, the being who had coloured all his existence. He was reminded at once of the grand epoch of his life, and of its utter unimportance. But these are the thoughts that would occur rather to us than him. Thought at that moment was an intolerable flash that burst on him for an instant, and then left all in darkness. He clung to the shattered corridor for support. Constance seemed touched and surprised by so overwhelming an emotion, and the habitual hypocrisy in which women are reared, and by which they learn to conceal the sentiments they experience, and affect those they do not, came to her assistance and his own.

"It is many years, Mr. Godolphin," said she, in a collected but soft voice, "since we met."

"Years!" repeated Godolphin, vaguely, and approaching her with a slow and faltering step; "years! *you* have not numbered them!"

Saville had retired a few steps on Godolphin's arrival, and had watched with a sardonic yet indifferent smile the proof of his friend's weakness. He joined Godolphin, and said,—

"You must forgive me, my dear Godolphin, for not apprising you before of Lady Erpingham's arrival at Rome; but a delight is perhaps the greater for being sudden."

The word Erpingham thrilled displeasingly through Godolphin's veins; in some measure it restored him to himself. He bowed coldly, and muttered a few ceremonious words; and while he was yet speaking, some stragglers that had belonged to Lady Erpingham's party came up. Fortunately, perhaps, for the self-possession of both, they, the once lovers, were separated from each other. But whenever Constance turned her glance to Godolphin, she saw those large, searching, melancholy eyes, whose power she well recalled, fixed unmovingly on her, as seeking to read in her cheek the history of the years which had ripened its beauties — for another.

CHAPTER XXXVI.

DIALOGUE BETWEEN GODOLPHIN AND SAVILLE. — CERTAIN EVENTS EXPLAINED. — SAVILLE'S APOLOGY FOR A BAD HEART. — GODOLPHIN'S CONFUSED SENTIMENTS FOR LADY ERPINGHAM.

"Good heavens! Constance Vernon once more free!"

"And did you not really know it? Your retreat by the lake must have been indeed seclusion. It is seven months since Lord Erpingham died."

"Do I dream?" murmured Godolphin, as he strode hurriedly to and fro the apartment of his friend.

Saville, stretched on the sofa, diverted himself with mixing snuffs on a little table beside him. Nothing is so mournfully amusing in life as to see what trifles the most striking occurrences to us appear to our friends.

"But," said Saville, not looking up, "you seem very incurious to know how he died, and where. You must learn that Erpingham had two ruling passions,—one for horses, the other for fiddlers. In setting off for Italy he expected, naturally enough, to find the latter, but he thought he might as well export the former. He accordingly filled the vessel with quadrupeds, and the second day after landing he diverted the tedium of a foreign clime with a gentle ride. He met with a fall, and was brought home speechless. The loss of speech was not of great importance to his acquaintance; but he died that night, and the loss of his life was!—for he gave very fair dinners — ah, bah!" And Saville inhaled the fragrance of a new mixture.

Saville had a very pleasant way of telling a story, particularly if it related to a friend's death, or some such agreeable incident. "Poor Lady Erpingham was exceedingly shocked; and well she might be, for I don't think weeds become her. She came here by slow stages, in order that the *illustrious* Dead might chase away the remembrance of the deceased."

"Your heart has not improved, Saville."

"Heart! What's that? Oh, a thing servant-maids have, and break for John the footman. Heart! my dear fellow, you are turned canter, and make use of words without meaning."

Godolphin was not prepared for a conversation of this order; and Saville, in a somewhat more serious air, continued: "Every person, Godolphin, talks about the world. The world! it conveys different meanings to each, according to the nature of that circle which makes his world. But we all agree in one thing,—the worldliness of the world. Now, no man's world is so void of affection as ours,—the polished, the courtly, the great world; the higher the air, the more pernicious to vegetation. Our very charm, our very fascination, depends upon a certain mockery; a subtle and fine ridicule on all persons and all things constitutes the essence of our conversation. Judge if that tone be friendly to the seriousness of the affections. Some poor dog among us marries, and household plebeianisms corrupt the most refined. Custom attaches the creature to his ugly wife and his squalling children; he grows affectionate, and becomes out of fashion. But we single men, dear Godolphin, have no one to care for but ourselves; the deaths that happen, unlike the ties that fall from the married men, do not interfere with our domestic comforts. We miss no one to make our tea, or give us our appetite-pills before dinner. Our losses are not intimate and household. We shrug our shoulders, and are not a whit the worse for them. Thus, for want of grieving and caring and fretting, we are happy enough to grow — come, I will use an epithet to please you — hard-hearted! We congeal into philosophy; and are we not then wise in adopting this life of isolation and indifference?"

Godolphin, rapt in reflection, scarcely heeded the voluptuary, but Saville continued; he had grown to that height in loneliness that he even loved talking to himself.

"Yes, wise! For this world is so filled with the selfish, that he who is not so labours under a disadvantage. Nor are we the worse for our apathy. If we jest at a man's misfortune, we do not do it to his face. Why not out of the ill, which is misfortune, extract good, which is amusement? Three men in this room are made cheerful by a jest at a broken leg in the next. Is the broken leg the worse for it? No; but the three men are made merry by the jest. Is the jest wicked, then? Nay, it is a benevolence. But some cry, 'Ay, but this habit of disregarding misfortunes blunts your wills when you have the power to relieve them.' Relieve! was ever such delusion? What can we relieve in the vast mass of human misfortunes? As well might we take a drop from the ocean, and cry, 'Ha, ha! we have lessened the sea!' What are even your public charities; what your best institutions? How few of the multitude are relieved at all; how few of that few relieved permanently! Men die, suffer, starve just as soon, and just as numerously; these public institutions are only trees for the public conscience to go to roost upon. No, my dear fellow, everything I see in the world says, *Take care of thyself*. This is the true moral of life; every one who minds it gets on, thrives, and fattens;

they who don't, come to us to borrow money, if gentlemen; or fall upon the parish, if plebeians. *I* mind it, my dear Godolphin; I have minded it all my life; I am very contented — content is the sign of virtue,— ah, bah!"

Yes; Constance was a widow. The hand of her whom Percy Godolphin had loved so passionately, and whose voice even now thrilled to his inmost heart and awakened the echoes that had slept for years, it was once more within her power to bestow, and within his to demand. What a host of emotions this thought gave birth to! Like the coming of the Hindoo god, she had appeared, and lo, there was a new world! "And her look," he thought, "was kind, her voice full of a gentle promise, her agitation was visible. She loves me still. Shall I fly to her feet? Shall I press for hope? And, oh, what, what happiness! but *Lucilla!*"

This recollection was indeed a barrier that never failed to present itself to every prospect of hope and joy which the image of Constance coloured and called forth. Even for the object of his first love, could he desert one who had forsaken all for him, whose life was wrapped up in his affection? The very coolness with which he was sensible he had returned the attachment of this poor girl made him more alive to the duties he owed her. If not bound to her by marriage, he considered with a generosity — barely in truth but justice, yet how rare in the world! — that the tie between them was sacred, that only death could dissolve it. And now that tie was, perhaps, all that held him from attaining the dream of his past life.

Absorbed in these ideas, Godolphin contrived to let Saville's unsympathizing discourse glide unheeded along, without reflecting its images on the sense, until the name of Lady Erpingham again awakened his attention.

"You are going to her this evening," said Saville; "and you may thank me for that; for I asked you if you were thither bound in her hearing, in order to force her into granting you an invitation. She only sees her most intimate friends,— you, me, and Lady Charlotte Deerham. Widows are shy of acquaintance during their first affliction. I always manage, however, to be among the admitted — caustic is good for some wounds."

"Nay," said Godolphin, smiling, "it is your friendly disposition that makes them sure of sympathy."

"You have hit it. But," continued Saville, "do you think Madame likely to marry again, or shall you yourself adventure? Erpingham has left her nearly his whole fortune."

Irritated and impatient at Saville's tone, Godolphin rose. "Between you and me," said Saville, in wishing him good-by, "I don't think she will ever marry again. Lady Erpingham is fond of power and liberty; even the young Godolphin — and you are not so handsome as you were — will find it a hopeless suit."

"Pshaw!" muttered Godolphin, as he departed. But the last words of Saville had created a new feeling in his breast. It was then possible, nay, highly probable, that he might have spared himself the contest he had undergone, and that the choice between Lucilla and Constance might never be permitted him.

"At all events," said he, almost aloud, "I will see if this conjecture be true; if Constance, yet remembering our early love, yet feeling for the years of secret pining which her ambition bequeathed me, should appear willing to grant me the atonement fate has placed within her power, then, then, it will be time for this self-sacrifice."

The social relations of the sex often make men villanous — they more often make them weak.

CHAPTER XXXVII.

AN EVENING WITH CONSTANCE.

Constance's heart was in her eyes when she saw Godolphin that evening. She had, it is true, as Saville observed, been compelled by common courtesy to invite him; and although there was an embarrassment in their meeting, who shall imagine that it did not bring to Constance more of pleasure than pain? She had been deeply shocked by Lord Erpingham's sudden death; they had not been congenial minds, but the great have an advantage denied to the less wealthy orders. Among the former, a husband and wife need not weary each other with constant companionships; different establishments, different hours, different pursuits, allow them to pass life in great measure apart, so that there is no necessity for hatred, and indifference is the coldest feeling which custom induces.

Still in the prime of youth and at the zenith of her beauty, Constance was now independent. She was in the enjoyment of the wealth and rank her early habits of thought had deemed indispensable, and she now for the first time possessed the power of sharing them with whom she pleased. At this thought how naturally her heart flew back to Godolphin! And while she now gazed, although by stealth, at his countenance, as he sat at a little distance from her, and in his turn watched for the tokens of past remembrance, she was deeply touched by the change (light as it seemed to others) which years had brought to him; and in recalling the emotion he had testified at meeting her, she suffered her heart to soften, while it reproached her in whispering, "Thou art the cause!" All the fire, the ardour of a character not then confirmed, which, when she last saw him spoke in his eye and mien, were gone forever. The irregular brilliancy of his conversation, the earnestness of his air and gesture, were replaced by a calm and even and melancholy composure. His forehead was stamped with the lines of thought; and the hair, grown thinner towards the temples, no longer concealed by its luxuriance the pale expanse of his brow. The air of delicate health which had at first interested her in his appearance still lingered, and gave its wonted and ineffable charm to his low voice, and the gentle expression of his eyes. By degrees, the conversation, at first partial and scattered, became more general. Constance and Godolphin were drawn into it.

"It is impossible," said Godolphin, "to compare life in a

southern climate with that which we lead in colder countries. There is an indolence, a *laissez aller*, a philosophical *insouciance*, produced by living under these warm suns, and apart from the ambition of the objects of our own nation, which produce at last a state of mind that divides us forever from our countrymen. It is like living amidst perpetual music,—a different kind of life, a soft, lazy, voluptuous romance of feeling, that indisposes us to action,—almost to motion. So far from a sojourn in Italy being friendly to the growth of ambition, it nips and almost destroys the germ."

"In fact, it leaves us fit for nothing but love," said Saville, — "an occupation that levels us with the silliest part of our species."

"Fools cannot love," said Lady Charlotte.

"Pardon me, love and folly are synonymous in more languages than the French," answered Saville.

"In truth," said Godolphin, "the love which you both allude to is not worth disputing about."

"What love is?" asked Saville.

"First love," cried Lady Charlotte; "is it not, Mr. Godolphin?"

Godolphin changed colour, and his eyes met those of Constance. She too sighed and looked down; Godolphin remained silent.

"Nay, Mr. Godolphin, answer me," said Lady Charlotte; "I appeal to you!"

"First love, then," said Godolphin, endeavouring to speak composedly, "has this advantage over others,— it is usually disappointed, and regret forever keeps it alive."

The tone of his voice struck Constance to the heart. Nor did she speak again — save with visible effort — during the rest of the evening.

CHAPTER XXXVIII.

CONSTANCE'S UNDIMINISHED LOVE FOR GODOLPHIN. — HER REMORSE AND HER HOPE. — THE CAPITOL. — THE DIFFERENT THOUGHTS OF GODOLPHIN AND CONSTANCE AT THE VIEW. — THE TENDER EXPRESSIONS OF CONSTANCE.

All that Constance heard from others of Godolphin's life since they parted increased her long-nursed interest in his fate. His desultory habits, his long absences from cities, which were understood to be passed in utter and obscure solitude (for the partner of the solitude and its exact spot were not known), she coupled with the quiet melancholy in his aspect, with his half-reproachful glances towards herself, and with the emotions which he had given vent to in their conversation. And of this objectless and unsatisfactory life she was led to consider herself the cause. With a bitter pang she recalled his early words, when he said, "My future is in your hands;" and she contrasted his vivid energies, his cultivated mind, his high talents, with the life which had rendered them all so idle to others and unprofitable to himself. Few, very few, know how powerfully the sentiment that another's happiness is at her control speaks to a woman's heart. Accustomed to dependence herself, the feeling that another depends on her is the most soothing aliment to her pride. This makes a main cause of her love to her children; they would be incomparably less dear to her if they were made independent of her cares. And years, which had brought the young countess acquainted with the nothingness of the world, had softened and deepened the sources of her affections, in proportion as they had checked those of her ambition. She could not, she did not, seek to disguise from herself that Godolphin yet loved her; she anticipated the hour when he would avow that love, and when she might be permitted to atone for all of disappointment that her former rejection might have brought to him. She felt, too, that it would be a noble as well as delightful task to awaken an intellect so brilliant to the natural objects of its display; to call forth into active life his teeming thought, and the rich eloquence with which he could convey it. Nor in this hope were her more selfish designs, her political schemings, and her desire of sway over those whom she loved to humble forgotten; but they made, however,— to be just,— a small part of her meditations. Her hopes were chiefly of a more generous order. "I refused thee," she thought, "when I was poor and dependent; now that I have wealth and rank, how gladly will I yield them to thy bidding!"

But Godolphin, as if unconscious of this favourable bias of her inclinations, did not warm from his reserve. On the contrary, his first abstraction and his first agitation had both subsided into a distant and cool self-possession. They met often, but he avoided all nearer or less general communication. She saw, however, that his eyes were constantly in search of her, and that a slight trembling in his voice when he addressed her belied the calmness of his manner. Sometimes, too, a word, or a touch from her, would awaken the ill-concealed emotions,— his lips seemed about to own the triumph of her and of the past; but, as if by a violent effort, they were again sealed; and not unoften, evidently unwilling to trust his self-command, he would abruptly depart. In short, Constance perceived that a strange embarrassment, the causes of which she could not divine, hung about him, and that his conduct was regulated by some secret motive, which did not spring from the circumstances that had occurred between them. For it was evident that he was not withheld by any resentment towards her from her former rejection; even his looks, his words, had betrayed that he had done more than forgive. Lady Charlotte Deerham had heard from Saville of their former attachment: she was a woman of the world, and thought it but common delicacy to give them all occasion to renew it. She always, therefore, took occasion to retire from the immediate vicinity of Constance whenever Godolphin approached, and, as if by accident, to leave them the opportunity to be sufficiently alone. This was a danger that Godolphin had, however, hitherto avoided. One day fate counteracted prudence, and a conference ensued which perplexed Constance and tried severely the resolution of Godolphin.

They went together to the Capitc , from whose height is beheld perhaps the most imposing landscape in the world. It was a sight pre-eminently calculated to arouse and inspire the ambitious and working mind of the young countess.

"Do you think," said she to Godolphin, who stood beside her, "that there lives any one who could behold these countless monuments of eternal glory, and not sigh to recall the triteness, or rather burn to rise from the level, of our ordinary life?"

"Nay," said Godolphin, "to you the view may be an inspiration, to others a warning. The arch and the ruin you survey speak of change yet more eloquently than glory. Look on the spot where once was the temple of Romulus: there stands the little church of an obscure saint. Just below you is the Tarpeian Rock: we cannot see it; it is hidden from us by a crówd of miserable houses. Along the ancient plain of the Campus Martius behold the numberless spires of a new religion, and the palaces of a modern race! Amidst them you see the triumphal columns of Trajan and Marcus Antoninus; but whose are the figures that crown their summits? Saint Peter's and Saint Paul's! And this awful wilderness of men's labours, this scene and token of human revolutions, inspires you with a love of glory; to me it proves its nothingness. An irresistible, a *crushing* sense of the littleness and brief life of our most ardent and sagacious achievements seems to me to float like a voice over the place!"

"And are you still, then," said Constance, with a half sigh, "dead to all but the enjoyment of the present moment?"

"No," replied Godolphin, in a low and trembling voice; "I am not dead to the regret of the past!"

Constance blushed deeply; but Godolphin, as if feeling he had committed himself too far, continued in a hurried tone.

"Let us turn our eyes," said he, "yonder among the olive groves. There —

"'Far from the madding crowd's ignoble strife' —

were the summer retreats of Rome's brightest and most enduring spirits. There was the retirement of Horace and Mæcenas; there Brutus forgot his harsher genius; and there the inscrutable and profound Augustus indulged in those graceful relaxations — those sacrifices to wit, and poetry, and wisdom — which have made us do so unwilling and reserved a justice to the crimes of his earlier and the hypocrisy of his later years. Here, again, is a reproach to your ambition," added Godolphin, smiling; "his ambition made Augustus odious; his occasional forgetfulness of ambition alone redeems him."

"And what, then?" said Constance, "would you consider inactivity the happiest life for one sensible of talents higher than the common standard?"

"Nay, let those talents be devoted to the discovery of pleasures, not the search after labours; the higher our talents, the keener our perceptions; the keener our perceptions, the more intense our capacities for pleasure:[1] — let pleasure, then, be our object. Let us find out what is best fitted to give our peculiar tastes gratification, and, having found out, steadily pursue it."

"Out on you! it is a selfish and ignoble system," said Constance. "You smile; well, I may be unphilosophical, I do not deny it. But give me one hour of glory, rather than a life of luxurious indolence. Oh, would," added Constance, kindling as she spoke, "that you, — you, Mr. Godolphin, — with an intellect so formed for high accomplishment, with all the weapons and energies of life at your command, — would that you could awaken to a more worthy estimate — pardon me — of the uses of exertion! Surely, surely, you must be sensible of the calls that your country, that mankind, have at this epoch of the world, upon all, — all, especially, possessing your advantages and powers. Can we pierce one inch beyond the surface of

[1] I suppose Godolphin by the word "pleasure" rather signifies "happiness."

society, and not see that great events are hastening to their birth? Will you let those inferior to yourself hurry on before you, and sit inactive while they win the reward? Will you have no share in the bright drama that is already prepared behind the dark curtain of fate, and which will have a world for its spectators? Ah, how rejoiced, how elated with myself I should feel, if I could win over one like you to the great cause of honourable exertion!"

For one instant Godolphin's eye sparkled, and his pale cheek burned; but the transient emotion faded away as he answered,—

"Eight years ago, when she who spoke to me was Constance Vernon, her wish might have moulded me according to her will. Now," and he struggled with emotion, and turned away his face,—"*now* it is too late!"

Constance was smitten to the heart. She laid her hand gently on his arm, and said, in a sweet and soothing tone, "No, Percy, not too late!"

At that instant, and before Godolphin could reply, they were joined by Saville and Lady Charlotte Deerham.

CHAPTER XXXIX.

LUCILLA'S LETTER.—THE EFFECT IT PRODUCES ON GODOLPHIN.

THE short conversation recorded in the last chapter could not but show to Godolphin the dangerous ground on which his fidelity to Lucilla rested. Never before—no, not in the young time of their first passion—had Constance seemed to him so lovely or so worthy of love. Her manners now were so much more soft and unreserved than they had necessarily been at a period when Constance had resolved not to listen to his addresses or her own heart, that the only part of her character that had ever repulsed his pride or offended his tastes seemed vanished forever. A more subdued and gentle spirit had descended on her surpassing beauty, and the change was of an order that Percy Godolphin could especially appreciate. And the world, for which he owned reluctantly that she yet lived too much, had, nevertheless, seemed rather to enlarge and animate the natural nobleness of her mind, than to fritter it down to the standard of its common votaries. When she spoke he delighted in, even while he dissented from, the high and bold views which she conceived. He loved her indignation of all that was mean and low, her passion for all that was daring and exalted. Never was he cast down from the height of the imaginative part of his love by hearing from her lips one petty passion or one sordid desire; much about her was erroneous, but all was lofty and generous, even in error. And the years that had divided them had only taught him to feel more deeply how rare was the order of her character, and how impossible it was ever to behold her like. All the sentiments, faculties, emotions, which, in his affection for Lucilla had remained dormant, were excited into full play the moment he was in the presence of Constance. She engrossed no petty portion she demanded and obtained the whole empire, of his soul. And against this empire he had now to contend! Torn as he was by a thousand conflicting emotions, a letter from Lucilla was suddenly put into his hands; its contents were as follows:—

LUCILLA'S LETTER.

"Thy last letter, my love, was so short and hurried, that it has not cost me my usual pains to learn it by heart; nor (shall I tell the truth?) have I been so eager as I once was to commit all thy words to my memory. Why, I know not, and will guess not, but there is something in thy letters since we parted that chills me; they throw back my heart upon itself. I tear open the seal with so much eagerness,—thou wouldst smile if thou couldst see me,—and when I discover how few are the words upon which I am to live for many days, I feel sick and disappointed, and lay down the letter. Then I chide myself and say, 'At least these few words will be kind!'—and I spell them one by one, not to hurry over my only solace. Alas! before I arrive at the end, I am blinded by my tears; my love for thee, so bounding and full of life, seems frozen and arrested at every line. And then I lie down for very weariness, and wish to die. O God, if the time has come which I have always dreaded, — if thou shouldst no longer love me! And how reasonable this fear is! For what am I to thee? How often dost thou complain that I can understand thee not, how often dost thou imply that there is much of thy nature which I am incapable — unworthy — to learn! If this be so, how natural is it to dread that thou wilt find others whom thou wilt fancy more congenial to thee, and that absence will only remind thee more of my imperfections!

"And yet I think that I have read thee to the letter; I think that my love, which is always following thee, always watching thee, always conjecturing thy wishes, must have penetrated into every secret of thy heart: only I want words to express what I feel, and thou layest the blame upon the want of feeling! I know how untutored, how ignorant, I must seem to thee; and sometimes — and lately very often — I reproach myself that I have not more diligently sought to make myself a worthier companion to thee. I think if I had the same means as others, I should acquire the same facility of expressing my thoughts; and my thoughts thou couldst never blame, for I know that they are full of a love to thee which — no, not the wisest — the most brilliant, whom thou mayest see could equal even in imagination. But I have sought to mend this deficiency since we parted; and I have looked into all the books thou hast loved to read, and I fancy that I have imbibed *now* the same ideas which pleased thee, and in which once thou imaginedst I could not sympathize. Yet how mistaken thou hast been! I see, by marks thou hast placed on the page, the sentiments that more especially charm thee; and I know that I have felt them much, oh! *how* much more deeply and vividly than they are there expressed, — only they seem to me to have no language; methinks that I have learned the language now. And I have taught myself songs that thou wilt love to hear when thou returnest home to me; and I have practised music, and I think — nay, I am sure — that time will not pass so heavily with *thee* as when thou wast last here.

"And when shall I see thee again? — forgive me if I press thee to return. Thou hast stayed away longer than thou hast been wont; but that I would not heed; it is not the number of days, but the sensations with which I have counted them, that make me pine for thy beloved voice, and long once more to behold thee. Never before did I so feel thy absence, never before was I so utterly wretched. A secret voice whispers me that we are parted forever. I cannot withstand the omens of my own heart. When my poor father lived, I did not, child as I was, partake of those sentiments with which he was wont to say the stars inspired us. I could not see in them the boders of fear and the preachers of sad tidings; they seemed to me only full of serenity and tenderness and the promise of enduring love! And ever when I looked on them, I thought of thee; and thy image to me then, as thou knowest it was from childhood, was bright with unimaginable but never melancholy spells. But now, although I love thee so far more powerfully, I cannot divest the thoughts of thee from a certain sadness; and so the stars, which are like thee, which are full of thee, have a sadness also! And this, the bed, where every morning I stretch my arms for thee, and find thee not, and have yet to live through the day, and on which I now write this letter to thee — for I, who used to rise with the sun, am now too dispirited not to endeavour to cheat the weary day — I have made them place nearer to the window; and I look out upon the still skies every night, and have made a friend of every star I see. I question it of thyself, and wonder, when thou lookest at it, if thou hast any thought of me. I love to look upon the heavens much more than upon the earth; for the trees and the waters and the hills around, thou canst not behold, but the same heaven which I survey is above thee also; and this, our common companion, seems in some measure to unite us. And I have thought over my father's lore, and have tried to learn it; nay, thou mayest smile, but it is thy absence that has taught me superstition.

"But tell me, dearest, kindest, tell me when — oh, when wilt thou return? Return only this once — if but for a day — and I will never persecute thee again. Truant as thou art, thou shalt have full liberty for life. But I cannot tell thee how sad and heavy I am grown, and every hour knocks at my heart like a knell! Come back to thy poor Lucilla — if only to see what joy is! Come — I know thou wilt! But should anything I do not foresee detain thee, fix at least the day — nay, if possible, the hour — when we shall meet, and let the letter which conveys such happy tidings be long and kind and full of thee, as thy letters once were. I know I weary thee, but I cannot help it. I am weak and dejected and cast down, and have only heart enough to pray for thy return."

"You have conquered! you have conquered, Lucilla!" said Godolphin, as he kissed this wild and reproachful letter, and thrust it into his bosom; "and I — I will be wretched rather than you shall be so!"

His heart rebuked him even for that last sentence. This pure and devoted attachment — was it indeed an unhappiness to obtain, and a sacrifice to return! Stung by his thoughts, and impatient of rest, he hurried into the air; he traversed the city; he passed St. Sebastian's Gate, gained the Appia Via, and saw, lone and sombre, as of old, the house of the departed Volktman. He had half unconsciously sought that direction, in order to strengthen his purpose, and sustain his conscience in its right path. He now hurried onwards, and stopped not till he stood in that lovely and haunted spot — the valley of Egeria — in which he had met Lucilla on the day that he first learned her love. There was a gloom over the scene now, for the day was dark and clouded: the birds were silent; a heavy oppression seemed to brood upon the air. He entered that grotto which is the witness of the most beautiful love-story chronicled even in the soft South. He recalled the passionate and burning emotions which, the last time he had been within that cell, he had felt for Lucilla, and had construed erroneously into real love. As he looked around, how different an aspect the spot wore! Then, those walls, that spring, even that mutilated statue, had seemed to him the encouragers of the soft sensations he had indulged. Now, they appeared to reprove the very weakness which hallowed themselves; the associations spoke to him in another tone. The broken statue of the river god, the desert silence in which the water of the sweet fountain keeps its melancholy course, the profound and chilling solitude of the spot,— all seemed eloquent, not of love, but the broken hope and the dreary loneliness that succeed it! The gentle plant (the capillaire) that overhangs the sides of the grotto, and nourishes itself on the dews of the fountain, seemed an emblem of love itself after disappointment,— the love that might henceforth be Lucilla's,— drooping in silence on the spot once consecrated to rapture, and feeding itself with tears. There was something mocking to human passion in the very antiquity of the spot; four-and-twenty centuries had passed away since the origin of the tale that made it holy — and that tale, too, was fable! What, in this vast accumulation of the sands of time, was a solitary atom! What, among the millions, the myriads, that around that desolate spot had loved and forgotten love. was the brief passion of one mortal, withering as it sprung! Thus differently moralizes the heart, according to the passion which bestows on it the text.

Before he regained his home, Godolphin's resolve was taken. The next day he had promised Constance to attend her to Tivoli; he resolved then to take leave of her, and on the following day to return to Lucilla. He remembered, with bitter reproach, that he had not written to her for a length of time treble the accustomed interval between his letters; and felt that, while at the moment she had written the lines he had now pressed to his bosom, she was expecting, with unutterable fondness and anxiety, to receive his lukewarm assurances of continued love, the letter he was about to write in answer to hers was the first one that would greet her eyes. But he resolved that in that letter, at least, she should not be disappointed. He wrote at length, and with all the outpourings of a tenderness reawakened by remorse. He informed her of his immediate return, and even forced himself to dwell upon it with kindly hypocrisy of transport. For the first time for several weeks, he felt satisfied with himself as he sealed his letter. It is doubtful whether that letter Lucilla *ever* received.

CHAPTER XL.

TIVOLI. — THE SIREN'S CAVE. — THE CONFESSION.

Along the deathly Campagna, a weary and desolate length of way, through a mean and squalid row of houses, you thread your course; and behold — Tivoli bursts upon you!

"Look! look!" cried Constance, with enthusiasm, as she pointed to the rushing torrent that, through matted trees and cragged precipices, thundered on.

Astonished at the silence of Godolphin, whom scenery was usually so wont to kindle and inspire, she turned hastily round, and her whole tide of feeling was revulsed by the absorbed but intense dejection written on his countenance.

"Why," said she, after a short pause, and affecting a playful smile, "why, how provoking is this! In general, not a common patch of green with an old tree in the centre, not a common rivulet with a willow hanging over it, escapes you. You insist upon our sharing your raptures, you dilate on the picturesque, you rise into eloquence; nay, you persuade us into your enthusiasm, or you quarrel with us for our coldness; and now, with this divinest of earthly scenes around us,— when even Lady Charlotte is excited, and Mr. Saville forgets himself, you are stricken into silence and apathy! The reason — if it be not too abstruse?"

"It is here!" said Godolphin, mournfully, and pressing his hand to his heart.

Constance turned aside; she indulged herself with the hope that he alluded to former scenes, and despaired of the future from their remembrance. She connected his melancholy with herself, and knew that, when referred to her, she could dispel it. Inspired by this idea, and exhilarated by the beauty of the morning, and the wonderful magnificence of nature, she indulged her spirits to overflowing. And as her brilliant mind lighted up every subject it touched, now glowing over description, now flashing into remark, Godolphin at one time forgot, and at another more keenly felt, the magnitude of the sacrifice he was about to make. But every one knows that feeling which, when we are unhappy, illumines (if I may so speak) our outward seeming from the fierceness of our inward despair,— that recklessness which is the intoxication of our grief.

By degrees Godolphin broke from his reserve. He seemed to catch the enthusiasm of Constance; he echoed back, he led into new and more dazzling directions, the delighted remarks of his beautiful companion. His mind, if not profoundly learned, at least irregularly rich, in the treasures of old times, called up a spirit from every object. The waterfall, the ruin, the hollow cave, the steep bank crested with the olive, the airy temple, the dark pomp of the cypress grove, and the roar of the headlong Anio,— *all* he touched with the magic of the past, clad with the glories of history and of legend, and decked ever and anon with the flowers of the eternal Poesy that yet walks, mourning for her children, amongst the vines and waterfalls of the ancient Tibur. And Constance, as she listened to him, entranced, until she herself unconsciously grew silent, indulged without reserve in that, the proudest luxury of love,— pride in the beloved object. Never had the rare and various genius of Godolphin appeared so worthy of admiration. When his voice ceased, it seemed to Constance like a sudden blank in the creation.

Godolphin and the young countess were several paces before the little party, and they now took their way towards the Siren's Cave. The path that leads to that singular spot is humid with an eternal spray; and it is so abrupt and slippery, that in order to preserve your footing, you must cling to the bushes that vegetate around the sides of the precipice.

"Let us dispense with our guide," said Godolphin. "I know every part of the way, and I am sure you share with me in dislike to these hackneyed indicators and sign-posts for admiration. Let us leave him to Lady Charlotte and Saville, and suffer me to be your guide to the cavern." Constance readily enough assented, and they proceeded. Saville, by no means liking the difficult and perilous path which was to lead only to a very cold place, soon halted, and suggested to Lady Charlotte the propriety of doing the same. Lady Charlotte much preferred the wit of her companion's conversation to the picturesque. "Besides," as she said, "she had seen the cave before." Accordingly, they both waited for the return of the more adventurous countess and her guide.

Unconscious of the defalcation of her friends, and not — from the attention that every step required — once looking behind, Constance continued. And now, how delightful to her seemed that rugged way, as, with every moment, Godolphin's care, Godolphin's hand, became necessary; and he, inspired, inflamed by her company, by her touch, by the softness of her manner, and the devotion of her attention — no, no! not *yet* was Lucilla forgotten!

And now they stood within the Siren's Cave. From this spot alone you can view that terrible descent of waters which rushes to earth like the coming of a god! The rocks dripped around them, the torrent dashed at their very feet. Down, down, in thunder, forever and forever, dashed the might of the maddening element; above, all wrath; below, all blackness; there, the cataract; here, the abyss. Not a moment's pause to the fury, not a moment's silence to the roar; forward to the last glimpse of the sun,— the curse of labour, and the soul of unutterable strength, shall be upon those waters! The demon, tormented to an eternity, filling his dread dwelling-place with the unresting and unearthly voice of his rage and despair, is the only type meet for the spirit of the cataract.

And there — amidst this awful and tremendous eternity of strife and power — stood two beings whose momentary existence was filled with the master-passion of humanity. And that passion was yet audible there: the nature without could not subdue that within. Even amidst the icy showers of spray that fell around, and would have frozen the veins of others, Godolphin felt the burning at his heart. Constance was indeed utterly lost in a whirl and chaos of awe and admiration, which deprived her of all words. But it was the nature of her wayward lover to be aroused only to the thorough knowledge of his powers and passions among the more unfrequent and fierce excitements of life. A wild emotion now urged him on; something of that turbulent exaggeration of mind which gave rise to a memorable and disputed saying,— "If thou stoodest on a precipice with thy mistress, hast thou ever felt the desire to plunge with her into the abyss? If so, thou hast loved!" No doubt the sentiment is exaggerated, but there are times when love is exaggerated too. And now Constance, without knowing it, had clung closer and closer to Godolphin. His hand at first, now his arm, supported her; and at length, by an irresistible and maddening impulse, he clasped her to his breast, and whispered in a voice which was heard by her even amidst the thunder of the giant waters, "Here, here, my early, my only love, I feel, in spite of myself, that I never utterly, fully, adored you until now!"

CHAPTER XLI.

LUCILLA. — THE SOLITUDE. — THE SPELL. — THE DREAM AND THE RESOLVE.

While the above events, so fatal to Lucilla, were in progress at Rome, she was holding an unquiet commune with her own passionate and restless heart, by the borders of the lake, whose silver quiet mocked the mind it had, in happier moments, reflected. She had now dragged on the weary load of time throughout the winter; and the early and soft spring was already abroad, smoothing the face of the waters, and calling life into the boughs. Hitherto this time of the year had possessed a mysterious and earnest attraction for Lucilla, — now all its voices were mute. The letters that Godolphin had written to her were so few and so restrained, in comparison with those which she had received in the former periods of absence, that — ever alive as she was to impulse, and unregulated by settled principles of hope — her only relief to a tearful and spiritless dejection was in paroxysms of doubt, jealousy, and despair.

It is the most common thing in the world, that, when we have once wronged a person, we go on in the wrong, from a certain soreness with which conscience links the associations of the injured party. And thus, Godolphin, struggling with the return to his early and never-forgotten love, felt an unwillingness that he could seldom successfully combat in playing the hypocrite to Lucilla. His very remorse made him unkind; the feeling that he ought to write often, made him write seldom: and conscious that he ought to return her expressions of eager devotion, he returned them with involuntary awkwardness and reserve. All this is very natural, and very evident to us; but a thousand mysteries were more acceptable to, more sought for and more clung to, by Lucilla than a conjecture at the truth.

Meanwhile she fed more and more eagerly on those vain researches which yet beguiled her time, and flattered her imagination. In a science so false and so unprofitable, it mattered, happily, little whether or not the poor disciple laboured with success; but I need scarcely tell to any who have had the curiosity to look over the entangled schemes and quaint figures of the art, how slender was the advancement of the daughter in the learning of the sire. Still it was a comfort and a soothing even to look upon the placid heaven, and form a conjecture as to the language of its stars. And, above all, while she questioned the future, she thought only of her lover. But day after day passed,—no letter, or worse than none; and at length Lucilla became utterly impatient of all rest: a nervous fever possessed her; the extreme solitude of the place filled her with that ineffable sensation of irritability which sometimes preludes the madness that has been produced in criminals by solitary confinement.

On the day that she wrote that letter to Godolphin which I have transcribed, this painful tension of the nerves was more than hitherto acute. She longed to fly somewhere; nay, once or twice, she remembered that Rome was easily gained, that she might be there as expeditiously as her letter. Although in that letter only we have signified that Lucilla had expressed her wish for Godolphin's return, yet in all her later letters she had (perhaps more timidly) urged that desire. But they had not taken the same hold on Godolphin; nor, while he was playing with his danger, had they produced the same energetic resolution. Lucilla could not, however, hope with much reason that the success of her present letter would be greater than that of her former ones; and, at all events, she did not anticipate an *immediate* compliance with her prayers. She looked forward to some excuses, and to some delay. We cannot, therefore, wonder that she felt a growing desire to follow her own epistle to Rome; and although she had been prevented before, and still drew back from absolutely favouring and enforcing the idea, by the fear of Godolphin's displeasure, yet she trusted enough to his gentleness of character to feel sure that the displeasure could scarcely be lasting. Still the step was bold, and Lucilla loved devotedly enough to be timid; and besides, her inexperience made her look upon the journey as a far more formidable expedition than it really was.

Debating the notion in her mind, she sought her usual retreat, and turned listlessly over the books which she had so lately loved to study. At length, in moving one she had not looked into before, a paper fell to the ground; she picked it up; it was the paper containing that figure, which it will be remembered, the astrologer had shown to his daughter, as a charm to produce dreams prophetic of any circumstance or person concerning whom the believer might be anxious to learn aught. As she saw the image, which, the reader will recollect, was of a remarkable design, the whole of her conversation with Volktman on the subject rushed into her mind, and she resolved that very night to prove the efficacy of the charm on which he had so confidently insisted. Fraught with the chimerical delusion, she now longed for the hours to pass, and the night to come. She looked again and again at the singular image and the portentous figures wrought upon the charm; the very strangeness of the characters inspired her, as was natural, with a belief in their efficacy; and she felt a thrill, an awe, creep over her blood, as the shadows of eve, deepening over the far mountains, brought on the time of trial. At length it was night, and Lucilla sought her chamber.

The hour was exceedingly serene, and the stars shone through the casement with a lustre that to her seemed ominous. With bare feet, and only in her night-robe, she stole tremblingly across the threshold. She paused for a moment at the window, and looked out on the deep and quiet night; and as she so stood, it was a picture that, had I been a painter, I would have devoted a youth to accomplish. Half in light, half in shadow, her undress gave the outline, and somewhat more, of a throat and breast whose roundness, shape, and hue never were surpassed. Her arms were lightly crossed above her bosom; and her long rich hair seeming darker by that light, fell profusely, yet not dishevelled, around her neck, parting from her brow. Her attitude at that moment was quite still, as if in worship,—and perhaps it was; her face was inclined slightly upward, looking to the heavens and towards Rome. But that face—*there* was the picture! It was so young, so infantine, so modest; and yet the youth and the timidity were elevated and refined by the earnest doubt, the preternatural terror, the unearthly hope, which dwelt upon her forehead, her parted lip, and her wistful and kindled eye. There was a sublimity in her loneliness and her years, and in the fond and vain superstition, which was but a spirit called from the deeps of an unfathomable and mighty love. And afar was heard the breaking of the lake upon the shore—no other sound! And now, among the unwaving pines, there was a silver shimmer as the moon rose into her empire, and deepened at once, along the universal scene, the loveliness and the awe.

Lucilla turned from the window, and kneeling down wrote with a trembling hand upon the figure one word,—the name of Godolphin. She then placed it under her pillow, and the spell was concluded. The astrologer had told her of the necessary co-operation which the mind must afford to the charm; but it will easily be believed that Lucilla required no injunction to let her imagination dwell upon the vision she expected to invoke. And it would have been almost strange, if, so intently and earnestly brooding as she had done over the image of Godolphin, that image had not, without recurring to any cabalistical spells, been present to her dreams.

She thought that it was broad noonday, and that she was sitting alone in the house she then inhabited, and weeping bitterly. Of a sudden the voice of Godolphin called to her; she ran eagerly forth, but no sooner had she passed the threshold than the scene so familiar to her vanished, and she was alone in an immense and pathless wilderness; there was no tree and no water in this desert; all was arid, solitary, and inanimate. But what seemed *most* strange to her was, that in the heavens, although they were clear and bright, there was neither sun nor stars; the light seemed settled and stagnant,—there was in it no life.

And she thought that she continued to move involuntarily

along the waste; and that, ever and anon, she yearned and strove to rest, but her limbs did not obey her will, and a power she could not control urged her onward.

And now there was no longer an utter dumbness and death over the scene. Forth from the sands, as from the bowels of the reluctant earth, there crept, one by one, loathly and reptile shapes; obscene sounds rang in her ears,—now in a hideous mockery, now in a yet more sickening solicitation. Shapes of terror thickened and crowded round her. She was roused by dread into action; she hurried faster and faster; she strove to escape; and ever as she fled, the sounds grew louder, and the persecuting shapes more ghastly,—abominations which her pure mind shuddered to behold presented themselves at every turn: there was no spot for refuge, no cave for concealment. Wearied and despairing, she stopped short; but then the shapes and sounds seemed gradually to lose their terror; her eye and ear became familiar to them; and what at first seemed foes grew into companions.

And now, again, the wilderness was gone; she stood in a strange spot, and opposite, and gazing upon her with intent and mournful eyes, stood Godolphin. But he seemed much older than he was, and the traces of care were ploughed deeply on his countenance; and above them both hung a motionless and livid cloud; and from the cloud a gigantic hand was stretched forth, pointing with a shadowy and unmoving figure towards a quarter of the earth which was enveloped in a thick gloom. While she sought with straining eyes to penetrate the darkness of the spot thus fearfully marked out, she thought Godolphin vanished, and all was suddenly and utter night,—night, but not stillness; for there was a roar as of many winds, and a dashing of angry waters, that seemed close beneath; and she heard the trees groan and bend, and felt the icy and rushing air: the tempests were abroad. But amidst the mingling of the mighty sounds, she heard distinctly the ringing of a horse's hoofs; and presently a wild cry, in which she recognized the voice of Godolphin, rang forth, adding to the wrath of nature the yet more appalling witness of a human despair. The cry was followed by the louder dashing of the waves, and the fiercer turmoil of the winds; and then her anguish and horror freeing her from the Prison of Sleep, she woke.

It was nearly day, but the serenity of the late night had gone; the rain fell in torrents, and the house shook beneath the fury of a violent storm. This change in the mood of nature had probably influenced the latter part of her dream. But Lucilla thought of no natural solution to the dreadful vision she had undergone. Her superstition was confirmed and ratified by the intense impression wrought upon her mind by the dream. A thousand unutterable fears — fears for Godolphin, rather than herself, — or if for herself, only in connection with him — bore irresistible despotism over her thoughts. She could not endure to wait, to linger any longer in the dark and agitated suspense she herself had created; the idea she before had nursed now became resolve; she determined forthwith to set out for Rome, — to see Godolphin. She rose, woke her attendant, and that very day she put her resolution into effect.

CHAPTER XLII.

JOY AND DESPAIR.

It was approaching towards the evening as Lucilla paused for a few seconds at the door which led to Godolphin's apartments. At length she summoned courage. The servant who admitted her was Godolphin's favourite domestic; and he was amazed, but overjoyed, to see her; for Lucilla was the idol of all who knew her, — save of him, whose love only she cared and lived for.

His master, he said, was gone out for a short time, but the next day they were to have returned home. Lucilla coloured with vivid delight to hear that her letter had produced an effect she had not hoped so expeditiously to accomplish. She passed on into Godolphin's apartment. The room bore evident signs of approaching departure; the trunks lay half-packed on the floor; there was all that importance of confusion around which makes to the amateur traveller a luxury out of discomfort. Lucilla sat down and waited, anxious and trembling, for her lover. Her woman, who had accompanied her, thinking of more terrestrial concerns than love, left her, at her desire. She could not rest long; she walked, agitating and expecting, to and fro the long and half-furnished chamber which characterizes the Italian palace. At length, her eye fell on an open letter on a writing-table at one corner of the room. She glanced over it mechanically,—certain words suddenly arrested her attention. Were those words—words of passion—addressed to her? If not, O Heaven! to whom? She obeyed, as she ever did, the impulse of the moment, and read what follows:—

"CONSTANCE,—As I write that word how many remembrances rush upon me! for how many years has that name been a talisman to my heart, waking its emotions at will! You are the first woman I ever really loved; you rejected me, yet I could not disdain you. You became another's,—but my love could not desert you. Your hand wrote the history of my life after the period when we met; my habits, my thoughts,—you influenced and coloured them all! And now, Constance, you are free; and I love you more fervently than ever! And *you*—yes, you would not reject me now; you have grown wiser, and learned the value of a heart. And yet the same Fate that divided us hitherto will divide us now; all obstacles but one are passed away,—of that one you shall hear and judge.

"When we parted, Constance, years ago, I did not submit tamely to the burning remembrance you bequeathed me; I sought to dissipate your image, and by wooing others to forget yourself. Need I say that to know another was only to remember you the more? But among the other and far less worthy objects of my pursuit was one whom, had I not seen you first, I might have loved as ardently as I do you; and in the first flush of emotion, and the heat of sudden events, I imagined that I *did* so love her. She was an orphan, a child in years and in the world; and I was all to her,—I *am* all to her. She is not mine by the ties of the Church; but I have pledged a faith to her equally sacred and as strong. Shall I break that faith; shall I betray that trust; shall I crush a heart that has always been mine,—mine more tenderly than yours, rich in a thousand gifts and resources, ever was or ever can be? Shal'

I, sworn to protect her, — I, who have already robbed her of fame and friends, rob her now of father, brother, lover, husband, the world itself, — for I am all to her? Never! never! I shall be wretched throughout life: I shall know that you are free — that you — oh, Constance! *you* might be mine! — but she shall never dream what she has cost me! I have been too cold, too ungrateful to her already, — I will make her amends. My heart may break in the effort, but it shall reward her. You, Constance, in the pride of your lofty station, your strengthened mind, your regulated virtue (fenced in by the hundred barriers of custom), you cannot, perhaps, conceive how pure and devoted the soul of this poor girl is! She is not one whom I could heap riches upon and leave; my love is all the riches she knows. Earth has not a consolation or a recompense for the loss of my affection; and even heaven itself she has never learned to think of, except as a place in which we shall be united forever. As I write this I know that she is sitting afar off and alone, and thinking only of one whose whole soul, fated and accursed as he is, is maddened by the love of another. My letters, her only comfort, have been cold and few of late; I know how they have wrung her heart. I picture to myself her solitude, her sadness, her unfriended youth, her ardent mind, which, not enriched by culture, clings, feeds, lives only on one idea. Before you receive this, I shall be on the road to her. Never again will I risk the temptation I have undergone. I am not a vain man; I do not deceive myself; I do not imagine, I do not insult you by believing, that you will long or bitterly feel my loss. I have loved you far better than you have loved me, and you have uncounted channels for your bright hopes and your various ambition. You love the world, and the world is at your feet! And in remembering me now, you may think you have cause for indignation. Why, with the knowledge of a tie that forbade me to hope for you, why did I linger round you; why did I give vent to any word, or license to any look, that told you I loved you still? Why, above all, on that fated yesterday, when we stood alone surrounded by the waters, — why did I dare forget myself; why clasp you to my breast; why utter the assurance of that love which was a mockery, if I were not about solemnly to record it?

"This you will ask; and if you are not satisfied with the answer, your pride will clothe my memory with resentment. Be it so, yet hear me. Constance, when, in my first youth, at the time when the wax was yet soft, and the tree might yet be bent; when I laid my heart and my future lot at your feet; when you, at the dictates of a worldly and cold ambition (disguise the name as you will, the reality is the same), threw me back on the solitary desert of life; when you rejected, forsook me,

— do you think that, although I loved you still, there was no anger mingled with the love? We met again: but what years of wasted existence, of dimmed hope, of deadened emotion, had passed over me since then! And who had thus marked them? — You! Do you wonder, then, that something of human pride asked for human vengeance? Yes! I pined for some triumph in my turn; I longed to try whether I was yet forgotten, — whether the heart which stung me had been stung also in the wound that it inflicted. Was not this natural? Ask yourself, and blame me if you can. But by degrees, as I gazed upon a beauty, and listened to a voice, softer in their character than of old, as I felt that you would not deny me retribution, this selfish desire for revenge died away, and, by degrees, all emotions were merged in one, — unconquered, unconquerable love. And can you blame me, if then — traitor to myself as to you — I lingered on the spot; if I had many struggles to endure before I could resolve on the sacrifice I now make? Alas! it has cost me much to be just. Can you blame me if at all times I could not control my words and looks? Nay, even in our last meeting, when I was maddened by the thought that we were about to part forever; when we stood alone; when no eye was near; when you clung to me in a delicious timidity; when your breath was on my cheek; when the heaving of your heart was heard by mine; when my hand touched that which could give me all the world in itself; when my arm encircled that glorious and divine shape — O Heaven! can you blame me, can you wonder if I was transported beyond myself; if conscience, reason, all were forgotten, and I thought — felt — lived — but for the moment and for you? No, you will feel for the weakness of nature; you will not judge me harshly.

"And why should you rob me of the remembrance of that brief moment, that wild embrace? How often shall I recall it! How often when the light step of her to whom I return glides around me, shall I cheat myself, and think it yours; when I feel her breath at night, shall I not start and dream it comes from your lips? And in returning her unconscious caress, let me fancy it is you whispers me the assurances of unutterable love! Forgive me, Constance, my yet adored Constance, whom I shall never see more, for these wild words, this momentary weakness. Farewell! Whatever becomes of me, may God give you all His blessings!

"One word more — no, I will not close this letter yet! You remember that you once gave me a flower — years ago. I have preserved its leaves to this day; but I will give no indulgence to a folly that will now wrong you, and be unworthy of myself. I will send you back those leaves; let them plead for me, as the memories of former days. I must break off now, for I can literally write no more. I must go forth and recover my self-command. And oh! may she whom I seek to-morrow, whose unsuspecting heart admonished by temptation I will watch over, guide, and shield, far, far more zealously than I have yet done, never know what it has cost me not to abandon and betray her!"

And Lucilla read over every word of this letter! How wholly impossible it is for language to express the agony, the hopeless, irremediable despair that deepened within her as she proceeded to the end! Everything that life had, or could ever have had for her, of common peace or joy, was blasted forever! As she came to the last word, she bowed her head in silence over the writing, and felt as if some mighty rock had fallen upon her heart and crushed it to dust. Had the letter breathed but one unkind, one slighting expression of her, it would have been some comfort, some rallying point, however forlorn and wretched; but this cruel tenderness, this bitter generosity!

And before she had read that letter, how joyously, how breathlessly she had anticipated rushing to her lover's breast! It seems incredible that the space of a few minutes should suffice to blight a whole existence,— blacken, without a ray of hope, an entire future!

She was aroused by the sound of steps, though in another apartment; she would not now have met Godolphin for worlds; the thought of his return alone gave her the power of motion. She thrust the fatal letter into her bosom; and then, in characters surprisingly distinct and clear, she wrote her name, and placed that writing in the stead of the epistle she took away. She judged rightly that that single name would suffice to say all she could not then say. Having done this, she rose, left the room, and stole softly and unperceived into the open street.

Unconscious and careless whither she went, she hurried on, her eyes bent on the ground, and concealing her form and face with her long mantle. The streets at Rome are not thronged as with us; nor does there exist, in a city consecrated by so many sublime objects, that restless and vulgar curiosity which torments the English public. Each lives in himself, not in his neighbour. The moral air of Rome is Indifference.

Lucilla, therefore, hurried along unmolested and unobserved, until at length her feet failed her, and she sank exhausted, but still unconscious of her movements and of all around, upon one of the scattered fragments of ancient pride that at every turn are visible in the streets of Rome. The place was quiet and solitary, and darkened by the shadows of a palace that reared itself close beside. She sat down; and shrouding her face as it drooped over her breast, endeavoured to collect her thoughts. Presently the sound of a guitar was heard; and along the street came a little group of the itinerant musicians who invest modern Italy with its yet living air of poetry: the reality is gone, but the spirit lingers. They stopped opposite a small house; and Lucilla, looking up, saw the figure of a young girl placing a light at the window as a signal well known, and then she glided away. Meanwhile, the lover (who had accompanied the musicians, and seemed in no very elevated rank of life) stood bare-headed beneath; and in his upward look there was a devotion, a fondness, a respect, that brought back to Lucilla all the unsparing bitterness of contrast and recollection. And now the serenade began. The air was inexpressibly soft and touching, and the words were steeped in that vague melancholy which is inseparable from the tenderness, if not from the passion, of love. Lucilla listened involuntarily, and the charm slowly wrought its effect. The hardness and confusion of her mind melted gradually away, and as the song ended she turned aside and burst into tears. "Happy, happy girl!" she murmured; "she is loved!"

Here let us drop the curtain upon Lucilla. Often, O Reader! shalt thou recall this picture; often shalt thou see her before thee, alone and broken-hearted, weeping in the twilight streets of Rome!

CHAPTER XLIII.

LOVE STRONG AS DEATH, AND NOT LESS BITTER.

When Godolphin returned home the door was open, as Lucilla had left it, and he went at once into his apartment. He hastened to the table on which he had left, with the negligence arising from the emotions of the moment, the letter to Constance; the paper on which Lucilla had written her name alone met his eye. While yet stunned and amazed, his servant and Lucilla's entered: in a few moments he had learned all they had to tell him; the rest Lucilla's handwriting did indeed sufficiently explain. He comprehended all; and in a paroxysm of alarm and remorse, he dispersed his servants, and hurried himself in search of her. He went to the house of her relations; they had not seen or heard of her. It was now night, and every obstacle in the way of his search presented itself. Not a clew could be traced; or, sometimes following a description that seemed to him characteristic, he chased, and found some wanderer — how unlike Lucilla! Towards daybreak he returned home, after a vain and weary search; and his only comfort was in learning from her attendant that she had about her a sum of money which he knew would in Italy always purchase safety and attention. Yet, alone, at night, in the streets, — so utter a stranger as she was to the world, so young and so lovely — he shuddered, he gasped for breath at the idea. Might she destroy herself? That hideous question forced itself upon him; he could not exclude it: he trembled when he recalled her impassioned and keen temper, and when, in remembering the tone and words of his letter to Constance, he felt how desperate a pang every sentence must have inflicted upon her. And, indeed, even his imagination could not equal the truth, when it attempted to sound the depths of her wounded feelings. He only returned home to sally out again. He now employed the police, and those most active and vigilant agents that at Rome are willing to undertake all enterprises; he could not but feel assured of discovering her.

Still, however, noon, evening came on, and no tidings. As he once more returned home, in the faint hope that some intelligence might await him there, his servant hurried eagerly out to him with a letter; it was from Lucilla, and it was worthy of her: I give it to the reader.

LUCILLA'S LETTER.

"I have read your letter to another! Are not these words sufficient to tell you all? All? no! you never, never, never can tell how crushed and broken my heart is! Why? Because you are a man, and because you have never loved as I loved. Yes, Godolphin, I knew that I was not one whom you *could* love. I am a poor, ignorant, untutored girl, with nothing at my heart but a great world of love which I could never tell. Thou saidst I could not comprehend *thee:* alas! how much was there — is there — in *my* nature, in *my* feelings, which have been, and ever will be, unfathomable to thy sight!

"But all this matters not; the tie between us is eternally broken. Go, dear, dear Godolphin! link thyself to that happier other one, seemingly so much more thine equal than the lowly and uncultivated Lucilla. Grieve not for me; you have been kind, most kind, to me. You have taken away hope, but you have given me pride in its stead; the blow which has crushed my heart has given strength to my mind. Were you and I left alone on the earth, we must still be apart: I could never, never live with you again; my world is not your world; when our hearts have ceased to be in common, what of union is there left to us? Yet it would be something if, since the future is shut out from me, you had not also deprived me of the past: I have not even the privilege of looking back! What! all the while my heart was lavishing itself upon thee; all the while I had no other thought, no other dream but thee; all the while I sat by thy side, and watched thee, hanging on thy wish, striving to foresee thy thoughts, — all the while I was the partner of thy days, and at night my bosom was thy pillow, and I could not sleep from the bliss of thinking thee so near me, *thy* heart was then indeed away from me; *thy* thoughts estranged; I was to *thee* only an encumbrance, — a burthen, from which *thy* sigh was to be free! Can I ever look back, then, to those hours we spent together? All that vast history of the past is but one record of bitterness and shame. And yet I cannot blame thee; it were something if I could: in proportion as you loved me not, you were kind and generous; and God will bless you for that kindness to the poor orphan. A harsh word, a threatening glance, I never had the affliction to feel from thee. Tracing the blighted past, I am only left to sadden at that gentleness which never came from love!

"Go, Godolphin — I repeat the prayer in all humbleness and sincerity — go to her whom thou lovest, perhaps as I loved thee; go, and in your happiness I shall feel at last something of happiness myself. We part forever, but there is no unkindness between us; there is no reproach that one can make against the other. If I have sinned, it has been against Heaven and not thee; and thou — why, even against Heaven *mine* was *all* the fault, the rashness, the madness! You will return to your native land; to that proud England, of which I have so often questioned you, and which, even in your answers, seems to me so cold and desolate a spot, — a land so hostile to love. There, in your new ties, you will learn new objects, and you will be too busy and too happy for your thoughts to turn to me again. Too happy? — No, I wish I could think you would be; but I, whom you deny to possess sympathies with you, — I have at least penetrated so far into your heart as to fear that, come what may, you will never find the happiness you ask. You exact too much, you dream too fondly, not to be discontented with the truth. What has happened to me must happen to my rival, will happen to you throughout life. Your being is in one world, your soul is in another. Alas! how foolishly I run on, as if seeking in your nature and not circumstances the blow that separates us.

"I shall hasten to a conclusion. I have gained a refuge in this convent; seek me not, follow me not, I implore, I adjure thee; it can serve no purpose. I would not see thee; the veil is already drawn between thy world and me, and it only remains, in kindness and in charity, to bid each other farewell. Farewell, then! I think I am now with thee; I think my lips have breathed aside thy long hair, and cling to thy fair temples with a sister's — that word, at least, is left me — *a sister's* kiss. As we stood together, at the gray dawn, when we last parted; as then, in sorrow and in tears, I hid my face in thy bosom; as then, unconscious of what was to come, I poured forth *my* assurances of faithful unswerving thought; as thrice thou didst tear thyself from me and didst thrice return, — and as, through the comfortless mists of morn I gazed after thee, and fancied for hours that thy last words yet rang in my ear, so now, but with different feelings, I once more bid thee farewell, — farewell forever!"

CHAPTER XLIV.

GODOLPHIN.

"No, signor, she will not see you!"

"You have given my note, given that ring?"

"I have, and she still refuses."

"Refuses? — and is that all the answer; no line to — to soften the reply?"

"Signor, I have spoken all my message."

"Cruel, hard-hearted! May I call again, think you, with a better success?"

"The convent, at stated times, is open to strangers, signor; but so far as the young signora is concerned I feel assured, from her manner, that your visits will be in vain."

"Ay, ay, I understand you, madam; you wish to entice her from the wicked world,— to suffer not human friendships to disturb her thoughts. Good heavens! and can she, so young, so ardent, dream of taking the veil?"

"She does not dream of it," said the nun, coolly; "she has no intention of remaining here long."

"Befriend me, I beseech you!" cried Godolphin, eagerly; "restore her to me; let me only come once to her within these walls and I will enrich your —"

"Signor, good-day."

Dejected, melancholy, and yet enraged amidst all his sorrow, Godolphin returned to Rome. Lucilla's letter rankled in his heart like the barb of a broken arrow; but the stern resolve with which she had refused to see him appeared to the pride that belongs to manhood a harsh and unfeeling insult. He knew not that poor Lucilla's eyes had watched him from the walls of the convent, and that while, for his sake more than her own, she had refused the meeting he prayed for, she had not the resolution to deny herself the luxury of gazing on him once more.

He reached Rome; he found a note on his table from Lady Charlotte Deerham, saying she had heard it was his intention to leave Rome, and begging him to receive from her that evening her adieus. "Lady Erpingham will be with me," concluded the note.

This brought a new train of ideas. Since Lucilla's flight, all thought but of Lucilla had been expelled from Godolphin's mind. We have seen how his letter to Lady Erpingham miscarried: he had written no other. How strange to Constance must seem his conduct, after the scene of the avowal in the Siren's Cave: no excuse on the one hand, no explanation on the other; and now what explanation *should* he give? There was no longer a necessity, for it was no longer honesty and justice to fly from the bliss that might await him,—the love of his early-worshipped Constance. But could he, with a heart yet bleeding from the violent rupture of one tie, form a new one? Agitated, restless, self-reproachful, bewildered, and uncertain, he could not bear thoughts that demanded answers to a thousand questions; he flung from his cheerless room, and hastened, with a feverish pulse and burning temples, to Lady Charlotte Deerham's.

"Good heavens! how ill you look, Mr. Godolphin!" cried the hostess, involuntarily.

"Ill!—ha, ha! I never was better; but I have just returned from a long journey: I have not touched food nor felt sleep for three days and nights. I—ha, ha! no, I 'm not ill;" and, with an eye bright with gathering delirium, Godolphin glared around him.

Lady Charlotte drew back and shuddered; Godolphin felt a cool, soft hand laid on his; he turned, and the face of Constance, full of anxious and wondering pity, was bent upon him. He stood arrested for one moment, and then, seizing that hand, pressed it to his lips, his heart, and burst suddenly into tears. That paroxysm saved his life; for days afterwards he was insensible.

CHAPTER XLV.

THE DECLARATION. — THE APPROACHING NUPTIALS. — IS THE IDEALIST CONTENTED?

As Godolphin returned to health, and, day after day, the presence of Constance, her soft tones, her deep eyes, grew on him, renewing their ancient spells, the reader must perceive that bourne to which events necessarily tended. For some weeks not a word that alluded to the Siren's Cave was uttered by either; but when that allusion came at last from Godolphin's lips, the next moment he was kneeling beside Constance, her hand surrendered to his, and her proud cheek all bathed in the blushes of sixteen.

"And so," said Saville, "you, Percy Godolphin, are at last the accepted lover of Constance, Countess of Erpingham. When is the wedding to be?"

"I know not," replied Godolphin, musingly.

"Well, I almost envy you; you will be very happy for six weeks, and that 's something in this disagreeable world. Yet, now I look on you, I grow reconciled to myself again; you do not seem so happy as that I, Augustus Saville, should envy you while my digestion lasts. What are you thinking of?"

"Nothing," replied Godophin, vacantly; the words of Lucilla were weighing at his heart, like a prophecy working towards its fulfilment: "*Come what may, you will never find the happiness you ask: you exact too much.*"

At that moment Lady Erpingham's page entered with a note from Constance, and a present of flowers. No one ever wrote half so beautifully, so spiritually, as Constance; and to Percy the wit was so intermingled with the tenderness!

"No," said he, burying his lips among the flowers; "no! I discard the foreboding; with you I must be happy!" But conscience, still unsilenced, whispered *Lucilla!*

The marriage was to take place at Rome. The day was fixed; and, owing to Constance's rank, beauty, and celebrity, the news of the event created throughout "the English in Italy" no small sensation. There was a great deal of gossip, of course, on the occasion; and some of this gossip found its way to the haughty ears of Constance. It was said that she had made a strange match,—that it was a curious weakness in one so proud and brilliant to look no loftier than a private and not very wealthy gentleman; handsome, indeed, and reputed clever; but one who had never *distinguished himself* in anything,—who never would!

Constance was alarmed and stung, not at the vulgar accusation, the paltry sneer, but at the prophecy relating to Godolphin: "He had never distinguished himself in anything,—he never would." Rank, wealth, power, Constance felt these she wanted not, these she could command of herself; but she felt also that a nobler vanity of her nature required that the man of her mature and second choice should not be one in repute of that mere herd, above whom in reality his genius so eminently exalted him. She deemed it essential to her future happiness that Godolphin's ambition should be aroused, that he should share her ardour for those great objects that she felt would forever be dear to her.

"I love Rome!" said she, passionately, one day, as accompanied by Godolphin, she left the Vatican; "I feel my soul grow larger amidst its ruins. Elsewhere through Italy we live in the present, but here in the past."

"Say not that that is the better life, dear Constance; the present—can we surpass it?"

Constance blushed, and thanked her lover with a look that told him he was understood.

"Yet," said she, returning to the subject, "who can breathe the air that is rife with glory, and not be intoxicated with emulation? Ah, Percy!"

"Ah, Constance! and what wouldst thou have of me? Is it not glory enough to be thy lover?"

"Let the world be as proud of my choice as I am."

Godolphin frowned; he penetrated in those words to Constance's secret meaning. Accustomed to be an idol from his boyhood, he resented the notion that he had need of exertion to render him worthy even of Constance; and sensible that it might be thought he had made an alliance beyond his just pretensions, he was doubly tenacious as to his own claims. Godolphin frowned, then, and turned away in silence. Constance sighed; she felt that she might not renew the subject. But after a pause Godolphin himself continued it.

"Constance," said he, in a low, firm voice, "let us understand each other. You are all to me in the world,—fame and honour and station and happiness. Am I, also, that all to you? If there be any thought at your heart which whispers you, 'You might have served your ambition better; you have done wrong in yielding to love and love only,'—then, Constance, pause; it is not too late."

"Do I deserve this, Percy?"

"You drop words sometimes," answered Godolphin, "that seem to indicate that you think the world may cavil at your choice, and that some exertion on *my* part is necessary to maintain *your* dignity. Constance, need I say, again and again, that I adore the very dust you tread on? But I have a pride, a self-respect, beneath which I cannot stoop; if you really think or feel this, I will not condescend to receive even happiness from you: let us part."

Constance saw his lips white and quivering as he spoke; her heart smote her, her pride vanished; she sank on his shoulder, and forgot even ambition; nay, while she inly murmured at his sentiment, she felt it breathed a sort of nobility that she could not but esteem. She strove then to lull to rest all her more worldly anxieties for the future; to hope that, cast on the exciting stage of English ambition, Godolphin must necessarily be stirred despite his creed; and if she sometimes doubted, sometimes despaired of this, she felt at least that his presence had become dearer to her than all things. Nay, she checked her own enthusiasm, her own worship of fame, since they clashed with his opinions; so marvellously and insensibly had Love bowed down the proud energies and the lofty soul of the daughter of John Vernon.

CHAPTER XLVI.

THE BRIDALS. — THE ACCIDENT. — THE FIRST LAWFUL POSSESSION OF LOVE.

It was the morning on which Constance and Godolphin were to be married; it had been settled that they were to proceed the same day towards Florence, and Constance was at her toilette when her woman laid beside her a large bouquet of flowers.

"From Percy — from Mr. Godolphin, I mean?" she asked, taking them up.

"No, my lady; a young woman outside the palace gave them me, and bade me in such pretty English be sure to give them to your ladyship; and when I offered her money, she would not take anything, my lady."

"The Italians are a courteous people," replied Constance; and she placed the flowers in her bosom.

As, after the ceremony, Godolphin assisted his bride into the carriage, a girl, wrapped in a large cloak, pressed forward for a moment. Godolphin had in that moment turned his head to give some order to his servant, and with the next the girl had sunk back into the throng that was drawn around the carriage — yet not before Constance had heard her murmur in deep, admiring, yet sorrowful tone: "Beautiful! *how* beautiful! — Ah me!"

"Did you observe what beautiful eyes that young girl had?" asked Constance, as the carriage whirled off.

"What girl? I saw nothing but you!"

"Hark! there is a noise behind."

Godolphin looked out; the crowd seemed collected round one person.

"Only a young woman fainted, sir!" said his servant, seated behind. "She fell down in a fit just before the horses; but they started aside, and did not hurt her."

"That is fortunate!" said Godolphin, reseating himself by his new bride; "drive on faster."

At Florence, Godolphin revealed to Constance the outline of Lucilla's history, and Constance shared somewhat of the feelings with which he told it.

"I left," said he, "in the hands of the abbess a sum to be entirely at Lucilla's control, whether she stay in the convent or not, and which will always secure to her an independence. But I confess I should like now once more to visit the convent, and learn on what fate she has decided."

"You would do well, dear Percy," replied Constance, who from her high and starred sphere could stoop to no vulgar jealousy; "indeed, I think you could do no less."

And Godolphin covered those generous lips with the sweet kisses in which esteem begins to mingle with passion. What has the earth like that first fresh union of two hearts long separated, and now blended forever? However close the sympathy between woman and her lover, however each thinks to have learned the other, what a world is there left *un*learned, until marriage brings all those charming confidences, that holy and sweet intercourse, which leaves no separate interest, no undivided thought! But there is one thing that distinguishes the conversation of young married people from that of lovers on a less sacred footing,—*they talk of the future!* Other lovers talk rather of the past; an uncertainty pervades *their* hereafter; they feel, they recoil from it; they are sensible that their plans are not one and indivisible. But married people are always laying out the "TO COME;" always talking over their plans: this often takes something away from the tenderness of affection, but how much it adds to its enjoyment!

Seated by each other, and looking on the silver Arno, Godolphin and Constance, hand clasped in hand, surrendered themselves to the contemplation of their future happiness. "And what would be your favourite mode of life, dear Percy?"

"Why, I have now no schemings left me, Constance. With you obtained, I have grown a dullard, and left off dreaming.

But let me see, a house in England — *you* like England — some ten or twenty miles from the great Babel; books, pictures, statues, and old trees that shall put us in mind of our Norman fathers who planted them; above all, a noisy, clear sunny stream gliding amidst them; deer on the opposite bank, half hidden amongst the fern, and rooks overhead; a privilege for eccentricity that would allow one to be social or solitary as one pleased; and a house so full of guests, that to shun them *all* now and then would be no affront to *one*."

"Well," said Constance, smiling, "go on."

"I have finished."

"Finished?"

"Yes, my fair Insatiable! What more would you have?"

"Why, this is but a country-life you have been talking of, — very well in its way for three months in the year."

"Italy, then, for the other nine," returned Godolphin.

"Ah, Percy! is pleasure, mere pleasure, vulgar pleasure, to be really the sole end and aim of life?"

"Assuredly."

"And action, enterprise,— are these as nothing?"

Godolphin was silent, but began absently to throw pebbles into the water. The action reminded Constance of the first time she had ever seen him among his ancestral groves; and she sighed as she now gazed on a brow from which the effeminacy and dreaming of his life had banished much of its early chivalric and earnest expression.

CHAPTER XLVII.

NEWS OF LUCILLA.

Godolphin was about one morning to depart for the convent to which Lucilla had flown, when a letter was brought to him from the abbess of the convent herself; it had followed him from Rome. Lucilla had left her retreat,— left it three days before Godolphin's marriage; the abbess knew not whither, but believed she intended to reside in Rome. She inclosed him a note from Lucilla, left for him before her departure. Short but characteristic, it ran thus: —

LUCILLA TO GODOLPHIN.

"I can stay here no longer; my mind will not submit to quiet; this inactivity wears me to madness. Besides, I want to see thy wife. I shall go to Rome; I shall witness thy wedding; and then — ah! what then? Give me back, Godolphin, oh, give me back the young pure heart I had ere I loved you! Then, I could take joy in all things; *now!* — But I will not repine; it is beneath me. I, the daughter of the stars, am no love-sick and nerveless minion of a vain regret; my pride is roused at last, and I feel at least the independence of being alone. Wild and roving shall be my future life; that lot which denies me hope has raised me above all fear. Love makes us all the woman; love has left me, and something hard and venturous, something that belongs to *thy* sex, has come in its stead.

"You have left me money — I thank you — I thank you — I thank you; my heart almost chokes me as I write this. Could you think of me so basely? For shame, man! if my child — *our* child were living (and O Percy, she had thine eyes!), I would see her starve inch by inch rather than touch one doit of thy *bounty!* But she is dead, thank God! Fear not for me, I shall not starve; these hands can support life. God bless thee, — loved as thou still art! If, years hence, I should feel my end draw near, I will drag myself to thy country, and look once more on thy face before I die."

Godolphin sank down, and covered his face with his hands. Constance took up the letter. "Ay, read it!" said he, in a hollow voice. She did so, and when she had finished, the proud Constance, struck by a spirit like her own, bathed the letter in her tears. This pleased, this touched, this consoled Godolphin more than the most elaborate comfortings. "Poor girl!" said Constance, through her tears, "this must not be; she must not be left on the wide world to her own despairing heart. Let us both go to Rome, and seek her out. *I* will persuade her to accept what she refuses from you."

Godolphin pressed his wife's hand, but spoke not. They went that day to Rome. Lucilla had departed for Leghorn, and thence taken her passage in a vessel bound to the northern coasts of Europe. Perhaps she had sought her father's land? With that hope, in the absence of all others, they attempted to console themselves.

CHAPTER XLVIII.

IN WHICH TWO PERSONS, PERMANENTLY UNITED, DISCOVER THAT NO TIE CAN PRODUCE UNION OF MINDS.

WEEKS passed on, and, apparently, Godolphin had reconciled himself to the disappearance and precarious destiny of Lucilla. It was not in his calm and brooding nature to show much of emotion; but there was often, even in the presence of Constance, a cloud on his brow, and the fits of abstraction to which he had always been accustomed grew upon him more frequently than ever. Constance had been inured for years to the most assiduous, the most devoted attentions; and now, living much alone with Godolphin, she began somewhat to miss them,—for Godolphin could be a passionate, a romantic, but he could not be a very watchful lover. He had no *petits soins*. Few husbands have, it is true; nor is it necessary for husbands in general. But Constance was not an ordinary woman; she loved deeply, but she loved according to her nature, as a woman proud and exacting must love. For Godolphin, her haughty step waxed timorous and vigilant; she always sprang forward the first to meet him on his return from his solitary ramblings, and he smiled upon her with his wonted gentleness,— but not so gratefully, thought Constance, as he ought. In truth, he had been too much accustomed to the eager love of Lucilla to feel greatly surprised at any proof of tenderness from Constance. Thus, too proud to speak, to hint a complaint, Constance was nevertheless perpetually wounded, and by degrees (although not loving her husband less) she taught that love to be more concealed. Oh, that accursed secretiveness in women, which makes them always belie themselves!

Godolphin, too, was not without *his* disappointments. There was something so bright, so purely intellectual about Constance's character, that at times, when brought into constant intercourse with her, you longed for some human weakness, some wild, warm error on which to repose. Dazzling and fair as snow, like snow your eye ached to gaze upon her. She had, during the years of her ungenial marriage, cultivated her mind to the utmost; few women were so accomplished,—it might be learned; her conversation flowed forever in the same bright, flowery, adorned stream. There were times when Godolphin recollected how hard it is to read a volume of that Gibbon who in a page is so delightful. Her affection for him was intense, high, devoted; but it was wholly of the same intellectual spiritualized order; it seemed to Godolphin to want human warmth and fondness. In fact, there never was a woman who, both by original nature and after habits, was so purely and abstractedly "mind" as was Constance; there was not a single trait or taste in her character that a sensualist could have sneered at. Her heart was wholly Godolphin's; her mind was generous, sympathizing, lofty; her person unrivalled in the majesty of its loveliness; all these, too, were Godolphin's, and yet the eternal something was wanting still.

"I have brought you your hat, Percy," said Constance; "you forget the dews are falling fast, and your head is uncovered."

"Thank you," said Percy, gently; yet Constance thought the tone might have been warmer. "How beautiful is this hour! Look yonder, the sun's ray still upon those immortal hills, that lone gray tower amongst the far plains, the pines around — hearken to their sighing! These are indeed the scenes of the Dryad and the Faun. These are scenes where we could melt our whole nature down to love: Nature never meant us for the stern and arid destinies we fulfil. Look round, Constance, in every leaf of her gorgeous book, how glowingly is written the one sentence, 'LOVE AND BE HAPPY!' You answer not; to these thoughts you are cold."

"They breathe too much of the Epicurean and his rose-leaves for me," answered Constance, smilingly. "I love better that stern old tower, telling of glorious strife and great deeds, than all the *softer* landscape, on which the present debasement of the South seems written."

"You and your English," said Godolphin, somewhat bitterly, "prate of the debasement of my poor Italians in a jargon that I confess almost enrages me." (Constance coloured and bit her lip.) "Debasement! why debasement? They enjoy themselves: they take from life its just moral; they do not affect the more violent crimes; they feel their mortality, follow its common ends, are frivolous, contented, and die! Well; this is debasement. Be it so. But for what would you exchange it? The hard, cold, ferocious guilt of ancient Rome; the detestable hypocrisy, the secret villany, fraud, murder, that stamped republican Venice? The days of glory that you lament are the days of the darkest guilt; and man shudders when he reads what the fair moralizers over the soft and idle Italy sigh to recall!"

"You are severe," said Constance, with a pained voice.

"Forgive me, dearest, but you are often severe on *my* feelings."

Constance was silent; the magic of the sunset was gone; they walked back to the house, thoughtful, and somewhat cooled towards each other.

Another day, on which the rain forbade them to stir from home, Godolphin, after he had remained long silent and meditating, said to Constance, who was busy writing letters to her political friends, in which, avoiding Italy and love, the scheming countess dwelt only on busy England and its eternal politics,—

"Will you read to me, dear Constance? my spirits are sad to-day; the weather affects them."

Constance laid aside her letters, and took up one of the many books that strewed the table: it was a volume of one of our most popular poets.

"I hate poetry," said Godolphin, languidly.

"Here is Machiavel's history of the Prince of Lucca," said Constance, quickly.

"Ah, read that, and see how odious is ambition," returned Godolphin.

And Constance read, but she warmed at what Godolphin's lip curled with disdain. The sentiments, however, drew him from his apathy; and presently, with the eloquence he could command when once excited, he poured forth the doctrines of his peculiar philosophy. Constance listened, delighted and absorbed; she did not sympathize with the thought, but she was struck with the genius which clothed it. "Ah," said she, with enthusiasm, "why should those brilliant words be thus spoken and lost forever? Why not stamp them on the living page, or why not invest them in the oratory that would render *you* illustrious and *them* immortal?"

"Excellent!" said Godolphin, laughing; "The House of Commons would sympathize with philosophy warmly!"

Yet Constance was right on the whole. But the curse of a life of pleasure is its aversion to useful activity. Talk of the genius that lies crushed and obscure in poverty! Wealth and station have also their mute Miltons and inglorious Hampdens.

Alas! how much of deep and true wisdom do we meet among the triflers of the world! How much that in the stern middle walks of life would have obtained renown, in the withering and relaxed air of loftier rank dies away unheeded! The two extremes meet in this,—the destruction of mental gifts.

CHAPTER XLIX.

THE RETURN TO LONDON. — THE ETERNAL NATURE OF DISAPPOINTMENT. — FANNY MILLINGER. — HER HOUSE AND SUPPER.

It was in the midst of spring, and at the approach of night, that our travellers entered London. After an absence of some duration, there is a singular emotion on returning to the roar and tumult of that vast city. Its bustle, its life, its wealth, — the tokens of the ambition and commerce of the Great Island Race,— have something of inconceivable excitement and power, after the comparative desertion and majestic stillness of Continental cities. Constance leaned restlessly forth from the window of the carriage as it whirled on.

"Oh, that I were a man!" said she, fervently.

"And why?" asked Godolphin, smilingly.

"Why! look out on this broad theatre of universal ambition, and read the why. What a proud and various career lies open in this free city to every citizen! Look, look yonder,— the old hereditary senate, still eloquent with high memories."

"And close by it," said Godolphin, sneering, "behold the tomb!"

"Yes, but the tomb of great men!" said Constance, eagerly.

"The victims of their greatness."

There was a pause; Constance would not reply, she would scarcely listen.

"And do you feel no excitement, Percy, in the hum and bustle, the lights, the pomp of your native city?"

"Yes; I am in the mart where all enjoyment may be purchased."

"Ah, fie!"

Godolphin drew his cloak round him, and put up the window.

"These cursed east winds!"

Very true — they *are* the curse of the country!

The carriage stopped at the stately portico of Erpingham House. Godolphin felt a little humiliated at being indebted to another, — to a woman, — for so splendid a tenement; but Constance, not penetrating into this sentiment, hastened up the broad stairs, and said, pointing to a door that led to her boudoir, —

"In that room Cabinets have been formed and shaken."

Godolphin laughed; he was alive only to the vanity of the boast, because he shared not the enthusiasm; this was Constance's weak point: her dark eye flashed fire.

There 's nothing bores a man more than the sort of uneasy quiet that follows a day's journey. Godolphin took his hat, and yawningly stretching himself, nodded to Constance, and moved to the door; they were in her dressing-room at the time.

"Why, what, Percy, you cannot be going out now?"

"Indeed I am, my love."

"Where, in Heaven's name?"

"To White's, to learn the news of the Opera, and the strength of the Ballet."

"I had just rung for lights to show you the house!" said Constance, disappointed, and half-reproachfully.

"Mercy, Constance! damp rooms and east winds together are too much. House, indeed! what can there be worth seeing in your English drawing-rooms after the marble palaces of Italy? Any commands?"

"None!" said Constance, sinking back into her chair, with the tears in her eyes. Godolphin did not perceive them; he was only displeased by the cold tone of her answer, and he shut the door, muttering to himself, "Was there ever such indelicate ostentation!"

"And thus," said Constance, bitterly, "I return to England; friendless, unloved, solitary in my schemes and my heart as I was before. Awake, my soul! *thou* art my sole strength, my sole support. Weak, weak that I was, to love this man in spite of — Well, well, I am not sunk so low as to regret."

So saying, she wiped away a few tears, and turning with a strong effort from softer thoughts, leaned her cheek on her hand, and gazing on the fire, surrendered herself to the sterner and more plotting meditations which her return to the circle of her old ambition had at first called forth.

Meanwhile Godolphin sauntered into the then arch-club of St. James's, that reservoir of idle exquisites and kid-gloved politicians. There are two classes of popular men in London, — the sprightly, joyous, good-humoured set; the quiet, gentle, sarcastic herd. The one are fellows called "devilish good," the other, fellows called "devilish gentlemanlike." To the latter class belonged Godolphin. As he had never written a book nor set up for a genius, his cleverness was tacitly allowed to be no impediment to his good qualities. Nothing atones for the sin, in the eyes of those young gentlemen who create for their contemporaries reputation, of having in any way distinguished oneself. "He 's such a d—d bore, that man with his books and poetry," said an arch-dandy of Byron, just after "Childe Harold" had turned the heads of the women. There happened to be a knot assembled at White's when Godolphin entered; they welcomed him affectionately.

"Wish you joy, old fellow," said one. "Bless me, Godolphin! well, I am delighted to see you," cried another. "So you have monopolized Lady Erpingham!— lucky dog!" whispered a third.

Godolphin, his vanity soothed by the reception he met with, spent his evening at the Club. The habit begun, became easy, — Godolphin spent *many* evenings at his club. Constance, running the round of her acquaintance, was too proud to complain. Perhaps complaint would not have mended the matter; but one word of delicate tenderness, or one *look* that asked for his society, and White's would have been forsaken! Godolphin secretly resented the very evenness of temper he had once almost overprized.

"Oh, Godolphin," one evening whispered a young lord,

"we sup at the little actress's,—*the* Millinger; you remember the Millinger? You must come; you are an old favourite, you know: she 'll be so glad to see you,—all innocent, by the way: Lady Erpingham need not be jealous"—jealous! Constance jealous of Fanny Millinger!—"all innocent. Come. I 'll drive you there; my cab is at the door."

"Anything better than a lecture on ambition," thought Godolphin; and he consented. Godolphin's friend was a lively young nobleman, of that good-natured, easy, uncaptious temper, which a clever, susceptible, indolent man often likes better than comrades more intellectual, because he has not to put himself out of his way in the comradeship. Lord Falconer rattled on, as they drove along the brilliant streets, through a thousand topics, of which Godolphin heard as much as he pleased; and Falconer was of that age and those spirits when a listener may be easily dispensed with.

They arrived at a little villa at Brompton. There was a little garden round it, and a little bower in one corner, all kept excessively neat; and the outside of the house had just been painted white from top to bottom; and there was a veranda to the house; and the windows were plate-glass, with mahogany sashes—only, here and there, a Gothic casement was stuck in by way of looking "tasty;" and through one window on the ground-floor, the lights shining within showed crimson silk and gilded chairs, and all sorts of finery,—Louis Quatorze in a nutshell! The reader knows the sort of house as well as if he had lived in it. Ladies of Fanny Millinger's turn of mind always choose the same kind of habitation. It is astonishing what a unanimity of taste they have; and young men about town call it "taste" too, and imitate the fashion in their own little *tusculums* in Chapel Street.

After having threaded a Gothic hall four feet by eight and an oval conservatory with a river-god in the middle, the two visitors found themselves in the presence of Fanny Millinger.

Godolphin had certainly felt no small curiosity to see again the frank, fair, laughing face which had shone on his boyhood, and his mind ran busily back to that summer evening when, with a pulse how different from its present languid tenor, and a heart burning with ardour and the pride of novel independence, the young adventurer first sallied on the world. He drew back involuntarily as he now gazed on the actress: she had kept the promise of her youth, and grown round and full in her proportions. She was extravagantly dressed, but not with an ungraceful, although a theatrical choice: her fair hands and arms were covered with jewels, and that indescribable air which betrays the stage was far more visibly marked in her deportment than when Godolphin first knew her; yet still there was the same freedom as of old, the same joyousness, and good-humoured carelessness in her manner, and in the silver ring of her voice as she greeted Falconer, and turned to question him as to his friend. Godolphin dropped his cloak, and the next moment, with a pretty scream, quite stage-effect, and yet quite natural, the actress had thrown herself into his arms.

"Oh, but I forgot," said she, presently, with a mock salutation of respect, "you are married now; there will be no more cakes and ale. Ah, what long years since we met; yet I have never quite forgotten you, although the stage requires all one's memory for one's new parts. Alas! your hair — it *was* so beautiful — it has lost half its curl, and grown thin. Very rude in me to say so, but I always speak the truth, and my heart warms to see you, so all its thoughts thaw out."

"Well," said Lord Falconer, who had been playing with a little muffy sort of dog, "you 'll recollect *me* presently."

"You! Oh, one never thinks of you, except when you speak, and then one recollects you — to look at the clock."

"Very good, Fanny — very good, Fan: and when do you expect Windsor? — He ought to be here soon. Tell me, do you like him really?"

"*Like* him?—yes, excessively; just the word for him — for you all. If *love* were thrown into the stream of life, my little sail would be upset in an instant. But in truth, what with dressing and playing and all the grave business of life, I am not idle enough to love. And oh, Godolphin, I 'm so improved! Ask Lord Falconer if I don't sing like an angel, although my voice is hardly strong enough to go round a lootable; but on the stage, one learns to dispense with all qualities. It is a curious thing, that fictitious existence, side by side with the real one! We live in enchantment, Percy, and enjoy what the poets pretend to."

The dreaming Godolphin was struck by the remark. He was surprised, also, to see how much Fanny remained the same. A life of gayety had not debased *her*.

Tom Windsor came next, an Irishman of five-and-forty, not like his countrymen in aught save wit. Thin, small, shrivelled, but up to his ears in knowledge of the world, and with a jest forever on his tongue; rich and gay, he was always popular, and he made the most of his little life without being an absolute rascal. Next dropped in the handsome Frenchman De Damville; next the young gambler St. John; next, two ladies, both actresses,—and the party was complete.

The supper was in keeping with the house; the best wines, excellent viands,—the actress had grown rich. Wit, noise, good-humour, anecdote, flashed round with the champagne; and Godolphin, exhilarated into a second youth, fancied himself once more the votary of pleasure.

CHAPTER L.

GODOLPHIN'S SOLILOQUY.—HE BECOMES A MAN OF PLEASURE AND A PATRON OF THE ARTS.—A NEW CHARACTER SHADOWED FORTH; FOR AS WE ADVANCE, WHETHER IN LIFE OR ITS REPRESENTATION, CHARACTERS ARE MORE FAINT AND DIMLY DRAWN THAN IN THE EARLIER PART OF OUR CAREER.

"YES," said Godolphin, the next morning, as he soliloquized over his lonely breakfast-table,—lonely, for the hours of the restless Constance were not those of the luxurious and indolent Godolphin, and she was already in her carriage; nay, already closeted with an intriguing ambassadress,—"yes; I have passed two eras of life,—the first of romance, the second of contemplation; once my favourite study was poetry, next philosophy. Now, returned to my native country, rich, settled, yet young, new objects arise to me; not that vulgar and troublous ambition (which is to make a toil of life) that Constance suggests, but a more warm and vivid existence than that I have lately dreamed away. Let luxury and pleasure now be to me what solitude and thought were. I have been too long the solitary, I will learn to be social."

Agreeably to this resolution, Godolphin returned with avidity to the enjoyment of the world; he found himself courted, he courted society in return. Erpingham House had been for years the scene of fascination: who does not recollect the yet greater refinement which its new lord threw over its circles? A delicate and just conception of the fine arts had always characterized Godolphin. He now formed that ardour for collecting, common to the more elegant order of minds. From his beloved Italy he imported the most beautiful statues; his cabinets were filled with gems; his walls glowed with the triumphs of the canvas; the showy but heterogeneous furniture of Erpingham House gave way to a more classic and perfect taste. The same fastidiousness, which, in the affairs of the heart, had characterized Godolphin's habits and sentiments, characterized his new pursuits; the same thirst for the Ideal, the same worship of the Beautiful, and aspirations after the Perfect.

It was not in Constance's nature to admit this smaller ambition: her taste was pure but not minute; she did not descend to the philosophy of detail. But she was glad still to see that Godolphin could be aroused to the discovery of an active object; and although she sighed to perceive his fine genius frittered away on the trifles of the virtuoso, although she secretly regretted the waste of her great wealth (which afforded to political ambition so high an advantage) on the mute marble, and what she deemed, nor unjustly, frivolous curiosities, she still never interfered with Godolphin's caprices, conscious that, to his delicacy, a single objection to his wishes on the score of expense would have reminded him of what she wished him most to forget,—namely, that the means of this lavish expenditure were derived from her She hoped that his mind, once fairly awakened, would soon grow sated with the acquisition of baubles, and at length sigh for loftier objects; and, in the mean while, she plunged into her old party plots and ambitious intrigues.

Erpingham House, celebrated as ever for the beauty of its queen and for the political nature of its entertainments, received a new celebrity from its treasures of art and the spiritual wit and grace with which Godolphin invested its attractions. Among the crowd of its guests there was one whom its owners more particularly esteemed,—Stainforth Radclyffe was still considerably under thirty, but already a distinguished man. At school he had been distinguished, at college distinguished, and now in the world of science distinguished also. Beneath a quiet, soft, and cold exterior, he concealed the most resolute and persevering ambition; and this ambition was the governing faculty of his soul. His energies were undistracted by small objects; for he went little into general society, and he especially sought in his studies those pursuits which nerve and brace the mind. He was a profound thinker, a deep political economist, an accurate financier, a judge of the intricacies of morals and legislation,—for to his mere book studies he added an instinctive penetration into men; and when from time to time he rejoined the world, he sought out those most distinguished in the sciences he had cultivated, and by their lights corrected his own. In him there was nothing desultory or undetermined; his conduct was perpetual calculation. He did nothing but with an eye to a final object; and when, to the superficial, he seemed most to wander from the road their prudence would have suggested, he was only seeking the surest and shortest paths. Yet his ambition was not the mere vulgar thirst for getting on in the world; he cared little for the paltry place, the petty power, which may reward what are called aspiring young men. His clear sight penetrated to objects that seemed wrapped in shade to all others; and to those only — distant, but vast and towering — he deigned to attach his desires. He cared not for small and momentary rewards; and while always (for he knew its necessity) uppermost on the tide of the hour, he had neither joy nor thought for the petty honours for which he was envied, and by which he was supposed to be elated. Always occupied and always thoughtful, he went, as I have just said, very little into the gay world, and was not very well formed to shine in it when there; for trifles require the whole man as much as matters of importance. He did not want either wit or polish, but he tasked his powers too severely on great subjects not to be sometimes dull upon small ones: yet, when he was either excited or at home, he was not without — what man of genius is? — his peculiar powers of conversation. There was in this young, dark, brooding, stern man that which had charmed Constance at first sight; she thought to recognize a nature like her own, and Radclyffe's venturous spirit exulted in a commune with hers. Their politics were the same; their ultimate ends not *very* unlike; and their common ambition furnished them with an eternity of topics and schemes. Radclyffe was Constance's guest; but Godolphin soon grew attached to the young politician, though he shrugged his shoulders at his opinions. In youth, Godolphin had been a Tory; now, if anything he was a Tory still. Such a political creed was perhaps the natural result of his philosophical belief. Constance, Whig by profession, ultra-Liberal in reality, still however gave the character to the politics of the house; and the easy Godolphin thought politics the veriest of all the trifles which a man could leave to the discretion of the lady of his household. We may judge, therefore, of the quiet, complacent amusement he felt in the didactics of Radclyffe or the declamations of Constance.

"That is a dangerous, scheming woman, believe me," said the Duchess of —— to her great husband, one morning, when Constance left her Grace.

"Nonsense! women are never dangerous."

CHAPTER LI.

GODOLPHIN'S COURSE OF LIFE. — INFLUENCE OF OPINION AND OF RIDICULE ON THE MINDS OF PRIVILEGED ORDERS.— LADY ERPINGHAM'S FRIENDSHIP WITH GEORGE THE FOURTH. — HIS MANNER OF LIVING.

THE course of life which Godolphin now led was exactly that which it is natural for a very rich intellectual man to indulge,— voluptuous but refined. He was arriving at that age when the poetry of the heart necessarily decays. Wealth almost unlimited was at his command; he had no motive for exertion; and he now sought in pleasure that which he had formerly asked from romance. As his faculties and talents had no other circle for display than that which "society" affords, so by slow degrees, society — its applause and its regard — became to him of greater importance than his "philosophy dreamt of." Whatever the circle we live amongst, the public opinion of that circle will, sooner or later, obtain a control over us. This is the reason why a life of pleasure makes even the strongest mind frivolous at last. The lawyer, the senator, the man of letters, all are insensibly guided, moulded, formed, by the judgment of the tribe they belong to, and the circle in which they move. Still more is it the case with the idlers of the great world, amongst whom the only main staple of talk is "themselves."

And in the last-named set, Ridicule being more strong and fearful a deity than she is amongst the cultivators of the graver occupations of life, reduces the inmates, by a constant dread of incurring her displeasure, to a more monotonous and regular subjection to the judgment of others. Ridicule is the stifler of all energy amongst those she controls. After a man's position in society is once established, after he has arrived at a certain age, he does not like to hazard any intellectual enterprise which may endanger the quantum of respect or popularity at present allotted to him. He does not like to risk a failure in parliament, a caustic criticism in literature; he does not like to excite new jealousies, and provoke angry rivals, where he now finds complaisant inferiors. The most admired authors, the most respected members of either House, now looked up to Godolphin as a man of wit and genius,— a man whose house, whose wealth, whose wife, gave him an influence few individuals enjoy. Why risk all this respect by provoking comparison? Among the first in one line, why sink into the probability of being second-rate in another?

This motive, which secretly governs half the aristocracy,— the cleverer half, namely, the more diffident and the more esteemed, which leaves to the obtuse and the vain a despised and unenviable notoriety, added new force to Godolphin's philosophical indifference to ambition. Perhaps, had his situation been less brilliant, or had he persevered in that early affection for solitude which youth loves as the best nurse to its dreams, he might now, in attaining an age when ambition, often dumb before, usually begins to make itself heard, have awakened to a more resolute and aspiring temperament of mind. But as it was, courted and surrounded by all the enjoyments which are generally the reward to which exertion looks, even an ambitious man might have forgotten his nature. No wound to his vanity, *no feeling that he was underrated* (that great spur to proud minds), excited him to those exertions we undertake in order to belie calumny. He was "the glass of fashion," at once popular and admired; and his good fortune in marrying the celebrated, the wealthy, the beautiful Countess of Erpingham was, as success always is, considered the proof of his genius, and the token of his merits.

It was certainly true, that a secret and mutual disappointment rankled beneath the brilliant lot of the husband and wife. Godolphin exacted from Constance more softness, more devotion, more compliance, than belonged to her nature; and Constance, on the other hand, ceased not to repine that she found in Godolphin no sympathy with her objects and no feeling for her enthusiasm. As there was little congenial in their pursuits, the one living for pleasure, the other for ambition, so there could be no congeniality in their intercourse. They loved each other still; they loved each other warmly; they never quarrelled, for the temper of Constance was mild, and that of Godolphin generous: but neither believed there was much love on the other side; and both sought abroad that fellowship and those objects they had not in common at home.

Constance was a great favourite with the reigning king; she was constantly invited to the narrow circle of festivities at Windsor. Godolphin, who avoided *the being bored* as the greatest of earthly evils, could not bow down his tastes and habits to any exact and precise order of life, however distinguished the circle in which it became the rule. Thirsting to be amused, he could not conjugate the *active* verb "to amuse." No man was more fitted to adorn a court, yet no man could less play the courtier. He admired the manners of the sovereign, he did homage to the natural acuteness of his understanding; but, accustomed as he was to lay down the law in society, he was too proud to receive it from another,—a common case among those who live with the great by right and not through sufferance. His pride made him fear to seem a parasite; and, too chivalrous to be disloyal, he was too haughty to be subservient. In fact, he was thoroughly formed to be the Great Aristocrat,—a career utterly distinct from that of the hanger-on upon a still greater man; and against his success at court, he had an obstacle no less in the inherent *fierté* of his nature than in the acquired philosophy of his cynicism.

The king, at first, was civil enough to Lady Erpingham's husband; but he had penetration enough to see that he was not adequately admired: and on the first demonstration of royal coolness, Godolphin, glad of an excuse, forswore Castle and Pavilion forever, and left Constance to enjoy alone the honours of the regal hospitality. The world would have insinuated scandal; but there was that about Constance's beauty which there is said by one of the poets to belong to an angel's,—it struck the heart, but awed the senses.

CHAPTER LII.

RADCLYFFE AND GODOLPHIN CONVERSE. — THE VARIETIES OF AMBITION.

"I DON'T know," said Godolphin to Radclyffe, as they were one day riding together among the green lanes that border the metropolis,— "I don't know what to do with myself this evening. Lady Erpingham is gone to Windsor; I have no dinner engagement, and I am wearied of balls. Shall we dine together, and go to the play quietly, as we might have done some ten years ago?"

"Nothing I should like better; and the theatre — are you fond of it now? I think I have heard you say that it once made your favourite amusement."

"I still like it passably," answered Godolphin; "but the gloss is gone from the delusion. I am grown mournfully fastidious. I must have excellent acting, an excellent play. A slight fault, a slight deviation from nature, robs me of my content at the whole."

"The same fault in your character pervading all things," said Radclyffe, half smiling.

"True," said Godolphin, yawning; "but have you seen my new Canova?"

"No: I care nothing for statues, and I know nothing of the Fine Arts."

"What a confession!"

"Yes, it is a rare confession; but I suspect that the Arts, like truffles and olives, are an acquired taste. People talk themselves into admiration where at first they felt indifference. But how can you, Godolphin, with your talents, fritter away life on these baubles?"

"You are civil," said Godolphin, impatiently. "Allow me to tell you that it is your objects *I* consider baubles. Your dull, plodding, wearisome honours; a name in the newspapers; a place, perhaps, in the ministry, purchased by a sacrificed youth and a degraded manhood; a youth in labour, a manhood in schemes. No, Radclyffe! give me the bright, the glad sparkle of existence; and ere the sad years of age and sickness, let me at least *enjoy.* That is wisdom! *Your* creed is — But I will not imitate your rudeness!" and Godolphin laughed.

"Certainly," replied Radclyffe, "you do your best to enjoy yourself. You live well and fare sumptuously; your house is superb, your villa enchanting. Lady Erpingham is the handsomest woman of her time; and, as if that were not enough, half the fine women in London admit you at their feet. Yet you are not happy."

"Ay; but who is?" cried Godolphin, energetically.

"I am," said Radclyffe, dryly.

"You! humph!"

"You disbelieve me?"

"I have no right to do so: but are you not ambitious? And is not ambition full of anxiety, care,—mortification at defeat, disappointment in success? Does not the very word ambition — that is, a desire to be something you are not — prove you discontented with what you are?"

"You speak of a vulgar ambition," said Radclyffe.

"Most august sage! — and what species of ambition is yours?"

"Not that which you describe. You speak of the ambition for self; my ambition is singular,— it is the ambition for others. Some years ago I chanced to form an object in what I considered the welfare of my race. You smile. Nay, I boast no virtue in my dream; but philanthropy was my hobby, as statues may be yours. To effect this object, I see great changes are necessary; I desire, I work for these great changes. I am not blind, in the meanwhile, to glory. I desire, on the contrary, to obtain it! but it would only please me if it came from certain sources. I want to feel that I may realize what I attempt; and wish for that glory that comes from the permanent gratitude of my species, not that which springs from the momentary applause. Now, I am vain, very vain: vanity was, some years ago, the strongest characteristic of my nature. I do not pretend to conquer the weakness, but to turn it towards my purposes. I am vain enough to wish to shine, but the light must come from deeds I think really worthy."

"Well, well!" said Godolphin, a little interested in spite of himself; "but ambition of one sort resembles ambition of another, inasmuch as it involves perpetual harassments and humiliations."

"Not so," answered Radclyffe; "because when a man is striving for what he fancies a laudable object, the goodness of his intentions comforts him for a failure in success, whereas your selfishly ambitious man has no consolation in *his* defeats; he is humbled by the external world, and has no inner world to apply to for consolation."

"O man!" said Godolphin, almost bitterly, "how dost thou eternally deceive thyself! Here is the thirst for power, and it calls itself the love of mankind!"

"Believe me," said Radclyffe, so earnestly, and with so deep a meaning in his grave, bright eye, that Godolphin was staggered from his scepticism,—"believe me, they may be distinct passions, and yet can be united."

CHAPTER LIII.

FANNY BEHIND THE SCENES. — REMINISCENCES OF YOUTH. — THE UNIVERSALITY OF TRICK. — THE SUPPER AT FANNY MILLINGER'S. — TALK ON A THOUSAND MATTERS, EQUALLY LIGHT AND TRUE. — FANNY'S SONG.

The play was "Pizarro," and Fanny Millinger acted Cora. Godolphin and Radclyffe went behind the scenes.

"Ah," said Fanny, as she stood in her white Peruvian dress, waiting her turn to re-enter the stage,—"ah, Godolphin! this reminds me of old times. How many years have passed since you used to take such pleasure in this mimic life! Well do I remember your musing eye and thoughtful brow bent kindly on me from the stage-box yonder! and do you recollect how prettily you used to moralize on the deserted scenes when the play was over? And you sometimes waited on these very boards to escort me home. Those times have changed. Heigh-ho!"

"Ay, Fanny, we have passed through new worlds of feeling since then. Could life be to us now what it was at that time, we might love each other anew. But tell me, Fanny, has not the experience of life made you a wiser woman? Do you not seek more to enjoy the present,— to pluck Time's fruit on the bough, ere yet the ripeness is gone? I do. I dreamed away my youth,— I strive to enjoy my manhood."

"Then," said Fanny, with that quickness with which, in matters of the heart, women beat all our philosophy,— "then I can prophesy that, since we parted, you have loved or lost some one. Regret, which converts the active mind into the dreaming temper, makes the dreamer hurry into activity, whether of business or of pleasure."

"Right," said Radclyffe, as a shade darkened his stern brow.

"Right," said Godolphin, thoughtfully, and Lucilla's image smote his heart like an avenging conscience. "Right," repeated he, turning aside and soliloquizing; "and those words from an idle tongue have taught me some of the motives of my present conduct. But away reflection! I have resolved to forswear it. My pretty Cora!" said he aloud, as he turned back to the actress, "you are a very De Staël in your wisdom: but let us not be wise; 't is the worst of our follies. Do you not give us one of your charming suppers to-night?"

"To be sure; your friend will join us. He was once the gayest of the gay, but years and fame have altered him a little."

"Radclyffe gay! Bah!" said Godolphin, surprised.

"Ay, you may well look astonished," said Fanny, archly; "but note that smile,— it tells of old days."

And Godolphin turning to his friend saw indeed on the

thin lip of that earnest face a smile so buoyant, so joyous, that it seemed as if the whole character of the man were gone; but while he gazed, the smile vanished, and Radclyffe gravely declined the invitation.

Cora was now on the stage; a transport of applause shook the house.

"How well she acts!" said Radclyffe, warmly.

"Yes," answered Godolphin, as with folded arms he looked quietly on; "but what a lesson in the human heart does good acting teach us! Mark that glancing eye, that heaving breast, that burst of passion, that agonized voice: the spectators are in tears! The woman's whole soul is in her child! Not a bit of it! She feels no more than the boards we tread on: she is probably thinking of the lively supper we shall have; and when she comes off the stage, she will cry, 'Did I not *act* it well?'"

"Nay," said Radclyffe, "she probably feels while she depicts the feeling."

"Not she; years ago she told me the whole science of acting was trick; and trick — trick — trick it is, on the stage or off. The noble art of oratory — noble forsooth! — is just the same; philosophy, poetry,— all, all hypocrisy! 'Damn the moon!' said B—— to me, as we once stood gazing on it at Venice; 'it always gives me the ague: but I have described it well in my poetry, Godolphin, eh?'"

"But —" began Radclyffe.

"But me no buts," interrupted Godolphin, with the playful pertinacity which he made so graceful. "You are younger than I am; when you have lived as long, you shall have a right to contradict my system,— not before."

Godolphin joined the supper party. Like Godolphin's, Fanny's life was the pursuit of pleasure; she lavished on it, in proportion to her means, the same cost and expense, though she wanted the same taste and refinement. Generous and profuse, like all her tribe,— like all persons who win money easily,— she was charitable to all and luxurious in herself. The supper was attended by four male guests,— Godolphin, Saville, Lord Falconer, and Mr. Windsor.

It was early summer; the curtains were undrawn, the windows were half opened, and the moonlight slept on the little grassplot that surrounded the house. The guests were in high spirits. "Fill me this goblet," cried Godolphin; "champagne is the boy's liquor; I will return to it *con amore.* Fanny, let us pledge each other: stay, a toast! What shall it be?"

"Hope till old age, and Memory afterwards," said Fanny, smiling.

"Pshaw! theatricals still, Fan?" growled Saville, who had placed a large screen between himself and the window; "no sentiment between friends."

"Out on you, Saville," said Godolphin; "as well might you say no music out of the opera; these verbal prettinesses colour conversation. But you *roués* are so d—d prosaic, you want us to walk to Vice without a flower by the way."

"Vice indeed!" cried Saville. "I abjure your villanous appellatives. It was in your companionship that I lost my character, and now you turn king's evidence against the poor devil you seduced."

"Humph!" cried Godolphin, gayly; "you remind me of the advice of the Spanish hidalgo to a servant: always choose a master with a good memory; for 'if he does not pay, he will at least remember that he owes you.' In future, I shall take care to herd only with those who recollect, after they are finally debauched, all the good advice I gave them beforehand."

"Meanwhile," said the pretty Fanny, with her arch mouth half-full of chicken, "I shall recollect that Mr. Saville drinks his wine without toasts — as being a useless delay."

"Wine," said Mr. Windsor, sententiously, "wine is just the reverse of love. Your old topers are all for coming at once to the bottle, and your old lovers forever mumbling the toast."

"See what you have brought on yourself, Saville, by affecting a joke upon me," said Godolphin. "Come, let us make it up; we fell out with the toast, let us be reconciled by the glass. Champagne?"

"Ay, anything for a quiet life, — even champagne," said

Saville, with a mock air of patience, and dropping his sharp features into a state of the most placid repose. "You wits are so very severe. Yes, champagne, if you please. Fanny, my love," and Saville made a wry face as he put down the scarce-tasted glass; "go on,—another joke, if you please; I now find I can bear your satire better, at least, than your wine."

Fanny was all bustle; it is in these things that the actress differs from the lady,—there is no quiet in her. "Another bottle of champagne; what can have happened to this?" Poor Fanny was absolutely pained. Saville enjoyed it, for he always revenged a jest by an impertinence.

"Nay," said Godolphin, "our friend does but joke. Your champagne is excellent, Fanny. Well, Saville, and where is young Greenhough? He is vanished. Report says he was marked down in your company, and has not risen since."

"Report is the civilest jade in the world. According to her all the pigeons disappear in my fields. But, seriously speaking, Greenhough is off—gone to America, over head and ears in debt,—debts of honour. Now," said Saville, very slowly, "there 's the difference between the gentleman and the *parvenu;* the gentleman, when all is lost, cuts his throat: the *parvenu* only cuts his creditors. I am really very angry with Greenhough that he did not destroy himself. A young man under my protection and all; so d—d ungrateful in him."

"He was not much in your debt, eh?" said Lord Falconer, speaking for the first time, as the wine began to get into his head.

Saville looked hard at the speaker.

"Lord Falconer, a pinch of snuff: there is something singularly happy in your question,—so much to the point; you have great knowledge of the world,—great. He *was* very much in my debt. I introduced the vulgar dog into the world, and he owes me all the thousands he had the honour to lose in good society!"

"Do you know, Percy," continued Saville, "do you know,

by the way, that my poor dear friend Jasmin is dead,—died after a hearty game of whist? He had just time to cry 'Four by honours,' when death *trumped* him. It was a great shock to me; he was the second best player at Graham's. Those sudden deaths are very awful,—especially with the game in one's hands."

"Very mortifying, indeed," seriously said Lord Falconer, who had just been initiated into whist.

"'T is droll," said Saville, "to see how often the last words of a man tally with his life ; 't is like the moral to the fable. The best instance I know is in Lord Chesterfield, whose fine soul went out in that sublime and inimitable sentence, 'Give Mr. Darrell a chair.'"

"Capital," cried Lord Falconer. "Saville, a game at *écarté*."

As the lion in the Tower looked at the lapdog, so in all the compassion of contempt looked Saville on Lord Falconer.

"Infelix puer!" muttered Godolphin; "infelix puer atque impar congressus Achilli."

"With all my heart," said Saville at last. "Yet, no; we 've been talking of death—such topics waken a man's conscience. Falconer, I never play for less than—"

"Ponies! I know it!" cried Falconer, triumphantly.

"Ponies! less than chargers!"

"Chargers—what are chargers?"

"The whole receipts of an Irish peer, Lord Falconer; and I make it a point never to lose the first game."

"Such men are dangerous," said Mr. Windsor, with his eyes shut.

"O Night!" cried Godolphin, springing up theatrically, "thou wert made for song, and moonlight, and laughter—but woman's laughter. Fanny, a song,—the pretty quaint song *you* sang me, years ago, in praise of a town love and an easy life."

Fanny, who had been in the pouts ever since Saville had blamed the champagne—for she was very anxious to be of *bon ton* in her own little way—now began to smile once

FANNY AND GODOLPHIN.

more; and as the moon played on her arch face, she seated herself at the piano, and, glancing at Godolphin, sang the following song: —

LOVE COURTS THE PLEASURES.

Believe me, Love was never made
In deserts to abide ;
Leave Age to take the sober shade,
And Youth the sunny side.

II.

Love dozes by the purling brook,
No friend to lonely places ;
Or, if he toy with Strephon's crook,
His Chloes are the Graces.

III.

Forsake "The Flaunting Town !" Alas!
Be cells for saints, my own love !
The wine of life 's a *social* glass,
Nor may be quaffed alone, love.

IV.

Behold the dead and solemn sea,
To which our beings flow;
Let waves that soon so dark must be
Catch every glory now.

V.

I would not chain that heart to this,
To sicken at the rest ;
The cage we close a prison is,
The open cage a nest.

CHAPTER LIV.

THE CAREER OF CONSTANCE. — REAL STATE OF HER FEELINGS TOWARDS GODOLPHIN. — RAPID SUCCESSION OF POLITICAL EVENTS. — CANNING'S ADMINISTRATION. — CATHOLIC QUESTION. — LORD GREY'S SPEECH. — CANNING'S DEATH.

While in scenes like these, alternated with more refined and polished dissipation, Godolphin lavished away his life, Constance became more and more powerful as one of the ornaments of a great political party. Few women in England ever mixed more actively in politics than Lady Erpingham, or with more remarkable ability. Her friends were out of office, it is true; but she saw the time approaching rapidly when their opinions must come into power. She had begun to love for itself the scheming of political ambition, and in any country but England she would have been a conspirator, and in old times might have risen to be a queen; but as it was, she was only a proud, discontented woman. She knew, too, that it was all she could be,— all that her sex allowed her to be,— yet did she not the less struggle and toil on. The fate of her father still haunted her; her promise and his death-bed still rose oft and solemnly before her; the humiliations she had known in her early condition, the homage that had attended her later career, still cherished in her haughty soul indignation at the faction he had execrated, and little less of the mighty class which that faction represented. That system of "fashion" she had so mainly contributed to strengthen, and which was originally by her intended to build up a standard of opinion, independent of mere rank and in defiance of mere wealth, she saw polluted and debased, by the nature of its followers, into a vulgar effrontery, which was worse than the more quiet dulness it had attempted to supplant. Yet still she was comforted by the thought that through this system lay the way to more wholesome changes.

The idols of rank and wealth once broken, she believed that a pure and sane worship must ultimately be established. Doubtless in the old French *régime* there were many women who *thought* like her, but there were none who *acted* like her, deliberately, and with an end. What an excellent, what a warning picture is contained in the entertaining Memoirs of Count Ségur! how admirably that agreeable gossip develops the state of mind among the nobility of France! — "merry censurers of the old customs," "enchanted by the philosophy of Voltaire," "ridiculing the old system," "embracing liberality as a fashion," and "gayly treading a soil bedecked with flowers, which concealed a precipice from their view!" In England, there are fewer flowers, and the precipice will be less fearful.

A certain disappointment which had attended her marriage with Godolphin, and the disdainful resentment she felt at the pleasures that allured him from her, tended yet more to deepen at once her distaste for the habits of a frivolous society, and to nerve and concentrate her powers of political intrigue. Her mind grew more and more masculine; her dark eye burned with a sterner fire; the sweet mouth was less prodigal of its smiles; and that air of dignity which she had always possessed grew harder in its character, and became *command.*

This change did not tend to draw Godolphin nearer to her; he, so susceptible to coldness, so refining, so exacting, believed fully that she loved him no more, that she repented the marriage she had contracted. His pride was armed against her; and he sought more eagerly those scenes where all for the admired, the gallant, the sparkling Godolphin wore smiles and sunshine.

There was another matter that rankled in his breast with peculiar bitterness. He had wished to raise a large sum of money (in the purchase of some celebrated works of art), which could only be raised with Lady Erpingham's consent. When he had touched upon the point to her, she had not refused, but she had hesitated. She seemed embarrassed, and, he thought, discontented. His delicacy took alarm, and he never recurred to the question again; but he was secretly much displeased with her reluctant manner on that occasion. Nothing the proud so little forget as a coolness conceived upon money matters. In this instance, Godolphin afterwards discovered that he had wronged Constance, and misinterpreted the cause of her reluctance.

Yet, as time flew on for both, both felt a yearning of the heart towards each other; and had they been thrown upon a desert island, had there been full leisure, full opportunity, for a frank, unfettered interchange and confession of thought, they would have been mutually astonished to find themselves still so beloved, and each would have been dearer to the other than in their warmest hour of earlier attachment. But when once in a very gay and occupied life a husband and wife have admitted a seeming indifference to creep in between them, the chances are a thousand to one against its after-removal. How much more so with a wife so proud as Constance and a husband so refining as Godolphin! Fortunately, however, as I said before, the temper of each was excellent; they never quarrelled; and the indifference, therefore, lay on the surface, not at the depth. They seemed to the world an affectionate couple, as couples go; and their union would have been classed by Rochefoucauld among those marriages that are very happy,—*il n'y a point de délicieux.*

Meanwhile, as Constance had predicted, the political history of the country was marked by a perpetual progress towards liberal opinions. Mr. Canning was now in office; the Catholic Question was in every one's mouth.

There was a brilliant meeting at Erpingham House. Those who composed it were of the heads of the party, but there were divisions amongst themselves; some were secretly for joining Mr. Canning's administration; some had openly done so; others remained in stubborn and jealous opposition. With these last was the heart of Constance.

"Well, well, Lady Erpingham," said Lord Paul Plympton, a young nobleman, who had written a dull history, and was therefore considered likely to succeed in parliamentary life,—"well, I cannot help thinking you are too severe upon Canning; he is certainly very liberal in his views."

"Is there one law he ever caused to pass for the benefit of the working classes? No, Lord Paul, his Whiggism is for peers, and his Toryism for peasants. With the same zeal he advocates the Catholic Question and the Manchester Massacre."

"Yet, surely," cried Lord Paul, "you make a difference between the just liberality that provides for property and intelligence, and the dangerous liberality that would slacken the reins of an ignorant multitude."

"But," said Mr. Benson, a very powerful member of the Lower House, "true politicians must conform to circumstances. Canning may not be all we wish, but still he ought to be supported. I confess that I shall be generous: I care not for office, I care not for power; but Canning is surrounded with enemies, who are enemies also to the people: for that reason I shall support him."

"Bravo, Benson!" cried Lord Paul.

"Bravo, Benson!" echoed two or three notables, who had waited an opportunity to declare themselves; "that 's what I call handsome."

"Manly!"

"Fair!"

"Disinterested, by Jove!"

Here the Duke of Aspindale suddenly entered the room. "Ah, Lady Erpingham, you should have been in the Lords to-night: such a speech! Canning is crushed forever!"

"Speech! from whom?"

"Lord Grey. Terrific: it was the vengeance of a life concentrated into one hour; it has shaken the ministry fearfully."

"Humph!" said Benson, rising; "I shall go to Brooks's and hear more."

"And I too," said Lord Paul.

A day or two after, Benson in presenting a petition alluded in terms of high eulogy to the masterly speech made "in another place;" and Lord Paul Plympton said, "It was indeed unequalled."

That 's what I call handsome.

Manly!

Fair!

Disinterested, by Jove!

And Canning died; his gallant soul left the field of politics broken into a thousand petty parties. From the time of his death the two great hosts into which the strugglers for power were divided have never recovered their former strength. The demarcation that his policy had tended to efface was afterwards more weakened by his successor, the Duke of Wellington; and had it not been for the question of Reform that again drew the stragglers on either side around one determined banner, it is likely that Whig and Tory would, among the many minute sections and shades of difference, have lost forever the two broad distinguishing colours of their separate factions.

Mr. Canning died; and now, with redoubled energy, went on the wheels of political intrigue. The rapid succession of short-lived administrations, the leisure of a prolonged peace, the pressure of debt, the writings of philosophers,—all insensibly yet quickly excited that popular temperament which found its crisis in the Reform Bill.

CHAPTER LV.

THE DEATH OF GEORGE IV.—THE POLITICAL SITUATION OF PARTIES, AND OF LADY ERPINGHAM.

The death of George the Fourth was the birth of a new era. During the later years of that monarch a silent spirit had been gathering over the land, which had crept even to the very walls of his seclusion. It cannot be denied that the various expenses of his reign, no longer consecrated by the youthful graces of the prince, no longer disguised beneath the military triumphs of the people, had contributed far more than theoretical speculations to the desire of political change. The shortest road to liberty lies through attenuated pockets!

Constance was much at Windsor during the king's last illness, one of the saddest periods that ever passed within the walls of a palace. The memorialists of the reign of the magnificent Louis XIV. will best convey to the reader a notion of the last days of George the Fourth. For, like that great king, he was the representation in himself of a particular period, and he preserved much of the habits of (and much too of the personal interest attached to) his youth, through the dreary decline of age. It was melancholy to see one who had played, not only so exalted, but so gallant a part, breathing his life away; nor was the gloom diminished by the many glimpses of a fine original nature, which broke forth amidst infirmity and disease.

George the Fourth died; his brother succeeded; and the English world began to breathe more freely, to look around, and to feel that the change, long coming, was come at last. The French Revolution, the new parliament, Henry Brougham's return for Yorkshire, Mr. Hume's return for Middlesex, the burst of astonished indignation at the Duke of Wellington's memorable words against reform, — all betrayed, while they ripened, the signs of the new age. The Whig ministry was appointed,— appointed amidst discontents in the city, suspicions amongst the friends of the people, amidst fires and insurrections in the provinces, convulsions abroad, and turbulence at home.

The situation of Constance in these changes was rather curious; her intimacy with the late king was no recommendation with the Whig government of his successor. Her power, as the power of fashion always must in stormy times, had received a shock; and as she had of late been a little divided from the main body of the Whigs, she did not share at once in their success, or claim to be one of their allies. She remained silent and aloof; her parties were numerous and splendid as ever, but the small plotting *réunions* of intriguers were suspended. She hinted mysteriously at the necessity of pausing, to see *what* reform the new ministers would recommend, and what economy they would effect. The Tories, especially the more moderate tribe, began to court her; the Whigs, flushed with their triumph, and too busy to think of women, began to neglect. This last circumstance the high Constance felt keenly, but with the keenness rather of scorn than indignation; years had deepened her secret disgust at all aristocratic ordinances, and looking rather at what the Whigs had been than what, pressed by the times, they have become, she regarded them as only playing with democratic counters for aristocratic rewards. She repaid their neglect with contempt, and the silent neutralist soon became regarded by them as the secret foe.

But Constance was sufficiently the woman to feel mortified and wounded by that which she affected to despise. No post at court had been offered to her by her former friends; the confidant of George the Fourth had ceased to be the confidant of Lord Grey. Arrived at that doubtful time of life when the beauty, although possessing, is no longer assured of, her charms, she felt the decay of her personal influence as a personal affront; and thus vexed, wounded, alarmed, in her mid-career, Constance was more than ever sensible of the peculiar disquietudes that await female ambition, and turned with sighs more frequent than heretofore to the recollections of that domestic love which seemed lost to her forever.

Mingled with the more outward and visible stream of politics there was, as there ever is, a latent tide of more theoretic and speculative opinions. While the practical politicians were playing their momentary parts, schemers and levellers were propagating in all quarters doctrines which they fondly imagined were addressed to immortal ends. And Constance began to turn with some curiosity to these charlatans or sages. The bright countess listened to their harangues, pondered over their demonstrations, and mused over their hopes. But she had lived too much on the surface of the actual world, her habits of thought were too essentially worldly, to be converted, while she was attracted, by doctrines so startling in their ultimate conclusions. She turned once more to herself, and waited, in a sad and thoughtful stillness, the progress of things, convinced only of the vanity of them all.

CHAPTER LVI.

THE ROUÉ HAS BECOME A VALETUDINARIAN. — NEWS. — A FORTUNE-TELLER.

MEANWHILE the graced Godolphin floated down the sunny tide of his prosperity. He lived chiefly with a knot of epicurean dalliers with the time, whom he had selected from the wittiest and the easiest of the London world. Dictator of theatres, patron of operas, oracle in music, mirror of entertainments and equipage,—to these conditions had his natural genius and his once dreaming dispositions been bowed at last! A round of dissipation, however, left him no time for reflection; and he believed (perhaps he was not altogether wrong) that the best way to preserve the happy equilibrium of the heart is to blunt its susceptibilities. As the most uneven shapes, when whirled into rapid and ceaseless motion, will appear a perfect circle, so, once impelled in a career that admits no pause, our life loses its uneven angles, and glides on in smooth and rounded celerity, with false aspects more symmetrical than the truth.

One day Godolphin visited Saville, who now, old, worn, and fast waning to the grave, cropped the few flowers on the margin, and jested, but with sourness, on his own decay. He found the actress (who had also come to visit the Man of Pleasure) sitting by the window, and rattling away with her usual vivacity, while she divided her attention with the labours of knitting a purse.

"Heaven only knows," said Saville, "what all these times will produce. I lose my head in the dizzy quickness of events. Fanny, hand me my snuff-box. Well, I fancy my last hour is not far distant; but I hope, at least, I shall die a gentleman. I have a great dislike to the thought of being revolutionized into a *roturier*. That 's the only kind of revolution I have any notion about. What do you say to all this, Godolphin? Every one else is turning politician; young Sunderland whirls his cab down to the House at four o'clock every day, dines at Bellamy's on cold beef, and talks of nothing but that d—d good speech of Sir Robert's! Revolution! faith, the revolution is come already. Revolutions only change the aspect of society; is it not changed enough within the last six months? Bah! I suppose you are bit by the mania?"

"Not I! while I live I will abjure the vulgar toil of ambition. Let others rule or ruin the State; like the Duc de Lauzun, while the guillotine is preparing, I will think only of my oysters and my champagne."

"A noble creed!" said Fanny, smiling: "let the world go to wreck, and bring me my biscuit! That 's Godolphin's motto."

"It is life's motto."

"Yes — a gentleman's life."

"Pish! Fanny, no, satire from you,— you, who are not properly speaking even a *tragic* actress! But there is something about your profession sublimely picturesque in the midst of these noisy brawls. The storms of nations shake not the stage; you are rapt in another life; the atmosphere of poetry girds you. You are like the fairies who lived among men, visible only at night, and playing their fantastic tricks amidst the surrounding passions,— the sorrow, the crime, the avarice, the love, the wrath, the luxury, the famine, that belong to the grosser dwellers of the earth. You are to be envied, Fanny."

"Not so; I am growing old."

"Old!" cried Saville: "ah, talk not of it! Ugh! Ugh! Curse this cough! But hang politics; it always brings disagreeable reflections. Glad, my old pupil, glad am I to see that you still retain your august contempt for these foolish strugglers,— insects splashing and panting in the vast stream of events, which they scarcely stir, and in which they scarcely drop before they are drowned — "

"Or the fishes, their passions, devour them," said Godolphin.

"News!" cried Saville; "let us have real news; cut all the politics out of the 'Times,' Fanny, with your scissors, and then read me the rest."

Fanny obeyed.

"'Fire in Marylebone!'"

"That 's not news! skip that."

"'Letter from Radical.'"

"Stuff! What else?"

"Emigration. 'No fewer than sixty-eight —'"

"Hold, for mercy's sake! What do I, just going out of the world, care for people only going out of the country? Here, child, give the paper to Godolphin; he knows exactly what interests a man of sense."

"'Sale of Lord Lysart's wines —'"

"Capital!" cried Saville; "*that* 's news; *that* 's interesting!"

Fanny's pretty hands returned to their knitting. When the wines had been discussed, the following paragraph was chanced upon: —

"There is a foolish story going the round of the papers about Lord Grey and his vision; the vision is only in the silly heads of the inventors of the story, and the ghost is, we suppose, the apparition of Old Sarum. By the way, there is a celebrated fortune-teller, or prophetess, now in London, making much noise. We conclude the discomfited Tories will next publish *her* oracular discourses. She is just arrived in time to predict the passing of the Reform Bill, without any fear of being proved an impostor."

"Ah, by the by," said Saville, "I hear wonders of this sorceress. She dreams and divines with the most singular accuracy; and all the old women of both sexes flock to her in hackney-coaches, making fools of themselves to-day in order to be wise to-morrow. Have you seen her, Fanny?"

"Yes," replied the actress, very gravely; "and, in sober earnest, she has startled me. Her countenance is so striking, her eyes so wild, and in her conversation there is so much enthusiasm, that she carries you away in spite of yourself. Do you believe in astrology, Percy?"

"I almost did once," said Godolphin, with a half sigh; "but does this female seer profess to choose astrology in preference to cards? The last is the more convenient way of tricking the public."

"Oh, but this is no vulgar fortune-teller, I assure you," cried Fanny, quite eagerly: "she dwells much on magnetism; insists on the effect of your own imagination; discards all outward quackeries; and, in short, has either discovered a new way of learning the future, or revived some forgotten trick of deluding the public. Come and see her some day, Godolphin."

"No, I don't like that kind of imposture," said Godolphin, quickly; and turning away, he sank into a silent and gloomy revery.

CHAPTER LVII.

SUPERSTITION,—ITS WONDERFUL EFFECTS.

It was perfectly true that there had appeared in London a person of the female sex who, during the last few years, had been much noted on the Continent for the singular boldness with which she had promulgated the wildest doctrines, and the supposed felicity which had attended her vaticinations. She professed belief in all the dogmas that preceded the dawn of modern philosophy; and a strange, vivid, yet gloomy eloquence that pervaded her language gave effect to theories which, while incomprehensible to the many, were alluring to the few. None knew her native country, although she was believed to come from the North of Europe. Her way of life was lonely, her habits eccentric; she sought no companionship; she was beautiful, but not of this earth's beauty; men admired, but courted not; she, at least, lived apart from the reach of human passions. In fact, the strange Liehbur, for such was the name the prophetess was known by (and she assumed before it the French title of Madame), was not an impostor, but a fanatic; the chords of the brain were touched, and the sound they gave back was erring and imperfect. She was mad, but with a certain method in her madness; a cold and preternatural and fearful spirit abode within her, and spoke from her lips; its voice froze herself, and she was more awed by her own oracles than her listeners themselves.

In Vienna and in Paris her renown was great, and even terrible. The greatest men in those capitals had consulted her, and spoke of her decrees with a certain reverence; her insanity thrilled them, and they mistook the cause. Besides, in the main, she was right in the principle she addressed: she worked on the imagination, and the imagination afterwards fulfilled what she predicted. Every one knows what dark things may be done by our own fantastic persuasions; belief insures the miracles it credits. Men dream they shall die within a certain hour; the hour comes, and the dream is realized. The most potent wizardries are less potent than fancy itself. Macbeth was a murderer, not because the witches predicted, but because their prediction aroused the thought of murder. And this principle of action the prophetess knew well; she appealed to that attribute common to us all, the foolish and the wise, and on that fruitful ground she sowed her soothsayings.

In London there are always persons to run after anything new, and Madame Liehbur became at once the rage. I myself have seen a minister hurrying from her door with his cloak about his face; and one of the coldest of living sages confesses that she told him what he believes, by mere human means, she could not have discovered. Delusion all! But what age is free from it?

The race of the nineteenth century boast their lights, but run as madly after any folly as their fathers in the eighth. What are the prophecies of Saint Simon but a species of sorcery? Why believe the external more than the inner miracle?

There were but a few persons present at Lady Erpingham's, and when Radclyffe entered, Madame Liehbur was the theme of the general conversation. So many anecdotes were told, so much that was false was mingled with so much that seemed true, that Lady Erpingham's curiosity was excited, and she resolved to seek the modern Cassandra with the first opportunity. Godolphin sat apart from the talkers, playing a quiet game at *écarté*. Constance's eyes stole ever and anon to his countenance; and when she turned at length away with a sigh, she saw that Radclyffe's deep and inscrutable gaze was bent upon her, and the proud countess blushed, although she scarce knew why.

CHAPTER LVIII.

THE EMPIRE OF TIME AND OF LOVE. — THE PROUD CONSTANCE GROWN WEARY AND HUMBLE. — AN ORDEAL.

About this time the fine constitution of Lady Erpingham began to feel the effects of that life which, at once idle and busy, is the most exhausting of all. She suffered under no absolute illness; she was free from actual pain; but a fever crept over her at night, and a languid debility succeeded it the next day. She was melancholy and dejected; tears came into her eyes without a cause; a sudden noise made her tremble; *her nerves were shaken*,— terrible disease, which marks a new epoch in life, which is the first token that our youth is about to leave us!

It is in sickness that we feel our true reliance on others, especially if it is of that vague and not dangerous character when those around us are not ashamed or roused into attendance; when the care and the soothing and the vigilance are the result of that sympathy which true and deep love only feels. This thought broke upon Constance as she sat alone

one morning in that mood when books cannot amuse, nor music lull, nor luxury soothe,—the mood of an aching memory and a spiritless frame. Above her, and over the mantelpiece of her favourite room, hung that picture of her father which I have before described; it had been long since removed from Wendover Castle to London, for Constance wished it to be frequently in her sight. "Alas!" thought she, gazing upon the proud and animated brow that bent down upon her; "alas! though in a different sphere, *thy* lot, my father, has been *mine*,—toil unrepaid, affection slighted, sacrifices forgotten; a *harder* lot in part; for thou hadst at least, in thy stirring and magnificent career, continued excitement and perpetual triumph. But I, a woman, shut out by my sex from contest, from victory, am left only the thankless task to devise the rewards which others are to enjoy; the petty plot, the poor intrigue, the toil without the honour, the humiliation without the revenge. Yet have I worked in thy cause, my father, and thou—thou, couldst thou see my heart, wouldst pity and approve me."

As Constance turned away her eyes, they fell on the opposite mirror, which reflected her still lofty but dimmed and faded beauty; the worn cheek, the dejected eye, those lines and hollows which tell the progress of years! There are certain moments when the time we have been forgetting makes its march suddenly apparent to our own eyes, when the change we have hitherto marked not stares upon us rude and abrupt; we almost fancy those lines, those wrinkles, planted in a single hour, so unperceived have they been before. And such a moment was this to the beautiful Constance; she started at her own likeness, and turned involuntarily from the unflattering mirror. Beside it, on her table, lay a locket, given her by Godolphin just before they married, and containing his hair; it was a simple trifle, and the simplicity seemed yet more striking amidst the costly and modern jewels that were scattered round it. As she looked on it, her heart, all woman still, flew back to the day on which, whispering eternal love, he hung it round her neck. "Ah, happy days! would that they could return!" sighed the desolate schemer; and she took the locket, kissed it, and softened by all the numberless recollections of the past, wept silently over it. "And yet," she said, after a pause, and wiping away her tears,—"and yet this weakness is unworthy of me. Lone, sad, ill, broken in frame and spirit as I am, he comes not near me; I am nothing to him, nothing to any one in the wide world. My heart, my heart, reconcile thyself to thy fate!—what thou hast been from thy cradle, that shalt thou be to my grave. I have not even the tenderness of a child to look to—the future is all blank!"

Constance was yet half yielding to, half struggling with, these thoughts, when Stainforth Radclyffe (to whom she was never denied) was suddenly announced. Time, which, sooner or later, repays perseverance, although in a deceitful coin, had brought to Radclyffe a solid earnest of future honours. His name had risen high in the science of his country; it was equally honoured by the many and the few; he had become a marked man, one of whom all predicted a bright hereafter. He had not yet, it is true, entered parliament, usually the great arena in which English reputations are won; but it was simply because he had refused to enter it under the auspices of any patron, and his political knowledge, his depth of thought, and his stern, hard, ambitious mind were not the less appreciated and acknowledged. Between him and Constance friendship had continued to strengthen, and the more so as their political sentiments were in a great measure the same, although originating in different causes,—hers from passion, his from reflection.

Hastily Constance turned aside her face, and brushed away her tears, as Radclyffe approached; and then seeming to busy herself amongst some papers that lay scattered on her escritoire, and gave her an excuse for concealing in part her countenance, she said, with a constrained cheerfulness, "I am happy you are come to relieve my *ennui;* I have been looking over letters written so many years ago, that I have been forced to remember how soon I shall cease to be young,—no pleasant reflection for any one, much less a woman."

"I am at a loss for a compliment in return, as you may

suppose," answered Radclyffe; "but Lady Erpingham deserves a penance for even hinting at the possibility of being ever less charming than she is; so I shall hold my tongue."

"Alas!" said Constance, gravely, "how little, save the mere triumphs of youth and beauty, is left to our sex! How much, nay, how entirely, in all other and loftier objects, is our ambition walled in and fettered! The human mind must have its aim, its aspiring; how can your sex blame us, then, for being frivolous, when no aim, no aspiring, save those of frivolity, are granted us by society?"

"And is love frivolous?" said Radclyffe. "Is the empire of the heart nothing?"

"Yes!" exclaimed Constance, with energy; "for the empire never lasts. We are slaves to the empire we would found; we wish to be loved, but we only succeed in loving too well ourselves. We lay up our all — our thoughts, hopes, emotions, all the treasures of our hearts — in one spot; and when we would retire from the deceits and cares of life, we find the sanctuary walled against us; we love, and are loved no longer!"

Constance had turned round with the earnestness of the feeling she expressed; and her eyes, still wet with tears, her flushed cheek, her quivering lip, struck to Radclyffe's heart more than her words. He rose involuntarily; his own agitation was marked; he moved several steps towards Constance, and then checked the impulse, and muttered indistinctly to himself.

"No," said Constance, mournfully, and scarcely heeding him, "it is in vain for *us* to be ambitious. We only deceive ourselves; we are not stern and harsh enough for the passion. Touch our affections, and we are recalled at once to the sense of our weakness; and I — I — would to God that I were a humble peasant girl, and not — not what I am!"

So saying, the lofty Constance sank down, overpowered with the bitterness of her feelings, and covered her face with her hands. Was Radclyffe a man that he could see this unmoved; that he could hear those beautiful lips breathe complaints for the want of love, and not acknowledge the love that burned at his own heart? Long, secretly, resolutely, had he struggled against the passion for Constance which his frequent intercourse with her had fed, and which his consciousness that in her was the only parallel to himself that he had ever met with in her sex, had first led him to form; and now lone, neglected, sad, this haughty woman wept over her unloved lot in his presence, and still he was not at her feet! He spoke not, moved not, but his breath heaved thick, and his face was as pale as death. He conquered himself. All within Radclyffe obeyed the idol he had worshipped, even before Constance; all within him, if ardent and fiery, was also high and generous. The acuteness of his reason permitted him no self-sophistries; and he would have laid his head on the block rather than breathe a word of that love which he knew, from the moment it was confessed, would become unworthy of Constance and himself.

There was a pause. Lady Erpingham, ashamed, confounded at her own weakness, recovered herself slowly and in silence. Radclyffe at length spoke; and his voice, at first trembling and indistinct, grew, as he proceeded, clear and earnest.

"Never," said he, "shall I forget the confidence your emotions have testified in my — my friendship; I am about to deserve it. Do not, my dear friend (let me so call you), do not forget that life is too short for misunderstandings in which happiness is concerned. You believe that — that Godolphin does not repay the affection you have borne him: do not be angry, dear Lady Erpingham; I feel it indelicate in me to approach that subject, but my regard for you emboldens me. I know Godolphin's heart; he may seem light, neglectful, but he loves you as deeply as ever, — he loves you entirely."

Constance, humbled as she was, listened in breathless silence; her cheek burned with blushes, and those blushes were at once to Radclyffe a torture and a reward.

"At this moment," continued he, with constrained calmness, "at this moment he fancies in you that very coldness you lament in him. Pardon me, Lady Erpingham; but Godolphin's nature is wayward, mysterious, and exacting. Have you consulted, have you studied it sufficiently? Note it well, soothe it; and if his love can repay you, you will be repaid. God bless you, dearest Lady Erpingham."

In a moment more Radclyffe had left the apartment.

CHAPTER LIX.

CONSTANCE MAKES A DISCOVERY THAT TOUCHES AND ENLIGHTENS HER AS TO GODOLPHIN'S NATURE. — AN EVENT, ALTHOUGH IN PRIVATE LIFE, NOT WITHOUT ITS INTEREST.

If Constance most bitterly reproached herself, or rather her slackened nerves, her breaking health, that she had before another — that other too, not of her own sex — betrayed her dependence upon even her husband's heart for happiness; if her conscience instantly took alarm at the error (and it was indeed a grave one) which had revealed to any man her domestic griefs, — yet, on the other hand, she could not control the wild thrill of delight with which she recalled those words that had so solemnly assured her she was still beloved by Godolphin. She had a firm respect in Radclyffe's penetration and his sincerity, and knew that he was one neither to deceive her nor be deceived himself. His advice, too, came home to her. Had she, indeed, with sufficient address, sufficient softness, insinuated herself into Godolphin's nature? Neglected herself, had she not neglected in return? She asked herself this question, and was never weary of examining her past conduct. That Radclyffe, the austere and chilling Radclyffe, entertained for her any feeling warmer than friendship, she never for an instant suspected; that suspicion alone would have driven him from her presence forever. And although there had been a time, in his bright and exulting youth, when Radclyffe had not been without those arts which win, in the opposite sex, affection from aversion itself, those arts doubled, ay, a hundredfold, in their fascination, would not have availed him with the pure but disappointed Constance, even had a sense of right and wrong very different from the standard he *now* acknowledged permitted him to exert them. So that his was rather the sacrifice of impulse than of any triumph that impulse could afterwards have gained him.

Many and soft and sweet were now the recollections of Constance. Her heart flew back to her early love among the shades of Wendover; to the first confession of the fair enthusiastic boy, when he offered at her shrine a mind, a genius, a heart capable of fruits which the indolence of after-life and the lethargy of disappointed hope had blighted before their time.

If he was now so deaf to what she considered the nobler, because more stirring, excitements of life, was she not in some measure answerable for the supineness? Had there not been a day in which he had vowed to toil, to labour, to sacrifice the very character of his mind, for a union with her? Was she, after all, was she right to adhere so rigidly to her father's dying words, and to that vow afterwards confirmed by her own pride and bitterness of soul? She looked to her father's portrait for an answer; and that daring and eloquent face seemed, for the first time, cold and unanswering to her appeal.

In such meditations the hours passed, and midnight came on without Constance having quitted her apartment. She now summoned her woman, and inquired if Godolphin was at home. He had come in about an hour since, and, complaining of fatigue, had retired to rest. Constance again dismissed her maid, and stole to his apartment. He was already asleep; his cheek rested on his arm, and his fair hair fell wildly over a brow that now worked under the influence of his dreams. Constance put the light softly down, and seating herself beside him, watched over a sleep which, if it had come suddenly on him, was not the less unquiet and disturbed. At length he muttered, "Yes, Lucilla, yes; I tell you, you are avenged. I have not forgotten you! I have not forgotten that I betrayed, deserted you! but was it my fault? No, no! Yet I have not the less sought to forget it. These poor excesses, these chilling gayeties,— were they not incurred for you? And now you come — you — ah, no — spare me!"

Shocked and startled, Constance drew back. Here was a new key to Godolphin's present life, his dissipation, his thirst for pleasure. Had he indeed sought to lull the stings of conscience? And she, instead of soothing, of reconciling him to the past, had she left him alone to struggle with bitter and unresting thoughts, and to contrast the devotion of the one lost with the indifference of the one gained? She crept back to her own chamber, to commune with her heart and be still.

"My dear Percy," said she, the next day, when he carelessly sauntered into her *boudoir* before he rode out, "I have a favour to ask of you."

"Who ever denied a favour to Lady Erpingham?"

"Not you, certainly; but my favour is a great one."

"It is granted."

"Let us pass the summer in —— shire."

Godolphin's brow grew clouded.

"At Wendover Castle?" said he, after a pause.

"We have never been there since our marriage," said Constance, evasively.

"Humph! — as you will."

"It was the place," said Constance, "where you, Percy. first told me you loved!"

The tone of his wife's voice struck on the right chord in Godolphin's breast; he looked up, and saw her eyes full of tears and fixed upon him.

"Why, Constance," said he, much affected, "who would have thought that you still cherished that remembrance?"

"Ah, when shall I forget it?" said Constance; "*then* you loved me!"

"And was rejected."

"Hush! but I believe now that I was wrong."

"No, Constance; you were wrong, for your own happiness, that the rejection was not renewed."

"Percy!"

"Constance!" and in the accent of that last word there was

something that encouraged Constance, and she threw herself into Godolphin's arms, and murmured,—

"If I have offended, forgive me; let us be to each other what we once were."

Words like these from the lips of one in whom such tender supplications, such feminine yearnings, were not common, subdued Godolphin at once. He folded her in his arms, and kissing her passionately, whispered, "Be always thus, Constance, and you will be more to me than ever."

CHAPTER LX.

THE REFORM BILL. — A VERY SHORT CHAPTER.

This reconciliation was not so short-lived as matters of the kind frequently are. There is a Chinese proverb which says, "How near are two hearts when there is no deceit between them!" And the misunderstanding of their mutual sentiments being removed, their affection became at once visible to each other. And Constance, reproaching herself for her former pride, mingled in her manner to her husband a gentle, even a humble sweetness, which, being exactly that which he had most desired in her, was what most attracted him.

At this time, Lord John Russell brought forward the Bill of Parliamentary Reform. Lady Erpingham was in the lantern of the House of Commons on that memorable night; like every one else, her feelings at first were all absorbed in surprise. She went home; she hastened to Godolphin's library. Leaning his head on his hand, that strange person, in the midst of events that stirred the destinies of Europe, was absorbed in the old subtleties of Spinosa. In the frank confidence of revived love, she put her hand upon his shoulder, and told him rapidly that news which was then on its way to terrify or delight the whole of England.

"Will this charm *you*, dear Constance?" said he, kindly; "is it a blow to the party *you* hate, and I sympathize with — or — "

"My father," interrupted Constance, passionately, "would to Heaven he had seen this day! It was this system, the patron and the nominee system, that crushed and debased and killed him. And now I shall see that system destroyed!"

"So, then, my Constance will go over to the Whigs in earnest?"

"Yes, because I shall meet there truth and the people!"

Godolphin laughed gently at the French exaggeration of the saying, and Constance forgave him. The fine ladies of London were a little divided as to the merits of the "Bill;" Constance was the first that declared in its favour. She was an important ally,— as important at least as a woman can be. A bright spirit reigned in her eye; her step grew more elastic; her voice more glad. This was the happiest time of her life, — she was happy in the renewal of her love, happy in the approaching triumph of her hate.

CHAPTER LXI.

THE SOLILOQUY OF THE SOOTHSAYER. — AN EPISODICAL MYSTERY, INTRODUCED AS A TYPE OF THE MANY THINGS IN LIFE THAT ARE NEVER ACCOUNTED FOR. — GRATUITOUS DEVIATIONS FROM OUR COMMON CAREER.

In Leicester Square there is a dim old house, which I have but this instant visited, in order to bring back more vividly to my recollection the wild and unhappy being who, for some short time, inhabited its old-fashioned and gloomy chambers.

In that house, at the time I now speak of, lodged the mysterious Liehbur. It was late at noon, and she sat alone in her apartment, which was darkened so as to exclude the broad and peering sun. There was no trick nor sign of the fallacious art she professed visible in the large and melancholy room. One or two books in the German language lay on the table beside which she sat; but they were of the recent poetry, and not of the departed dogmas, of the genius of that tongue. The enthusiast was alone; and, with her hand supporting her chin, and her eyes fixed on vacancy, she seemed feeding in silence the thoughts that flitted to and fro athwart a brain which had for years lost its certain guide,—a deserted mansion, whence the lord had departed, and where spirits not of this common life had taken up their haunted and desolate abode. And never was there a countenance better suited to the character which this singular woman had assumed. Rich, thick, auburn hair was parted loosely over a brow in which the large and full temples would have betrayed to a phrenologist the great preponderance which the dreaming and the imaginative bore over the sterner faculties. Her eyes were deep, intense, but of the bright and wandering glitter which is so powerful in its effect on the beholder, because it betokens that thought which is not of this daily world, and inspires that fear, that sadness, that awe, which few have looked on the face of the insane and not experienced. Her features were still noble, and of the fair Greek symmetry of the painter's Sibyl; but the cheeks were worn and hollow, and one bright spot alone broke their marble paleness; her lips were, however, full, and yet red, and by their uncertain and varying play gave frequent glimpses of teeth lustrously white; which, while completing the beauty of her face, aided—with somewhat of a fearful effect—the burning light of her strange eyes, and the vague, mystic expression of her abrupt and unjoyous smile. You might see when her features were, as now, in a momentary repose, that her health was broken, and that she was not long sentenced to wander over that world where the soul had already ceased to find its home; but the instant she spoke, her colour deepened, and the brilliant and rapid alternations of her countenance deceived the eye, and concealed the ravages of the worm that preyed within.

"Yes," said she, at last breaking silence, and soliloquizing in the English tongue, but with somewhat of a foreign accent; "yes, I am in his city; within a few paces of his home; I have seen him, I have heard him. Night after night, in rain, and in the teeth of the biting winds, I have wandered round his home. Ay! and I could have raised my voice, and shrieked a warning and a prophecy, that should have startled him from his sleep as the trumpet of the last angel! but I hushed the sound within my soul, and covered the vision with a thick silence. O God! what have I seen and felt and known, since he last saw me! But we shall meet again; and ere the year has rolled round, I shall feel the touch of his lips and die! *Die!* what calmness, what luxury in the word! The fiery burthen of this dread knowledge I have heaped upon me shuffled off; memory no more; the past, the present, the future exorcised; and a long sleep, with bright dreams of a lulling sky, and a silver voice, and his presence!"

The door opened, and a black girl of about ten years old, in the costume of her Moorish tribe, announced the arrival of a new visitor. The countenance of Madame Liehbur changed at once into an expression of cold and settled calmness; she ordered the visitor to be admitted; and presently Stainforth Radclyffe entered the room.

. . . .

"Thou mistakest me and my lore," said the diviner; "I meddle not with the tricks and schemes of the worldly; I show the truth, not garble it."

"Pshaw!" said Radclyffe, impatiently; "this jargon cannot deceive me. You exhibit your skill for money. I ask one exertion of it, and desire you to name your reward. Let us talk after the fashion of this world, and leave that of the other to our dupes."

"Yet thou has known grief too," said the diviner, musingly, "and those who have sorrowed ought to judge more gently of each other. Wilt thou try my art on thyself, ere thou askest it for others?"

"Ay, if you could restore the dead to my dreams."

"I can!" replied the soothsayer, sternly.

Radclyffe laughed bitterly. "Away with this talk to me; or, if you would convince me, raise at once the spectre I desire to see!"

"And dost thou think, vain man," replied Liehbur, haughtily, "that I pretend to the power thou speakest of? Yes; but not as the impostors of old (dull and gross, appealing to outward spells, and spells wrought by themselves alone) affected to do. I can bring the dead before thee, but thou thyself must act upon thyself."

"Mummery! What would you drive at?"

"Wilt thou fast three days, and for three nights abstain from sleep, and then visit me once again?"

"No, fair deluder; such a preliminary is too much to ask of a Neophyte. Three days without food, and three nights without sleep! Why, you would have to raise myself from the dead!"

"And canst thou," said the diviner, with great dignity, "canst thou hope that thou wouldst be worthy of a revelation from a higher world, that for thee the keys of the grave should unlock their awful treasure, and the dead return to life, when thou scruplest to mortify thy flesh and loosen the earthly bonds that cumber and chain the spirit? I tell thee that only as the soul detaches itself from the frame, can its inner and purer sense awaken, and the full consciousness of the invisible and divine things that surround it descend upon its powers."

"And what," said Radclyffe, startled more by the countenance and voice than the words themselves of the soothsayer, — "what would you then do, supposing that I perform this penance?"

"Awaken to their utmost sense, even to pain and torture, the naked nerves of that Great Power thou callest the IMAGINATION, — that Power which presides over dreams and visions; which kindles song, and lives in the Heart of Melodies; which inspired the Magian of the East and the Pythian voices, and in the storms and thunder of savage lands originated the notion of a God and the seeds of human worship; that vast presiding Power which, to the things of mind, is what the Deity is to the Universe itself, — the creator of all. I would awaken, I say, that Power from its customary sleep where, buried in the heart, it folds its wings, and lives but by fits and starts, unquiet, but unaroused; and by that Power thou wouldst see, and feel, and know, and through it only thou wouldst exist. So that it would be with thee as if the body were not,—as if thou wert already all-spiritual, all-living. So thou wouldst learn in life that which may be open to thee after death; and so, soul might now, as hereafter, converse with soul, and revoke the Past, and sail prescient down the dark tides of the Future. A brief and fleeting privilege, but dearly purchased: be wise, and disbelieve in it; be happy, and reject it!"

Radclyffe was impressed, despite himself, by the solemn novelty of this language, and the deep mournfulness with which the soothsayer's last sentence died away.

"And how," said he, after a pause,—"how, and by what arts, would you so awaken the imaginative faculty?"

"Ask not until the time comes for the trial," answered Liehbur.

"But can you awaken it in all,—the dull, the unideal, as in the musing and exalted?"

"No! but the dull and unideal will not go through the necessary ordeal. Few besides those for whom fate casts her great parts in life's drama ever come to that point when I can teach them the Future."

"Do you mean that your chief votaries are among the great? Pardon me, I should have thought the most superstitious are to be found among the most ignorant and lowly."

"Yes; but they consult only what imposes on their credulity, without demanding stern and severe sacrifice of time and enjoyment, as I do. The daring, the resolute, the scheming, with their souls intent upon great objects and high dreams,—those are the men who despise the charms of the moment, who are covetous of piercing the far future, who know how much of their hitherward career has been brightened, not by genius or nature, but some strange confluence of events, some mysterious agency of fate. The great are always fortunate, and therefore mostly seekers into the decrees of fortune."

So great is the influence which enthusiasm, right or wrong, always exercises over us, that even the hard and acute Radclyffe—who had entered the room with the most profound contempt for the pretensions of the soothsayer, and partly from a wish to find materials for ridiculing a folly of the day, partly, it may be from *the desire to examine* which belonged to his nature — began to consider in his own mind whether he should yield to his curiosity, now strongly excited, and pledge himself to the preliminary penance the diviner had ordained.

The soothsayer continued,—

"The stars and the clime and the changing moon have power over us,— why not? Do they not have influence over the rest of Nature? But we can only unravel their more august and hidden secrets by giving full wing to the creative spirit which first taught us their elementary nature, and which, when released from earth, will have full range to wander over their brilliant fields. Know, in one word, the Imagination and the Soul are *one*,— one indivisible and the same; on that truth rests all my lore."

"And if I followed your precepts, what other preliminaries would you enjoin?"

"Not until thou engagest to perform them, will I tell thee more."

"I engage!"

"And swear?"

"I swear!"

The soothsayer rose — and —

. . . .

CHAPTER LXII.

IN WHICH THE COMMON LIFE GLIDES INTO THE STRANGE, — EQUALLY TRUE, BUT THE TRUTH NOT EQUALLY ACKNOWLEDGED.

It was on the night of this interview that Constance, coming into Godolphin's room, found him leaning against the wall, pale and agitated and almost insensible. "Percy,

Percy, you are ill!" she exclaimed, and wound her arms round his neck. He looked at her long and wistfully, breathing hard all the time, until at length he seemed slowly to recover his self-possession, and seating himself, motioned Constance to do the same. After a pause, he said, clasping her hand,—

"Listen to me, Constance. My health, I fear, is breaking; I am tormented by fearful visions; I am possessed by some magic influence. For several nights successively, before falling asleep, a cold tremor has gradually pervaded my frame; the roots of my hair stand on end; my teeth chatter; a vague horror seizes me; my blood seems turned to a solid substance, so curdled and stagnant is it. I strive to speak, to cry out, but my voice clings to the roof of my mouth; I feel that I have no longer power over myself. Suddenly, and in the very midst of this agony, I fall into a heavy sleep; then come strange bewildering dreams, with Volktman's daughter forever presiding over them; but with a changed countenance, calm, unutterably calm, and gazing on me with eyes that burn into my soul. The dream fades, I wake with the morning, but exhausted and enfeebled. I have consulted physicians; I have taken drugs; but I cannot break the spell,—the previous horror and the after-dreams. And just now, Constance, just now—you see the window is open to the park, the gate of the garden is unclosed; I happened to lift my eyes, and lo! gazing upon me in the sickly moonlight, was the countenance of my dreams,—Lucilla's, but how altered! Merciful Heaven! is it a mockery, or can the living Lucilla really be in England? And have these visions, these terrors, been part of that mysterious sympathy which united us ever, and which her father predicted should cease but with our lives?"

The emotions of Godolphin were so rarely visible, and in the present instance they were so unaffected and so roused, that Constance could not summon courage to soothe, to cheer him; she herself was alarmed and shocked, and glanced fearfully towards the window, lest the apparition he had spoken of should reappear. All without was still; not a leaf stirred on the trees in the Mall; no human figure was to be seen.

She turned again to Godolphin, and kissed the drops from his brow, and pressed his cheek to her bosom.

"I have a presentiment," said he, "that something dreadful will happen shortly. I feel as if I were near some great crisis of my life, and as if I were about to step from the bright and palpable world into regions of cloud and darkness. Constance, strange misgivings as to my choice in my past life haunt and perplex me. I have sought only the present; I have abjured all toil, all ambition, and laughed at the future; my hand has plucked the rose-leaves, and now they lie withered in the grasp. My youth flies me, age scowls on me from the distance,—an age of frivolities that I once scorned; yet—yet, had I formed a different creed, how much I might have done! But—but, out on this cant! My nerves are shattered, and I prate nonsense. Lend me your arm, Constance; let us go into the saloon, and send for music!"

And all that night Constance watched by the side of Godolphin, and marked in mute terror the convulsions that wrung his sleep, the foam that gathered to his lip, the cries that broke from his tongue. But she was rewarded when, with the gray dawn, he awoke, and, catching her tender and tearful gaze, flung himself upon her bosom, and bade God bless her for her love!

CHAPTER LXIII.

A MEETING BETWEEN CONSTANCE AND THE PROPHETESS.

A STRANGE suspicion had entered Constance's mind, and for Godolphin's sake she resolved to put it to the proof. She drew her mantle round her stately figure, put on a large disguising bonnet, and repaired to Madame Liehbur's house.

The Moorish girl opened the door to the countess; and her strange dress, her African hue and features, relieved by the long, glittering pendants in her ears, while they seemed suited to the eccentric reputation of her mistress, brought a slight smile to the proud lip of Lady Erpingham, as she conceived them a part of the charlatanism practised by the soothsayer. The girl only replied to Lady Erpingham's question by an intelligent sign; and running lightly up the stairs, conducted the guest into an anteroom, where she waited but for a few moments before she was admitted into Madame Liehbur's apartment.

The effect that the personal beauty of the diviner always produced on those who beheld her was not less powerful than usual on the surprised and admiring gaze of Lady Erpingham. She bowed her haughty brow with involuntary respect, and took the seat to which the enthusiast beckoned.

"And what, lady," said the soothsayer, in the foreign music of her low voice,—"what brings thee hither? Wouldst thou gain, or hast thou lost, that gift our poor sex prizes so dearly beyond its value? Is it of love that thou wouldst speak to the interpreter of dreams and the priestess of the things to come?"

While the bright-eyed Liehbur thus spoke, the countess examined through her veil the fair face before her, comparing it with that description which Godolphin had given her of the sculptor's daughter, and her suspicion acquired new strength.

"I seek not that which you allude to," said Constance; "but of the future, although without any definite object, I would indeed like to question you. All of us love to pry into dark recesses hid from our view, and over which you profess the empire."

"Your voice is sweet, but commanding," said the oracle; "and your air is stately, as of one born in courts. Lift your veil, that I may gaze upon your face, and tell by its lines the fate your character has shaped for you."

"Alas!" answered Constance, "life betrays few of its past signs by outward token. If you have no wiser art than that drawn from the lines and features of our countenances, I shall still remain what I am now,—an unbeliever in your powers."

"The brow and the lip and the eye and the expression of each and all," answered Liehbur, "are not the lying index you suppose them."

"Then," rejoined Constance, "by those signs will I read your own destiny, as you would read mine."

The sibyl started, and waved her hand impatiently; but Constance proceeded,—

"Your birth, despite your fair locks, was under a southern sky; you were nursed in the delusions you now teach; you were loved, and left alone; you are in the country of your lover. Is it not so,—am I not an oracle in my turn?"

The mysterious Liehbur fell back in her chair, her lips apart and blanched, her hands clasped, her eyes fixed upon her visitant.

"Who are you?" she cried at last, in a shrill tone; "who, of my own sex, knows my wretched history? Speak, speak! in mercy speak! tell me more! convince me that you have but vainly guessed my secret, or that you have a right to know it!"

"Did not your father forsake, for the blue skies of Rome, his own colder shores?" continued Constance, adopting the heightened and romantic tone of the one she addressed; "and, Percy Godolphin — is that name still familiar to the ear of Lucilla Volktman?"

A loud, long shriek burst from the lips of the soothsayer, and she sank at once lifeless on the ground. Greatly alarmed, and repenting her own abruptness, Constance hastened to her assistance. She lifted the poor being, whom *she* unconsciously had once contributed so deeply to injure, from the ground; she loosened her dress, and perceived that around her neck hung a broad ivory necklace wrought with curious characters, and many uncouth forms and symbols. This evidence that, if deluding others, the soothsayer deluded herself also, touched and affected the countess; and while she was still busy in chafing the temples of Lucilla, the Moor, brought to the spot by that sudden shriek, entered the apartment. She seemed surprised and terrified at her mistress's condition, and poured forth, in some tongue unknown to Constance, what seemed to her a volley of mingled reproach and lamentation. She seized Lady Erpingham's hand, dashed it indignantly away, and, supporting herself the ashen cheek of Lucilla, motioned to Lady Erpingham to depart; but Constance, not easily accustomed to obey, retained her position beside the still insensible Lucilla; and now, by slow degrees, and with quick and heavy sighs, the unfortunate daughter of Volktman returned to life and consciousness.

In assisting Lucilla, the countess had thrown aside her veil, and the eyes of the soothsayer opened upon that superb beauty, which once to see was never to forget. Involuntarily she again closed her eyes, and groaned audibly; and then, summoning all her courage, she withdrew her hand from Constance's clasp, and bade her Moorish handmaid leave them once more alone.

"So, then," said Lucilla, after a pause, "it is Percy Godolphin's wife, his English wife, who has come to gaze on the fallen, the degraded Lucilla; and yet," sinking her voice into a tone of ineffable and plaintive sweetness — "yet I have slept on his bosom, and been dear and sacred to him as thou! Go, proud lady, go! — leave me to my mad and sunken and solitary state. Go!"

"Dear Lucilla!" said Constance, kindly, and striving once more to take her hand, "do not cast me away from you. I have long sympathized with your generous although erring heart,— your hard and bitter misfortunes. Look on me only as your friend,— nay, your sister, if you will. Let me persuade you to leave this strange and desultory life; choose your own home: I am rich to overflowing; all you can desire shall be at your command. *He* shall not know more of you unless (to assuage the remorse that the memory of you does, I know, still occasion him) you will suffer him to learn, from your own hand, that you are well and at ease, and that you do not revoke your former pardon. Come, dear Lucilla!" and the arm of the generous and bright-souled Constance gently wound round the feeble frame of Lucilla, who now, reclining back, wept as if her heart would break.

"Come, give me the deep, the grateful joy of thinking I

can minister to your future comforts. I was the cause of all your wretchedness; but for me, Godolphin would have been yours forever,—would probably, by marriage, have redressed your wrongs; but for me you would not have wandered an outcast over the inhospitable world. Let me in something repair what I have cost you. Speak to me, Lucilla!"

"Yes, I will speak to you," said poor Lucilla, throwing herself on the ground, and clasping with grateful warmth the knees of her gentle soother; "for long, long years—I dare not think how many—I have not heard the voice of kindness fall upon my ear. Among strange faces and harsh tongues hath my lot been cast; and if I have wrought out from the dreams of my young hours the course of this life (which you contemn, but not justly), it has been that I may stand alone and not dependent,—feared and not despised. And now you, you whom I admire and envy, and would reverence more than living woman (for he loves you and deems you worthy of him),—you, lady, speak to me as a sister would speak, and —and—" Here sobs interrupted Lucilla's speech; and Constance herself, almost equally affected, and finding it vain to attempt to raise her, knelt by her side, and tenderly caressing her, sought to comfort her, even while she wept in doing so.

And this was a beautiful passage in the life of the lofty Constance. Never did she seem more noble than when, thus lowly and humbling herself, she knelt beside the poor victim of her husband's love, and whispered to the diseased and withering heart tidings of comfort, charity, home, and a futurity of honour and of peace. But this was not a dream that could long lull the perturbed and erring brain of Lucilla Volktman; and when she recovered, in some measure, her self-possession, she rose, and throwing back the wild hair from her throbbing temples, she said, in a calm and mournful voice,—

"Your kindness comes too late. I am dying fast,—fast. All that is left to me in the world are these very visions, this very power—call it delusion if you will—from which you would tear me. Nay, look not so reproachfully, and in such wonder. Do you not know that men have in poverty, sickness, and all outer despair clung to a creative spirit within — a world peopled with delusions — and called it POETRY; and that gift has been more precious to them than all that wealth and pomp could bestow? So," continued Lucilla, with fervid and insane enthusiasm, "so is this, *my* creative spirit, my imaginary world, my inspiration, what poetry may be to others. I may be mistaken in the truth of my belief. There are times when my brain is cool, and my frame at rest, and I sit alone and think over the *real* past, when I feel my trust shaken, and my ardour damped; but that thought does not console but torture me, and I hasten to plunge once more among the charms and spells and mighty dreams that wrap me from my living self. Oh, lady! bright and beautiful and lofty as you are, there may come a time when you can conceive that even madness may be a relief. For" (and here the wandering light burned brighter in the enthusiast's glowing eyes), "for, when the night is round us, and there is peace on earth, and the world's children sleep, it is a wild joy to sit alone and vigilant, and forget that we live and are wretched. The stars speak to us then with a wondrous and stirring voice; they tell us of the doom of men and the wreck of empires, and prophesy of the far events which they taught to the old Chaldeans. And then the Winds, walking to and fro as they list, bid us go forth with them and hear the songs of the midnight spirits; for you know," she whispered with a smile, putting her hand upon the arm of the appalled and shrinking Constance, who now saw how hopeless was the ministry she had undertaken, "that this world is given up to two tribes of things that live and have a soul,— the one bodily and palpable as we are; the other more glorious, but invisible to our dull sight — though I have seen them,— Dread Solemn Shadows, even in their mirth; the night is their season as the day is ours; they march in the moonbeams, and are borne upon the wings of the winds. And with them, and by their thoughts, I raise myself from what I am and have been. Ah, lady, wouldst thou take this comfort from me?"

"But," said Constance, gathering courage from the gentleness which Lucilla's insanity now wore, and trying to soothe, not contradict her in her present vein, "but in the country, Lucilla, in some quiet and sheltered nook, you might indulge these visions without the cares and uncertainty that must now perplex you; without leading this dangerous and roving life, which must at times expose you to insult, to annoyance, and discontent you with yourself."

"You are mistaken, lady," said the astrologer, proudly; "none know me who do not fear. I am powerful, and I hug my power,—it comforts me; without it, what should I be,—an abject, forsaken, miserable woman. No! that power I possess,—to shake men's secret souls,—even if it be a deceit; even if I should laugh at them, not pity,—reconciles me to myself and to the past. And I am not poor, madam," as, with the common caprice of her infirmity, an angry suspicion seemed to cross her; "I want no one's charity,—I have learned to maintain myself. Nay, I could be even wealthy if I would!"

"And," said Constance, seeing that for the present she must postpone her benevolent intentions, "and he—Godolphin—you forgive him still?"

At that name, it was as if a sudden charm had been whispered to the fevered heart of the poor fanatic; her head sank from its proud bearing; a deep, a soft blush coloured the wan cheek; her arms drooped beside her; she trembled violently, and, after a moment's silence, sank again on her seat, and covered her face with her hands. "Ah," said she, softly, "that word brings me back to my young days, when I asked no power but what love gave me over one heart; it brings me back to the blue Italian lake, and the waving pines, and our solitary home, and my babe's distant grave. Tell me," she cried, again starting up, "has he not spoken of me lately,—has he not seen me in his dreams; have I not been present to his soul when the frame, torpid and locked, severed us no more, and in the still hours I charmed myself to his gaze? Tell me, has he not owned that Lucilla haunted his pillow? Tell me; and if I err, my spells are nothing, my power is vanity, and I am the helpless creature thou wouldst believe me!"

Despite her reason and her firm sense, Constance half shuddered at these mysterious words, as she recalled what Percy had told her of his dreams the preceding evening, and the emotions she herself had witnessed in his slumbers when she watched beside his bed. She remained silent, and Lucilla regarded her countenance with a sort of triumph.

"My art, then, is not so idle as thou wouldst hold it. But — hush! — last night I beheld him, not in spirit, but visibly, face to face; for I wander at times before his home (*his* home was once mine!), and he saw me, and was smitten with fear; in these worn features he could recognize not the *living* Lucilla he had known. But go to him! — thou, his wife, his own — go to him; tell him — no, tell him *not* of me. He must not seek me; *we* must not hold parley together: for oh, lady" (and Lucilla's face became settled into an expression so sad, so unearthly sad, that no word can paint, no heart conceive, its utter and solemn sorrow), "when we two meet again to commune, to converse, when once more I touch that hand, when once more I feel that beloved, that balmy breath, — *my* last hour is at hand, and danger — imminent, dark, and deadly danger — clings fast to *him!*"

As she spoke, Lucilla closed her eyes, as if to shut some horrid vision from her gaze; and Constance looked fearfully round, almost expecting some apparition at hand. Presently Lucilla, moving silently across the room, beckoned to the countess to follow: she did so. They entered another apartment; before a recess there hung a black curtain. Lucilla drew it slowly aside, and Constance turned her eyes from a dazzling light that broke upon them. When she again looked, she beheld a sort of glass dial marked with various quaint hieroglyphics and the figures of angels, beautifully wrought; but around the dial, which was circular, were ranged many stars, and the planets, set in due order. These were lighted from within by some chemical process, and burned with a clear and lustrous, but silver light. And Constance observed that the dial turned round, and that the stars turned with it, each in a separate motion; and in the midst of the dial were the hands as of a clock, that moved, but so slowly, that the most patient gaze alone could observe the motion.

While the wondering Constance regarded this singular device, Lucilla pointed to one star that burned brighter than the rest; and below it, half-way down the dial, was another, a faint and sickly orb, that, when watched, seemed to perform a much more rapid and irregular course than its fellows.

"The bright star is his," said she; "and yon dim and dying one is the type of mine. Note: in the course they both pursue they must meet at last; and *when* they meet, the mechanism of the whole halts,—the work of the dial is forever done. These hands indicate hourly the progress made to that end; for it is the mimicry and symbol of mine. Thus do I number the days of my fate; thus do I know, even almost to a second, the period in which I shall join my Father that is in heaven!

"And now," continued the maniac (though *maniac* is too harsh and decided a word for the dreaming wildness of Lucilla's insanity), as, dropping the curtain, she took her guest's hand and conducted her back into the outer room,—"and now, farewell! You sought me, and, I feel, only from kind and generous motives. *We* never shall meet more. Tell not your husband that you have seen me. He will know soon, too soon, of my existence. Fain would I spare him that pang and," growing pale as she spoke, "that *peril;* but Fate forbids it. What is writ, is writ; and who shall blot God's sentence from the stars, which are His book? Farewell! high thoughts are graved upon your brow: may they bless you; or, where they fail to bless, may they console and support. Farewell! I have not yet forgotten to be grateful, and I still dare to pray."

Thus saying, Lucilla kissed the hand she had held, and turning hastily away, regained the room she had just left; and, locking the door, left the stunned and bewildered countess to depart from the melancholy abode. With faltering steps she quitted the chamber, and at the foot of the stairs the little Moor awaited her. To her excited fancy there was something eldrich and preternatural in the gaze of the young African, and the grin of her pearly teeth, as she opened the door to the visitant. Hastening to her carriage, which she had left at a corner of the square, the countess rejoiced when she gained it; and throwing herself back on the luxurious cushions, felt as exhausted by this starry and weird incident in the epic of life's common career, as if she had partaken of that overpowering inspiration which she now almost incredulously asked herself, as she looked forth on the broad day and the busy streets, if she had really witnessed.

CHAPTER LXIV.

LUCILLA'S FLIGHT. — THE PERPLEXITY OF LADY ERPINGHAM. —A CHANGE COMES OVER GODOLPHIN'S MIND. — HIS CONVERSATION WITH RADCLYFFE. — GENERAL ELECTION. — GODOLPHIN BECOMES A SENATOR.

No human heart ever beat with more pure and generous emotions, when freed from the political fever that burned within her (withering, for the moment, the chastened and wholesome impulses of her nature), than those which animated the heart of the queenly Constance. She sent that evening for the most celebrated physician in London,—that polished and courtly man who seems born for the maladies of the drawing-room, but who beneath so urbane a demeanour conceals so accurate and profound a knowledge of the disorders of his unfortunate race. I say accurate and profound comparatively, for positive knowledge of pathology is what no physician in modern times and civilized countries really possesses. No man cures us,— the highest art is not to kill! Constance, then, sent for this physician, and, as delicately as possible, related the unfortunate state of Lucilla, and the deep anxiety she felt for her mental and bodily relief. The physician promised to call the next day; he did so, late in the afternoon: Lucilla was gone. Strange, self-willed, mysterious, she came like a dream, to warn, to terrify, and to depart. They knew not whither she had fled, and her Moorish handmaid alone attended her.

Constance was deeply chagrined at this intelligence; for she had already begun to build castles in the air, which poor Lucilla, with a frame restored and a heart at ease and nothing left of the past but a soft and holy penitence, should inhabit. The countess, however, consoled herself with the hope that Lucilla would at least write to her, and mention her new place of residence; but days passed, and no letter came.

Constance felt that her benevolent intentions were doomed to be unfulfilled. She was now greatly perplexed whether or not to relate to Godolphin the interview that had taken place between her and Lucilla. She knew the deep, morbid, and painful interest which the memory of this wild and visionary creature created in Godolphin; and she trembled at the feeling she might re-awaken by even a faint picture of the condition and mental infirmities of her whose life he had so darkly shadowed. She resolved, therefore, at all events for the present, and until every hope of discovering Lucilla once more had expired, to conceal the meeting that had occurred. And in this resolve, she was strengthened by perceiving that Godolphin's mind had become gradually calmed from its late excitement, and that he had begun to consider, or at least appeared to consider, the apparition of Lucilla at his window as the mere delusion of a heated imagination. His nights grew once more tranquil, and freed from the dark dreams that had tormented his brain; and even the cool and unimaginative Constance could scarcely divest herself of the wild fancy that, when Lucilla was near, a secret and preternatural sympathy between Godolphin and the reader of the stars had produced that influence over his nightly dreams which paled and receded and vanished, as Lucilla departed from the actual circle in which he lived.

It was at this time, too, that a change was perceptible in Godolphin's habits, and crept gradually over the character of his thoughts. Dissipation ceased to allure him, the light wit of his parasites palled upon his ear; magnificence had lost its gloss, and the same fastidious, exacting thirst for the ideal which had disappointed him in the better objects of life, began now to discontent him with its glittering pleasures.

The change was natural and the causes not difficult to fathom. The fact was, that Godolphin had now arrived at that period of existence when a man's character is almost invariably subject to great change,—the crisis in life's fever, when there is a new turn in our fate, and our moral death or regeneration is sealed by the silent wavering or the solemn decision of the HOUR. Arrived at the confines of middle age, there is an outward innovation in the whole system; unlooked-for symptoms break forth in the bodily, unlooked-for symptoms in the mental, frame. It happened to Godolphin that, at this critical period, a chance, a circumstance, a straw, had reunited his long interrupted but never stifled affections to the image of his beautiful Constance. The reign of passion, the magic of those sweet illusions, that ineffable yearning which possession mocks, although it quells at last, were indeed forever over; but a friendship more soft and genial than exists in any relation save that of husband and wife had sprung up, almost as by a miracle (so sudden was it), between breasts for years divided. And the experience of those years had taught Godolphin how frail and unsubstantial had been all the other ties he had formed. He wondered, as sitting alone with Constance, her tenderness recalled the past, her wit enlivened the present, and *his* imagination still shed a glory and a loveliness over the future, that he had been so long insensible to the blessings of that communion which he now experienced. He did not perceive what in fact was the case,—that the tastes and sympathies of each, blunted by that disappointment which is the child of experience, were more willing to concede somewhat to the tastes and sympathies of the other; that Constance gave a more indulgent listening to his beautiful refinements of an ideal and false epicurism; that he, smiling still, smiled with kindness, not with scorn, at the sanguine politics, the worldly schemes, and the rank ling memories of the intriguing Constance. Fortunately, too, for her, the times were such, that men who never before dreamed of political interference were roused and urged into the mighty conflux of battling interests, which left few moderate and none neuter. Every *coterie* resounded with political war-cries; every dinner rang, from soup to the coffee, with the merits of *the Bill;* wherever Godolphin turned for refuge, Reform still assailed him; and by degrees the universal feeling, that was at first ridiculed, was at last, although reluctantly, admitted by his mind.

"Why," said he, one day, musingly, to Radclyffe, whom he met in the old Green Park,—for since the conversation recorded between Radclyffe and Constance the former came little to Erpingham House,—"why should I not try a yet *un*tried experiment? Why should I not live like others in their graver as in their lighter pursuits? I confess, when I look back to the years I have spent in England, I feel that I calculated erroneously. I chalked out a plan, I have followed it rigidly. I have lived for self, for pleasure, for luxury; I have summoned wit, beauty, even wisdom around me. I have been the creator of a magic circle, but to the magician himself the magic was tame and ignoble. In short, I have dreamed, and am awake. Yet what course of life should supply this, which I think of deserting? Shall I go once more abroad, and penetrate some untravelled corner of the earth? Shall I retire into the country, *and write,* draining my mind of the excitement that presses on it; or lastly, shall I plunge with my contemporaries into the great gulf of actual events, and strive and fret and struggle; or — in short, Radclyffe, you are a wise man: advise me!"

"Alas!" answered Radclyffe, "it is of no use advising one to be happy who has no object beyond himself. Either enthusiasm or utter mechanical coldness is necessary to reconcile men to the cares and mortifications of life. You must feel nothing, or you must feel for others. Unite yourself to a great object; see its goal distinctly; cling to its course courageously; hope for its triumph sanguinely; and on its majestic progress you sail, as in a ship, agitated indeed by the storms, but unheeding the breeze and the surge that would appall the individual effort. The larger public objects make us glide smoothly and unfelt over our minor private griefs. To be happy, my dear Godolphin, you must forget yourself. Your refining and poetical temperament preys upon your content. Learn benevolence,— it is the only cure to a morbid nature."

Godolphin was greatly struck by this answer of Radclyffe, — the more so, as he had a deep faith in the unaffected sincerity and the calculating wisdom of his adviser. He looked hard in Radclyffe's face, and, after a pause of some moments, replied slowly, "I believe you are right after all; and I have learned in a few short sentences the secret of a discontented life."

Godolphin would have sought other opportunities of conversing with Radclyffe, but events soon parted them. Parliament was dissolved! What an historical event is recorded in those words! The moment the king consented to that measure, the whole series of subsequent events became, to an ordinary prescience, clear as in a mirror. Parliament dissolved in the heat of the popular enthusiasm, a majority, a great majority of Reformers, was sure to be returned.

Constance perceived at a glance the whole train of consequences issuing from that one event,— perceived and exulted. A glory had gone forever from the party she abhorred. Her father was already avenged. She heard his scornful laugh ring forth from the depths of his forgotten grave!

London emptied itself at once. England was one election. Godolphin remained almost alone. For the first time a sense of littleness crept over him,— a feeling of insignificance, which wounded and galled his vain nature. In these great struggles he was nothing. The admired, the cultivated, *spirituel*, the splendid Godolphin sank below the commonest adventurer, the coarsest brawler,— yea, the humblest freeman, who felt his stake in the State, joined the canvass, swelled the cry, and helped in the mighty battle between old things and new, which was so resolutely begun. This feeling gave an impetus to the growth of the new aspirations he had already suffered his mind to generate; and Constance marked, with vivid delight, that he now listened to her plans with interest, and examined the political field with a curious and searching gaze.

But she was soon condemned to a disappointment proportioned to her delight. Though Godolphin had hitherto taken no interest in party politics, his prejudices, his feelings, his habits of mind, were all the reverse of democratic. When he once began to examine the bearings of the momentous question that agitated England, he was not slow in coming to conclusions which threatened to produce a permanent disagreement between Constance and himself.

"You wish me to enter parliament, my dear Constance," said he, with his quiet smile; "it would be an experiment dangerous to the union re-established between us. I should vote against your Bill."

"You!" exclaimed Constance, with warmth; "is it possible that you can sympathize with the fears of a selfish oligarchy,— with the cause of the merchants and traffickers of the plainest right of a free people,— the right to select their representatives?"

"My dear Constance," returned Godolphin, "my whole theory of Government is aristocratic. The right of the people to choose representatives! — you may as well say the right of the people to choose kings or magistrates and judges — or clergymen and archbishops! The people have, it is true, the abstract and original right to choose all these, and every year to chop and change them as they please; but the people, very properly, in all States, mortgage their elementary rights for one catholic and practical right,— the right to be well governed. It *may* be no more to the advantage of the State that the People (that is, the majority, the populace) should elect uncontrolled all the members of the House of Commons than that they should elect all the pastors of their religion. The sole thing we have to consider is, will they be better governed?"

"Unquestionably," said Constance.

"Unquestionably! — Well, I question it. I foresee a more

even balance of parties,—nothing else. When parties are evenly balanced States tremble. In good government there should be somewhere sufficient power to carry on, not unexamined but at least with vigour, the different operations of government itself. In free countries, therefore, one party ought to preponderate sufficiently over the other. If it do not, all the State measures are crippled, delayed, distorted, and the State languishes while the doctors dispute as to the medicines to be applied to it. You will find by your Bill, not that the Tories are destroyed, but that the Whigs and the Radicals are strengthened; the Lords are not crushed, but the Commons are in a state to contest with them. Hence party battles upon catchwords, struggles between the two chambers for things of straw. You who desire progress and movement will find the real affairs of this great Artificial Empire, in its trade, commerce, colonies, internal legislation, standing still while the Whigs and the Tories pelt each other with the quibbles of faction. No, I should vote against your Bill! I am not for *popular* governments, though I like *free* States. All the advantages of democracy seem to me more than counterbalanced by the sacrifice of the peace and tranquillity, the comfort and the grace, the dignity and the charities of life, that democracies usually entail. If the object of men is to live happily,—not to strive and to fret; not to make money in the market-place, and call each other rogues on the hustings,—who would not rather be a German than an American? I own I regret to differ from you. For—but no matter—"

"For!—what were you about to say?"

"For—then, since you must know it—I am beginning to feel interest in these questions,—excitement is contagious. And, after all, if a man really deem his mother-country in some danger, inaction is not philosophy, but a species of parricide. But to think of the daily and hourly pain I should occasion to you, my beloved and ardent Constance, by shocking all your opinions, counteracting all your schemes, working against objects which your father's fate and your early associations have so singularly made duties in your eyes,—to do all this is a patriotism beyond me. Let us glide out of this whirlpool, and hoist sail for some nook in the country where we can hear gentler sounds than the roar of the democracy."

Constance sighed, and suffered Godolphin to quit her in silence. But her generous heart was touched by his own generosity. This is one of the great curses of a woman who aspires to the man's part of political controversy. If the man choose to act, the woman, with all her wiles, her intrigues, her arts, is powerless. If Godolphin were to enter parliament a Tory, the great Whig rendezvous of Erpingham House was lost, and Constance herself a cipher,—and her father's wrongs forgotten, and the stern purpose of her masculine career baffled at the very moment of success. She now repented that she had ever desired to draw Godolphin's attention to political matters. She wondered at her own want of foresight. How, with his love for antiquity, his predilections for the elegant and the serene, his philosophy of the "Rose-garden," could she ever have supposed that he would side with the bold objects and turbulent will of a popular party in a stormy crisis?

The subject was not renewed. But she had the pain of observing that Godolphin's manner was altered: he took pleasure in none of his old hobbies,—he was evidently dissatisfied with himself. In fact, it is true that he, for the first time in his life, felt that there is a remorse to the mind as well as to the soul, and that a man of genius cannot be perpetually idle without, as he touches on the middle of his career, looking to the past with some shame and to the future with some ambition. One evening, when he had sat by the open window in a thoughtful and melancholy, almost morose, silence for a considerable time, Constance, after a violent struggle with herself, rose suddenly, and fell on his neck.

"Forgive me, Percy," she said, unable to suppress her tears,—"forgive me. It is past; I have no right that you, so superior to myself, should be sacrified to my — my *prejudices* you would call them — so be it. Is it for your wife to condemn you to be inglorious? No, no, dear Godolphin; fulfil your destiny,—you are born for high objects. Be active, be distinguished, and I will ask no more!"

John Vernon, in that hour you were forgotten! Who among the dead can ever hope for fidelity, when love to the living invites a woman to betray?

"My sweet Constance," said Godolphin, drawing her to his heart, and affected in proportion as he appreciated all that in that speech his wife gave up for his sake,—the all, far more than the lovely person, the splendid wealth, the lofty rank that she had brought to his home,—"my sweet Constance, do not think I will take advantage of words so generously but hastily spoken. Time enough hereafter to think of differences between us. At present let us indulge only the luxury of the new love, the holiness of the new nuptials, that have made us as one Being. Perhaps this restlessness, so unusual to me, will pass away; let us wait a while. At present 'Sparta has many a worthier son.' One other year, one sweet summer, of the private life we have too much suffered to glide away, enjoyed, and then we will see whether the harsh realities of Ambition be worth either a concession or a dispute. Let us go into the country,—to-morrow if you will."

And as Constance was about to answer, he sealed her lips with his kiss.

But Lady Erpingham was not one of those who waver in what they deem a duty. She passed the night in stern and sleepless commune with herself; she was aware of all that she hazarded, all that she renounced; she was even tortured by scruples as to the strange oath that had almost unsexed her. Still, in spite of all, she felt that nothing would excuse her in suffering that gifted and happy intellect, now awakened from the sleep of the Sybarite, to fall back into its lazy and effeminate repose. She had no right to doom a human soul to rot away in its clay. Perhaps, too, she hoped, as all polemical enthusiasts do, that Godolphin, once aroused, would soon become her convert. Be that as it may, she delayed, on various pretences, their departure from London. She went secretly the next day to one of the proprietors of the close Boroughs, the existence of which was about to be annihilated, and a few days afterwards Godolphin received a letter informing him that he had been duly elected member for ——. I will not say what were his feelings at these tidings. Perhaps, such is man's proud and wayward heart, he felt shame to be so outdone by Constance.

CHAPTER LXV.

NEW VIEWS OF A PRIVILEGED ORDER. — THE DEATH-BED OF AUGUSTUS SAVILLE.

This event might indeed have been an era in the life of Percy Godolphin, had that life been spared to a more extended limit than it was; and yet, so long had his ambition been smoothed and polished away by his peculiarities of thought, and so little was his calm and indifferent tone of mind suited to the hot contests and nightly warfare of parliamentary politics, that it is not probable he would ever have won a continuous and solid distinction in a career which requires either obtuseness of mind or enthusiasm of purpose to encounter the repeated mortifications and failures which the most brilliant *débutant* ordinarily endures. As it was, however, it produced a grave and solemn train of thought in Godolphin's breast. He mused much over his past life, and the musing did not satisfy him. He felt like one of those recorded in physiological history who have been in a trance for years: and now slowly awakening, he acknowledged the stir and rush of revived but confused emotions. Nature, perhaps, had intended Godolphin for a poet; for, with the exception of the love of glory, the poetical characteristics were rife within him; and over his whole past existence the dimness of unexpressed poetical sensation had clung and hovered. It was this which had deadened his soul to the active world, and wrapped him in the land of dreams; it was this which had induced that vague and restless dissatisfaction with the Actual which had brought the thirst for the Ideal; it was this which had made him fastidious in love, repining in pleasure, magnificent in luxury, seeking and despising all things in the same breath. There are many, perhaps, of this sort, who, having the poet's nature, have never found the poet's vent to his emotions; have wandered over the visionary world without chancing to discover the magic wand that was stored within the dark chamber of their mind, and would have reduced the visions into shape and substance. Alas! what existence can be more unfulfilled than that of one who has the soul of the poet and not the skill; who has the susceptibility and the craving, not the consolation or the reward?

But if this cloud of dreamlike emotion had so long hung over Godolphin, it began now to melt away from his heart; a clearer and distincter view of the large objects of life lay before him; and he felt that he was standing, half stunned and passive, in the great crisis of his fate.

The day was now fixed for their departure to Wendover, when Saville was taken alarmingly ill; Godolphin was sent for, late one evening. He found the *soi-disant* Epicurean at the point of death, but in perfect possession of his senses. The scene around him was emblematic of his life: save Godolphin, not a friend was by. Saville had some dozen or two of natural children — where were they? He had abandoned them to their fate; he knew not of their existence, nor they of his death. Lonely in his selfishness, was he left to breathe out the small soul of a man of *bon ton!* But I must do Saville the justice to say, that if he was without the mourners and the attendants that belong to natural ties, he did not require them. His was no whimpering exit from life: the champagne was drained to the last drop; and Death, like the true boon companion, was about to shatter the empty glass.

"Well, my friend," said Saville, feebly, but pressing with weak fingers Godolphin's hand,— "well, the game is up, the lights are going out, and presently the last guest will depart, and all be darkness!" Here the doctor came to the bedside with a cordial. The dying man, before he took it, fixed upon the leech an eye which, although fast glazing, still retained something of its keen, searching shrewdness.

"Now, tell me, my good sir, how many hours more can you keep in this — this breath?"

The doctor looked at Godolphin.

"I understand you," said Saville; "you are shy on these points. Never be shy, my good fellow; it is inexcusable after twenty: besides, it is a bad compliment to my nerves, — a gentleman is prepared for every event. Sir, it is only a *roturier* whom death, or anything else, takes by surprise. How many hours, then, can I live?"

"Not many, I fear, sir; perhaps until daybreak."

"*My* day breaks about twelve o'clock, p. m.," said Saville, as dryly as his gasps would let him. "Very well; give me the cordial. Don't let me go to sleep, — I don't want to be cheated out of a minute. So, so! I am better. You may withdraw, doctor. Let my spaniel come up. Bustle, Bustle! poor fellow! poor fellow! Lie down, sir! be quiet! And now, Godolphin, a few words in farewell. I always liked you greatly; you know you were my *protégé*, and you have turned out well. You have not been led away by the vulgar passions of politics and place and power. You have had power over power itself; you have not office, but you have fashion. You have made the greatest match in England; very prudently not marrying Constance Vernon, very prudently marrying Lady Erpingham. You are at the head and front of society; you have excellent taste, and spend your wealth properly. All this must make your conscience clear, — a wonderful consolation! Always keep a sound conscience; it is a great blessing on one's death-bed; it is a great blessing to me in this hour, for I have played my part decently, eh? I have enjoyed life, as much as so dull a possession can be enjoyed; I have loved, gamed, drunk, but I have never lost my character as a gentleman: thank Heaven, I have no remorse of that sort! Follow my example to the last and you will die as easily. I have left you my correspondence and my journal: you may publish them if you like; if not, burn them. They are full of amusing anecdotes; but I don't care for fame, as you well know, — especially posthumous fame. Do as you please, then, with my literary remains. Take care of my dog — 't is a good creature; and let me be quietly buried. No bad taste, no ostentation, no epitaph. I am very glad I die before the d—d Revolution that must come; I don't want to take wine with the member for Holborn Bars. I am a type of a system; I expire before the system; my death is the herald of its fall."

With these expressions — not continuously uttered, but at short intervals — Saville turned away his face: his breathing became thick: he fell into the slumber he had deprecated; and, after about an hour's silence, died away as insensibly as an infant. "Sic transit gloria mundi!"

The first living countenance beside the death-bed on which Godolphin's eye fell was that of Fanny Millinger; she (who had been much with Saville during his latter days, for her talk amused him, and her good-nature made her willing to amuse any one) had been, at his request, summoned also with Godolphin at the sudden turn of his disease. She was at the theatre at the time, and had only just arrived when the deceased had fallen into his last sleep. There, silent and shocked, she stood by the bed, opposite Godolphin. She had not stayed to change her stage-dress; and the tinsel and mock jewels glittered on the revolted eye of her quondam lover. What a type of the life just extinguished! What a satire on its mountebank artificialities!

Some little time after, she joined Godolphin in the desolate apartment below. She put her hand in his, and her tears — for she wept easily — flowed fast down her cheeks, washing away the lavish rouge which imperfectly masked the wrinkles that Time had lately begun to sow on a surface Godolphin had remembered so fair and smooth.

"Poor Saville!" said she, falteringly; "he died without a pang. Ah, he had the best temper possible!"

Godolphin sat by the writing-table of the deceased, shading his brow with the hand which the actress left disengaged.

"Fanny," said he, bitterly, after a pause, "the world is indeed a stage. It has lost a consummate actor, though in a small part."

The saying was wrung from Godolphin, — and was not said

unkindly, though it seemed so, for he too had tears in his eyes.

"Ah," said she, "the play-house has indeed taught us, in our youth, many things which the real world could not teach us better."

"Life differs from the play only in this," said Godolphin, some time afterwards, — "it has no plot; all is vague, desultory, unconnected, till the curtain drops with the mystery unsolved."

Those were the last words that Godolphin ever addressed to the actress.

CHAPTER LXVI.

THE JOURNEY AND THE SURPRISE. — A WALK IN THE SUMMER NIGHT. — THE STARS, AND THE ASSOCIATION THAT MEMORY MAKES WITH NATURE.

This event detained Godolphin some days longer in town. He saw the last rites performed to Saville, and he was present at the opening of the will.

As in life Saville had never lent a helping hand to the distressed, as he had mixed with the wealthy only, so now to the wealthy only was his wealth devoted. The rich Godolphin was his principal heir; not a word was even said about his illegitimate children, not an inquiry ordained towards his poor relations. In this, as in all the formula of his will, Saville followed the prescribed customs of the world.

Fast went the panting steeds that bore Constance and Godolphin from the desolate city. Bright was the summer sky, and green looked the smiling fields that lay on either side their road. Nature was awake and active. What a delicious contrast to the scenes of Art which they left behind! Constance exerted herself to the utmost to cheer the spirits of her companion, and succeeded. In the small compass which confined them together, their conversation flowed in confidence and intimate affection. Not since the first month of their union had they talked with less reserve and more entire love — only there was this difference in their topics: they then talked of the future only, they now talked more of the past. They uttered many a fond regret over their several faults to each other; and, with clasped hands, congratulated themselves on their present reunion of heart. They allowed how much all things independent of affection had deceived them, and no longer exacting so much from love, they felt its real importance. Ah, why do all of us lose so many years in searching after happiness, but never inquiring into its nature! We are like one who collects the books of a thousand tongues, and knowing not their language, wonders why they do not delight him.

But still, athwart the mind of Constance one dark image would ever and anon obtrude itself; the solitary and mystic Lucilla, with her erring brain and forlorn fortunes, was not even in happiness to be forgotten. There were times, too, in that short journey, when she felt the tale of her interview with that unhappy being rise to her lips; but ever when she looked on the countenance of Godolphin, beaming with more heartfelt and homeborn gladness than she had seen for years, she could not bear the thought of seeing it darkened by the pain her story would inflict, and she shrank from embittering moments so precious to her heart.

All her endeavours to discover Lucilla had been in vain; but an unquiet presentiment that at any moment that discovery might be made, perhaps in the presence of Godolphin, constantly haunted her, and she even now looked painfully forth at each inn where they changed horses, lest the sad, stern features of the soothsayer should appear, and break that spell of happy quiet which now lay over the spirit of Godolphin.

It was towards the evening that their carriage slowly wound up a steep and long ascent. The sun yet wanted an hour to its setting; and at their right, its slant and mellowed beams fell over rich fields, green with the prodigal luxuriance of June, and intersected by hedges from which, proud and frequent, the oak and elm threw forth their lengthened shadows. On their left the grass less fertile and the spaces less inclosed were whitened with flocks of sheep; and far and soft came the bleating of the lambs upon their ear. They saw not the shepherd nor any living form; but from between the thicker groups of trees the chimneys of peaceful cottages peered forth, and gave to the pastoral serenity of the scene that still and tranquil aspect of life which alone suited it. The busy wheel in the heart of Constance was at rest, and Godolphin's soul, steeped in the luxury of the present hour, felt that delicious happiness which would be heaven could it *outlive* the hour.

"My Constance," whispered he, "why, since we return at last to these scenes, why should we ever leave them? Amidst them let us recall our youth!" Constance sighed, but with pleasure, and pressed Godolphin's hand to her lips.

And now they had gained the hill, a sudden colour flushed over Godolphin's cheek.

"Surely," said he, "I remember this view. Yonder valley! This is not the road to Wendover Castle; this — my father's home! — the same, and not the same!"

Yes! Below, basking in the western light, lay the cottage in which Godolphin's childhood had been passed. There was the stream rippling merrily; there the broken and fern-clad turf, with "its old hereditary trees;" but the ruins! — the shattered arch, the mouldering tower, were left indeed; but new arches, new turrets had arisen, and so dexterously blended with the whole that Godolphin might have fancied the hall of his forefathers restored,— not indeed in the same vast proportions and cumbrous grandeur as of old, but still alike in shape and outline, and such even in size as would have contented the proud heart of its last owner. Godolphin's eyes turned inquiringly to Constance.

"It should have been more consistent with its ancient dimensions," said she; "but then it would have taken half our lives to have built it."

"But this must have been the work of years?"

"It was."

"And *your* work, Constance?"

"For you."

"And it was for this that you hesitated when I asked you to consent to raising the money for the purchase of Lord ——'s collection?"

"Yes; am I forgiven?"

"Dearest Constance," said Godolphin, flinging his arms around her, "how have I wronged you! During those very years, then, of our estrangement, during those very years in which I thought you indifferent, you were silently preparing this noble revenge on the injury I did you. Why, why did I not know this before? Why did you not save us both from so long a misunderstanding of each other?"

"Dearest Percy, I was to blame; but I always looked to this hour as to a pleasure of which I could not bear to rob myself. I always fancied that when this task was finished, and you could witness it, you would feel how uppermost you always were in my thoughts, and forgive me many faults from that consideration. I knew that I was executing your father's great wish; I knew that you always, although unconsciously, perhaps, sympathized in that wish. I only grieve that, as yet, it has been executed so imperfectly."

"But how," continued Godolphin, gazing on the new pile as they now neared the entrance, "how was it this never reached my ears through other quarters?"

"But it did, Percy; don't you remember our country neighbour, Dartmour, complimenting you on your intended improvements, and you fancied it was irony, and turned your back on the discomfited squire?"

They now drove under the gates surmounted with Godolphin's arms; and in a few minutes more, they were within the renovated halls of the Priory.

Perhaps it was impossible for Constance to have more sensibly touched and flattered Godolphin than by this surprise. It affected him far more than the political concession which to her had been so profound a sacrifice; for his early poverty had produced in him somewhat of that ancestral pride which the poor only can gracefully wear; and although the tie between his father and himself had not possessed much endearment, yet he had often, with the generosity that belonged to him, regretted that his parent had not survived to share in his present wealth, and to devote some portion of it to the realization of those wishes which he had never been permitted to consummate. Godolphin, too, was precisely of a nature to appreciate the delicacy of Constance's conduct, and to be deeply penetrated by the thought that, while he was following a career so separate from hers, she, in the midst of all her ambitious projects, could pause to labour, unthanked and in concealment, for the delight of this hour's gratification to him; the delicacy and the forethought affected him the more, because they made not a part of the ordinary character of the high and absorbed ambition of Constance. He did not thank her much by words, but his looks betrayed all he felt, and Constance was overpaid.

Although the new portion of the building was necessarily not extensive, yet each chamber was of those grand proportions which suited the magnificent taste of Godolphin, and harmonized with the ancient ruins. Constance had shown her tact by leaving the ruins themselves (which it was profane to touch) unrestored; but so artfully were those connected with the modern addition, and thence with the apartments in the cottage, which she had not scrupled to remodel, that an effect was produced from the whole far more splendid than many Gothic buildings of greater extent and higher pretensions can afford. Godolphin wandered delightedly over the whole, charmed with the taste and judgment which presided over even the nicest arrangement.

"Why, where," said he, struck with the accurate antiquity of some of the details, "where learned you all these minutiæ? You are as wise as Hope himself upon cornices and tables."

"I was forced to leave these things to others," answered Constance; "but I took care that they possessed the necessary science."

The night was exceedingly beautiful, and they walked forth under the summer moon among those grounds in which Constance had first seen Godolphin. They stood by the very rivulet, they paused at the very spot! On the murmuring bosom of the wave floated many a water-flower; and now and then a sudden splash, a sudden circle in the shallow stream, denoted the leap of the river-tyrant on his prey. There was a universal odour in the soft air,—that delicate, that ineffable fragrance belonging to those midsummer nights which the rich English poetry might well people with Oberon and his fairies; the bat wheeled in many a ring along the air; but the gentle light bathed all things, and robbed his wanderings of the gloomier associations that belong to them; and ever and ever, the busy moth darted to and fro among the flowers, or misled upwards by the stars whose beam allured it, wandered, like Desire after Happiness, in search of that light it might never reach. And those stars still, with their soft, unspeakable eyes of love, looked down upon Godolphin as of old, when, by the Italian lake, he roved with her for whom he had become the world itself. No, not now, nor ever, could he gaze upon those wan, mysterious orbs, and not feel the pang that reminded him of Lucilla! Between them and her was an affinity which his imagination could not sever. All whom we have loved have something in nature especially devoted to their memory,—a peculiar flower, a breath of air, a leaf, a tone. What love is without some such association,—

> "Striking the electric chain wherewith we 're bound?"

But the dim and shadowy and solemn stars were indeed meet remembrances of Volktman's wild daughter; and so intimately was their light connected in Godolphin's breast with that one image, that their very softness had, to his eyes, something fearful and menacing,—although as in sadness, not in anger.

CHAPTER LXVII.

THE FULL RENEWAL OF LOVE. — HAPPINESS PRODUCES FEAR, AND IN TO-DAY ALREADY WALKS TO-MORROW.

O, FIRST Love! well sang the gay minstrel of France, that we return again and again to thee. As the earth returns to its spring, and is green once more, we go back to the life of life and forget the seasons that have rolled between! Whether it was — perhaps so — that in the minds of both was a feeling that their present state was not fated to endure; whether they felt, in the deep calm they enjoyed, that the storm was already at hand,— whether this was the truth I know not; but certain it is that during the short time they remained at Godolphin Priory, previous to their earthly separation, Constance and Godolphin were rather like lovers for the first time united than like those who have dragged on the chain for years. Their perfect solitude, the absence of all intrusion, so unlike the life they had long passed, renewed all that charm, that rapture in each other's society, which belong to the first youth of love. True that this could not have endured long; but Fate suffered it to endure to the last of that tether which remained to their union. Constance was not again doomed to the severe and grating shock which the sense of estrangement brings to a woman's heart; she was sensible that Godolphin was never so entirely, so passionately her own, as towards the close of their mortal connection. Everything around them breathed of their first love. This was that home of Godolphin to which, from the splendid halls of Wendover, the young soul of the proud orphan had so often and so mournfuly flown with a yearning and wistful interest; this was that spot in which he, awaking from the fever of the world, had fed his first dreams of *her*. The scene, the solitude, was as a bath to their love,— it braced, it freshened, it revived its tone. They wandered, they read, they thought together; the air of the spot was an intoxication. The world around and without was agitated; they felt it not: the breakers of the great deep died in murmurs on their ear. Ambition lulled its voice to Constance; Godolphin had realized his visions of the ideal. Time had dimmed their young beauty, but their eyes saw it not; they were young, they were all beautiful, to each other.

And Constance hung on the steps of her lover — still let that name be his! She could not bear to lose him for a moment: a vague indistinctness of fear seized her if she saw him not. Again and again, in the slumbers of the night, she stretched forth her arms to feel that he was near; all her pride, her coldness seemed gone, as by a spell; she loved as the softest, the fondest, love. Are we, O Ruler of the future! imbued with the half-felt spirit of prophecy as the hour of evil approaches,— the great, the fierce, the irremediable evil of a life? In this depth and intensity of their renewed passion, was there not something preternatural? Did they not tremble as they loved? They were on a spot to which the dark waters were slowly gathering; they clung to the Hour, for eternity was lowering round.

It was one evening that a foreboding emotion of this kind weighed heavily on Constance. She pressed Godolphin's hand in hers, and when he returned the pressure, she threw herself on his neck, and burst into tears. Godolphin was alarmed; he covered her cheek with kisses, he sought the cause of her emotion.

"There is no cause," answered Constance, recovering herself, but speaking in a faltering voice, "only I feel the impossibility that this happiness can last; its excess makes me shudder."

As she spoke, the wind rose and swept mourningly over the large leaves of the chestnut-tree beneath which they stood; the serene stillness of the evening seemed gone; an unquiet and melancholy spirit was loosened abroad, and the chill of the sudden change which is so frequent to our climate came piercingly upon them. Godolphin was silent for some moments, for the thought found a sympathy in his own.

"And is it truly so?" he said at last. "Is there really to be no permanent happiness for us below? Is pain always to tread the heels of pleasure? Are we never to say the harbour is reached, and we are safe? No, my Constance," he added, warming into the sanguine vein that traversed even his most desponding moods, "no! let us not cherish this dark belief; there is no experience for the future; one hour lies to the next; if what has been seem thus chequered, it is no type of what may be. We have discovered in each other that world that was long lost to our eyes; we cannot lose it again; death only can separate us!"

"Ah, *death!*" said Constance, shuddering.

"Do not recoil at that word, my Constance, for we are yet in the noon of life; why bring, like the Egyptian, the spectre to the feast? And, after all, if death come while we thus love, it is better than change and time,—better than custom which palls, better than age which chills. Oh," continued Godolphin, passionately, "oh, if this narrow shoal and sand of time be but a breathing spot in the great heritage of immortality, why cheat ourselves with words so vague as life and death? What is the difference? At most, the entrance in and the departure from one scene in our wide career. How many scenes are left to us! We do but hasten our journey, not close it. Let us believe this, Constance, and cast from us all fear of our disunion."

As he spoke, Constance's eyes were fixed upon his face, and the deep calm that reigned there sank into her soul, and silenced its murmurs. The thought of futurity is that which Godolphin (because it is so with all idealists) must have revolved with the most frequent fervour; but it was a thought which he so rarely touched upon that it was the first and only time Constance ever heard it breathed from his lips.

They turned into the house: and the mark is still in that page of the volume which they read, where the melodious accents of Godolphin died upon the heart of Constance. Can she ever turn to it again?

CHAPTER LXVIII.

THE LAST CONVERSATION BETWEEN GODOLPHIN AND CONSTANCE. — HIS THOUGHTS AND SOLITARY WALK AMIDST THE SCENES OF HIS YOUTH. — THE LETTER. — THE DEPARTURE.

They had denied themselves to all the visitors who had attacked the Priory; but on their first arrival, they had deemed it necessary to conciliate their neighbours by concentrating into one formal act of hospitality all those social courtesies which they could not persuade themselves to relinquish their solitude in order singly to perform. Accordingly, a day had been fixed for one grand *fête* at the Priory; it was to follow close on the election, and be considered as in honour of that event. The evening for this gala succeeded that which I have recorded in the last chapter. It was with great reluctance that they prepared themselves to greet this sole interruption of their seclusion; and they laughed, although they did not laugh cordially, at the serious annoyance which the giving a ball was for the first time to occasion to persons who had been giving balls for a succession of years.

The day was remarkably still and close; the sun had not once pierced through the dull atmosphere, which was charged with the yet silent but gathering thunder; and as the evening came on, the sullen tokens of an approaching storm became more and more loweringly pronounced.

"We shall not, I fear, have propitious weather for our festival to-night," said Godolphin; "but after a general election, people's nerves are tolerably hardened. What are the petty fret and tumult of nature, lasting but an hour, to the angry and everlasting passions of men?"

"A profound deduction from a wet night, dear Percy," said Constance, smiling.

"Like our friend C——," rejoined Godolphin, in the same vein, "I can philosophize on the putting on one's gloves, you know;" and therewith their conversation flowed into a vein singularly contrasted with the character of the coming events. Time fled on as they were thus engaged until Constance started up, surprised at the lateness of the hour, to attend the duties of the toilette.

"Wear this, dearest," said Godolphin, taking a rose from a flower-stand by the window, "in memory of that ball at Wendover Castle, which, although itself passed bitterly enough for me, has yet left so many happy recollections." Constance put the rose into her bosom; its leaves were then all fresh and brilliant,—so were her prospects for the future. He kissed her forehead as they parted,—they parted for the last time.

Godolphin, left alone, turned to the window, which, opening to the ground, invited him forth among the flowers that studded the grass-plots which sloped away to the dark and unwaving trees that girded the lawn. That pause of nature which precedes a storm ever had a peculiar attraction to his mind; and instinctively he sauntered from the house, wrapped in the dreaming, half-developed thought which belonged to his temperament. Mechanically he strayed on until he found himself beside the still lake which the hollows of the dismantled park embedded. There he paused, gazing unconsciously on the gloomy shadows which fell from the arches of the Priory and the tall trees around. Not a ripple stirred the broad expanse of waters; the birds had gone to rest; no sound, save the voice of the distant brook that fed the lake beside which, on the first night of his return to his ancestral home, he had wandered with Constance, broke the universal silence. That voice was never mute. All else might be dumb; but that living stream, rushing through its rocky bed, stilled not its repining music. Like the soul of the landscape is the gush of a fresh stream; it knows no sleep, no pause: it works forever,—the life, the cause of life to all around. The great frame of nature may repose, but the spirit of the waters rests not for a moment. As the soul of the landscape is the soul of man; in our deepest slumbers its course glides on, and works unsilent, unslumbering, through its destined channel.

With slow step and folded arms Godolphin moved along. The well-remembered scenes of his childhood were all before him; the wild verdure of the fern; the broken ground, with its thousand mimic mounts and valleys; the deep dell overgrown with matted shrubs and dark as a wizard's cave; the remains of many a stately vista, where the tender green of the lime showed forth, even in that dusky light, beneath the richer leaves of the chestnut,— all was familiar and home-breathing to his mind. Fragments of boyish verse, forgotten for years, rose hauntingly to his remembrance, telling of wild thoughts, unsatisfied dreams, disappointed hopes.

"But I am happy at last," said he, aloud,— "yes, happy. I have passed that bridge of life which divides us from the follies of youth; and better prospects and nobler desires extend before me. What a world of wisdom in that one saying of Radclyffe, 'Benevolence is the sole cure to idealism;' to live for others draws us from demanding miracles for ourselves. What duty as yet have I fulfilled? I renounced ambition as unwise, and with it I renounced wisdom itself. I lived for pleasure,— I lived the life of disappointment. Without one vicious disposition, I have fallen into a hundred vices; I have never been *actively* selfish, yet always selfish. I nursed high thoughts — for what end? A poet in heart, a voluptuary in life. If mine own interest came into clear collision with that of another, mine I would have sacrificed; but I never asked if the whole course of my existence was not that of a war with the universal interest. Too thoughtful to be without a leading principle in life, the one principle I adopted has been one error. I have tasted all that imagination can give to earthly possession,— youth, health, liberty, knowledge, love, luxury, pomp. Woman was my first passion,— what woman have I wooed in vain? I imagined that my career hung upon Constance's breath,— Constance loved and refused me. I attributed my errors to that refusal; Constance became mine: — how have I retrieved them? A vague, a dim, an unconfessed remorse has pursued me in the memory of Lucilla; yet, why not have redeemed that fault to her by good to others? What is penitence not put into action but the great fallacy in morals? A sin to one, if irremediable, can only be compensated by a virtue to some one else. Yet was I to blame in my conduct to Lucilla? Why should conscience so haunt me at that name? Did I not fly her? Was it not herself who compelled our union? Did I not cherish, respect, honour, forbear with her more than I have since with my wedded Constance? Did I not resolve to renounce Constance herself, when most loved, for Lucilla's sake alone? Who prevented that sacrifice, who deserted me, who carved out her own separate life?—Lucilla herself. No, so far, my sin is light. But ought I not to have left all things to follow her, to discover her, to force upon her an independence from want, or possibly from crime? Ah, there was my sin, and the sin of my nature; the sin, too, of the children of the world,—*passive sin.* I could sacrifice my happiness, but not my indolence; I was not ungenerous, I was inert. But is it too late? Can I not yet search, discover her, and remove from my mind the anxious burthen which her remembrance imposes on it? For, oh, one thought of remorse linked with the being who has loved us is more intolerable to the conscience than the gravest crime!"

Muttering such thoughts, Godolphin strayed on until the deepening night suddenly recalled his attention to the lateness of the hour. He turned to the house and entered his own apartment. Several of the guests had already come. Godolphin was yet dressing, when a servant knocked at the door and presented him a note.

"Lay it on the table," said he to the valet; "it is probably some excuse about the ball."

"Sir," said the servant, "a lad has just brought it from S——," naming a village about four miles distant; "and says he is to wait for an answer. He was ordered to ride as fast as possible."

With some impatience Godolphin took up the note; but the moment his eye rested on the writing, it fell from his hands; his cheek, his lips, grew as white as death; his heart seemed to refuse its functions; it was literally as if life stood still for a moment, as by the force of a sudden poison. With a strong effort he recovered himself, tore open the note, and read as follows: —

Percy Godolphin, the hour has arrived, — once more we shall meet. I summon you, fair love, to that meeting, — the bed of death. Come!

LUCILLA VOLKTMAN.

"Don't alarm the countess," said Godolphin to his servant, in a very low, calm voice; "bring my horse to the postern, and send the bearer of this note to me."

The messenger appeared,— a rough country lad, of about eighteen or twenty.

"You brought this note?"

"I did, your honour."

"From whom?"

"Why, a sort of a strange lady, as is lying at the Chequers, and not expected to live. She be mortal bad, sir, and do run on awesome."

Godolphin pressed his hands convulsively together.

"And how long has she been there?"

"She only came about two hours since, sir; she came in a chaise, sir, and was taken so ill that we sent for the doctor directly. He says she can't get over the night."

Godolphin walked to and fro, without trusting himself to speak, for some minutes. The boy stood by the door, pulling about his hat, and wondering and staring and thoroughly stupid.

"Did she come alone?"

"Eh, your honour?"

"Was no one with her?"

"Oh, yes! a little nigger girl; she it was sent me with the letter."

"The horse is ready, sir," said the servant; "but had you not better have the carriage brought out? It looks very black; it must rain shortly, sir; and the ford between this and S—— is dangerous to cross in so dark a night."

"Peace!" cried Godolphin, with flashing eyes, and a low

convulsive laugh. "Shall I ride to that death-bed at my ease and leisure?"

He strode rapidly down the stairs, and reached the small postern door; it was a part of the old building. One of the grooms held his impatient horse,— the swiftest in his splendid stud; and the dim but flaring light, held by another of the servitors, streamed against the dull heavens and the imperfectly seen and frowning ruins of the ancient pile.

Godolphin, unconscious of all around, and muttering to himself, leaped on his steed. The fire glinted from the courser's hoofs; and thus the last lord of that knightly race bade farewell to his father's halls. Those words which he had muttered, and which his favourite servant caught and superstitiously remembered, were the words in Lucilla's note,—"*The hour has arrived!*"

CHAPTER THE LAST.

A DREAD MEETING. — THE STORM. — THE CATASTROPHE.

On the humble pallet of the village inn lay the broken form of the astrologer's expiring daughter. The surgeon of the place sat by the bedside, dismayed and terrified, despite his hardened vocation, by the wild words and ghastly shrieks that ever and anon burst from the lips of the dying woman. The words were, indeed, uttered in a foreign tongue unfamiliar to the leech,— a language not ordinarily suited to inspire terror; the language of love and poetry and music, the language of the sweet South. But, uttered in that voice where the passions of the soul still wrestled against the gathering weakness of the frame, the soft syllables sounded harsh and fearful; and the dishevelled locks of the sufferer, the wandering fire of the sunken eyes, the distorted gestures of the thin, transparent arms, gave fierce effect to the unknown words, and betrayed the dark strength of the delirium which raged upon her.

One wretched light on the rude table opposite the bed broke the gloom of the mean chamber; and across the window flashed the first lightnings of the storm about to break. By the other side of the bed sat, mute, watchful, tearless, the Moorish girl, who was Lucilla's sole attendant,— her eyes fixed on the sufferer with faithful, unwearying love; her ears listening, with all the quick sense of her race, to catch, amidst the growing noises of the storm, and the tread of hurrying steps below, the expected sound of the hoofs that should herald Godolphin's approach.

Suddenly, as if exhausted by the paroxysm of her disease, Lucilla's voice sank into silence; and she lay so still, so motionless, that, but for the faint and wavering pulse of the hand, which the surgeon was now suffered to hold, they might have believed the tortured spirit was already released. This torpor lasted for some minutes, when, raising herself up, as a bright gleam of intelligence stole over the hollow cheeks, Lucilla put her finger to her lips, smiled, and said, in a low, clear voice, "Hark! he comes!"

The Moor crept across the chamber, and opening the door, stood there in a listening attitude. *She*, as yet, heard not the tread of the speeding charger. A moment, and it smote her ear; a moment more it halted by the inn-door. The snort of the panting horse, the rush of steps, Percy Godolphin was in the room, was by the bedside; the poor sufferer was in his arms; and softened, thrilled, overpowered, Lucilla resigned herself to that dear caress; she drank in the sobs of her choked voice; she felt still, as in happier days, burning into her heart, the magic of his kisses. One instant of youth, of love, of hope, broke into that desolate and fearful hour, and silent and scarcely conscious tears gushed from her aching eyes, and laved, as it were, the burthen and the agony from her heart.

The Moor traversed the room, and, laying one hand on the surgeon's shoulder, pointed to the door. Lucilla and Godolphin were alone.

"Oh!" said he, at last finding voice, "is it thus — thus we meet? But say not that you are dying, Lucilla! have mercy, mercy upon your betrayer, your —"

Here he could utter no more; he sank beside her, covering his face with his hands, and sobbing bitterly.

The momentary lucid interval for Lucilla had passed away; the maniac rapture returned, although in a wild and solemn shape.

"Blame not yourself," said she, earnestly; "the remorseless stars are the sole betrayers: yet, bright and lovely as they once seemed when they assured me of a bond between thee and me, I could not dream that their still and shining lore could forbode such gloomy truths. Oh, Percy! since we parted, the earth has not been *as* the earth to me: the *Natural* has left my life; a weird and roving spirit has entered my breast, and filled my brain, and possessed my thoughts, and moved every spring of my existence. The sun and the air, the green herb, the freshness and glory of the world, have been covered with a mist in which only dim shapes of dread were shadowed forth. But thou, my love, on whose breast I have dreamed such blessed dreams, wert not to blame. No! the power that crushes we cannot accuse; the heavens are above the reach of our reproach; they smile upon our agony; they bid the seasons roll on, unmoved and unsympathizing, above our broken hearts. And what has been my course since your last kiss on these dying lips? Godolphin," — and here Lucilla drew herself apart from him, and writhed, as with some bitter memory, — "these lips have felt other kisses and these ears have drunk unhallowed sounds, and wild revelry and wilder passion have made me laugh over the sepulchre of my soul. But I am a poor creature; poor, poor — mad, Percy, — mad, — they tell me so!" Then, in the sudden changes incident to her disease, Lucilla continued: "I saw your bride, Percy, when you bore her from Rome, and the wheels of your bridal carriage swept over me, for I flung myself in their way; but they scathed me not: the bright demons above ordained otherwise, and I wandered over the world; but you shall know not," added Lucilla, with a laugh of dreadful levity, "whither or with whom, for we must have concealments, my love, as you will confess; and I strove to forget you, and my brain sank in the effort. I felt my frame withering, and they told me my doom was fixed, and I resolved to come to England, and look on my first love once more; so I came, and I saw you, Godolphin; and I knew, by the wrinkles in your brow, and the musing thought in your eye, that your proud lot had not brought you content. And then there came to me a stately shape, and I knew it for her for whom you had deserted me: she told me, as you tell me, to live, to forget the past. Mockery, mockery! But my heart is proud as hers, Percy, and I would not stoop to the kindness of a triumphant rival; and I fled, what matters it whither? But listen, Percy, listen; my woes have made me wise in that science which is not of earth, and I knew that you and I must meet once more, and that that meeting would be in this hour; and I counted, minute by minute, with a savage gladness, the days that were to bring on this interview and my death!" Then raising her voice into a wild shriek, "Beware, beware, Percy! — the rush of waters is on my ear — the splash, the gurgle! Beware! — *your* last hour, also, is at hand!"

From the moment in which she uttered these words, Lucilla relapsed into her former frantic paroxysms. Shriek followed shriek; she appeared to know none around her, not even Godolphin. With throes and agony the soul seemed to wrench itself from the frame. The hours swept on; midnight came; clear and distinct the voice of the clock below reached that chamber.

"Hush!" cried Lucilla, starting. "Hush!" and just at that moment, through the window opposite, the huge clouds, breaking in one spot, discovered high and far above them a solitary star.

"Thine, thine, Godolphin!" she shrieked forth, pointing to the lonely orb; "it summons thee. Farewell, but not for long!"

. . . .

The Moor rushed forward with a loud cry; she placed her hand on Lucilla's bosom; the heart was still, the breath was gone, the fire had vanished from the ashes: that strange unearthly spirit was perhaps with the stars for whose mysteries it had so vainly yearned.

Down fell the black rain in torrents; and far from the mountains you might hear the rushing of the swollen streams, as they poured into the bosom of the valleys. The sullen, continued mass of cloud was broken, and the vapours hurried fast and lowering over the heavens, leaving now and then a star to glitter forth ere again "the jaws of darkness did devour it up." At the lower verge of the horizon, the lightning flashed fierce, but at lingering intervals; the trees rocked and groaned beneath the rain and storm; and immediately above the bowed head of a solitary horseman broke the thunder that, amidst the whirl of his own emotions, he scarcely heard.

Beside a stream, which the rains had already swelled, was a gypsy encampment; and as some of the dusky itinerants, waiting perhaps the return of a part of their band from a predatory excursion, cowered over the flickering fires in their tent, they perceived the horseman rapidly approaching the stream.

"See to yon gentry cove," cried one of the band; "'t is the same we saw in the forenight crossing the ford above. He has taken a short cut, the buzzard! and will have to go round again to the ford; a precious time to be gallivanting about!"

"Pish!" said an old hag; "I love to see the proud ones tasting the bitter wind and rain as we bear alway; 't is but a mile longer round to the ford. I wish it was twenty."

"Hallo!" cried the first speaker; "the fool takes to the water. He 'll be drowned; the banks are too high and rough to land man or horse yonder. Hallo!" and with that painful sympathy which the hardest feel at the imminent peril of another when immediately subjected to their eyes, the gypsy ran forth into the pelting storm, shouting to the traveller to halt. For one moment Godolphin's steed still shrunk back from the rushing tide; deep darkness was over the water, and the horseman saw not the height of the opposite banks. The shout of the gypsy sounded to his ear like the cry of the dead whom he had left; he dashed his heels into the sides of the reluctant horse, and was in the stream.

"Light — light the torches!" cried the gypsy; and in a few moments the banks were illumined with many a brand from the fire, which the rain however almost instantly extinguished; yet by that momentary light they saw the noble animal breasting the waters, and perceived that Godolphin, discovering by the depth his mistake, had already turned the horse's head in the direction of the ford. They could see no more, but they shouted to Godolphin to turn back to the place from which he had plunged; and, in a few minutes afterwards, they heard, several yards above, the horse clambering up the rugged banks, which there were steep and high, and crushing the boughs that clothed the ascent. They thought, at the same time, that they distinguished also the splash of a heavy substance in the waves; but they fancied it some detached fragment of earth or stone, and turned to their tent, in the belief that the daring rider had escaped the peril he had so madly incurred. That night the riderless steed of Godolphin arrived at the porch of the Priory, where Constance, alarmed, pale, breathless, stood exposed to the storm, awaiting the return of Godolphin, or the messengers she had despatched in search of him.

At daybreak his corpse was found by the shallows of the ford; and the mark of violence across the temples, as of some blow, led them to guess that in scaling the banks his head had struck against one of the tossing boughs that overhung them, and the blow had precipitated him into the waters.

LETTER FROM CONSTANCE, COUNTESS OF ERPINGHAM, TO ——

August, 1832.

I have read the work you have so kindly compiled from the papers transmitted to your care, and from your own intimate knowledge of those to whom they relate. You have in much fulfilled my wishes with singular success. On the one hand, I have been anxious that a History should be given to the world, from which lessons so deep and, I firmly believe, salutary, may be generally derived; on the other hand, I have been anxious that it should be clothed in such disguises that the names of the real actors in the drama should be forever a secret. Both these objects you have attained. It is impossible, I think, for any one to read the book about to be published without being impressed with the truth of the moral it is intended to convey, and without seeing, by a thousand infallible signs, that its spring and its general course have flowed from reality and not fiction. Yet have you, by a few slight alterations and additions, managed to effect that concealment of names and persons, which is due no less to the living than to the memory of the dead.

So far I thank you from my heart; but in one point you have utterly failed. You have done no justice to the noble character you meant to delineate under the name of Godolphin; you have drawn his likeness with a harsh and cruel pencil; you have enlarged on the few weaknesses he might have possessed, until you have made them the foreground of the portrait; and his vivid generosity, his high honour, his brilliant intellect, the extraordinary stores of his mind, you have left in shadow. O God! that for such a being such a destiny was reserved! and in the prime of life, just when his mind had awakened to a sense of its own powers and their legitimate objects! What a fatal system of things, that could for thirty-seven years have led away, by the pursuits and dissipations of a life suited but to the beings he despised, a genius of such an order, a heart of such tender emotions![1] But on this subject I cannot, cannot write. I must lay down the pen; to-morrow I will try and force myself to resume it.

Well, then, I say, you have not done justice to *him*. I beseech you to remodel that character, and atone to the memory of one whom none ever saw but to admire, or knew but to love.

Of me, — of me, the vain, the scheming, the proud, the unfeminine cherisher of bitter thoughts, of stern designs, — of me, on the other hand, how flattering is the picture you have drawn! In that flattery is my sure disguise; therefore I will not ask you to shade it into the poor and unlovely truth. But while, with agony and shame, I feel that you have rightly described that seeming neglectfulness of one no more, which sprang from the pride that believed *itself* neglected, you have not said enough — no, not one millionth part enough — of the *real love* that I constantly bore to him, — the only soft and redeeming portion of my

1 The reader will acquit me of the charge of injustice to Godolphin's character when he arrives at this sentence; it conveys exactly the impression that my delineation, faithful to truth, is intended to convey, — the influences of our actual world on the ideal and imaginative order of mind, when that mind is without the stimulus of pursuits at once practical and ennobling.

nature, But who can know, who can describe what another feels? Even I knew not what I felt, until death taught it me.

Since I have read the whole book, one thought constantly haunts me, — the strangeness that I should survive his loss; that the stubborn strings of my heart have not been broken long since; that I live, and live, too, amidst the world! Ay, but not one *of* the world; with that consciousness I sustain myself in the petty and sterile career of life. Shut out henceforth and forever from all the tenderer feelings that belong to my sex; without mother, husband, child, or friend; unloved and unloving, I support myself by the belief that I have done the little suffered to my sex in expediting the great change which is advancing on the world. And I cheer myself by the firm assurance that, sooner or later, a time must come when those vast disparities in life which have been fatal, not to myself alone, but to all I have admired and loved; which render the great heartless, and the lowly servile; which make genius either an enemy to mankind or the victim to itself; which debase the energetic purpose; which fritter away the ennobling sentiment; which cool the heart and fetter the capacities, and are favourable only to the general development of the Mediocre and the Lukewarm, shall, if never utterly removed, at least be smoothed away into more genial and unobstructed elements of society. Alas! it is with an aching eye that we look abroad for the only solace, the only occupation of life, — Solitude at home, and Memory at our hearth.

THE END.

www.ingramcontent.com/pod-product-compliance
Lightning Source LLC
Chambersburg PA
CBHW022148010726
47493CB00002B/388
9781434429407